CU00722880

About the Author

Born in the city of Coventry, and schooled within her deep love for history and writing, the author entered university later in life. This re-stirred the passion of writing that had flown in and out of her life since childhood, allowing her to pull the reader into her characters' lives.

For my sister

Emily Edwards

The 'Art' of Deception

AUSTIN MACAULEY PUBLISHERS™

LONDON • CAMBRIDGE • NEW YORK • SHARJAH

A CIP catalogue record for this title is available from the British Library.

ISBN 978-1-78629-681-8 (Paperback)
ISBN 978-1-78629-682-5 (Hardback)
ISBN 978-1-78629-683-2 (EBook)

www.austinmacauley.com

First Published (2017)
Austin Macauley Publishers Ltd.
25 Canada Square
Canary Wharf
London
E14 5LQ

With grateful thanks to

Jim Coape-Arnold
Skin City,
Leicester

Who confirmed my research

It is claimed, 'A girl's got to do what a girl's got to do' please, do not believe it.

From childhood, I had fought against the conventional class system, chosen the impossible, discarded the obvious.

In my mind this pragmatic rationing became the centre of my adult life. Through disrespect of all things 'feminine', and with a clear understanding (my own take on life and love) that life equalled obstinate, and love equalled fantasy I allowed myself the right to manoeuvre through a minefield of guilt. I chose the road that led to deception.

It began when my friend Jimmy, whom I had met at university, vowed in a quirky moment of drunkenness to seal a pact in the search for love and freedom. Ten years we promised, campaigning for the oppressed, visiting different cultures, uncovering our own version of the seven lettered word. After those ten years, if neither had discovered our own nirvana, we would part on Millennium eve.

How was I to know this 'dare and do' promise would deliver me into the hands of a traitor, and at the same time an exceptional body artist? That the Berlin Wall, the Forgotten City of China, the romanticism of Paris, and the heart stopping sights of America would lead me on a trail of deceit, fabrication, and heartache?

My body became the canvas to a scenic jigsaw, where dreams and nightmares collided, and family values were torn apart. The seed that was planted on that drunken night opened the door to a journey, an intrepid trek of discovery of joy, pain, and realisation that life is not quite that fairy-tale we imagine it to be.

We all believe we can judge a character – now is your chance.

In Honesty,
Rhia Bryant.

Part One

'Oh, what a tangled web we weave,
when first we practise to deceive'

(Sir Walter Scott 1771-1832)

1

New Year's Day, 2000

I rise from my bed, feel my way to the bathroom, plunge for the toilet, and throw up. The cold enamel beneath my trembling hands stirs something deep inside me. A memory, a pain, an emotion, something so tangible I fight to keep it hidden. Flushing away my misery I stagger to the sink and peer into the oval mirror above the cream basin. I gasp.

Before me is the face of a woman, drawn and sallow; a thirty plus woman whose skin shows slight (yet definite) signs of wear and tear.

'A good age,' you may say. *'An age when a young woman can look back at the first marks she has left on the world.'*

I snigger, hold my stomach in despair, and croak, "Not this woman!"

I stare again, then cover my face, cursing the dim light of the bulb glaring down from its home in a single spot-lighter.

I hate mornings – especially in the winter. The grey shabby clouds hanging as if pegged to an old fashioned washing line, swaying over an unsuspecting world, waiting to divulge their burden of moisture onto the scattering creatures below. Cold nipping at fingers and toes, no matter how tightly they are wrapped in woollen gloves and tights.

Oh yes believe me, January is a month to hibernate – and right now, I wish to fall down a squirrel hollow forever.

Slowly I peep from behind clammy fingers, screwing my wild green eyes into the tightest slits possible. Anything, to avoid the bright pink rouged cheeks smudged from tears and mascara, and the tousled mass of red hair falling across my face. I touch my lips, feel the sting from last night's forceful kiss, catch a quick glimpse of the silk pink pyjamas I tore from the untidy shelf in the airing cupboard, sitting on my voluptuous frame in the most haphazard way. Their job – oh hell – supposedly to hide the lavish swirls of black ink etched onto my torso; act as a cover for the secret life I had allowed myself to follow. My body moves, ripples against the constricting fabric, demanding to be free. I pause, inhale deeply, and with quivering fingers unbutton the hooks and eyes of the jacket. Help me, please – nothing is left to the imagination.

As the material falls from my shoulders to the stone coloured tiles of the floor I heave with disbelief. My body – a tear falls – sensuous in all the right places, is a backdrop for tattooed art.

Oh, do not look so surprised.

My breasts, midriff, back, buttocks, thighs and upper arms display objects or landscapes of every dimension. They are a moving, living art gallery!

In pain I turn left, then right, my stomach churning with each movement. I scan the blatant, yet tasteful work. ten years of memories, some interesting and beautiful, others frightening and challenging. Times and places I would rather forget, taunting me, haunting me with the thought of how I could have been so foolish. Another tear escapes, sliding down my face, nestling in the creases of the foundation cream I had not bothered to remove. I stumble to a seat, an icon of past days resting on its spindly frame by the bathroom wall, and snatch the jacket from the floor. Swathing myself in its silky softness I pray, beg, for those heady days of youth and the disappointment of adulthood to disappear;

I shout, "Take away this night of horror."

Not to be. Nausea grips my throat, forcing me to reach for the nearest receptacle. Wave after wave of involuntary retching pushes my head down.

Catching sight of the past actions of my life in black and white; years when this world and I were at odds, yet could have sworn we were in perfect harmony. Thinking back, I was constantly on the edge of that emotional insanity. Add this to my crazy drinking habit, and I promise you it equals – today.

This day was always coming – *always* – in the depth of my subconscious, like a ghost on a mission. I see the troubled look in your eyes, that question of fact or fiction.

Don't bother. My life runs like that. What is true, what is false – could I – should I?

First let me say, I surrender to all; put my hands high in the air, like a cowboy surprised by the law.

I *am* the lost cause you hear about when the media have nothing better to print. That daily story that makes a reader go 'ahh' or 'ohh', then 'she deserves it'.

Yet, I am unsure how I can bear it.

How can I admit to myself, let alone anyone else, that startling fact?

I, Rhia Bryant, had lost the battle!

'Battle,' you are bound to repeat. *'What battle?'*

I promise, you will know soon enough.

I cough, gagging from the taste of bile residing on my tongue. Turning toward the bath I twist the cold tap, splash water onto my face, breathe deeply. If I did not feel so ill I would have likened the droplets running down my cheeks, slithering down my neck, cradling in the dip between my collar bones to gentle rain – soft and caressing. A waterfall washing away the drought of my sorrow. Thinking of those times when I laughed with joy and cried with frustration I wish I could raise a smile. Whether it be sarcastic or otherwise, it is impossible. I cannot even raise my head properly, let alone use the muscles of my face. Besides, I must be honest, what is there to smile about?

Today. I hated everyone. Hate – detest – loathe – all the words I can fit into my world of anger.

I wanted to scream, pierce the air around me in sheer frustration, use a whip like the monks of old in retribution for my stupidity.

I had lost a loved one.

Not in death. Oh no, far more damaging than that. I had lied and cheated ...

Pain shot through my chest, threatening me, holding me to ransom; up once more into my throat – up, up, up.

—

Last night the world crashed at my feet, splintering in front of me; fired by that egotistical nature that had driven me since I was a child.

You giggle, in the way most people do when they read an embarrassing admission. Half heartedly, believing the story teller is being over severe and tyrannical about themselves. Please don't –

I do not deserve your sympathy or expect it.

My undoing is purely my own fault. It is I who ostracised my dearest friend and confidante. I who offered my body to be sketched like a masterpiece. I who now suffer the consequence of my actions. I am no fool.

There are those lovers of post-modernist thinking that say the painter is among the greatest God given talent that lives. Believe his or her work to be a psychological insight into the human mind. This may be true, and as my body art can be classed in this mould I should be flattered yet scared.

My problem – at this very moment – all I wish to think about is Jimmy: true, steadfast Jimmy. Through fantasy, vanity – call it what you will, I came to lose him.

Funny really, when tribulation stares you in the face – you wish to run. Keep going, anywhere, until your feet are so sore you can run no more. I do not even have that luxury. My bank account indicates empty, and my energy is at its lowest pitch ever.

Your face crinkles into confusion. I am sorry if the logic of my pain is not clear.

Here are the facts.

Jimmy has never seen my tattoos, not full on anyway. I often wondered if he glimpsed bits and pieces, in the swimming pool, on a hot day, who knows. If so, he did not comment.

You see, Jimmy was not my lover, *he* was my best friend in the world.

Here I gulp.

'Ah.' The expression escapes your lips, as if the complete picture unfolds before you.

Trust me, it does not.
Nothing, and I stress this word, is that simple.

It is because I wanted it all – lover, friend, adventure – that I am left with nothing.

I see your frown.

Please have the patience to hear me out.

My friend has deserted me – gone – taken his lean body, brown hair, angular features and cheeky smile with him. Leaving me – the tears start to fall again – with the pangs of alcohol sickness and a heartache as deep as the Grand Canyon.

I kick the bath panel, hear the 'crack' of the bevelled plastic and sob for all I am worth. The root of my desolation has got to be that silly pact. A creation of post university euphoria, when over-awed students search for common ground.

Jimmy and I – we were freedom seekers.

Surprise you – me too – with my hot temper and short fuse.

It did not matter where, or in what form the main objective took us. Our vow was to travel, march, protest, listen, discover the meaning of freedom.

To compile this inane scheme, we drew blood and promised to complete our search by the dawning of the new Millennium, or say 'goodbye' forever.

Daft? You bet.

'Who invented that?' your query pierces my brain.

"I did," I shout. "It was a joke." (well, I thought it was) "I did!"

To tell you the truth the whole promise thing is a blur. Taken at a mad party I can just about remember. Not for one moment did I think my friend would keep to it.

There again, I suppose he had no choice. Stupid, needless bloody pact!

I grab the bath tap again. Here I must groan, as loud as possible. The implementation of the deed floods my mind. The cutting of our fingers, the mixing of blood – straight from the pages of a medieval scroll. Hands up, I was young. Some would say naïve, others would class me as arrogant and selfish. In defence, if I dare, looking back I would call myself a dreamer, one of those people who align life with fiction, and believe me, that is far too kind.

Moving uncomfortably on the flimsy sixties chair I try to rest my thumping head against the wall. Tiny black dots float in front of my eyes, blurring my vision, tightening the hold.

I had experienced days such as this before – many. 'Hangover dramas,' my mother called them. 'Self-induced sickness.'

I guess she was right. However, this time the main miscreant was an emotion more in keeping with my beloved grandmother's way of thinking.

'That naughty arrow of Eros has landed. The heart has discovered what the head foolishly dismissed.'

A wise woman? You decide.

The room spins. I must stop my mind from rambling. It is getting me nowhere.

Here I am, six o' clock on the first day of the new Millennium, the church bell ringing, joyous, happy, stomach turning cheerful, and I have no will-power to move.

Scientists quote the brain as the most brilliant piece of human creation; an organ to be amazed at.

If I could shout, I would shout that they are so right, it is an instrument of pride or destruction. In my case, the latter calls.

What can I do?

Help me.

———

Alone, the idea would have escaped me.

My task is simple – given to me as a child by my beloved grandmother.

'Your Grandmother?' you query.
Oh yes, *'Write, read, heal,'* she would say.

That is it, a true conversation between my subconscious and myself. I will call it a journal: you, dear reader, can be my judge and jury.

'What will you write?' Anticipation is growing.

Everything, of course.

Easing myself from the chair I run my fingers along the smooth plaster painted walls – wobble once or twice. My aim – the sanctum of the bedroom.

I feel my way across the lounge. Past a sofa scattered with cushions, books and half my wardrobe. Marvel at how nothing has really changed from the previous day.

You remind me there has been no Millennium bug set free in the country's electrical appliances. No alien life over-running the capital. No hand that has suddenly stopped the world from turning. My flat still looked and smelt the same. Its occupant no tidier than back in 1999.

I want to scream. I have changed!! I crawl into the chaotic mess I choose to call a bedroom.

Oh bed, receive this wretched mortal.

I feel no need to close the window blind. Surplus activity in the world cannot be halted, even though all and sundry will be recovering from the dire after effects of too much drink, too much food. A few maybe nursing a broken heart – like mine.

Rummaging in the drawers that stand at the side of my bed I gather all the blank paper I can find. Taking up a pen, from between my underwear at the bottom of the drawer I exercise my hand into the writing position. With a tenacity even I was unaware I owned, I begin to scribble, starting from the onset of my troubles when I knew nothing, yet thought I knew everything.

Scanning the first line of hurried script, I sink deeper beneath the hotchpotch I have the cheek to label my life.

'This, dear reader, is the case for the prosecution. The case of Bryant versus Conscious.'

October 1989

From a distance I could hear the slow 'drip, drip, drip' of trickling condensation. Spattering onto wood, before 'pitter, pattering' downwards towards its destination on the floor. Struggling to gain consciousness, the consistent repetitiveness irritated my thumping head and drove my muffled brain crazy. I knew snuggling back under the eiderdown was impossible, partly due to the noise and partly due to the problem I was having with opening my eyes. Do not giggle, but they had secured themselves tight. This problem, I have to admit, was my fault: vast amount of eyelash glue. I so wanted the long black spider legs that were the 'in thing' of the day, but this morning, after swallowing every mixture of alcohol offered, they angered me. I would have to spit on my finger, then wet the confounded things as much as I could.

I began, the gooey substance sticking to my fingers, locking them together, forcing me to spit more. Once done, I stared round the room. It was decorated in colours of bright orange and pink. My psychedelic den. An announcement to the world that this girl is her 'own' woman. Glancing in the direction of the window I noticed a tiny puddle of water forming on the newly painted bedroom windowsill. Translucent H20 glistening in the glare of the bright winter sun.

First thought: 'the bloody window is leaking.'

Second thought: 'who cares.'

Feeling the sting of an over-rubbed nose I sniff, inhaling the overpowering smell of stale cigarette smoke. It causes me to gag. The pungent odour is on my pillow, my sheets, my hair, even on my crumpled clothes.

"Unjust," was my instant reaction. "Bloody unjust."

Why does someone have to end up resembling an ashtray when all they had wanted was to enjoy what I dubbed, 'a night on the tiles', or in layman's language, 'an alcoholic binge'? I can vaguely recall someone singing (maybe shouting) 'Congratulations' and 'Celebrations' over and over again.

Oh Lord – that had got to be me, hence the dry aching throat.

I must have tumbled into bed at some ungodly hour, dishevelled and exhausted, the boom, boom, boom of the dance music pounding in my head.

I really want to laugh, if only my mouth would move in that direction, as little bits of memory float in and out of my banging head. Friends and family cavorting around a hired room like idiots, (sorry, grabbing the smelly pillow to splutter at the resurrected sight), arms holding aloft drinks in crystal glasses; (splutter again at my mother's snobbery and stupidity); sights never to be mentioned again within the realm of 'proper family gatherings'. You see, it was my mother's idea, this so-called get-together. A double whammy for her newly graduated daughter in her twenty first year. I will dub it the Grand Hotel pompous bash, an 'up your nose' mission.

'Not fair,' you say.

Don't spare your sympathy. I know my mother!

All my relatives, on her side, came from hard working backgrounds. *She* was the sister, aunt, or cousin, whose fate had inspired her to marry the wealthy banker. Talk about rubbing their faces into the class system mud. She had no idea. With her flame coloured bob, (yep, her fault mine is the colour of New England's leaves in the fall) my snooty mother had no idea at all to the hard graft it took to put a crust of bread in their mouth. How many pay-days it took to save for a dress or suit to make them feel acceptable in surroundings such as these. They were a trillion miles away from her cheque book and newly acquired credit card. Even so, she neither questioned or showed interest in their ongoing struggles.

I will sum it up as a case of 'heaven forbid' if she had to shop anywhere but the finest delicatessen or boutique in the high street. My mother was a paragon of 'class division'. and she revelled in it. All the same I loved her in my way. She amused me. Her constant declaration of 'keeping up with the Joneses' (whoever the Joneses were), turned snobbery into a farce.

It was far more humorous than any comic book character.

To be honest I am the constant disappointment. The son she had craved arrived in the guise of female gender, and once her sylph like body had been distorted by pregnancy first time

21

around there was no chance of a sister or brother. As I grew, her derision grew. I am not saying she did *not* love me, she just saw me as the genuine 'care about nothing, express my opinion, do as I please' rich bitch.

She would quip, "Her father's shadow. No room for improvement."

For the record, I would not have envisaged any other life.

—

I peer from under my striking pink overlay, squinting at the watery droplets starting to drip in swifter rotation onto the striking pink carpet. Mother will perspire a bucket load of sweat trying to dry the large stain. What the heck.

I have more important things to deal with. Phantoms that keep rotating in my inebriated brain. Bleached out jeans and mid length T shirts, vibrant dresses with large shoulder pads, gaudy miniskirts worn with black, brown, white or pink leggings. Fluffy (Madonna copied) hair, large earrings of various colours, worn with variegated pieces of glass jewellery. Guys of every nationality, dressed as replicas of the television series 'Miami Vice', plying me with drinks, and good wishes "Well done. Good for you. Bottom up".

The list could go on.

I stretch my body. It hurt. Every muscle screamed – stop. I obeyed. Snuggling further into the feather filled pillow I conjure up a face I am safe with. Jimmy. Jimmy Grant. My best, *best* friend in all the world, even if he is from the 'council house' estate. Actually, Mother liked him – a lot. Funny, you bet! Matter of fact I would go as far as naming him a 'bedmate' (metaphorically speaking) in the ongoing student search for freedom.

Stop it this instant.

You frown.

The nodding and winking I mean. Jimmy and I are friends, nothing more or less.

It was pure good luck that we had gelled from day one of our university life. No soppy romance, no quick satisfaction, just real, close friendship. By that, as anyone who has a guy for a mate will agree I mean harmony. That special bond of integrity and openness; a knowledge, some say, of what the other is thinking. Okay, we argued. Waved our banner. Marched in every protest we could find, and laughed so much our faces would go into a spasm. A true friendship forged in the name of freedom.

Here, I must share a secret – my marching was tinged with a little (OK, big) distraction – blonde hair, blue eyes.

No, not my friend. His colouring was definitely the opposite.

"Sad," you intersperse. "Especially as you bind so well."

I will laugh, say "That's life," turn over and moan.

—

My toes are restricted by something bound around my legs and feet.

"Hell, what f – hand has grabbed my legs."

I struggled harder, promising to pummel the joker into the ground.

My hand shot down the bed, ready for the warmth of other flesh. I was grabbing, clutching raised nylon flowers. 'Eek.' I feel again – lace – wound about my incarcerated legs tights – those things that kept the knickers hidden, and made female legs a bonus to look at (my father's opinion). For me, at this precise moment, I wished to know what maniac had invented such things. It had got to be male. Their self-satisfaction produced these items of torture to be tight around the legs, and even *tighter* over the tiny blobs of flesh and bone at the end of feet.

I needed to stretch, free myself from these cages of nylon frippery. I wrenched my hot legs – nothing budged.

"Good workmanship," you giggle.

I fight like a demon possessed. "Bloody nuisance," I shriek back.

I try to stretch again. This time the vivid fuchsia top (purchased deliberately to annoy my mother) bit into my fleshy arms. The one inch straps, adorned with deeper pink sequins were pushing my ample bosom upward, and outward by the minute.

I swear female clothes are designed to fight with our conscious.

'Is my bum too big?' 'Should I buy a padded dress?' 'Where has my waist gone?'

Fat frame, thin frame, it does not matter. We all get sucked into the three-way mirror. Who knows better than me?

I rub my stinging face. I needed sleep, not this constant aching that every organ within my body felt obliged to come up with. I wished to stop remembering, not confront the clothing on my bottom half.

'It' had got to be bad.

"How do you know?" Your voice is smooth.

"My rebellious nature," I whisper.

Pulling the covers as high to my chin as possible I search the depths of the ruffled bed. Guess what? I am blinded. Sparkling trousers are laughing back at me, gold lamé culottes. Heavy, hot, and twisted round my jumping legs. Their voluminous panels were strangling my size fourteen plus size thighs; equal measure to the pink straps cutting my shoulders. This *was* my hour of expiration. I was being killed by clothes.

How was this so? I was a freedom fighter – well, something of that sort.

I would not be soli – solid – solidified to this bed.

Hands up if you have heard the continuous thump of a blacksmith's hammer? Its forceful smashing down onto an iron anvil? If you can say yes, then know my pain.

My fault or not, I am suffering in slow motion.

Rubbing my black smudged eyes, I pray for release. Ask to be anything – the sea dragging inland the shale – sand kissing the shore – a tiny boat bobbing on the distant horizon – **Anything!**

Grant this, and like the preachers in history who brand drink the 'Curse of the Devil', I will agree. Never, never again.

—

From the black mist of my stupor the voice thundered.

"Rhia, telephone, please come down this instant."

Then, silence. A nightmare. I return to that dense oblivion.

"Rhia." This time the voice was louder, more distinct, a booming in my ear.

My arms flail, hit out at the sound that appears to be attacking my head, my eyes shoot open, vaguely make out the blurred shadow leaning over me.

I am right, this is my time. My slow slide downhill to the fiery pit. A devil has come to kidnap me.

I gesture for the figure to recede, back into the shadows of its parallel world.

"Go, go," I command from my position in the pit.

A voice. "If I repeat myself once more I will spray you with water."

"Ahh," my dry throat moans.

This is cruel, even if it is a nightmare.

Holding my head with both hands I try to focus better, but the more I closed and re-opened my eyes the blur was becoming – scary!! I screamed.

The sight before me pained my booze muddled brain. Swathed in a pale blue bath robe, hair tightly wound around spiky rollers, face imprisoned by a green cream mask, stood my mother; a simile for what the majority of the human race would presume an extra-terrestrial alien looked like.

"Rhia," I could tell her patience was growing thin. "Please get up." (my mother never forgot her position), "It is nearly five o' clock, and Jimmy is over excited."

"Jimmy, over excited. Why. how?"

Arms were being wafted in the direction of the door. Thin red lips were twitching, trying hard not to crack the smooth paste covering her chin. "I do not know. Poor boy, I should imagine he can guess what state you are in."

It took me a moment or two in registering what she was saying. Cheek.

I counted five slowly, counted again, then grasped the hand extended my way. Hoisting myself upward I tugged at the pink top.

The eyes, reminding me of a person posing behind a cardboard figure at the funfair, stared in disbelief. "Oh dear, Rhia, you look dreadful – again."

Here we go; wait for it; admonishment; moan; derision; disappointment.

Looking away in disgust the green face took in the huge stain on the carpet.

"Oh no." Tiny lines appeared down the side of her mouth. "You have allowed the room to get overheated."

The figure ran to the window, threw it open (more than cruel: tyrannical), bent down and rubbed vigorously, using anything she could get her hands on (namely my clean towels). A minute or two later the figure returned, the cream mask a mass of broken pieces.

"Stand." The voice was loud.

I began to shiver, the cool air circulating the room, and finding me on my bed.

I am telling you – if you have ever heard the phrase, 'split the head or ears'- this was it.

Mother (I cannot keep calling her 'the figure', although I must say it suited her better) screamed at top 'C'.

"You have got to sort yourself out, young lady. Here you are, a graduate (yeah, yeah), your father a prominent banker (grab that), and you – you are in a state of drunken sloth."

I thought she was going to cry. Decided I needed to be a trifle more helpful.

Grabbing a good chunk of the blue seersucker robe I hauled myself from the bed.

It all happened so quickly that even now on writing I can scarcely believe it, so I will ask. Why is it that when you need to stand, your legs have other ideas!

I felt each bubble and dip in the gown slipping through my trembling fingers. Reaching instinctively for the belt tied loosely around my mother's waist I missed my hold, dipped, snaked, slid my way toward the floor. Bump. crumpling into a pile at the startled woman's feet. The expletive springing from my dribbling mouth doubled itself as backward I reeled – thump – my banging head connecting with the bright pink carpet. In one hand Mother's blue seersucker dressing gown, in the other a clutch of carpet tuft trying to free itself from my grip. Without hesitation, and certainly with no thought for my well-being, my mother upped the shrill squeal.

"Get up, Rhia, this instant. You should be ashamed of yourself."

Glaring at me from her vantage point of five foot seven, the mouth opening and closing with a barrage of disdain, the cracked green face bristled with contempt.

I wanted to take hold of her foot, and call out, "I am your daughter. Have pity."

Nothing, apart from incoherent gaggling.

The blue robe was moving, slipping from my fingers with each pull of Mother's wrist. She was shivering as she towered above me in her silk shift.

"No good will come of all this ridiculous behaviour. A sticky end, my girl – you mark my words."

With that my green faced monster disengaged herself from my grip and flung the door as wide as possible. I heard the feet pounding down the stairs, returning the dressing gown to its rightful place, and calling my father in that trumped up voice used only when she was really mad.

Thinking of Jimmy I croaked, "Wait for me. I am on my way."

—

It took ten painful minutes to crawl on my hands and knees down the stairs. The descent was tricky. Each step a mountain, each dip a ravine to fall into. Reaching the hall, I stumbled my way to the walnut table and Mother's precious white telephone. Clutching the receiver with a shaking hand I gasped into it, "Hello."

A thunderous guffaw penetrated my head. I could not sit. To do that would create bedlam in my stomach and possible catastrophe on the parquet floor. Instead I sprawled myself across the back of Mother's padded chair, conveniently placed by the main door for telephone chatting to her socialite friends.

"Rhia, you're plastered." More thunderous laughter as he slurred his voice in fun.

"Very funny," I hissed. "What do you want? What is so important that it cannot wait until tomorrow?"

Jimmy rattled his teeth; an infuriating habit my friend knew would capture my attention.

"Ah, my news," he hesitated. "It is like this."

Off he went, sentences flying back and forth. Only the odd word made sense, striking an impact from the jumbled meanings. Among them – pact, break, passport, Berlin.

Everything else – zero.

My friend spoke so quick that I found the panting of his breath far more fascinating to listen to than his conversation. I would later swear he had passed through the barrier of sound; he had become an athlete of speech.

Willing him to finish I held fast to the wall (a reference to my future), relieved when he had completed the lengthy narrative.

"Right," I hiccupped.

Jimmy was not amused. He vowed to come over the next day, in expectation of my answer.

What answer!!

I replaced the receiver.

"And?" came the freshly washed face round the kitchen door.

"Not sure," I stuttered.

"Really, you are impossible." My mother drew breath. "One of these days you will wish you had taken notice."

I could sense her feet in the starting blocks to argue, prayed she would not.

"Mrs Wallace is popping round from next door for wine and cake. I am sure she does not want to be greeted by you."

"The Joneses – how quaint," I whispered.

Mother's brow held her severest scowl. Time to pull my generous bottom up the stairs.

–

I began to crawl upwards with greater observation than coming down. Not because I felt better; as a matter of fact I was beginning to lose my fight with my inner organs, but my right hand kept throbbing. As I listened to Jimmy (OK, OK, I really tried – **I did**) my eyes noticed red swollen skin around a thin jagged line cut into the fleshy part of my thumb. The sight of the angry contusion caused me to retch, as it was now. Squatting in hope of the nausea subsiding, I searched for tell-tale blood stains on Mother's white carpet (I know, a ridiculous colour, however expensive it was), searched again – could not find a spot. Stretching out my fingers I looked for other cuts and scratches. None. Strange.

Pressing around the offending mark it ached, yet it could not be fresh. I ruled out foul play today – think. A careless knife wound at the party? Maybe. A broken glass? probably. Yet surely I would have a small inkling. No, the inch and half wound was a complete puzzle.

I dismissed any more recollections. Thinking was hard work, and continual looking at the wound was creating a sea-sickness effect.

"Breathe deep," Jimmy would say. "Fall foul of the dreaded nausea, and the boat goes down."

Silly boy!

Even so, everything would have to wait. It was becoming crucial to visit the bathroom, and after if there would be an after – I would sleep.

2

The world had gone crazy, lost its balance. That was how I summed up the events that unfolded the day after Jimmy's telephone call. I had risen early, dazed, dry mouthed, and still very hung over. Dressing quickly I tried, with my fingers, to de-matt my hair, before applying a little artificial colour to my pale cheeks. Wandering downstairs I noticed the large grandfather clock in the hall striking midday. Rushing into the kitchen I closed the door, quickly deciding my mother's nattering would be far more acceptable to my painful head than the noise emanating from that huge family heirloom. The room was empty. Silence – no Mother, no radio, no nattering! Perfect peace.

In gratitude I sat down. Placing my head in cupped hands I spotted the neat folded white paper propped against the vase of white dahlias in the middle of the table. I stared at it, dreading its revelations: 'so and so is coming, please tidy yourself up', or 'be back soon, please do not be sick again in the bathroom!' I knew my mother. So when I read, 'See you later,' signed, 'Mother', I was positively on a high.

I spent the next four hours watching a swirl of milk play 'catch up' with wheat puffs around a ceramic dish, listening to soothing music, and practising what I would say to my friend when, and if he arrived.

What troubled me, and to be truthful I am not sure why, was the word 'pact'. It was just a four lettered word, and the only one to have fixated itself in my head from Jimmy's phone call. Maybe it was something I had said to him on my party night, something he found really funny. Maybe it was something he had said to me. That's it, a joke, phew! Yet what peeved me most was the hold it seemed to carry. Almost as though we had promised something to each other, made a vow, cut ourselves in honour –

Noooo, please I hate blood!

By this time the 'puffs' were playing 'catch up' with the milk at such speed it was a miracle they were not floundering on Mother's squeaky clean floor. Slamming the dish to the sink – (oops, it is Mother's best china) I think ok the words Jimmy had gabbled. Thought, but could not fully remember. The 'pact' word was chasing everything else from my brain, when the clock in the hall chimed four thirty as the doorbell rang. It had got to be Jimmy, for let's be honest, Mother would not be seen dead standing ringing the bell if she had forgotten her key. She would phone, make sure I knew the exact time of her arrival, open the door, and greet her for all the neighbours to see.

I eased the heavy door ajar. Along with the vast majority of young Mothers in the street fetching their children from school (I bother to mention this for the floods of laughter that will follow). I began to laugh, splutter in astonishment at the 'thing' before me. My friend stood in the porch swaddled in what I can only describe as the most ridiculous hooded anorak I had ever seen. Pockets bulging, sleeves too long, the outline of his face hidden within a mass of straggly green fur. He looked, and I believe all those onlookers would agree, like that elusive 'Yeti.' I was beside myself with ongoing spontaneous laughter (told you). Sweeping past me, Jimmy kicked the heavy wooden door with his foot. There followed an almighty bang as the gaudy gold lock crashed into its gaudy gold niche. Pulling down the offending hood, Jimmy ran his fingers through his mop of dark curly hair.

"Funny hey," my friend leant toward me casting a dark brown eye over my fatigued features. "You may not think so a week down the line."

He watched as the quizzical scowl travelled across my brow.

"Ah," he sighed. "Not spoken to your parents yet?"

Parents? Spoken – whatever did he mean? Please, brain, enlighten me.

Jimmy was miffed, to say the least. He threw himself down onto the chair. Sat there eyeing me in that arrogant male way. You know the one, where the nose and chin are tilted upwards and the whole persona claims to have the upper hand in any argument.

My head swam, as the shrug of my shoulders and his impatience collided.

"OK, OK. Last night you obviously did not take in anything I told you, too far gone as usual."

Cheeky sod, how could he? Friend and all that.

"The letting of blood," Jimmy was shouting. **"This."**

He held his thumb aloft. My stomach lurched. Across the fleshy part of his right thumb was a small jagged cut exactly replica to my own. I raised my own thumb.

"Bingo," he hissed. "That tanked up body felt something."

I wanted to bellow.

"I can't remember a bloody thing," I sniffled.

Nothing, no sympathy, no consideration for my head. My green swaddled friend wore the puffed up air associated with a champion gladiator.

"Mixed the red stuff," he was saying, spiteful when I am so queasy, wagging the digit in front of my nose.

I swallowed hard. "Do not mention blood," I managed to gulp.

A sticky moment when Jimmy's scowl was as black as the sky outside, then my friend laughed, putting his wounded pride back in order, looked at me in that way he knew I could not fathom. "I will give you this, girl, you come up with some idiotic suggestions. Still, as your best friend I will go along with it."

Go along with it. Go along with what!

He circled his reddened thumb around my face. I took a step backwards fighting for a composure that was alluding me.

I so wanted to scream. Was it my fault I could not recall our conversation of the day before, believe me, I had other, more important things on my mind. I could not bring to mind that silly 'pact' word still running round my brain as if the devil himself had set it free, also the promise I was supposed to have made to Jimmy. So, was it really my fault I forgot it in the mist of drink?

Jimmy was muttering. "Even if it means our parting, who am I to argue?"

The expression on his face hit me like an express train shooting through an abandoned station. Now, I was really lost!

Jimmy noted my blank reaction. "The millennium parting?" his voice held an icy expression.

"I am not sure –" I began.

He stopped me short, temper wobbling on the edge of explosion. "You, Rhia, *you* – made me promise that if by the year 2000 we had not found the secret to the freedom we seek, we would say 'goodbye'."

To put it politely, I was gob smacked.

"Good-bye" I stuttered. "Good-bye." The shriek sounded around the hallway. It had got to be a sick, ridiculous joke. Of course we would never be anything but friends, I did not fancy *him,* but part – *never.* I searched my friend's eyes. Looked for the tell-tale signs that appeared when he was mucking about. Nothing. He was serious.

I swallowed hard. "*My* suggestion?"

"Oh yes," he nodded. "*You* insisted."

"I was drunk?"

"So, so." he returned

"Not serious then." I threw my head back in relief.

"Indeed it was, we drew blood."

"NO – ooooo" The horrible sound reverberated around the minimalistic hall.

Jimmy's voice had become gruff. "You were in earnest all right. Whatever was going on in that foggy head of yours did not include me. As a matter of fact you laid down the hour and time. Midnight on Millennium eve."

My eyes lifted themselves upward, my mouth shot out the first remark it latched onto.

"Thank God, a prank. Ten years. Phew."

My friend stood up, removed the anorak, laid it across the back of Mother's chair (she will kill him), and without a backward glance waltzed into the kitchen.

I stood there, my eyes following his back like a fish out of water.

—

Reader, I have to think. At the end of everyone's dark tunnel it is said there is light. My grandmother told me that when I was four, and frightened of the dark.

I am now twenty-one. Thirty something is a long, long way off. I must be sensible. The 'goodbye' debate would never happen.

'How do you know?' I hear you ask.

Well, as I have already said, Jimmy and I are best of friends. Friends do not part.

'Right.' you whimper.

Can you not see? Jimmy and I are modern day Robin Hoods, seeking out the true meaning of freedom. We require our own emancipation as much as others. We alone are the crusaders of our destiny. That means we call the shots, not some silly bloodletting pact. Please do not look at me in that way. I was in a state of dipsomania the night my mouth ran away with itself.

'Answer.' you screech.

Answer? of course. I know the solution. Clever, I think. Use every part of my feminine psyche. Play to my friend's ego. Oh yes, coercion grand style.

You frown.

Okay, any damn thing then, that would make my best friend forget such nonsense.

—

I wandered into the kitchen. Jimmy was sitting at the table shaping Mother's note into a boat, whizzing it around the table, before securing it once more to its home at the base of the dahlia vase. His face held the usual tomboyish grin until he heard my movements. Playing a game? Two can join in.

I slithered to his side (supposedly every inch the Mata Hari. I know, she was slinky – so what), and ruffled the top of his head.

"Dear friend, you know me so well. My mind is a blur. Come to my rescue."

Do not let anyone tell you that the male ego is tiny. Not true.

Jimmy instantly put down his paper toy and turned my way. His words tumbled into the air: the party, coloured fairy lights, flowing drink, two friends, a pen knife, bloodletting, a vow, sealed and bound, a promise to search for the true meaning of freedom for ourselves and others, finally interjections of the pact – and – a name. Jimmy said 'Kurt', Berlin wall, protest – listen, Rhia, this is important.

My attention was secured.

"You don't mind putting up with Kurt in Berlin?" Jimmy was asking.

"Pardon?" I whispered.

"For goodness sake, Rhia, take note. Kurt has had a tip off the Berlin Wall is opening on the night of November 9th. He has invited us over. Do you mind putting up with that ego centred nosey-parker for a couple of days?"

Putting up with Kurt, was my friend mad? Our blue eyed German mate had been the figment of my nightly excursions since university.

My guilt, reader, Jimmy did not know.

I hesitated, to make the moment look good, and yes, I can hear you, best friends and all that. Come on, there are certain things a girl cannot disclose.

I continued to ruffle his hair, letting the name 'Kurt' flow over me like sweet honey. What more could a girl want than a protest march with the male of her dreams. Drawing an image of the six foot blonde in my mind I remembered our arguments. Kurt and I against Jimmy, harmless fun – at least that was my take on the political gibberish.

Jimmy moved his head from my hand. "You do mind. Drat. I have told the clod it would be great."

I smiled as sweetly as I could. "No, you have got it wrong. I will put up with him."

Jimmy twirled me round until I landed in his lap, then gave me the biggest hug he could manage. "Great. Promise, we need never see him again after that. I know he is an obnoxious prat. He actually troubles me, almost as though he holds a secret."

I forced a giggle. Secrets. I breathed long and hard. The only thing wrong with Kurt was his reluctance to ask me out.

Returning my friend's hug, I whispered, "Let us forget the pact. Pretend it did not happen."

Jimmy sat bolt upright, moved me to the edge of his knee "But it did."

Why was the male so simple? We are in the twentieth century, not the medieval age. We are not knights of old where a pact is sacrosanct. Yep, I hear you – Yesterday I compared us to knights of old. Well, that was then, and this is now.

"It was a prank Jimmy, my prank."

"Even so, a promise is a promise."

I struggled to understand his insistence on the subject. A crazy, drunken pact. Could he not see I would promise anything when under the influence? (Mother's choice of expression when she does not want to say her daughter is drunk.) I would say Jimmy was punishing me for being rich, but that is not fair, he knew from day one, and did not care. Could he then be on Mother's side, agree with her when she thundered I needed to take responsibility? No longer a care-free, speak to the hand, teenager, but a young woman.

'Maybe,' you nod.

Sitting on the fence, are we?

Tell me, reader, have you never had a friend that you tell most, and I underline most, of your secrets to?

I wait for you to agree. Silence.

Do you know what, I am not going to argue with you. I have to use my energy thinking about Kurt, lovely, dreamy, to die for Kurt.

A frown passes over your face.

I suppose you are considering lies and stratagems, contrivances and guile.

What the heck, do not worry, I will work it out. Jimmy will come under the same deviation as my mother. It works in the end.

'This is not your mother,' you remind me.

I choose to ignore you.

3

Frantic is the word I will use in describing the remaining two weeks before Jimmy and I departed for Berlin. My parents were not happy. They moaned and complained, grumbled and groaned, lamented their only child was marching into a conflict of war, dramatic or what. Mother saw this 'adventure' as I will put it, to be a rebellious part of student indulgence. A far right attitude to avoid work. Father finally conceded he had wished me to travel, but not particularly flanked by two young men, and definitely not in a country where the atmosphere would be volatile.

I asked him if he would like me to fly to the moon.

His answer – use your imagination!

Both questioned me over behaviour and welfare. I testily assured them both would be at the top of my list, whilst nursing Kurt's overpowering proximity within my heart. He was all I could really think about.

Jimmy had taken to arriving daily in that larger than life anorak. Parading up and down the hallway in front of my mother. His excuse, to explain the coat's virtues of warmth and protection. Distraught over what she nick-named it's 'common' look my mother tried to suggest various alternatives. One idea was an all in one leather (top quality) bikers outfit, with a flag, scarf, bobble hat and furry gloves. Thanks to my father she was soon voted down on that. Enlightened, I would have been mistaken for an overdressed fool more than a serious protester. Another of her fanciful suggestions found itself in the area of an astronaut suit, a flame resistant, Velcro zapped material which on its own, without any other clothes, would have boiled me to a frazzle. In the end, after much consoling from my friend, the woman gave in, travelled out of town to an 'upper class' shop, where she purchased a 'named' anorak as near to Jimmy's as possible. Still, much to Mother's disgust, father was in stitches. The first time he had allowed himself to laugh since being told about the march. At least I can own up to wearing the most 'classy' fur anorak, with a backpack to match.

Jimmy guaranteed my parents their daughter would come home intact. By that he meant no missing arms or legs (made you wonder, me too at the time). He was so earnest that I could not stop myself whacking him on the foot with my flag pole. What was he going to do, tie my arm to his, use glue to make sure I stayed by his side? Anyway, it worked, I was given their blessing. Two days before our departure Jimmy received a letter from Kurt. I quivered at the thought, grew impatient for my friend to show me, or read it to me. It was a fact sheet, information of where to meet, a place to stay, news of the city, no snippet or two to ask over me. Shame.

Kurt suggested we book a couple of beds in a youth hostel a few streets away from the west to east checkpoint known as 'Charlie'. Although he had no idea what the place was like, he promised to meet us around midday on the 9th of November. He explained how busy the city would be, as from what he gathered people would attack the wall with gusto. He also wrote that if his countrymen would only stop and consider, things were not really that bad, and opening the wall may 'open a can of worms'. Jimmy was furious at this comment. He protested that Kurt was being ridiculous. He lived in the city, had eyes and ears to hear the screams of the ordinary people and the condemnation of the world's press.

I put it down to political agitating. Kurt tormenting my friend.

Kurt continued to berate the Americans for manning the western side of 'Charlie', making another passing comment to the future of his nation. How the loss of discipline, and the mixing of culture would destroy the ordered pattern. Jimmy really moaned at that. Again, I came to my dream's defence, expressing my opinion that my friend did not understand German political rhetoric, therefore we should keep our thoughts to ourselves. Kurt concluded by stating that everything to do with the wall was a secret. He had found out through an informant (sounds really MI5 don't you think), who if discovered would lose his life (what is it with men and drama), so please say nothing. He ended in wishing us a safe journey, and that he was looking forward to our company – you bet.

Jimmy stuffed the letter into his pocket, muttering something like, "Bloody fool," under his breath. Part of me was concerned that our visit would be overtaken by Jimmy and Kurt arguing or political nonsense, and to be truthful I had other things in mind. The other part could not help but wonder if Kurt was not quite in favour of the wall being dismantled. I felt guilty that this thought should ever concern me. In practical terms, why would Kurt invite us to witness the wall in all probability being demolished and torn down – does not make sense. No, this disturbance in my mind is down to Jimmy and his stupid talk.

"Kurt's on the level, trust me."

My friend pulled a face (sour grapes if you ask me), and shook his head. "He is not to be trusted."

I laughed, "And you are?"

Jimmy looked deep into my eyes, decided not to retaliate, and turned to speak with my father who had herded Mother through the front door along with her multitude of shopping bags.

"I have new underwear for you to pack." Mother grabbed my arm, pulling me from hallway into the lounge.

My heart was already walking a tight line to keep it in control. The nearer November crept forward, the more I think of Kurt. In my heart the guy was lovely.

I know, a feminine word. Well, I don't care. *He* is lovely, *lovely,* **lovely.**

The day of departure came. Sad to say, neither set of parents came to the ferry port to wave us 'bon voyage'. Mine, they were still cross at their failure to intercept my will-power. Both feigned work and social events, yet both were constantly asking us questions. Jimmy's, they really did have to work. Even so, it would have been great to wave to someone. Stepping onto that ferry my stomach lurched, somersaulted as never before. I took it to be partly due to the rough sea, partly from expectation. Gripping Jimmy's arm I held fast to my rucksack and banner while pressing my face to the distant horizon.

—

From Calais we boarded a bus that would carry us to Germany. I say a 'bus', more like an old chunting train carriage. It was packed – so much for 'something' that was supposed to be a secret (Kurt's words), it had spread at the speed of lightning. Travelled so quickly that one could only take a guess into 'how' or 'by who'.

Pushing and shoving our way onto this ramshackle bus, using shoulders, elbows, bags and feet Jimmy and I rammed, trust me this phase is correct, into the first empty seat. Scrunching ourselves tight up against the window we were soon joined by a young boy. The driver's demand of three people sharing two seats did not take into consideration the weight or height of the occupiers. The boy was large (and yes, I am robust myself) but it appeared he was determined to squeeze his way to comfortability. To add to our humility, he had the largest flag you could imagine. He poked the bright yellow pennant under our nose as he positioned it across all three laps, the black letters, 'Freedom', sticking into my ribs like a skewer.

I wanted to slap him, grab his bold banner and snap it at least to the size of ours, which was not small, but lay at our feet in trampled pity. The boy, once settled, jarred my ears with his constant stream of dribble and crunching teeth. Food was entering his mouth at the rate of a meteorite falling from space. I had not slept for around twelve hours, due to excitement and expectation, and this boy was irritating me beyond words. The prolonged agony of being skewed, dribbled on, shook around as the bus rattled its way through the early November morning, came to a disastrous end, puttering to a stop down a long dark street. By this time the boy, whose bottom had become lodged in the seat was snoring his head off, along with my red faced friend.

It was me who could neither lean forward or backward. The pain in my ribs was completely overpowering any sensible thought, to the point that I made a silent promise that any poor chicken in my hands would not be trussed up for barbecuing, instead I would give it a more enlightened end to its miserable life. I thumped Jimmy in the arm. My friend jumped, causing the kid to shoot upright in his tiny space, grasping and pulling the end of his precious flag. You can imagine what this did to the pole – and my ribs. I let out one almighty scream.

Jimmy shot forward, causing the bloody pole to ram even further into my side. This time the scream pierced the stale air of the bus, making the kid's eyes grow larger; balls of shining

41

crystals in a face of waxy cream. To help this process two women appeared, equally the same size, the same chewing mouths, babbling on about 'their boy' being disturbed. Jeering at my discomfort the two women pulled hard on the boy's shoulders. He leapt to his feet, popping from his resting place like a champagne cork. At this point I let myself sink into slight sorrow. It registered: the kid was going to throw up. His round hamster face began to contort, his mouth gurgling with what I decided was bile. The round stomach moved in conjunction with his mouth. Easing the wretched pole out from my sore midriff I shrunk as far back as possible, anywhere to distance myself from the forthcoming projectile vomit.

'You may be in the firing line,' you say in an unconvincing tone.

My answer: 'Not if I can help it, not on your life!'

I threw myself (as best as I could) behind Jimmy's protruding arm, just in time. The boy coughed, choked, gagged, I thought the stench would choke me.

Burying my nose into Jimmy's sweaty armpit (save me from the extremes of the male), the boy started to move down the bus. Mopping his brow, the women glared at us, before turning on him with a certain degree of self-indulgence, telling him off for gorging his own lunch box and theirs. Struggling to free ourselves from the rancid smell Jimmy took my hand, snatched the bags from the overhead rack, and led the way out of the seat, tiptoeing down the aisle. Sorry to leave our flag behind we manoeuvred side to side until we reached the door. The driver was none too pleased, waving us out onto the pavement in disgust: his sacred bus had been soiled.

The cool air tickled our heated cheeks and stinging eyes. Amid a crowd as excited as ourselves I threw my arms up to the sky (which did not help my aching ribs) and clasped my hands together. We were here, in Germany. Okay, we had vomit sprayed onto our anoraks (yuk), lost our banner, felt slightly queasy ourselves, yet nonetheless elated. Believe me when I say the coat could be sponged, but the adventure of a lifetime lay before me.

We could make another flag, although Jimmy was moaning over his masterpiece, blaming everything in his way, including me, silly ass.

Searching in my bag for the 'essential wipes' Mother had packed I started to clean our anoraks, briskly brushing from top to bottom in a rhythmic movement. As I rubbed Jimmy's sleeves (he was directly in the line of fire, please help my stomach) I caught the look passing over my friend's face. He was pointing to a building in front of us.

"Kurt, you idiot, I am responsible for Rhia."

I looked from my friend to the door half hidden within the crumbling brickwork, paint peeling and broken. It hung at such an angle to suggest it had been kicked by heavy boots. My first thought was a raid, my second, drugs, my third, I can look after myself.

The neon sign flashing read, 'Hostel', the colour of bright pink a bit seedy. My mouth fell open. This could not be *our* hostel. Not the one Kurt had suggested. Edging nearer we saw a purple swathed lampshade throwing its murky light onto identical painted walls and carpet.

"Smutty." Jimmy wiggled his nose.

"But, Kurt –"

Jimmy stopped me in my tracks "I know, stupid clot, I am sorry Rhia, I know you don't care for him."

What? I have never uttered a word. Dare not now.

"It is revolting," I managed to say.

Jimmy nodded, passing his eyes over our wet coats. "Worse than these."

A smile forced its way onto my lips. I could hear my mother's voice wailing into her handkerchief, berating my father for supplying me with money to let me come.

Moving nearer to the door I cast my glance up the unkempt carpet. Jimmy followed, twitched his nose, his face taking on the guise of disbelief. "Marijuana, let's go."

Grabbing my arm, he pulled me down the street. "Your parents will kill me. Wait until I get my hands on our mate."

"Kurt?"

"Right."

His fury and sarcasm were at their height.

"Well, it's obvious," I said in a haughty manner. "Kurt would not know."

Jimmy made no reply, just threw his hands up to the heavens.

Trying to steer his thoughts away from adorable Kurt I expressed my horror in an exaggerated mode. "The kid – the women – not there?"

Jimmy was unable to stay mad. "Who knows, it's cheap. Sometimes that's all that matters."

My friend giggled in an attempt to ease our worry. We strained our eyes on the building.

"If it was only me, then."

I was astounded, which made him laugh louder.

"You have got to be kidding," I said. "How long before Kurt meets us?"

"An hour, maybe two," my friend replied in a distraught voice.

"That's it, we cannot stay here, not in this state."

Jimmy eyed me "And, what does my good friend propose?"

As usual he was baiting me, firmly being his pompous self, challenging me with his command stance. 'You think of something.'

I let my mind wander, take in the early morning workers. Everywhere would be busy, bursting to the seams with this 'secret' affair. I thought, pondered Jimmy's smug face, thought again, then shrieked, "Eureka."

It had taken a moment or two to register the intention. Outrageous, very much so, downright cheeky if you must know. Jimmy would not be pleased.

'Well?' you shriek.

"Do you know where Kurt lives?" I gabbled.

Jimmy lifted one eyebrow. "Yes, why?"

"We will go there."

"To his house?" Incredulous describes the note in his voice. "His house?"

"Yes."

"No."

"Yes."

"We couldn't."

"We must. Need to change. Where else. In the street?"

The convoluted sentence did the trick.

Believe me when I say fluster is more a female cover up. For a male, very, very unbecoming. Jimmy made excuses, crossed the 't', dotting the 'i'; any pretext that would come up with another solution. At last, thank the heavens, Jimmy, bags and I set off to find a taxi rank. My friend deep in thought.

The weight of contrived sin fled – for the time being, anyhow.

4

Berlin
November 9th 1989

The taxi slipped into a district that was a far cry from the seedy down-town street we had just left. Each house, two to three storeys high, all designed in the same style. Picture windows, dressed in expensive brocade curtains. Embossed solid wood arched doors, stained or painted a glossy white. Smooth painted walls, catching the early morning sunshine. Gardens, laid out in the new fashionable square design that was becoming so popular outside London, edged by meticulously measured white fences: the earth neatly spaded, its colour dark, rich, nutritious, a gardener's dream. Scrubbed pathways, no stains or gum like back home. It was as if everything had to be in order, pristine, and unbelievingly precise.

I could not help but think the sheer opulence of this sub-district would have set my own Mother's heart racing. Jimmy did not speak. He sat crunched up on the leather seat of the taxi in stony silence, focusing hard on the letter in his hand. Every now and then I glanced sideways. Saw again the bold loop of the writing that was undeniably individual to Kurt. The address at the top of the page, the signature at the bottom, and allowed a thrill to run all the way through me.

Depositing us at one of these houses tucked into a corner of the street, the taxi driver mumbled an amount, cleared his throat and proffered his hand. Jimmy dropped what he called 'the extravagant amount' into the outstretched palm. Hauling our bags from where they had lain in the footwell we walked up the path. The taxi turned and disappeared before I stretched for the door knocker; an emblem of an eagle, with eyes that made you feel as though the bird was watching you. I knocked. The door clicked open. *He* (heart started to pound) stepped into the breaking sunlight, fair hair glistening in the dawn light. Behind him a woman, smothered (only word that seems to fit) in an apron of pure white. She was so thin, it would not be wrong of me to say she could have been an apparition.

"Mamma," the voice was one of surprise. "My friends have arrived."

The woman hesitated, then as quickly restored her manners. "Please come in. You are welcome."

Her wobbly voice full of broken English aroused my curiosity, while helping me warm to her. I instantly thought her old, yet 'not old'. 'Worn' would describe her better. She wore her hair stretched back in the tightest bun, highlighting the sallowness of her complexion. Tiny lines flared out from the corners of the hooded pale blue eyes, accompanied by a sag of skin that continually forced her to squint. Her aquiline nose pointed downward reminding me of witches' noses in fairy-tale books. The dry cracked lips were thin and displayed a bluish tinge, hopefully more from the cold than heart trouble. She wore no make-up, not even a hint of powder or lipstick. Her appearance was deliberately nondescript, and after years spent watching my mother's meticulous care, I found this odd. It was almost as if the woman wished to fade into the background, go unnoticed, pass in a crowd as a shadow. What did strike me, and to this day I swear it was genuine, was the radiance of that smile. Jimmy, as you have gathered by now forever the pessimist, would later call her a play actor. For this I branded him a gloom merchant. A person who found fault in everyone.

Jimmy dumped the bags on the other side of the threshold, and once inside the hall we explained our dilemma. Kurt apologised, capturing my gaze and causing that hot infusion that every woman has experienced in times of confusion. To his Mother, who stood with her head bent, he spoke in his native tongue. Once finished he slapped Jimmy on the back (much to my friend's annoyance) saying, "My mistake, you are welcome, hey, Mamma?"

The woman nodded, not once taking her shrewd eyes from her son's face. He offered we look around with an elaborate swing of his arms. "Home."

My eyes travelled from the glass chandelier hanging above our heads, to the old walnut furniture, down to the ash wood parquet floor. Prosperity was screaming at me from oiled and water-colour paintings to expensive trinkets. I tapped Jimmy's arm, as my glance fell on the staircase. Black and white snapshots of children. Children playing, children posing, children laughing. Every size, every age; tall, small, and now and again cute baby snaps. No square inch was uncovered, just rows and rows of faces, the straightness of the frames almost militarised in position. Catching my surprise the woman smiled that smile, directed Kurt to speak. "Welcome to the family album."

It was the catalyst for us all to speak at once.

"A gallery?" Jimmy.

"Memories." Kurt.

"My children, sister's children, cousin's children," his mother tried hard to intervene.

"Wow," I stuttered.

It was during this outburst that I spied the picture. A man with a child of around twelve. Nothing unusual, you say, in which you are correct, apart from one small detail. This man was in uniform of some sort of high command, and man and boy were saluting.

"This one," I pointed to the 10x8 inch frame. "Who is that?"

The woman gasped, implored her son to help. Kurt took my hand (yeah), began to lead me to a room at the end of the hall. "That old thing. A bit of fun, a laugh."

Jimmy glared, retreated into his 'sour grapes' attitude.

"Tea?" Kurt asked.

"Lovely," I sighed.

He indicated to his Mother to prepare tea, who scurried away to the kitchen.

"Sit, sit." Kurt promptly pulled a chair away from the table, indicating me to accept.

To be honest I was grateful. My legs, arms, head, and especially my ribs still ached. I will swear to this day that kid's banner penetrated my lungs.

Jimmy would laugh out loud at that statement, for a punctured lung evidently would create more than bruising; my friend is a know all!

What really troubled me were the unexplainable emotions raging through me.

Removing his anorak Jimmy flung himself down on a chair, bemoaning a pain in his head.

My thoughts: he was the pain. I was tired, but rude, never.

Kurt stepped forward to help me with my coat.

"Sick," I indicated to the marks the baby wipes had not smeared. "Boy on the bus."

Kurt nodded, put out his hand for Jimmy's coat then followed his Mother out the door, and into the kitchen.

Jimmy watched him leave, then leant my way. "I knew it, both are a bit miffed, don't you think? Uncomfortable with us being here."

"Don't be ridiculous. It is their way."

Jimmy shrugged. "I thought they were both touchy over the picture."

"Not at all, we did snoop a bit, and land on their doorstep out of the blue."

"Whose idea?" he growled. My friend gave me one of his long, 'why are you making excuses,' looks, cupped his mouth and whispered in what I must record as a warning tone.

"You say the daftest things. Even a child could see they are wary."

That was it. In my tired, aching state enough was enough.

"If you say one more word I will hit you."

Jimmy pulled a face: horror, ridiculously scary, stupidly silly. I really cannot pen how daft he was acting

"Was that your answer?" I kept my voice as low as possible.

Jimmy scanned the room he was in. Stared at the door to the kitchen. Leant further my way.

"One day, dear girl, your ignorance will land you in hot water."

Hot water? Hot passion I hope. I did not allow my thoughts, hopes, wishes to leave my lips.

Reader, I must add at this point I adore my friend, in the friendly aspect as aforementioned, yet have to outline his defects. He can be surly if he cannot fathom out a problem, whatever that problem is. Half the time I do not know. Mind, the last time he was travelling this pathway was at university – him, Kurt, and me.

I am in no mood for this discussion, it is ending now – This instant, and besides, this girl is otherwise preoccupied.

—

I could not believe how hungry we were. Our cup of tea turned out to be a full English breakfast.

'Your queasy tummy,' you protest.
Blow that. I mimic the need to eat.

Kurt and his Mother chatted endlessly, sometimes drawing us in (Kurt), other times in the tongue that was beyond our weary comprehension. Tiredness began to overtake me, that and the need for a good wash. Putting down my knife and fork I raised my head just in time to catch Jimmy's comment. "Your father at work?"

The atmosphere prickled. Kurt's Mother collected our plates. Kurt sighed.

"It upsets mama that my father is always at work. Today of all days he is working the late shift." He lit a cigarette, jauntily dangling it from his sensuous lips.

"Does he know about the wall?" Jimmy reminded me of a dog gnawing on a bone.

There came a clang, followed by what I presumed to be a swear word in German. Kurt hurried to his Mother's side, retrieved what I could only think to be a kettle that had clattered to the floor. Returning to the dining room doorway he doused the cigarette.

"My father's job is most frustrating. All work, no play. As we know life deals a card," he took a deep breath "We join in the game' choose, work, choose, history, whichever we choose we cannot win." The blonde head shook.

Jimmy scowled.

Me, I was entranced, figuratively speaking; sprawled at the feet of my hero.

My friend's consistent battering was not only beginning to get to me, but to put it in plain language I did not bloody care. All that mattered to me was Kurt.

"Jimmy, this is our hostess's husband you are banging on about."

Now, Jimmy hates being stopped in full flow. The guy believes it is his right to finish whatever he has started. Well, not this time boy. I will overlook the 'if looks could kill' scenario. My friend backed down, changed the subject in the speed of light, praised Kurt's Mother on her dexterity, told Kurt how proud he should be, asked me if I had noticed.

Noticed? for goodness sake, she had prepared, cooked and served us food, took what appeared to be a very stressful telephone call, returned three herself, then washed and cleaned up.

Gold medallist I would say.

I begin to yawn just as the clock on the dresser chimed ten o' clock. Jimmy and I had been awake for twenty-four hours. Kurt flashed me a smile. Everything shuddered.

"My mother has suggested you may like to wash and rest before tonight. We have to go out, but you are welcome to stay."

My heart beat so fast I thought it would leave my body.

Jimmy let out a wheeze. "Great, mate. Sleep and a fresh up is overdue, that right, Rhia?"

"Thank you." was my simple answer.

Jimmy slid his chair away from the table, stretched his arms and headed for the door where Kurt's Mother waited. Her son eased my chair, apologised, "Pardon me" as his fingers caught the back of my neck.

I wobbled. "Whoops" and fell straight into his arms.

I can sense your snigger – so – what would you do?

His arms encircled my waist, tightening their hold, before leading me from the room into the hall, and up the stairs. I could see the anger in Jimmy's eyes as he watched our slow progress.

Longer the better to me.

Could my friend not grasp that his ridiculous 'insight' into the human character got on my nerves? Apart from him having no experience, or qualification in psychology (he said it was intuition) I thought it was complete rot!

As we passed that picture of man and child saluting I could not stop the involuntary shiver passing through me. The darkness of the black uniforms portrayed against the stark white of the photographic cloth created something – sinister. I could not quite figure it out. Maybe it was the way man and child looked into the camera, forceful, severe, even menacing. Maybe it was the insignia on the uniforms, for they were definitely military. Whatever it was, it made me think of my father. Our snaps had never been that formal. We had laughed, gestured funny things, come across as a 'right pair'. That picture was different. Somewhere in my tired brain, thinking back, I am sure a bell would be ringing. At this time, tiredness convinced me otherwise.

Kurt came to rest by an open door. His Mother bidding me to enter.

Throwing a quick glance at her son she headed to a door on the opposite side of the landing with Jimmy at her heels.

Kurt's gaze travelled across my flushed face. "You are tired?"

I nodded.

"Then sleep, my little one. Refresh yourself for tonight's adventure. I will be here for you at six o' clock."

His mother tapped his back, and together they descended the stairs.

'Little one' – the innuendo in his voice made my spine tingle.

I closed the door and sank onto the bed – sprang from it – sat down – stood up – if you have seen a jack in the box – I'm here.

I could not control my jittery legs. My heart raced, breath was leaving my mouth in short rasps. I gave no thought to my friend across the corridor. My one priority – the urgent need to satisfy a yearning I neither understood or could explain. I thought of splashing water onto my burning face to ease this inner longing. Drawing the long brocade curtains closed (this bedroom overlooked the street) I took a towel from the stand and stood in front of the basin tucked into the corner of the room. Draping it onto the floor I removed my boots, socks, jeans and jumper. The oval mirror, balanced at an angle to catch the light above the sink, highlighted the redness of my skin. It was like a creeping disease. An emotional fire, ardent, eager, all consuming. My only certainty – it was impossible to control.

I began to sponge myself, trickled water over my eyes, down my throat, sizzling in my mind, as the droplets scattered over my breasts. I breathed deeply, the dizziness in my head affecting my thoughts. I began to float, blonde hair, blue eyes dashing before me like a car speedometer. Want, need, want, need – must have.

I ceased my sponging. Never had I given virginity a second thought. Far too busy fighting one cause or another. My hand brushed against my nipple.

I watched the water fight its way down the sink-hole, my eyes slowly closing. Throwing myself between the bed covers the flames of destruction were already licking at my bones.

5

The sound was harsh and deep, one of those throaty vibrating voices echoing in authoritarian force, demanding in the language of its birth for another person to be quiet. I sat upright in the bed – listened – silence – then, again, the thundering sound. This time, if possible, the voice was harsher, bouncing around outside my door, rebounding off the walls of the long narrow hallway. I strained my ears to catch the clipped words travelling up the stairs, the noise invading my space, almost as if the perpetrator was standing beside me. Logic told me to ignore it.

Impossible, this voice was angry. It frightened me, drove me to move my shaking legs from the warm bed. Ease my feet to the floor, and make my way to the door. Gently turning the handle of the door, I pull it slightly ajar. Presumption was spot on. A man and woman were arguing. More than that, raging at each other in earnest.

'*Nosiness.*' I hear your condemnation. '*A private argument.*'

A person has got the right to be aware of what is going on around them, especially in a strange city.

They were shouting in angry unison. Pausing now and again to scream the name, 'Kurt' in broken English. On the intake of a breath the man would (to me who could not see anyone, but imagined what was taking place) shake the woman, shout, 'friends, sleep, work' as she cried. Fear held me in its grip, for I knew that meant Jimmy and me. Letting go of the handle I stood with my back to the wall. This was no ordinary male voice. Whoever it was knew control. He was accustomed to every command barked being carried through.

I thought of creeping onto the landing, spy over the bannister, make sure what I was hearing fitted with my vivid imagination. I could not. Fear strapped me to the bedroom wall, prevented me from bending, stretching or leaning in any direction.

To all you theologians. If Lot had turned me to stone I could not have been more rigid.

Closing my eyes against the ramifications of my mind a memory nudged my subconscious. The man in the picture up the stairway wall – and the more I focused, the more the voice became synonymous with that image. Oh gosh – was it him?

The lacerating tongue bit into my mind. Who was he?

Someone started to sob. Heart wrenching cries drawn from the pit of their stomach. Dear God, it was the woman. Her pleading tore at my heart.

The man was a brute, a damn bully.

I picked up courage to move from the wall and sit on the edge of the bed. No matter how I held my legs I could not stop them trembling. I really was becoming Lot's wife; stiff, cold, and very, very frightened. The clock was wavering around four o' clock. Afternoon – I had slept for around five hours. Heard no-one leave the house, or enter, so could the two voices locked in war be his Mother and father?

'*War? Come on, an exaggeration on your part.*'

Look here reader, my parents bicker, at least once a week. Raised voices, Mother cries, father gives in, pours her a drink, ruffles her hair. These two, they are feral cats – wild.

The clock hands move in slow formation, slide into the next hour, the voices berating my brain like a blacksmith's hammer. The argument continued – domination, determination, demand after demand. Jimmy sprang into my mind. Had my friend heard? Straining my ears, I listened for the turn of a door handle, the step of a foot on the landing – not a sound. No rustling or door creaking.

Dear Lord, had prying not got the better of him. Some friend, sleeping through the noise. I might have been in mortal danger. What did he care?

'*He was tired,*' you quip.

Tired – the silly fool is supposed to be protecting me – yeah, yeah.

'Shame, poor guy. Don't abuse him.'

Abuse him? I say use whatever your mind latches onto, be it simple or prolific!

The clock struck five. I shivered. Although I did not know it then, the striking of a clock would follow me for a very long time to come.

—

I was still sitting on the edge of the bed an hour later when a knock rattled my door. I froze.

"Rhia," came the whisper. "Time to get up."

Kurt – tripping over my feet I opened the door, threw myself onto him.

"Wow, steady, are you ready?" Kurt grinned.

"Nearly," I whispered, looking over his shoulder for signs of activity.

His eyes rolled over my uncovered curves. "Mmmm, so I see."

Embarrassed, I slid further into my room. "Give me ten minutes."

Kurt grinned, "OK, I will knock Jimmy. You slept well?"

"Slept – well." I stopped.

"Sure?" he queried.

It was not so much the furtive glance, but the way he said it – a statement.

"Yes, of course I did. Thank you."

Whether he was content, who could tell, actually who cared? Kurt was here. He whistled as he headed across the landing.

Closing the door, I heard him knock Jimmy's door. Time to go. Grabbing clean jeans and a thick jumper I quickly fastened the bulging back-pack and made my way onto the landing. Jimmy and Kurt were waiting. I was glad Jimmy had not witnessed the earlier 'riot' that had taken place downstairs, for if he had he would certainly be re-telling it by now. I had no doubt Jimmy kept nothing to himself, every little detail brought to life. Smiling Kurt took my hand, led me down the stairs into the hallway. Jimmy followed, not uttering one word – strange. That was until we reached the kitchen.

"No Mother?" my friend's voice resounded around the quiet room.

"Out," Kurt returned. "Visiting family – tonight is history."

"Ah," was all my friend responded.

"Let's eat out," Kurt said. "I know just the place."

Jimmy nodded.

"Great," I answered.

I so needed to get out of this house. Leave that fierce argument behind. My legs were still like jelly and my mind a den of expectation and fear. The terrible booming voice had unsettled me. Still clinging on to Kurt's long fingers I thrilled at their warmth and strength. All may be calm now, but trust me, I required his re-assurance – or (blushing madly) something of the sort.

—

The city was abuzz with anticipation. Complete strangers would stop, put aside their inhibitions, and hug the nearest bystander. No-one protested. It appeared each and every inhabitant of this great city had become a part of the moment. Wherever we walked there were people, congregating in small groups on street corners, in the entrances to shops, out of the windows and doors of houses, under the street lamplight. I jokingly called them 'the bowed heads', for each small group huddled tightly together in earnest contemplation. Jimmy laughed, telling me the real reason for their downcast faces was partly down to fear. I queried this, so Jimmy being Jimmy spelt it out for me.

Fear that the rumour was a lie.

Fear that the night would turn into a blood bath.

Fear that the men in charge of the east would run amok, and capture them. Drag innocent victims to a place of no return.

Kurt agreed with him (mark it up).

Jimmy just grunted.

I must write here: if those people felt the fear I had felt earlier then I pity them.

As we forged deeper into the city children were squealing with delight. Holding tight to the strong parental hand pulling them forcefully onward. Dogs were barking, cats meowing; candles were spinning around like sparklers in the hands of those who carried them. I truly believed the universal menagerie of human life had congregated tonight in Berlin. Excitement, replacing the loathing of this afternoon, made my eyes seek Kurt. I willed him to look at me. When he did, my heart raced so hard I could hardly breathe. Jimmy insisted he carry the banner Kurt had made while on his outing. It was rough, more than that: the red material was daubed with the word 'Freedom' in hurried black paint. My ungrateful friend snorted as he took hold of it, shot a glance my way, and tried hard to stuff it under his newly sponged anorak. I wondered if it was the colour, knowing Jimmy he would have linked it to some political no-go.

"Where are we going?" I asked on a lighter note.

"The café," Kurt shouted. "The Café Alder – the one and only."

"Lead on," I smiled, casting a 'behave' scowl at my moody friend.

—

In exhilarated mood, I entered the café. It was bursting at the seams; noisy would be an understatement. How we acquired a window seat I could not say, it just became vacant. Easing our belongings under the table we stared out of the large pane of glass onto what was obviously the best panoramic view along Friedrichstrasse Street; the walkway to the checkpoint known as Charlie. Kurt sauntered up to the tiny counter, ordered food and three Cokes. I could see my blonde-haired dream chatting to the man behind the counter. Kurt would say something, lean closer over the counter, then the guy serving would peer over Kurt's shoulder at Jimmy and me, screwing his eyes up as though they shared a confidence or joke. Every now and again they would pause, the server mouthing the word, 'sir', and nod in agreement. I smiled at this emphasis on the formal, accepting the guy's politeness as a matter of fact part of his job. Hearing the grating of my friend's teeth (it does annoy me) I knocked his arm. "How about him," dipping my head towards the counter. "Polite or what?"

"Got it," was all my friend replied.

"Café manners," I added.

"Maybe," a sound similar to that of a bleating sheep made its exit from Jimmy's mouth.

'Best ignored,' was my decision, 'put your attention to lighter things'.

I rotated my body full square to the view outside the window. Flames, torches, lanterns; a vast sea of artificial light. People were unfurling reams of material, swinging these homemade banners above their heads chanting 'Freedom,' 'Freedom,' 'Come, come, come,' 'come – come – come' over and over again. All of a sudden, the street went silent, then from somewhere deep inside the eastern block of the city an answer could be heard. The heart jerking reply of, 'We are coming, we are coming,' filled the air with its throbbing chorus. I listened to the pulsating sound. The rumour had got to be true. It would be unforgivable if the barriers did not rise tonight. This was a once in a lifetime chance for many of the residents of Berlin to meet family and friends interred by circumstance.

A man stopped outside the window, leant on the glass, took a rosary out of his pocket, and prayed, imploring the Mother of God to let the rumour be true. I rubbed my eyes, the hot stinging tears threatening to fall. It was then my gaze fell on a figure darting in and out of the alleyways.

"Look," I squealed.

To my own ears, it vibrated around the busy café; to everyone else it must have pealed a warning. Silence descended.

It was Jimmy who put my thoughts into words...

"Henchman," his voice was non-committal. "No doubt marking those that lead any procession."

Kurt took a gulp of his drink. He had returned to the table soon after I began scanning the street. Sitting next to Jimmy his eyes (I am sure) had bored a hole in my back.

Both dragged their attention to where my finger rubbed eagerly at the mist on the window.

"Henchman?" I gazed at my friend.

Kurt stiffened, Jimmy sighed. "For goodness sake, Rhia. Stasi."

I was amazed he had mentioned the word. According to my father anything to do with 'those' people was best whispered in secret, or imitated at by action. They were dangerous. His warning: "Watch out for the dark, communist henchmen."

"Shush," I warned, pointing once again in the direction of the long black mac, scurrying in and out of shop doorways.

Kurt stiffened as he watched my finger make marks on the window. My heart leapt. He had to be afraid, after all he was German, and all German people were afraid when they caught sight of these persecutors.

"Do not worry," Jimmy soothed. "I doubt any instrument of doom could shake the crowd's resolve tonight, hey Kurt?"

The blue eyes lost their stare, took his Coke and saluted it our way.

"Tonight," was his simple gesture.

My whole being tingled.

"Now, eat," he commanded, offering the assorted meat and salad delivered to our table. We ate as though our lives depended upon it, well – Jimmy and me. Kurt nibbled.

The town hall clock chimed nine o' clock. Kurt rose from the table.

"Pardon me, I have a meeting. I will be fifteen minutes – promise." His gaze took in my disappointment.

"A meeting, mate, at this hour?" Jimmy sounded surprised.

"I know, funny time, but this guy lives near the checkpoint. He is a colleague, and will know exactly what is going on."

"Right." Jimmy had a knack of sounding sarcastic. "Shall we tag along?"

"No, no," was the hurried reply. "As I say, I will not be more than fifteen minutes. Stay, drink, be merry."

"Be merry," Jimmy imitated him. "Sure thing."

Kurt pretended he had not heard the catch in Jimmy's voice, instead he stooped to purr in my ear, "Miss me."

"You bet," slipped past my lips.

Kurt was gone.

"I smell a fish," Jimmy barked.

"What is wrong with you? Let him be. If whoever he has gone to see can feed him information that's fine." I was mad.

Jimmy gave a wry smile. "Do you believe him? Informant indeed – a pretext. The whole of Berlin senses history in the making. What can he know they don't?"

"A whole lot more than you," I snapped back "Anyway, what does it matter if he has gone to see a pal?" I hesitated "At least he has one."

'Ooch,' you mutter.

I know, probably unfair, but Jimmy was starting to get to me. What had Kurt said wrong?

"It was your idea to come here in the first place. Now Kurt, who may I remind you has been more than helpful, can do nothing right."

My friend shifted, took another swig from his Coke bottle, looked at me in a way I could neither fathom nor understand.

Something had to give here. I tweaked his ear in a bid to be playful. "You are just miffed Kurt will not tell us where he has gone."

Jimmy twirled his bottle in quick rotation, proceeded to utter the 'p' word he always used when in a tricky situation, before looking me straight in the eye. "OK, you win, I give up." His hands floated upward in front of him marking submission. And I say, "Thank heaven for that!"

Kurt returned to the café at nine thirty. He was out of breath, and a good deal paler in colour than when he left.

"The border gate will be opened around midnight," he shouted.

No secret this time then.

"Are you sure?" I moved closer to him as he thumped down beside me.

"Yes, that is what I have been told."

"Lucky to have information on the inside," Jimmy mumbled.

"Pardon?" I said.

"Yes, it is," quipped Kurt.

The smoke-filled venue erupted. Everyone jumped to their feet, clapping, singing, crying, laughing. Rushing from table to table clinking Coke bottles, slamming fists onto the scrubbed wooden tops. A man with an accordion started to play. His fingers strumming out the strain of a haunting tune. Men stood to attention, women joined their stand, all began to hum and sway, clasping a shaking hand to their chest.

"Beautiful," I murmured.

Kurt indicated to a group not far from our table.

"They are singing Hoffmann's, 'My Thoughts Remain Free'. It has been sung by sections of German countrymen in the face of tyranny."

"How beautiful," I said again, shook from my reverie by the sharpness of Jimmy's enquiry "Have you ever sung it?"

Kurt's eyes narrowed. "I personally do not deal with sentimentality."

"Thought so," Jimmy whistled.

"Meaning?" Kurt sounded annoyed.

Jimmy shook his head. "Oh, this and that."

That was it. Friend or not, Jimmy was really starting to get on my nerves. Does male testosterone never take a holiday? I remember at university these two had their encounters, but I have got to say, nothing as edgy as this. Kurt threw Jimmy a sidelong glance, and as far as Jimmy was concerned I was seriously beginning to think there was a screw missing in his head. I had never known him be so rude, his face so contorted with fury. He was edging for a fight – why?

Lucky break – the proprietor of the café cleared the floor by the counter for customers to dance. This was my opportunity. Throwing an arm around Kurt's shoulder I teased him from his seat, leading him into the small space.

Squeezing our way through clasped arms and hugging bodies we danced; smooched would be the more correct term, his aftershave hung around him fresh and sensual, while his warm fingers sunk into the flesh of my neck. My body burnt, my mind alive with strong heroes and frail damsels. I dare not glance at Jimmy.

Ten o' clock ... the café grew noisier, hotter. Clinking glasses and riotous cheering drowning out Jimmy's comment thrown our way.

"Time for a stiff drink," Kurt whispered in my ear.

Trust me when I say this girl had sworn to herself 'never again'. Did I mean it? – Of course – At the time. So you can imagine my horror as I whispered back to Kurt and then called to Jimmy, "Good idea, come on." (you cannot... shame.)

Kurt made his way to the door. I smiled in what any onlooker would describe as a 'provocative' way. Jimmy scooped up our belongings, vehemently pushing past bodies only too eager to take over the vacated seats. Once in the open, we brushed ourselves down, eyed one another up, laughing as if there would be no tomorrow. Jimmy laughed the loudest. This is true reader, my friend's mood had flipped, from persistent grumbler full circle to overjoyed protester. I should be pleased, for it meant Jimmy would not be on Kurt's back all the time. Yet, all did not feel right. What I found odd, and even at this stage you will probably have a clearer insight into what was going on than me, was Jimmy's willingness to 'put up, and shut up'. I confess, a pathway he had never travelled before.

'*If you cannot beat them, then join them,*' you remark.

Maybe – Using that penetrating stare he was famous for Jimmy's gaze found mine; nodding at Kurt we followed his lead.

6

Winding down the back streets and alleyways, leaving the cheering voices behind us, we quickened our pace to keep up with our guide. The night sky was heavy and oppressive; odd for November. It constricted my breathing to the point when all I could picture was a summer evening where only a storm broke the overbearing humidity. Jimmy was curious, asked where we were going. Kurt told us to trust him.

Trust him. I would follow him to the end of the earth!

For a second Jimmy's mask of 'pleasant' slipped, to be replaced by a scowl, then as quickly by the silliest grin anyone could imagine. We chatted about university, the parties, the pub crawls, anything but the upcoming opening of the wall. Some would dub it 'small talk' – messy prattle that covers huge amounts, yet in all honesty, talks of very little.

Halfway down the street we entered a dark building with entrance doors of dark mahogany. Oh, it was seedy looking, but only on first glance. Get past the entrance and oh boy ... you were hit by damask walls, a barrage of glass chandeliers, huge mirrors, cream blinds, and numerous fairy lights. This was a grotto – a grotto without Santa Claus!

No sooner had we made ourselves comfortable on the high stools at the bar than arms were raised and salutes given. Kurt shook hands and saluted back.

"A game," he whispered out the corner of his mouth. "Fun to play along."

All the customers were dressed in grey and black uniforms. They all spoke fluent German, at a pace even a linguist would have trouble interpreting. They all threw schnapps and vodka down their throat at a speed unknown to me. The men slapped Kurt on his back, the women kissed him on each cheek, before embracing Jimmy and me in a tight bear hug. Funny really, for the outfits reminded me of the picture hanging in Kurt's home.

Actually sent a shiver through me; made me think of those black and white news reels where a riotous rendering of the song, 'Lily Marlene', would any minute pour from their mouths.

The bar tender, same outfit, same salute, placed six vodka shots in front of us. He demanded we drink them straight down. In Kurt's view, a *must* party game. Putting the tiny glass to my lips I jolted (true) the contents down my throat. Talk burn, it gushed as hot lava from a volcano. I gasped for breath. The barman laughed, willing the others to join in. I relaxed a little, after all it was 'fancy dress' night in honour of the wall, and I was sitting as close as possible to my dream. I glanced at Jimmy; he shrugged, bared his teeth, and looked away from me, silly fool. The barman proffered another glass my way. Talking became impossible, it was easier to nod for 'yes' and shake my head for 'no'. So, guess how many nods I gave, six.

By eleven fifteen (the ornamental clock behind the bar chimed every quarter hour) six vodkas and four schnapps had somehow found their route to my stomach.

This was some party.

Out of nowhere a 'low life' (it is imperative I call him this so you can picture for yourself how sleazy he was) appeared by my side. His shoulders bore the insignia of rank (this need for every other person to be a sergeant, a captain, or a general was beginning to bore me). His fat hands held me in his grip. Pretend or not, this man began to slobber all over me, laughing like a jackal about to devour his prey. He signalled the bar tender to supply three more glasses, mimicking I drink as one.

My fuzzy brain was lost, and when I refused he demanded, barked a command, reminding me of the man at the house this afternoon.

I retaliated, shoved him backward. He wobbled, he dipped up and down, holding on to the bar for all he was worth.

Play-acting? this slug was taking it a bit too far.

I searched for Kurt; he was busy chatting to a man with treble insignia on his arm

Jimmy, no luck; he did not pause in chatting up the buxom blonde to his left.

The man demanded again, helping me tip the vodka down my throat, slamming the glasses upside down on the bar.

I burped. Loud.

The slob's arms came around me, his fat lips covered mine. The smell of his boozy breath made me gag and suffocate.

I searched for Jimmy; back towards me, no interest whatsoever in my problem, then just as I thought I would faint, my teeth bit into the skin sagging across my mouth.

The grotty swine yelped, drew his mouth from mine, and let me go.

It is unfit to write the abuse from those oversized leather lips.

He screamed so long and loud that Kurt whispered something in his ear. Something that made him back off faster than a hyena faced with the snarl of a hunting cat.

This damsel buried her throbbing head into the shoulder of her brave war-lord.

At eleven forty there came a stampede for the door as the bar tender shouted, 'time', and proceeded to shut up shop.

"Ran out of drink," my sardonic pitch screeched.

Kurt clapped a hand across my mouth. The bar tender leant across the shiny top until his head was but an inch from mine.

"Non," his face was bright red. "How do you say – Ran out of time."

I smacked Kurt's hand away, yelled a loud, "Ohhhh," before saluting in the most hideous way. "Did you hear that boys? A pub with no time. Hic."

The barman glared. The slob, about to shut the back door gave it a hefty kick, the blonde hiccupped (I knew it... she had accepted too many drinks from *my* friend), and Kurt kept apologising.

This was a party, for heaven's sake, an overrated dress up at that. I, by this time, was on a high; unlike those so-called revellers who stood in a straight serious line glaring at me. Where was their sense of fun? Why was this chaotic party not turning into a riotous free for all?

Kurt and Jimmy lifted me, one by my arms, the other by my legs, and carried me kicking and spluttering to the door. The bar tender jeered, the blonde cheered, the slob (from what I could see) raised his fingers in the sign of victory – cheek.

If only I could have raised my voice enough to shout, "Up yours, up yours."

I did not have the energy.

Once outside, the cooler air (though still oppressive) hit me. I felt myself steadied against a wall, my head pushed between my knees. The world spun, slipping the moorings of my brain until the transparent liquid found its resting place on the cobbles below. Lifting my head I took the bottled water held in front of me, rolled the cool sap around my mouth, and splashed the residue over my face.

"Better?" Kurt quizzed.

I nodded. "What kind of celebration was that?"

Jimmy interrupted Kurt's answer. "Forget it, let's go, high five." He stretched his hand out in mid-air. He was waiting for the obligatory hand clap. Left, right, to the top, down below, the prologue of many a student rally.

My head, still mulling over the 'party' behind the now bolted doors, joined in with zest. Linking our arms together we three began to march, striding out in defiant approval that history was about to be made. I felt my lungs expand as we began to run. It was everything I had imagined. Jimmy, shouting at the top of his voice, Kurt by my side, my feet hardly touching the ground. 'Gott sei Dank,' 'Long live Freedom,' vibrated through the crowd.

"Not far now." Kurt gripped my arm tighter.

"Hurry." Jimmy quickened his pace.

Before me that pathway that lead to a heart's desire. How we arrive there is through the choices made on a night such as this.

The town hall clock struck eleven forty-five.

—

There it was – the famous border crossing known as Checkpoint Charlie. Fifty by fifty metres, hewn out of the streets surrounding it. Equal to the Brandenburg Gate that once allowed east and west to integrate, now a forbidden walled zone. Charlie was larger than I had imagined, with guards patrolling the tall watchtower; strolling in a nonchalant way along the wall, marked at intervals by the scribbled names of those who had died trying to escape. I focused on the bridge where those same guards marched up and down to the command of an officer's voice. It stretched as far as the eye scanned. A solitary walkway overhung by wooden shafts and railings. From the gate on the west side there was a thirty metre stretch to another gate on the east side. This was affectionately (if you could use that term) known as 'No Man's Land'. Here, apart from the concrete pylons that served as a labyrinth for vehicles going in, or coming out the east gate, it was deserted. A coldness hung over the space, and I was immediately transported into the spy films of another era my father was so fond of.

Although I had been told the main checkpoint for the exchange of prisoners was BornholmerStrasse on the North side of the city, I could not stop myself from imagining the plight of a captive on this bridge. In my mind's eye, they were leaving the east to return to the west, or part of an exchange from west to east. Whichever, the walk across that desolate gap had to be the same: fear and isolation impossible to fathom. The protester inside me wanted to rush forward, scream at the guards, sacrifice myself for the universal pain freedom fighter's experience. Chain myself to the railings until the barrier was stripped away. How could they have done such a thing? This beautiful city, carved into four border sections by the British, American, French and Russian armies after talks collapsed in 1961. Were they too up their political noses to see it bore cruel, cruel marks of division?

Crowds were gathering, ten to twenty rows deep. Shouting, screaming, rattling whatever tin or bracket they could lay their hands on. People were crying, howling out names of those trapped beyond the wall. Cringing as they pointed to a spot dubbed the 'Bullet Run' where guns decided who lived or who died; brave men and women who had tried to escape from an enemy whose greed for power matched that of many tyrannical governments.

Without warning, bright yellow beams begun to sweep above our heads in a sequence of circular movements. Dipping and swaying, the spotlights easing every five to ten seconds to linger on an upturned face in the crowd. I followed the light to its source, a solitary uniformed figure of East Germany's secret police known as the Ministry for State Security (SSD for short), otherwise the Stasi. German men and women employed by the Communist regime to spy and inform on anyone, including family and friends, who did not walk their political tightrope. As previously mentioned these so-called 'night ghosts' were despised and feared by the ordinary citizen with the same repulsion given to the SS in the Second World War. Their job was to torture, maim, and kill to gain information. Vultures of the dark, who lived and hid in the west. What intrigued me as I stood before the wall of terror: 'Had these tyrants managed to hatch an escape plan if this crossing opened, or would they linger for their fellow countrymen to kill them, hang the traitors from the nearest tree, tar and feather them as France had done to collaborators, boil them in oil!' From a recess deep in my mind a slob of a man appeared, grey and black uniforms, bold jokes, raucous laughter, saluting, a voice calling 'time', a locking pub door.

I despatched the memory back whence it came.

We stood, the three of us, Jimmy waving the banner, shouting at the top of his voice. Kurt, quiet, locked in a world of his own. Myself following the yellow streams of light on their journey, ducking and diving to avoid any static beam. The atmosphere crackled with electricity.

What happened next was so quick that to this day I swear destiny staged it.

The crowd behind us lurched forward. "Freedom, Cowards," "Freedom, Cowards ..."

Words in rapid succession pouring over my head toward that beam of light. Kurt's body lunged into mine, his arms gripping tight round my waist to prevent him falling. His lips tickled my cheekbone. A firework exploded, shooting sparkling stars amid the array of artificial light. All thought of traitors and killing fled my mind. I could not stop myself. I snuggled closer, breathing in the faint aroma of his eau-de-Cologne.

In that moment the world held two people, Kurt and me, lost in an oasis of our own.

—

It was Jimmy's voice that distracted me, caused me to break free from Kurt's embrace. Someone had shunted my friend forward, and his gabble of profanity in the direction of the spotlights held an undercurrent of accusation so volatile that if not checked, it could be dangerous.

Stretching past the woman in front of me I struggled to grab his sleeve. Tugging hard I hissed, "What the hell are you doing?"

He gave me that 'on your bike' look he usually saved for the perpetrator not the protester and stormed, "This night belongs to the people. Come on, join in."

I gazed into the beam; still moving, still marking certain heads in the crowd, and pulled tighter on the green anorak. "I can understand your excitement, but should you not be a little careful?" pointing to the bright spectre searching at random. I added, "Best to keep your head down."

Jimmy glared. "Keep my head down? Is that what Kurt told you to say?"

I reeled. "Kurt? no –"

"Then who?" he snarled.

"Me, I *am* telling you. They –" again I shook my head toward the light, "will arrest you."

Jimmy nudged the young boy to his right as he stared at me. "She's a friend, such a numpty! It is over for them, tell her."

The boy, I am convinced too afraid to do any other, spoke in the best broken English he could muster. "He right, they would not dare leave post."

The boy let out a sarcastic groan. "Americans on our side, guarding wall."

Jimmy sneered. "Hey girl, told you. No need to worry."

I was hurt. The way he had ignored me at the party gnawed inside me. All I could think to say was, "I'm a numpty (a woolly brained simpleton), am I?"

"Yep," Jimmy flippantly threw back. "You can be."

My friend swung the banner higher above his head. The yellow beam came to rest on the vivid red material, shining on the black letters, 'FREEDOM'. It hovered there, swooping across it, swinging and bowing as if to pinpoint its location.

I drew back to Kurt. A sigh of resignation filled the night air. "Me, a numpty. Right."

Kurt noticed my distress, pulled on Jimmy's anorak. "Let me try to sort this, Jimmy mate, calm down."

Deep breath, for I am sure you have seen it on the television. Imagine a Chinese dragon rocket, the furious pace it can fly.

Jimmy whizzed (believe me, it fits) in the direction of Kurt. His voice was on fire. "Hunt the dogs down. String them up. No mercy."

I was petrified. Kurt tried again. "Keep your voice down, mate. You never know who is in the crowd."

"Do you?" the scream shot across heads stretched in all directions to his right and left.

Kurt put his fingers to his lips. "Please, you are mad, *they –* " his head moved to where the yellow beam lay, "will string you up."

Jimmy sniggered. "What? Don't be a fool, they have far more to worry about than me. Anyway, they have got to catch me first, know who I am. Will you tell?"

I gasped, pulled Kurt back to me, felt the struggle of his arm in my clasp as he plunged forward once more. "Tell of you? What are you saying, you crazy idiot?"

Jimmy blinked, the thunderous mask of anger etching his features. "Those bastards need to run before they themselves are shot."

"Shot," bellowed Kurt. "Shot?" grappling with the woman's coat in front of him. "You are the one they should shoot to keep your bloody mouth shut."

"Get here and say that," I could see Jimmy's mouth opening like a black cavern, the noise was ear screeching. Both faced up to each other.

Is it remotely possible that reading this you could understand my indignation, my concern and fear? On one side my best ever friend, on the other the guy who erupted my emotions to jelly. Please believe me when I say I am in West Germany, in the middle of a crowd torn by base emotion, and two supposedly educated guys are mauling each other like lions over territory. On top of all that – if they had the sense to think – to shoot anyone at this precise second would bring about a bloody massacre. Talk revolution – think backlash. Got it – right, can I ask who is the numpty now!

Wriggling under arms and over legs I managed to get between Kurt and Jimmy. Fists were flying: well, one fist with Jimmy, the other hand did not let go of the banner.

"A weapon?" I queried.

Both ignored me.

"Do not judge what you do not understand." Kurt was spitting.

"Understand." Jimmy exploded. "Understand? What is there to understand? People like you get rich on pain."

I raised my eyes to heaven. Jimmy was babbling.

Kurt looked murderous. He was seething.

I looked at both men (a term it appears they are not ready for), had I missed something?

Next round of the fight.

Jimmy: "Freedom is but a shout away, and those dogs are still trying to rule with an iron fist."

Kurt: "Those dogs have family."

Jimmy: "Yeah, as bad as they I bet."

Kurt: "That is your opinion."

Jimmy: "Yeah, dead right."

Kurt: "Fool."

Jimmy: "Idiot."

Kurt: "Blast you to hell."

Jimmy: "Fuck you."

Kurt: "Keep your stupid ass away from me."

Jimmy glared: "Let's sort this out. Come on."

My mouth fell open, believe me this was getting way out of hand. The crowd were beginning to take sides, the majority, funnily enough, chanting for Jimmy.

Determined to put an end to this nonsense I placed one hand on my friend, the other on my idol. "Shut up," I shouted. "We are protesting for the same thing."

Jimmy eyed me. "You are with him on this?"

I hesitated, then – I cannot, even now, admit to jumping in that gaping black hole we dig for ourselves. "He is our host."

"Oh, man, do you know what you are saying – host, you say? Host?"

I reeled at the bellow of his voice. Okay, two can play that game. "Jimmy," my bellow pierced my own ears, goodness knows what it did to those inquisitive people standing gaping in mock delight. "Please, **shut up**."

Jimmy flinched. "Shut up you say. Why?"

"Because – because we are all friends," I stumbled.

The angry look on his face stopped me from uttering another word. Could my friend not see we were fighting like children, sparring to get the better of each other? Mind, I did not miss the pleading look as Jimmy searched my face. The defeated whimper as he thrust the banner higher in the air, scarcely missing the poor woman behind him. He did not hear her comment. "A red flag. Oh my."

Jimmy turned to face Kurt nose to nose.

"Thank your lucky stars *she* is still *your* mate."

With that he manoeuvred deeper into the crowd. Kurt's reply fell flat. "The enemy within the state is better than you."

I held my breath. No retort from Jimmy. He had been lifted onto the shoulders of two burly men and all together they were yelling, "Stasi- out, out, out."

I watched as the receding back of my friend bobbed above the crowd. Torn between my loyalty to follow and the strange stabbing emotions in the pit of my stomach, tears started to spill down my cheeks. It was plain I had missed something of importance. That was obvious to everyone but me.

An accusation – a lurid comment?

Something I may have had the power to stop?

—

"Come with me."

Kurt was holding out his hand.

The crowd surged forward.

Kurt started to move. "It is time to leave."

"Jimmy," I croaked

"Do not worry over him, he will be fine after he finishes shouting."

I felt the warmth of his fingers slip into mine. I could not help myself.

"The police – a cell – hurt him." – The warm tears stroked my cold cheeks.

Kurt smiled (it suited him better).

"There, there, my lovely. Not tonight. I was taunting. It was my joke. Do not worry about him. We have more important things."

Had he really called me 'lovely'? I shivered at the thought. Kurt steered me through the jostling crowd, sidestepping the masses still making their way to the checkpoint. We did not speak, there was no need, the firmness of his hold said everything. Once or twice I threw a backward glance, caught the red blob in the distance; a stalwart beacon on the horizon before Kurt found a deserted alleyway, and pulled me into it.

The clock struck eleven fifty-five.

—

How long does it take to fulfil one's adolescent dreams?

The clumsy fumbling of first love washed aside any warning my brain may have stored. I was carried on the heat of the moment. Overtaken by the recklessness of Kurt's kisses, to my eyes, my ears, my cheeks, my throat. I tasted the salt of his lips, smouldered in each rhythmic movement of his body, drenched myself in the seductiveness of his power. The groping became more frantic, the hill I was climbing, steep. I was re-living every magazine article and puerile dream as a teenager I had held sacred. There was no separation between fantasy and fact, and when I heard the cry of 'freedom' over and over again I craved my fulfilment.

Lost in that concrete alleyway my heart, accompanied by the cheering voices of a city freed from imprisonment, rose to its heavenward pinnacle. The vibrant sound grated in my ear, soft and gentle at first, then louder and louder, matching the waves of abandonment engulfing my arching body. I gripped tighter to the embodiment of my dream and entered the hallowed vestibule of pubescent yearning, the gate to my juvenile fantasy was opening, as gluttony dismissed everything but the saturated act of passion.

The clock struck midnight.

7

"Hallelujah."

People were running through the alleyway, creating a wave of cool air to swish around my hot body. Out of the corner of my eye I saw people hurtling at breakneck speed past us, blowing trumpets, swinging rattles. Not one took any notice of the dishevelled couple pressed hard against the concrete wall. Kurt moaned, released his hold on me, and started to rearrange his clothes. The moon slinking from behind a cloud allowed me to see the contours of my lover's face. Through misty eyes I caught what I thought was a touch of irritation.

Oh reader, that had to be my mind playing tricks.

Barely a moment ago we had locked ourselves together in a bond of mutual passion. Yet, if you have ever caught a rabbit trapped in a car headlamp – furtive, sly ...

Despondency took hold of me. Had I given myself too easily? Possibly, but in defence, this was a special occasion. Weak excuse, I know.

Quickly arranging my clothes, thank heaven for the sponged huge anorak, I placed my hand in Kurt's. It was shaking, his whole body was shaking.

"You –" I began, only to be halted by the hard press of his fingers on my mouth.

"Shush." The command (in an odd way) thrilled me. "Follow me, who knows who is around."

Who is around? Oh Kurt, I would say most of Berlin tonight. I giggled.

Roughly he led me down the alleyway, not caring this time about discarded cans or forsaken food.

As I followed the back of my lover I could hear the yelling and whistling of excited crowds. Emerging into the street I blinked. It was so bright after the darkness of the alley. People were snaking their way toward the checkpoint, carrying torches and flame carriers. Men, women and children were twisting their bodies round and round, singing, laughing, clapping their hands; picking up on anything that made a noise. Accordions played, car horns honked, toy drums banged under tiny hands of squealing children. Trumpets, rattles, whistles, paper horns, all blown, swung and banged so hard they made the eardrum tingle. The city had come alive.

A woman stopped in front of me and held out her arms.

"Be among us," she beckoned. "Praise heaven for the miracle."

She was not German, no more than I, but her excitement showed.

A tremor shot through my body. "Do you hear that, Kurt? Shall we join them?"

No reply.

I spoke again, squeezing my fingers to gain warmth from his grip. "It is time, my love, to celebrate."

My fingers fumbled, no warmth, no flesh, save that of my own. I scoured left and right, behind me, up and down the street. Kurt had disappeared. I had not felt his fingers leave mine. Frantically I foraged back into the dark alley. I screamed. "Kurt. Kurt. Please do not play games."

Nothing.

I screamed again, louder this time. "Kurt, where are you?"

My lover had vanished.

"Kurt, Kurt." My lungs hurt as I tried to raise my voice above the noise drifting into the alleyway from the street. Desolation filled my soul, it was obvious we had been torn from one another, someone had drawn him into the crowd, buried him in their midst.

'*He could find his way back,*' you whisper.
Logic? Who needs logic now?

I was beside myself. I screamed again and again. Rushed out into the street, hurled myself into the centre of the jubilant throng, my tearful howling mistaken for a protest.

"Glad you have joined us," said the woman who had approached me before. "Shout away, my dear. The day of judgement for the wicked has arrived."

Swinging her banner to and fro she grasped my arm. "We are protesters, you and I are the chosen ones."

Just my luck. I had fallen into the arms of a religious fanatic.

Around me the world was spinning out of orbit.

"Are you crying with joy, my child?"

The woman, in the brightest flowered kaftan I had ever seen, persisted in repeating, "The Lord will bless you," whilst running her hand through her grey flowing locks.

I began to cry, howl if I was truthful.

Taking my hand, she waved it up in the air. "I know, this moment we all should cry. The sheer joy of its history."

I had no strength to fight. My one thought: how wrong can a person be!

Never in my life have I wished another person would disintegrate. Well, maybe my mother now and again. Oops. What you must understand – I was in torment.

"Freedom has been granted. Tell me your role in all this." The blasted woman would not go away.

This time I snapped, "I have lost someone."

She paused, slid her arm across my shoulder. The tears poured down my cheeks.

"Do not cry, poor child. When we reach Charlie we will talk, find your lost one together."

"I have another friend among the crowd," I managed to croak.

At this point I thought she was going to hug me, heaven forbid. I searched the crowd, found myself actually praying she would leave me alone.

Prayer answered, a girl appeared at her side.

"There you are, Mother. Come, we are congregating further down the line. It is important when we reach the checkpoint our voices will be heard."

The woman turned towards me. "Child, if you wish me to stay –" she began.

I cut her short. "No, no, you go. Your work is of the essence. How else can celebration be heard."

"Bless you, my child." and she was gone.

Please forgive me saying, "Thank you" to whoever heard my prayer.

Now, where was Kurt, and if it came to it, where was Jimmy? Both had deserted me.

—

Confusion is all I can say about the sight that greeted me at the checkpoint. People were howling, crying, singing, shouting, dancing, laughing; every emotion that highlights joy and sorrow as a closely linked sentiment. The steel barrier had lifted. The focus of oppression, that for the last twenty-eight years had kept west and east separated, was pointing skyward. People were streaming over the bridge. Women carrying babies in their arms, dragging small children at their heels. Men laden down with bags and bedding; their first step onto democratic soil, sinking to the ground. Old and young alike thanking God in whatever form they saw fit. They hugged and kissed whoever they passed, sighing, beating their chest to release the pent-up emotion. Those that had spent a lifetime waiting to be reunited with a mother, father, brother, sister, aunt, uncle, cousin, friend; isolated humans at last on the soil of the free 'promised land'.

My eyes scanned the wall. People of every age were climbing on top of it, smashing it down with any tool or brick they could find. They hit with loose bricks, they kicked with hard boots, some smashed hammers as they cursed and cried, some holding spades above their heads, beat the wall in uncontrollable rage, many clawed at the cement with bare hands, blood pouring from fingers and nails.

The broad walk-way where the guards had patrolled, inspired the crowd to kick, thump, jump and batter their weight down upon it, venting anger against the regime that had controlled their lives, the regime that were now discarding uniforms and long black belted macs in a hurry to escape the justice awaiting them. Figures jumped into the murky water; their fate, a battle with barbed wire and broken glass. Others crouched behind the glass of the lookouts, their frightened eyes darting here and there. From watching the crowd I would say those Stasi escaping were the lucky ones, for the majority left behind it would surely be reprisal; a confrontation where duty and obedience could not save them.

It was the hour of what my father called Armageddon: judgement of the wicked, chaotic and lawless.

—

I had not stopped searching for Kurt. All the way to the checkpoint I had stretched my neck as far as I could, peering along the line ahead of me for a blonde head. In truth, there were plenty, just not the one I was looking for. I began to shiver as the temperature dropped. An easterly wind blew, chilling me to the bone, even with my large warm anorak. I was tired and lonely, my mind clouded with lovemaking and loss. Pulling the fur trimmed hood further around my face I walked up and down the stretch of the wall, stopping now and again to watch as brick upon brick clattered to the ground accompanied by howling cheers; the people spouting their own special propaganda.

By the time the teeniest chink of dawn poked through the sky I felt sick with worry. No Jimmy, no Kurt. Just me, afraid and alone. People were still mounting the wall, still clattering across the bridge with suitcases in their hands; stragglers giving off an aura of uncertainty, furtively looking back across their shoulder to catch a glimpse of someone – anyone – herding them up, and returning them to the east. I stopped one or two in passing, described Jimmy and Kurt, but nobody acknowledged my plight. Whether it was my desperate handling of the language, or their wariness of foreign visitors I have no idea.

At five am I collapsed at the side of the bridge, too tired and heartbroken to think. I had failed in my attempt to find my friend or lover. Snuggling my head in the cradle of my arms, resting them on my two bent legs, I closed my eyes. If I missed the home-bound bus Mother would panic – yet how would I explain, through fantasy, and overpowering need, that I had left Jimmy to his fate?

—

Hearing a sound beside me I cautiously peeped between my arms. Two dusty brown male walking boots held my attention. First thought: Kurt. My heart flipped, sweat ran down my back. I knew it, my lover had found me as I knew he would. The ache in the pit of my stomach contracted, how could I have doubted?

Jerking my head upwards I met dark brown eyes: Jimmy!

"Here you are, girl. I thought you were lost to me."

His features had softened since our last encounter. Disappointment, relief, call it what you will, the tears I thought to have controlled spilled onto my cheeks, coursed earthward as rain in a monsoon.

"Where have you been?" I bawled.

"Here and there, mainly around the checkpoint, although I did venture onto the bridge."

"You silly ass, I thought you had been arrested."

His eyebrows lifted. "No, what would they want with me?"

Jimmy did not take his eyes from mine.

Thinking back, my whole body could have been under scrutiny. Fear filled my mind. Had my friend guessed? Please, no. What could I do, think?

Flippancy was the tool to hand.

"You were going some before midnight."

He laughed. "Yes, I was, and for a damn good reason, but that can be dealt with later. For now, let's get a drink. By the way, where is Kurt?"

My world rotated out of orbit. The name alone caused me to quiver. I had got to tell him. It would not be easy, Jimmy being my real best friend. Yet we had always agreed, sharing was honest.

"I ..." The words were having difficulty forming.

"Gone?" my friend queried.

I was a bit put out by the sharpness. "So it seems," was all I could find to say.

Jimmy said nothing. The moment had passed.

He offered me his hand, pulled me to my feet, and pointed toward the horizon. Mocking my mother's voice, he said, "A hot drink, *darling,* that is what is required. In my footsteps, one, two ..."

I wiped my hand over my eyes, it was impossible not to join in his frivolity.

Lucky for us the Café Alder had either opened early, or not closed from the night before. Throwing myself into the same window seat I gazed onto that same street. The hubbub of noise had quietened down, and apart from those people on their way to work, the world appeared normal. So much so that I wanted to shout, scream out loud, "Where is my lover?"

Latching onto my friend zigzagging his way from the counter, stepping over the remnants of party hats and balloons, I noticed the serious frown drawn across his brow. Placing the hot drinks on the table in front of me he fixed his eyes on mine, guessed my need.

"I did not bring a sandwich, you never asked."

I sighed. Why does the male always have to be asked? Why for once can they just not bring?

Sitting down he nodded toward the street.

"I could not believe I had lost you. I promise it was not intentional."

Guilt flooded my body. "It was an argument we should never have had."

Jimmy sipped his tea. "True, but emotion was sky-high."

This I had to agree with. "I know. That is why I thought it best you cooled down."

Okay, a blatant lie, or I could say, a misrepresentation of the truth!

Another gulp of tea, then he queried, "Where did you go?"

My eyes stung from the heat rising. "Nowhere special."

Jimmy was looking at me, through me. "You must have wandered somewhere."

'*Now,*' you will whisper, '*Now is your chance. Trust your friendship.*'

This was it. I took my friend's hand, fumbled. "We got lost in the crowd."

"Together?" The pitch in his tone grew higher.

Crossing my fingers, I took the first step down that road psychologists call deceit.

"No, how could we? The crowd pushed us apart. I looked for you once I was unceremoniously dumped. Could I find you? No." I picked up the sugar bowl, scooped four teaspoons into my tea, forcing myself to act casual.

Jimmy took hold of the teaspoon, "Slow down. You will be sick," then, "You were lucky not to be seen with *him*."

This, I could not believe. "There you go," I groaned "Nasty digs at a mate."

My friend's cup rattled in its saucer. "A mate, Rhia, you do not know do you?" Jimmy lent across the table, spoke in a hushed voice. "Our so called 'mate' was a party member."

Quizzical furrows raced across my brow. "A party member?"

Jimmy nodded, furtively looking around us, as if he was afraid someone might hear.

"Grey uniforms, a salute," he mouthed.

If he had not been serious I would have laughed. Bile rose in my gut.

"You mean ..."

Again he nodded. (Similar to those dogs people have in the back of the car.)

"There was an argument at the house yesterday afternoon. You must have been asleep (little did he know), and from my bedroom window I saw the man leave the house. Grey uniform, maroon lapels, the agitated walk of someone in command. A dead give-away. Stasi. Not wishing to upset you, and more importantly land both of us in 'very hot water', I said nothing. (Thanks) Agreed to go to the pub – need I carry on? Heart of the SSD if ever."

"The slob," I stuttered.

"Him, he was certainly high ranking. Got his eye on you."

Jimmy slowed down, let out a 'phew' through his teeth.

"Good thing, and I say this with real sarcasm, was the fact Kurt's father was higher," Jimmy stopped as he noticed the quizzical frown appear on my brow again; let his fingers fall on his shoulders. "His lapels, commander insignia."

"Oh," I managed to say.

He carried on, not even slowing down to acknowledge my surprise. "Mind, afterwards I beat my brain for 'our mate's' agenda, especially as he confronted a senior officer – not done. Oh no." Exhausted, Jimmy slumped backwards.

I was confused, irritated. "You said nothing."

"Nope." Flippant. "Although I had an idea at uni."

"At uni, and you did not think it was important to tell me?" my voice throbbed with the emotion it could not conceal.

"It was only certain things he said, papers he read, and besides I thought you liked him, as in *like*."

The hot cup burnt my hand. "*Like* him." My lips quivered. "He is – was – a mate – that's all."

'*Penance,*' you cry.

Jimmy expressed what I can undoubtedly say was relief. "That's good. No need to worry then?"

"Worry?"

"Oh yes, the German authorities are gathering up anyone who had dealings with those swine, whether it be friendly or otherwise."

He had to be joking.

I looked straight at the counter. "The proprietor of this café saw us together."

"Fear will keep him 'numb'- fear that some have got away."

"Kurt?" I had to know.

My lover had taken me to the playground of my dreams. Fulfilled the illusions of my youth. Supplied me with the reality of my bitter-sweet fantasies. Now, he was gone, and I was left with a yearning.

Jimmy blew his tea, round and round the cup, not slowing down as the splashes dribbled into the saucer. "His father was a general, very high ranking. Escaped yesterday evening, along with other top brass."

"Him?" I urged again.

"The word on the street is someone hid him away, until he could run."

My heart thumped, beat so hard within my chest I expected it to break through the skin.

"The mother?" My voice was pathetic.

"She of all people deserved to escape, yet was caught."

"You know a lot." I did not mean it to sound accusing.

He closed his eyes. "They were known assassins, especially the father."

"Oh."

My friend laughed. "I bet you're glad you lost him in the crowd."

Glad? If Jimmy knew, what would he think, let alone do? – look upon me with disgust, walk away from me in horror? He must never, and I mean **never** know.

I throw the cold tea down my throat, recline into the shifting dawn, and wait for Jimmy's summons to run for the bus.

8

May 1990

Six months passed. Months when routine became synonymous with an aching heart. Mother had been pleased her daughter came home from 'that place of peasants and soldiers' in one piece and unharmed. My father was a different matter. He eyed me suspiciously. Always on the brink of asking what I thought to be 'that question', then changed his mind. We all agreed I needed to work, earn my own money – or as Mother put it: "Show the world you can do silly things off your own back, for no doubt you will."

My father suggested a temporary position at his bank. Kept on and on until reluctantly I gave in. To be honest, I didn't care. My one aim in life was to find the perpetrator of my youthful longing, and give him the rough side of my tongue. (Jimmy's term: a good telling off to you and me).

Before you interrupt here, possibly with the most practical statement you will make, I have to say my heart knows Jimmy is the best friend a girl could ask for, steady, reliable, honest, sincere, yet the fire Kurt ignited will not go out. My head recognises the path he treads is dangerous, but risky is exciting, don't you agree?

I had started at the bank in January, collecting money, stamping bills, dispensing people's hard earned cash, and feeling like a fish out of water. Tedious – would be a good word to describe my day-time existence. Evenings – not much better.

Jimmy had taken a job at the local museum.

'Fantastic,' is your reaction.

Yes, well, he had the knowledge, no-one is denying that, but they stuck him in an office with two older men, grey trousers, cardigans, fossil brained. Jimmy loved it. He refused to accept my joke teasing him about growing into an old relic. Insisted these old boys would fill him so full of knowledge, promotion would be adjacent to running up a set of stairs. Whatever.

What annoyed me were the hours he spent studying. Apart from Saturday and Sunday nights I was a recluse. I suppose the good thing, and I write this in gratitude, was my friend never mentioned Berlin. It was as though a veil had been drawn over our 'protest' visit. Almost as if he wished to forget it. Now and again the television news would record the capture of past Stasi members. Then his ears would prick, causing him to jump and shout like a twelve-year-old boy. I listened to his raving, kept quiet, never once uttered what was on my mind. It suited my guilt-ridden conscience.

The problem I have discovered – by not confessing an act, small or large at the time it occurs, it expands from a seed to a tree; something developing from nothing. Anyway, six months on how could I explain to my loyal friend that while he was waving his banner, and doing his utmost to bring down an oppressive regime, I was screwing our German mate?

—

The weather on this particular Saturday in May suited the dispirited feeling hanging over me. It was raining. One of those fine showery downpour days that intentionally, or not, soak you to the skin. I had decided to shop, mainly to avoid Mother's constant nattering. She had taken of late the path of reminding me that I should be grateful for a job, any job was better than none in the uncertain economic climate surrounding us. Followed by a tirade of 'dos' and 'don'ts' concerning how I spent my money. I came to the conclusion that she was so egocentric that my own inner turbulent cravings, shown in endless snapping and crying were misunderstood for tantrums. They ran over her like smooth plaster: a case of once covered over, the tantrum never happened.

On the Kurt front there was still no news. While this really irked me, in fairness he did not know my address, and according to Jimmy, if ever Kurt came out of hiding, he would be arrested immediately.

Me, I just wanted to re-live that ten minute fantasy.

You gasp.
I smirk: sackcloth and ashes, the very thing to alleviate my guilt.

Aimlessly I roam in and out of my mother's coveted shops. Brand names, designer names; today all were one (Jasper Conran please forgive me, I am in a sulk). Dodging the prolonged watery outbursts I found an old cobbled street, and dawdled down it. Jumping puddles, I spotted an old-fashioned Coffee Shoppe, its window crammed with groaning cream buns. Fabulous, I needed to rest, lift my sodden feet from my flat pumps, and survey this strange tucked-away world. Choosing a table by the window (can life be telling me something?) I order a coffee and a bun (the word resisting is not part of my vocabulary) and begin to search the street beyond the glass.

Rows of shops stand to attention; soldiers on parade. Coloured neon lights seduce the weary customer. A sweet shop, candy displayed on pretty paper lined shelves – alongside a wedding boutique with expensive white gowns sparkling with stitched diamanté crystals. A classy crockery store, full of designer plates, cups, saucers and dishes – partnered a handbag shop, each leather item accompanied by the same coloured hat and shoes. Lingerie shops, jewellery shops, and a small, but important, city bank.

Feeling the sensation of hot coffee slide down my throat I warmed toward the knowledge that here, in this tiny back street, my mother was totally unaware of 'her kind of shops'. This pleased me.

'*Nasty,*' you say.
'Not at all,' is my retort, this is my secret location, a hideaway for myself.

I bit a piece of gooey bun, licking the oozing cream from around my mouth. The cream melted on my tongue, tingling my lips with each gulp. I scanned **my** street, focusing on another large neon sign at the bottom of the street. The word 'Studio' twinkled into the dull afternoon sky. I was entranced. Maybe it was the iridescent colours chasing each other that intrigued me, or the solid pink light shining from its window. Whatever it was I was drawn as a firefly to the flame. Finishing my bun and coffee I paid what I owed and closed the door onto the drizzling street. Tiptoeing (shoes were soaked) in the direction of the light I stood outside the shop window. Draped in pure white nets (quite daring for a shop), tiny spotlights sparkled at special advantage points, while the most amazing drawings lined the walls. Without considering if the work was for sale, I pushed open the plain glass door.

The tinkling of a brass bell spread a delicate sound around the neat waiting area, intermingling with the soft lilting tones of classical repertoire. Instantly I was hit by warmth; a blissful welcome, may I say, from the damp outside. The reception area, if that was what it was, stood empty. No assistant sat at the old oak desk set against the huge oval mirror on the back wall, or customers sitting on the pink velour two seater sofa reclining in front of the window. The pine clad wooden floor was scrupulously clean, as were the small side tables tucked either side of the settee. Don't ask why, I had an overwhelming feeling to remove my shoes. This I did while sinking into the smooth inviting cushions of pink velour.

Embraced by the warm air, I questioned the reason I had crept into the shop. One could say to dry off, remove my shoes, rest after those scrumptious cream buns, but I knew the real reason was the art. Art as I had never seen before. Trying to stand I suddenly let out the loudest, "Ouch"; my stiff red toes refused to move. Annoyed, I sat back down and began to rub them. How dare my feet not move, at this moment when I craved to have a closer look at those excellent drawings lining the walls. Landscape impressions of the Seine in Paris, the Golden Gate bridge in the U.S. of A – the Berlin Wall.

My heart jumped, acknowledged that whoever was the artist was one of immaculate precision. Unable to move I strained my eyes for a price tag: none. I could not see one pound or dollar sign anywhere, underneath, to the side, stuck to the frames. With no-one to ask I cast my eyes to a sign on the desk. There in italic handwriting a white and black vintage sign: '*Specialist in Tattooing*'.

Talk flabbergasted. This 'master' of art was a tattoo specialist.

Let down? You bet.

The only tattooed bodies I had encountered were burly men who wore vests in the summer, their bodies covered with blue or black dragons, names and insignias.

I did not hear a door creak in the corner behind the desk, did not register a footfall gently sliding my way, until the sight of two bare feet stood astride my own, causing me to jerk my head upwards.

"Hi." A soft voice.

"Oh." I scrambled for my discarded pumps. "It is wet outside."

The voice shook with humour. "Leave your feet bare. They will dry faster."

I watched as the thin body, clothed in brown cord trousers, white shirt, and flowered waistcoat, threw his arms above his head. An image straight from my mother's 'flower power' photos, a 'hippie' without a doubt. His long brown hair was swept into a ponytail by elastic fluorescent bands, kept in place by a flowery bandanna. On his chin a vague stubble, not unpleasant but again a reference to the era, in his left ear a small gold hoop ear-ring.

Honestly if I told my mother, she would swoon!

What startled me the most was the sensitivity of his grey eyes. They did not stare at me with the eagerness of someone selling their trade, but with the genuine gaze of a painter. It crossed my mind he looked into my soul. Watching him amble across the room to the desk, he rang a small brass bell. A girl appeared – disappeared – re-appeared with a steaming mug in her hand. She handed me the mug.

"Peppermint tea. Let it infuse your body and mind."

"Thank you."

By this time I was mesmerised, my eyes following the girl back to the desk.

In tune with the man before me, her clothes mirrored his own. Aged seventeen, eighteen at a push, her dyed black hair, scraped from her face, highlighting the fine cheek bones and amber eyes, which followed his every move.

Neither sturdy nor thin, but one of those figures that could wear anything, and sadly look damn good in it. Her face held an expression that my mother would label 'doe-like'; a fawning that was obviously for the man she worked with.

'Moony,' came into my head. 'Besotted,' full on entrapped.

'A pity,' I thought, for the guy was full of his own self-importance.

He moved to sit beside me, flapping his hands in the air, generating a movement of elegant grace.

"You found me by spiritual vibes. Most important clientele do."

I sat up straight, this guy thinks I am clientele. Hold on a minute. "It was wet," I stuttered.

"Yes, but you have an idea springing into your head."

Now, you can call me a fool, an idiot, anything you recognise as a numpty but, he was right. How, I have no idea.

He was ignoring the flummoxed face, the irritation of my feet to move.

"Let me introduce myself. I am Alexander Cromwell."

My mouth fell open. What I said next was, I swear, not me making fun, but the nervous reaction of one stuck in a hole. "After Oliver Cromwell, the Puritan commander?"

His face screwed into a mass of crevices, the gentle voice taking on a more belligerent tone. "I am sure if I bothered to look up my family tree it would take me back that far. Mind, I am the one with no warts etc."

"I did not mean –"

"Of no importance. Your request is what matters."

"Request? No, no, no. Forgive me, I am sorry to have bothered you. It was curiosity, the drawings. I love art."

"Exactly. The art."

I stood, this time steadier, able to wiggle my toes. Alexander stood, pointing toward the girl at the desk. "That is always how my customers find me. Rosie, prepare my studio."

"I must go, my mother would kill me."

He steadied my stumbling. "Come, come no need to tell her."

"Tell her, she will see it."

"Not at all. You are a grown woman. I presume you bathe on your own."

He laughed in a voice deep with meaning.

"Yes. Look, I can see how brilliant you are (head for the male ego), but –"

"Thank you." He bowed. "I must say that is your opinion, others are not so generous. They have no peace or love in their hearts."

My eyes fell on the window, and out to the street. The rain was still pouring down, streaking the glass like shards from a waterfall. What was I doing here, a tattoo parlour. I gazed again at the drawing of the Berlin wall, felt the weight of my secret, heard the, "ahh," as his eyes caught mine. My gaze fell on the neon signs flashing in unison with the driving rain. I took a deep breath, thought of this man's inspiration to create an aesthetic mysticism. Is that what I needed right now, the sackcloth and ashes? Dragging my eyes from the drenched street I whispered, "Your critics are fools."

"We think so," was his hushed reply. "Come, tell me your story."

In my mind I saw Jimmy waving his banner. Felt my heart melt at the touch of Kurt's lips. Brushed my eyes against the threat of falling tears.

Alexander took my hand and gently guided me past the desk into the sterile ante-room.

—

Since childhood I had imagined a tattoo room to be dark and ridiculously unclean. Maybe it was the shabby streets they had always seemed to occupy, or the gloom that sat over the shop itself. Either way, on entering Alexander's studio my concerns were deemed inaccurate and way off target. I walked into a room that was bright, white, and the next best thing to a sanitation unit. The long couch, placed at an angle in the middle of the room reminded me more of a sun-bed than a piece of furniture where torture (my childish fear) took place. Beside it stood a surgical lamp attached to a moving arm connected to the ceiling, a high stool, and a glass trolley laden with row upon row of sterile swabs and fine instruments in plastic see-through containers. Behind the stool was a machine (very similar to a dental one) with various tubes. These, the girl informed me, were to hold the instruments that would help create my work of art. In one corner of the room a Japanese screen hid what I presumed were clothes pegs and a chair; a space to recuperate? I was informed it was to rest for a few minutes, and fill in a questionnaire. Very professional and efficient.

Beside all this, the tranquil ambience (created by the piped music and the stark white walls) was an anaesthetized state in itself, lulling those who chose to hover between consciousness and sleep. Jimmy would insist it was an emotional self-deception, induced by the artist.

Jimmy was a step away from joining some kind of Lenin movement!

By the screen, Rosie (that's what her boss had called her) stood to attention, holding a white wrap around gown in my direction. She induced me to step behind and remove my top clothes. My eyes must have shot open wide for a faint smile stole around the red painted mouth.

I could not help it, this girl entranced me to a point that I gave her the representation of being a Russian Matryoshka doll; when one is taken away the second appears, and so on until there is only the smallest replica left.

Cruel – we will see.

I tried whilst changing to envisage her and Alexander as a couple. He was easily a good fifteen years her senior. I concluded she was deluding herself, then allowed myself the maybe, maybe not argument. True, interaction between the two left a lot to be desired, for in the short span of time I had been here her boss neither spoke to her in any tone but polite. He gave orders in that light airy pitch, neither admiring or saluting her quick actions. Instead, he positively ignored her, hardly spoke or glanced in her direction, declining the most basic of her suggestions.

Edging myself around the screen Alexander invited me to sit on the couch. This I did, fretting constantly over my parents' and best friend's horror if they ever found out. Alexander talked nonstop (makes the Rosie debate a little unsteady, but remember this is work), giving his point of view, asking for mine, digesting all he wanted to know. Somewhere in between chatting, I must have explained about the wall, skirting around the pleasure and the pain. Rosie let her mouth fall into that banana shape, pleased no doubt that I had my own guy to worry about. Alexander said nothing, just asked me to lay face down on the couch, demanding Rosie cover my lower body with what she spurted out was a 'modesty cloth'. Her boss was not impressed, shooing her away in haste.

Drifting into that cavity of the mind where argument and common sense clash I tried not to show my fear of anything in the least needle-wise.

9

I need not have worried. My sculptor's digit dexterity proved to be quick and skilful. A Monet or Matisse – take your choice!

Apart from the pricking sensation of the linear needle, the odd tingle and the rubbing of Alexander's hand there was no pain. He worked in his world of silence, lost in meditation. Ink and instruments swept across my back in the same way an artist's brush kissed the canvas. From my flat-out position on the comfortable couch I heard Rosie padding across the wooden floor. I counted her coming and going to be twenty. Carrying instruments, delivering fresh ink, and generally running here and there. Not once did I hear a, 'Thank-you', or even, 'Well done'. You can imagine it did not take me long to decide the girl was taken for granted; a servant to her ardent employer. Subconsciously I re-named her the 'Bumble-bee' due to her speed round the room. Little did I know this label would stick; a fond, yet acrimonious gesture on my part. I had stumbled into a battlefield.

His, the protestations of a rejected artist. Hers, the devoted admirer.

There came a moment of respite when Alexander asked me if I wished him to add colour to his drawing. This I declined, with haste – solid black ink would replicate my mood. Besides, it was far more suitable for my guilt-ridden conscience. No more was said until he balanced a mirror on his lap, urging me to approve. Easing myself up to elbow level I warily peeped into the crystal-clear glass – and gasped. It was all there, around my shoulder blades, zigzagging down my spine, dotted over the fleshy expanse of my back. Buildings, bridges, tiny matchstick people, freedom banners, crumbling bricks. The remnants of an oppressive era, bold against my pale skin. It was exact to that night – without the alleyway.

Alexander ran his ink stained hand across his forehead. "You are angry?"

Angry? With the 'Bumble-bee' around?

"No, shocked, that's all."

"Too big, too bold?"

The 'Bumble-bee' flew to his side.

The pair stared my way. I gulped.

"Yes, it is big. Larger than I thought a tattoo to be, yet very – interesting."

"Interesting?" her voice quivered.

Alexander raised himself from the stool, pushed past the indignant girl.

"That is fine," his tone was cool, non-committal. "My work is my life, and I draw as I see life. From what you told me it matches your pain."

Pain? I had said nothing of pain.

"It is brilliant." The words shot through the stunned silence.

Alexander turned, Vaseline in his hand. "Good."

Swiftly moving to a door at the end of the room marked 'Sterilizer' the girl disappeared.

She was mad, I could tell. Alexander, smoothed Vaseline over the tattoo, covering it with an absorbent cloth secured by medical tape, handing me a list of what, or what not to do. I dressed, paid the fee, and without another word swiftly left the studio. I was glad to be free, away from Alexander and the 'Bumble Bee' – a hornet's nest indeed, never to return. The tattoo, I could live with it –

My parents and Jimmy – that was something else!

—

The bell in the town spire rang out 5pm. Shoppers were hurrying to catch a bus, or collect their cars from where they had hastily parked them. Many clutched colourful bags, some designated with a desired name or crest of a favourite store, others plain and bulging with food or household basics as they stepped around the water congregating on the pavement. For the moment the rain had stopped, although large grey clouds were scurrying across the sky in rapid formation. "A warning," I mused. "Just a warning."

One blessing was my pumps had dried out as best they could, but as you must know waterlogged material shrinks, so due to this tightening of foot space the more I instructed my feet to go faster, the less they obeyed.

Yet, my biggest problem – supporting the weight of my shoulder bag – a nightmare.

Each step sent an ache through my upper back, a strange awareness of my skin being unable to stretch, caused by the medical tape. No matter what angle I held myself the tape would not slacken.

'Guilt having its pound of flesh,' you chuckle.

I snort and keep imagining my mother's face if I expose my back. The scream that would leave her contoured lips, would be heard in Australia. Actually, it is easier to ask you to conceptualise a child's paddy, and even that would have nothing on her showdown if I flung the word 'tattoo' into the circle. What did I say earlier about tantrums?

"Only common people have such marks," would be her first stinging jibe, followed by, "How can a child of mine embarrass me so?"

Not for one moment would my social climbing Mother remember the Chinese lettering adorning her own brother-in-law and sister-in-law's arms.

I rid myself of her image allowing another tall dark haired figure to take her place. He was my main worry. For instance, if I was not careful *he* (by that I mean Jimmy) would be clever, take one glimpse at my back and guess the parody. *He* hated Kurt. I would lose him, pact or not, and for an odd reason that upset me. I really could not allow that to happen.

Stop furrowing your brow. I know you are dying to ask why I am concerned over my friend. I don't know.

Go ahead, tell me I let him down. I know.

Rub it in that my action was deceitful. I know.

But, for the last time let me make this quite clear – I *am*- he *is* – only my best friend.

I stand still, well as still as my back will permit. A strategy is required. One that is simple, yet will not take a great deal of thinking about. Simple – of course – no more lounging around in skimpy tops, no greeting my friend in Pjs. I will become a well-dressed woman of the world – in a sort of, 'I really do not care' way.

It starts to rain again. Large drops falling in sequence from the darkening grey heaven. Umbrellas shoot up. People begin to scatter; always intrigues me why the human race fall into the category of small darting mice when water is involved. Children splash mischievously, dogs join in, all around me is a world of splashing chaos. My partially wet body (I forgot my umbrella) finds an alleyway covered by an awning to a side shop doorway. It makes me think of Kurt (not that he was ever far from my mind), and I know it is time for plan 'B'. I could not spoil my mother's social flight up the staircase of imaginary status, or take the chance of losing Jimmy. No, it had to be fabrication all the way. I am sure you will agree; for everyone's sanity, of course.

I arrive home to find Jimmy, my mother and father patiently waiting in the kitchen. The atmosphere was tense. Greeting me with delight (eerie) my mother flew round her post-modern kitchen filling the kettle, grabbing cups and slicing cake. The grin spreading across her face made it double eerie. Someone or something had put her into this frame of mind. The last time I had witnessed such joyous behaviour was a few months ago, when my father announced a substantial rise in pay, along with a 'step up the ladder'.

Suppressing the urge to shout, "Have you won the football pools?" I noticed similar grins on Jimmy and my father's lips. Rudely twisting my finger to the side of my head (the insignia for people acting silly) I eased my hot back onto an upright steel backed seat protruding out from the table. Three heads turned my way. Three sets of eyes stared at mine. My first thought: 'Oh boy, they have guessed. They know what I have done and flipped. Three are out for my blood. What can I do?'

My father was the first to speak. "Where have you been?"

"Shopping," I replied as calmly as I could.

Mother made sure the pretty rosebud cups were safely balancing on their identical saucers.

"No bags," she noted.

"No." I held fire for a second gathering my breath, trying to calm the rising tumult inside me. "Nothing much took my fancy. Thought we could try together another day."

What was I saying? My mother and me in the same shop. I gulped.

Father screwed his eyes up; fathoms of greenish grey sparkling in the kitchen spotlight. Jimmy wriggled his nose. My mother poured tea – cut cake.

I looked from one to another. The smile I had encountered when I had arrived was now a huge beaming grin spreading across each face in turn. Letting out an exasperated sigh, one to ease the tightness in my chest, two for the ridiculous behaviour of these so-called adults, I began to moan. "What is the matter? Have you gone mad? I will go to my bedroom."

Jimmy stepped up behind me, throwing his arms about my wet body.

"Ugh, you are soaked. Where have you been?"

"To the shops, already told you," my temper rising.
I winced within his hold, chafing the skin underneath the already displaced covering over my back. Hastily catching the dejection in his eyes, I added, "For goodness sake, it is raining, and daffy here forgot her umbrella. Silly me."

He let me go, casting a quick glance at my father.

Oh dear, there comes a time in every girl's life when the truth must out.

Mother passed me cake. She also eyed Jimmy and my father before saying, very matter of factly, "Go and change. You will catch your death of cold, and ruin your skin."

A nervous giggle rose within me. If only she had X-ray eyes. Still, I should be grateful of her concern. Easing myself from the seat (they must have thought my joints had seized), I was about to walk from the room when a shriek of laughter burst from three sets of lips.

This time they had guessed. Laughter was hiding an explosion of anger.

"You find it funny?" I bawled. "Let me say –" then stopped.

Each hand was holding some kind of ticket mid-air. Waving it around like the politicians do at their meetings in parliament. I was stunned, thrown into a quandary at what to do next.

They roared louder, protruding the paper my way, flapping them round my nose as if my numbed brain could conclude their meaning. My back stung, pulling in a way that was unexplainable to those who have not had a large tattoo. Leaning by the cupboards I slammed my hand down on the worktop.

"OK, no more teasing." Jimmy spoke first. "Your mother and father have won a holiday" He sighed with pure pleasure. "Walking the Great Wall of China."

Have you heard the aphorism, 'knocked down by a feather?' A silly saying you might say, and yes, any other time I would agree, but to be honest, looking at my mother and father poising to scream at the top of their lungs, I believed it to be true.

They were scrutinizing every flicker crossing my startled face. Suddenly I began to laugh; laugh until tears ran rapidly over my cheeks.

You wince, probably too eager to point out their excitement at winning. Repeat, 'Come on. **The Great Wall of China'**.

I plead for your understanding. Ask you to imagine my mother walking – hauling a backpack – trudging up dusty slopes in massive hiker boots, rolled down woollen socks – sun cream thick on her stuck-up nose, and to end it all – bedding down under the stars.

The more I visualise short pants and walking sticks, the harder it was to quell the laughing.

"Rhia," Jimmy exploded.

I caught the severity in his eyes.

"Sorry, could not help myself. The two of you in boots and hats. Does that include the swinging pom-poms to keep the flies away?"

I broke forth again.

My father put down his ticket and slumped into a chair. "Sad to say, Rhia, this attitude is you all over." He picked up his cup in a dejected manner, sipping the hot tea, eyeing Jimmy in resignation.

"You have got to see the funny side," I spluttered. "It was –
"

"We do not want to know," they all chimed together.

My eyes roamed over the trio.

"When?" I said, telling myself to calm down.

"July," Jimmy intervened.

I picked up on his hesitation. Something wrong? The way he pondered for a moment; and then as if he was running on the spot.

He began to gabble. "And, and I thought it a good idea if we went with them – at least to Beijing."

Repeat. Repeat. How many times do I have to say it? The impact jarred in my ears. A deathly silence descended over the kitchen.

Mother began to wipe any excess water dripping onto her precious floor. Swishing the cloth round my feet. She huffed and puffed. I sidestepped her rubbing.

"Your clothes –" she spat.

My, she was angry. "Sorry, Mother, sod my wet clothes, compared to this bolt from the blue they can wait."

Jimmy came and stood next to me. With a thud, he laid his ticket on the worktop along with another piece of paper.

"This is your ticket, paid for by your father. We were more than fortunate to get same day bookings at this late stage. It is a fantastic chance to visit the Forbidden City and the Summer Palace. All those places of oppression we have talked about."

"You did not ask," straight to my father.

"No, I did not. You were shopping. I foolishly fooled myself into thinking you would be delighted."

How much older he looked at that precise second. Guilt wrapped its cloak around me. My mind felt trapped. It was one of those moments when a person grasps at anything. "I have to work." The splutter sounded pathetic, even to me.

"Sorted," my father barked.

It would be, I thought, he was my manager.

I need another excuse – got it. "I have no clothes."

"Then buy," my father was tipping on the edge of exasperation.

Mother slapped the cloth over my feet, making me jump.

"Your jacket?"

"Sorry." The apology was genuine.

Removing my wet jacket I threw it in the sink, the cloth covering my back slipped further. How could my father forget the last holiday the three of us spent together? The Italian Lakes. A two week break of family pleasure Mother had promised. Wrong!

The hotel had been simple and clean. 'Ordinary' is the word I am looking for, and to be honest, what more could a tourist ask for?

Ah, but then we had not taken into account my mother. She was no 'ordinary' tourist.

She complained, ridiculed every aspect of the down to earth proprietors. Wore down my father and I until we actually became her accomplices in moaning.

The holiday turned out to be two weeks of sheer hell – hell without any barriers.

I did not even have Jimmy to help me see sense, too busy camping with his family (lucky him) in the Lake District. The other guests avoided us, as a matter of fact we were ostracised.

"They are not our type," Mother kept saying.

Our type – they were definitely my type. They drank, sat in the bar, joined in any music playing, they made merry. Normal, wouldn't you say?

I was never more grateful than when the plane taxied to a halt on home soil.

Now this.

With no regard to my back I motioned Jimmy by shaking my head like a ravaged dog. My friend. *He* paid no attention, just started talking.

"I have heard the palace is beautiful, and the history of the Chinese empresses and concubines fascinating. Think about it, Rhia, long years of repression at the bid of an emperor where freedom was denied or given on a whim. Imagine," Jimmy was getting excited, "how good it will be for us to include eastern history in our pact. Spend five days discovering what made these people tick."

Five days. Half way round the world for five days. I was under attack. This trio wanted an answer, now. Submission on my part.

All I wanted was the lucidity of my mind to be restored. Common sense to kick in. After what I had just done.

'*Your fault.*' I can hear the anger in your voice.
What can I say, what can I do?

"You are mad, all three of you."

Jimmy stood his ground. "No, Rhia you are. This is an opportunity for us to visit another era. Weigh up the values we hold to be oppressive. Come, don't come. I am going."

My heart raced. The argument was failing me. Jimmy grabbed the tickets and headed for the door. "We must confirm," a glance in my direction.

Please think about capitulation. I was. That feeling where the heart and head disagree, but the mind resigns to failure.

My tone was flat. "You win. China, here we come. Now let me be."

I stomped to the door; a trail of wet droplets falling behind me.

Throwing a glance at Jimmy, I swear he was smiling.

10

China, July 1990

Our hotel was situated in the centre of Beijing; a mixture of old and modern custom side by side. Sedan chairs hoisted aloft by traditionally clothed carriers, vying with the bicycle and motor car. Shops ablaze with vibrant materials recreating the days of old, complimented by the more down to earth jeans and T shirt. Chinese language amalgamated with a variety of Mother tongues, and modern and traditional music floated out from car radios, and shop speakers. Posters that invited you to visit past eras via theatre or museum, whilst offering up-to-date venues that served present day food and drink. It was fascinating.

The journey had been a tetchy ride into the city with Jimmy gazing out the bus window in what I can only explain as another black mood (no different to the flight). Now and again he drummed his thumb on the narrow sill, deep in solitary thought. The tap, tapping made my deduction of Mother's insistence on 'how mature' he was growing a hasty evaluation.

Me ... I refused to speak.

I will tell you why. My friend *had* kissed my fingers. Grabbed them, like you would a stick of rock, and draped his lips across them. He gave no reason why, or even an apology for his action. As a matter of fact, heaven alone knew. This was new, even for him. By that I mean Jimmy had mucked around before (my take on his teasing) – certainly, but not so direct as this. His way of annoying me? anybody's guess, but this I do know, it both brought back memories I would rather hide, besides the *action* disturbed me.

Setting foot in the foyer on our arrival we were greeted by sunny yellow sprigs of jasmine everywhere. In vases on the reception desk, draped across coffee tables and windowsills, even in tall huge pots languishing in darken corners. The smell was overpowering; beautiful, but overpowering. I did not know it yet, but this flower would haunt me whenever this holiday came to mind, conjure up images I would rather forget. Our maid, spruce in her black and white outfit informed us dinner would be served (if we wished) on the terrace adjacent to the dining room, overlooking the neat enclosed gardens at the rear. Drinks would be on the house, and Chinese dragon dancers would perform on the square clipped grass. In what appeared to be preoccupied musing we all signalled our agreement as we were shown to our rooms.

Heading for the bathroom I twist the taps, fill my lungs with the steamy vapour as the water gushes into the white sunken bath. Slipping from my sticky clothes I slide beneath its inviting depth. It was hot, biting into my scoured back: although healed, I still could not look. Over the past months I had avoided all mirrors, be it a bathroom or bedroom mirror. What one cannot see, one does not need to think about. Now, thinking was attacking me and I needed a diversion. It was then Mother's outfit to walk the Great China Wall brought me out in a tittering sweat.

'*Callous,*' you throw my way.

Not at all. I lay my head on the supplied bath pillow and remember two days ago, when my mother had slithered round my bedroom door in khaki shorts, a long-sleeved top, brown rolled down socks, large sand coloured walking boots, and what I can only describe as a sun-hat fit for the paddy fields. She stood there preening, posing, far from the serious-minded woman I was used to; totally unprepared for a hard five day trek.

Knowing her reflection was rebounding from the dressing table mirror where I sat, she croaked, "Do you think I will do?"

Hand on heart I promise you the sight of that lady's get-up was, and still is, seriously hilarious; a picture of vaudeville comedy.

The face carefully cemented with the best Dior make-up, bright diamond stud earrings glinting in her ears, a khaki blouse and trousers cut to perfection, rolled up to her knees.

Catching my hesitation, she tilted her chin upwards. "A girl must be prepared to look good and expensive at all costs."

I nodded, more out of manners than certainty. "Well?" my mother twirled again.

I had to say something – comment or rebuke.

'No,' you gasp.

Do not worry. I know which side my bread is buttered.

I asked. "Have you rubbed expensive cream into every crook and cranny? Have you packed a pair of cotton 'trakki' bottoms? (sorry, she was no fan of that phrase, placing track-suits with a certain element of social class. I told you – a snob). Have you a make-up barrier for the sun?"

Flapping in her usual manner, I inquired after my father. No sooner had the question left my mouth than this figure resembling a 1930 boy scout scampered into the doorway. That was it – will power gave up. I pretended to pick something up from the floor, dusting the carpet with the back of my hand. They managed to make the famous Morecambe and Wise duo in their Christmas sketch look like schoolboys in drag!

Re-setting my face I managed to ask about their bags.

My mother looked proud. "Your father has the larger back-pack. I have the smaller designer one." She scurried out into the hallway to return on the instant with a sleek silver item trimmed flamboyantly by a well-known name.

I snorted rather ungracefully. "Do you not think it will attract the sun, and even worse," I paused, "those who are not quite honest?"

She flicked her bobbed head, the red hair expensively groomed to her liking.

"As usual you are positively negative." (Oxymoron – even my mother's brain goes to sleep now and again.)

My father gave a drawn out twirl, winking in my direction. Mother glared.

"Henry, stop acting, this is our holiday of a lifetime."

Not wishing to get myself into another family discussion I hugged them both.

"You will do." Pretending was becoming second nature.

"Good," Mother acknowledged, "and yourself – please behave. Come along Henry, let's hike!"

She grabbed her 'exclusive' bag, he edged backwards to the door and both disappeared.

The bath had suddenly gone cold. Dragging myself from its soapy depths, I wrap the fluffy towel round my ample proportions, and plod into the Jasmine scented room, notice the hands of the clock are at eight. Late again, the trio will be waiting. I quickly dress in a high neck blouse and long skirt, pile my unruly red hair on top of my head, reach for the powder and paint. Time for my mask: lipstick, foundation, eye-liner, eye-shadow and rouge, emerge a sophisticated young woman.

The stage is set, the play will begin.

The Forbidden City

Mystical austerity, a sense of stepping from this very modern world we live in, to one that was steeped in grandeur and obedience. I could sense the long vanished hand of power. I could hear the muted whimpers of condemned men and women as the decree to execute flows down through the centuries. I mingled with the young girls and old women whose cries for freedom were swallowed up by the elaborate trappings of an enforced life. Females, who accepted that the fragility of submission was ultimately their strength in keeping them alive.

The many gates and beautiful walls hid a torrid past: masters, servitude, and obedience.

The pamphlet in my hand said so and I believed it.

Following Jimmy through one of the side gates where at one time ordinary men and women were herded through for pleasure or pain; the court's plaything, or a sentence of death. Here, they met the Captain of the Imperial Guard and sentence was passed.

In the middle of these imperious gates stood the 'Meridian Gate', an impressive portal thrown open only for the many palanquins carrying the young empress and her attendants arriving for her wedding. This girl, no older than fourteen or fifteen, knew before she entered that this day would be her last glimpse of the outside world. Overtaken by palace rules and feminine training, life became a constant round of audiences, dressing up, sewing, painting, poetry, prayers and waiting – waiting to be summoned to the emperor's bed.

Along with his chosen concubine (the favourite either being the empress's friend, or enemy) the young girl would live a life of extreme luxury, bestowing on her family higher status and extra money. If the girl learnt well the ways to delight her husband (also applied to his concubines), she was ranked among the highest ladies in the land. If not, although her life was secured as empress, she may never lay with her husband again. If she, or a concubine produced a son their life became a template of riches and authority, whilst a child of the female line meant very little. Forced into a life of sexual gratuitousness or hasty extinction, their division was one of favouritism or birth. The former on a whim, the latter by selection. No matter what, all were ruled by the officials of China, under the auspicious hand of the boy or man known as, 'The Son of Heaven'.

—

Meandering in and out of the regal buildings, the sun beating down onto the yellow upturned roofs, I could not stop the desolation of these women washing over me. The orb of their life rotated on 'if'. It covered every area of their life, what life they had!

I was surprised at the stunning architecture of the 1420 buildings, and in the midst of such beauty the melancholy silence that laid siege to each room. Running my fingers over the splendour of the stonework (holding my breath I would not be reproved by a guard) it certainly made me think. If I lived for 570 years I would not be anywhere near as grandiose. The sumptuous decoration alone, and the regal ambience left a mark on us tourists trailing through, to be confronted in the end with the administrative throne; the power seat of twenty-four Chinese emperors.

It did not matter what age the boy ascended the throne. With the help of astrologers, military aides, soothsayers, and the rare favourite concubine, this 'Son of Heaven' ruled with an iron rod. To all, this male had been born of the heavens, and if my pamphlet was to be believed he more than once returned in that direction by whatever foul means a jealous rival displayed.

Deep in thought we wandered from room to room, sensing bygone days, reliving what again the pamphlet quoted as 'Days rich in historical awe and wonder'. It did not take me long to admit my wayward spirit would not have survived incarceration in a place such as this, beautiful or not. We continued to walk in silence, both deep in thought, aggrieved at the blatant oppression that had been part of life back then, thrilled by the beauty and sense of history.

Stepping from the Imperial Palace Jimmy seated himself on one of the many steps. Unhooking his camera from where he had slung it around his neck back at the hotel, he began to click away in that annoying fashion that tourists had; an irritating 'cannot wait' to get everything on celluloid. My reasoning – let the mind's eye store it for them.

He put the camera down, scanned the lines of the impressive architecture, then turned my way. He was about to speak when he caught the inquisitive scowl across my face. "Penny for them," he queried.

I inclined my head toward the Meridian Gate. "I was observing that gateway. If ever there was an entrance to Hell."

He followed my gaze. "Ah, can you not recognise it as a passageway to Heaven?"

I lashed out. "A young girl's life. Hang on, we will say – what the heck!"

Jimmy sat up straight, patted my shoulder. "Come on, many concubines lived in the shadow of death, sharing the man they often learnt to love. It taught them how to be cunning and manipulative. In the words of the pamphlet, 'If they were lucky to bear a son their role would become that of advisor to the emperor, through this came freedom.' Not bad really."

Not bad?

If ... sorry, reader, I am in the mood to use this contentious conjunction, and ask, can my friend not see these poor women had to deceive and lie just to stay alive? May I hit him now!

It rankled, as we had discussed this very topic the evening before over dinner. Jimmy and I sat on the terrace, discussing the subject of women residing in the Forbidden City. I mentioned the difficult journey for the son of a concubine. Jimmy sprang to his feet in defence of this male's position, and how he would benefit. I sprang to my feet as well, arguing at the top of my voice, When I tell you that a silence descended over the other diners, your hand finds your mouth to stifle the giggle.

Well, so be it, but you have no idea how everyone else on that terrace filtered away to another bar, or another area – we had both become pariahs of society. I will say one word – Mother (think about it!)

Jimmy clapped his hands, bowed in a hilarious manner, clinked the china (joke!!!) cups, and roared like a lion.

Okay, his humour can be 'off the wall', even sarcastic to the point of annoying, but it seemed to me, my best friend was being downright smug.

I so wanted to scream, 'Think you're clever, guess what? I have a secret, something that will stop you in your tracks.'

Anyway, we continue.

I was referring to the child's main upbringing by the empress, not his Mother. The odd time a concubine rose in the ranks, such as Empress Cixi (1835-1908) for example a chosen concubine with influence the pamphlet stated, had become the power behind the dynastic throne of the last emperor (her son, then her nephew) in the nineteenth century. Although Cixi had given birth she had no Motherly duties to the young boy, that was in the hands of the empress. Later she would restore the Summer Palace in her son's name, (Jimmy and I would visit in two days' time,) declaring herself an historical figure. Yet still I believed these young girls were no more than incumbent slaves; pawns in their master's sexual games.

Trust me when I write that Jimmy was tormenting me, this I know, but his sanctimonious preening – another matter.

Pulling myself back into the present Jimmy had begun clicking again (give me strength), moving his camera upwards, sideways, zooming onto a specific building, not even bothering to stop annoying me.

"People in this country," he was saying, "lived in poverty. To be put in an existence of grandeur – lucky, I would say."

"Blatant submissiveness," I slammed back at him.

Jimmy whistled through his teeth (hate it). Aiming the camera my way he pressed the button for the shutter to open, taking the picture before I could look away. His dark head bouncing in various directions, allowing the hint of pale stubble growing from the determined chin to glint in the sun. My friend had changed, more argumentative would be my conclusion. 'Growing,' my mother would say.

Suddenly Jimmy linked his hand in mine, and began to pull me back up the steps to the Imperial Palace.

"Come on, misery, you will be glad you came in the end."

I followed, feeling the warmth of his touch, my mind on fire, burning with a guilt I could not explain – nor wished to.

Each step that I climbed I experienced the fear of a past century, aligned myself with my persecuted sisters.

—

Two to three hours later we ambled out into the courtyard once more, weary, foot sore, and overcome by the knowledge given. I had not spoken since lunchtime. Jimmy, he had given up trying to make me see how 'lucky' the women of the Forbidden City were. Instead, he just placed his finger on a certain passage of the pamphlet every so often as we entered a special room. At one point, goodness knows why, he hugged me to him. I strained against his hold, telling myself the back may be healed, yet if nudged or prodded it pains like hell. All in the mind? I know.

Feeling the heat of the afternoon enclose around us we began to find the parts of the courtyard that were sheltered. Determined not to set my friend off on another round of explaining I became what is known in school terms as a 'shadow partner', the other half of a three-legged race. Where he walked, so did I, when he stood still, so did I, and so on. It seemed to last forever. As you have discovered I am not good at shutting up, therefore when 5pm came and our tourist party began to filter through the 13 metre high walls I whooped in joy, much to everyone's entertainment. Passing the Gate of Supreme Harmony (how many gates are there?), and out into the throng of present day life. Jimmy broke his silence.

"The gate," he prodded my arm, "where the emperor met his military officials."

"Um," was the only thing I could say.

"Freedom and oppression *can* live together. To oppose one is to gain the other, whatever century a person inhabits."

I thought of Kurt. I missed him. A good case of freedom and oppression, I ask – don't you agree?

Once more Jimmy eyed me suspiciously, raised my fingers to his lips (here I am lost for words), and led me to the coach for our journey back to Beijing.

11

"Bloody men."

The harshness rang throughout the large bedroom. The knock on the door came louder. I raised my head from where I had thrown it the night before, and swallowed hard on spotting the mess I had left behind on the pillow.

"Hello," I called, trying hard to escape the disorientated world I was thrashing about in.

"Are you ready?"

The remark sounded far away, yet near, if that makes any sense at all.

"Ready?"

"For the Summer Palace."

Summer Palace. Ready.

"Ten minutes, Rhia."

I knew that voice, it was touching a chord, igniting powers of recollection. Jimmy.

"Oh no."

I scrambled out of bed, switching on lights, throwing my pyjamas onto a chair. Everything was moving, from the television to the dressing table. All had legs, all were walking toward me. I thought of a horror film. This was that step further on. It was real.

I headed for the bathroom, slapping water over my face, gargling mouthwash as if it were a drink. Looked in the mirror, ugh, looked away. My reflection confirmed my fear. I had sunk into that pit again. My emotional longing had eased with a drink, then another, and another. It was no use trying to count, I would fail.

Sticking out my tongue I felt my stomach turn at the white fur. Heard my croaky voice plead with it to stay put. The little man in my head thumped away, slamming down on his anvil with a monotonous rhythm. What worried me as I sped from bathroom to wardrobe to bed to bathroom was how much blabbering had taken place. How many secrets had left me and fallen onto my friend's ears. If my brain was to be trusted, and usually it was not, Jimmy had been completely absorbed in my chattering. Was it his vision that was haunting me, leaning over the small round terraced table almost grasping the words from my mouth. He could have got no nearer without sitting on my lap.

The faintest smile crosses your lips, and I demand: Do not even go there. Friends do not have to make excuses for sidling up close, only lovers do that.

Returning to the subject of gossip, I beseech my brain, *please let Kurt have stayed put in my subconscious.* My head is swimming its own 'freestyle' race. I fight to make sure all the buttons on my trousers are secure. It was not until I made my way down the staircase to where Jimmy was waiting that I realised my choice of colours were maybe a little, shall we say, on the loud side.

"Hey, girl," my friend quipped. "Where are you going, a carnival?"

Passing the huge glass mirror positioned on the wall by the main entrance (I can say without a doubt these 'eyes of the world' are certainly not – repeat not – my friend. Hate them –) I notice this blob of red, gold and green bouncing back at me. Here, you can create your own picture, flaming red hair, gold 'midi' pants, red T shirt and green zipped jacket. Thank Heaven my parents were trekking, Mother would have passed out, exclaiming I represent a painting of bad taste.

Perching the dark sunglasses across my tired eyes I made my way onto the pavement to join the line climbing aboard the two-tier bus. Boy, was it rickety. Jimmy laughed at my wobbly ascent, whispered the passengers might find my faux pas in fashion amusing.

Rotten friend.

Not funny really, I branded my mother and father the comedy duo.

Let's hope he has left his camera behind. If not, he and I will certainly fall out.

Jimmy scowled as he bumped down beside me.

"Careful," I hissed from the side of my mouth.

"Head still thumping?" He slammed the book-like map and guide into my hands.

"Yes." The squeak was hardly above a whisper.

"Oh dear, when will you learn?"

"Me?" Who was he to sit in judgement. "It was you who ordered the drink."

"Yes, but how much did *I* drink?"

"As much as me." Jimmy shook his head. "Half then?"

"Nope" he rubbed his fingernail down the lapel of his jacket in the style of a good schoolboy. "I know my limit, shame you don't."

I sneered. "I do not profess to be a goody-goody."

Jimmy eyed me through tight wrinkled slits.

"Me neither." His voice was strained, then in a lighter tone, "Though in light of where we are heading I must invoke the emperor's rule. You, my friend, are female, so what else could I expect? Avaricious in everything, clothes, perfume, money, drink." He stopped.

How dare he.

A smile spread across the familiar face, pompous ass.

Unsure of how much heart-talk had passed between us the night before I thought it best not to answer. Instead I eased myself into the cushioned seat, closed my eyes and settled down for the journey, my mind in turmoil.

—

Dating from the Manchu rule over China (1644-1911) the gardens surrounding the Summer Palace were designed as a restful retreat for the emperor and his family. The later addition of the palace, initially built in the reign of Emperor Qianlong (1711-99) was specifically constructed of coloured glazed bricks. Referred to as 'No Beam Hall', due to its lack of timber, it miraculously survived a raid by Anglo/French forces in 1860 who were fighting against the country's opium laws. These raiders torched the gardens, destroying the holy statue of Amitayus Buddha and 1,008 smaller figures. For the Chinese, a catastrophe. For the west, a severed relationship with the east. It was left to the Dowager Empress Cixi after the death of the emperor, to influence her son and later her nephew, in the restoration of these beautiful grounds. Not for this woman a simple garden of flowers. She created a private village built on a huge lake.

Moving slowly to the East Gate our guide hurried us through. Once accepted as the exclusive entrance for the Emperor, Empress and Dowager Empress, he assured us to pass this way was an honour. Let me say, when speaking about gates a person automatically describes thick, square shaped wood or iron. Not this one: this gate was the most ornamental entrance I had ever been privileged to walk through. The doors alone were carved and curved wood and glass, easily expanding the width of a road back home. Either side were two smaller doors, used in the past for extended Royal Family and court officials. It was not hard to admit I was impressed.

Throughout the journey my friend had looked at me, looked away, opened his mouth, closed it; what was going on?

What was my friend thinking?

Arriving, we parked in the large tourist car park. Scrambling from the bus Jimmy strode past me, a grin of self-satisfaction hovering about his lips.

"Hey, not so quick," I called. "It pains to run."

The 'tut, tut,' was all I could hear, followed by, "Do keep up. We will lose our guide."

Is it a crime to slap a friend in a garden of such provocative beauty!

Following the bobbing back of our traditionally dressed guide it was hard to put into words the feelings that overcame me. I will try.

Raw adulation is the expression I must use. Rapture, the kind that leaves a person fighting for breath. I have no doubt these were the emotions that overtook the crowd grouped closely together in the 796.2 yard long corridor our guide had led us down. Not one murmur could be heard. Everywhere I looked there was beauty. From the layered blue of the sky above our heads, to the colour formation of the sweeping flower beds.

We came to a standstill, all eyes surveying the painted corridor.

Lavish and wonderful – words are inadequate to describe the scene I found myself in. I had to remove the dark glasses. Supported by a quartet of double cove octagonal pavilions, a story unfolded of the four seasons.

The first represented spring, with white and pink blossoms encircled by leaf buds.

The second emblazoned with orange, mauve, crimson and cream orchids; their elegant heads standing tall to greet the hazy dappled days of summer.

Autumn was represented by tricolour leaves, falling and spreading across a background of russet and grey, while winter's frozen lakes and snow clad mountains forced the eye to focus on a darkened sky riven with icy lace particles.

From the guidebook, I read how the emperor's entourage would leave the privacy of the palace, walk the length of this corridor, and go their separate way to an assortment of outer buildings. How the young concubine made her way through this tunnel of beauty to her lord's bed. Required on a nightly test. If she failed (that word again) she would walk the long passageways of the 273 rooms in the palace, slowly, yet stealthily away from the 'Son of Heaven's' quarters.

I thought of her fear, shuddered for her consequences.

The tall trees and bushy shrubs bordering the corridor allowed my dreaming a far more exciting tale. They were the ideal hiding places to liaise with a lover.

He, a military official. She, from the emperor's vast harem.

They met, fell into one another's arms, fused in the moment.

'Comic book romance,' you inject. 'Imagine the outcome.'
I turn from your scorn.

Jimmy nudges me. I moved forward, lost in my dreams. Our guide stops, his shrill voice breaking my trail of thought.

"Symbolic of everlasting happiness."

He shrieked, his scraggy finger pointing in the direction of the lush gardens.

"Present from Empress Cixi," he shrieked again, bowing up and down in the mode of a slave begging for his life.

My two contrived figures, hidden among the erotic scents, began to shrink. How could I even consider romance? There would have been guards everywhere. In each paragraph of the guide book any form of deceit was reported to the dowager. In return, a trumped up court of officials ruled – death. Often in the most terrifying manner.

Another shriek told us Empress Cixi had changed the garden's old name. 'The Garden of Clear Ripples' became, 'Yiheyan, The Garden of Good Health and Harmony.'

A woman of her status taught caution, and caution gave freedom?

Following at a quicker pace (no thought for my head), we entered the palace at 'Inviting Moon Gate'. Here the guide explained we would pass through the Long Gallery (Changlang), and various halls. He advised us to, "Soak up past atmosphere, and when we finally stood in the 'Shizhang Pavilion,'" (his tone changed to one of pride), "Please to admire the classical Chinese paintings on the walls and ceilings."

His breath came in short excited pants as he begged us to take time from the busy tour to stand still and listen to the historical fables, re-live the days of the imperial family, and inspect the landscapes sculptured onto horizontal supports.

"This," he noted, "could take at least three hours."

He stood still with the hugest grin creasing the otherwise pale face.

"Then you eat lunch!"

—

The tour had been exhausting. We had walked-stopped-walked-stopped for give or take three hours, sauntering through so many rooms that it was a miracle we had not emerged on the Great China Wall and joined my mother. What was it with Chinese architecture that the passages were long, the rooms large, and the atmosphere electrifying?

Our guide joined us once more as we stood in the 'Shizhang Pavilion', speaking relentlessly about the sadness of a bygone dynasty. I have got to be truthful and admit a tear or two settled in the eyes, yet was I glad when we emerged into the sunlight once more, and sat at the foot of 'Longevity Hill', leading up to the 'Hall of Benevolent Longevity'. Jimmy perched himself on a lower step to mine, reading aloud from the guide book.

"From the Hall of Benevolent Longevity, the Dowager Empress Cixi and her son Emperor Guangxu dealt with state affairs. Outside the hall bronze animals, cauldrons and phoenixes are placed for good luck. Among these honourable ornaments the most revered treasure can be found – a Kylin.

This is symbolic to Chinese prophecy as it bears the dragon head, lion tail, deer's antlers, ox's hooves and a body covered in fish scales. The awesome creature fends off evil from the outside world. Inside this magnificent hall resides the Sandalwood throne, seat of the 'Son of Heaven'. Engraved with nine dragons, it is looked upon as the symbol of supreme power. To its left and right, occasionally held by two servants, are two large peacock feather fans. Raised above the throne is an inscription: 'Those who show benevolence in the government of the people will live a long life.'

"That must have calmed the prisoner's spirit," Jimmy joked. "Just utter the right words."

How right my friend was. Life in the Summer Palace, and if it came to that the Forbidden City, hung on the slip of the tongue.

Munching a bar of melting chocolate we had quickly slipped into our bag (sweating within the restrictive foil) we lodged ourselves on a bench underneath the largest jasmine tree possible, the smell, divine. Jimmy was still reading. Others in our group were complimenting the guide on his knowledge, thanking him for a job well done. The man bowed, clasped his hands in appreciation, and waited for our return of appreciation.

I did not move.

"Displeased at his hard work," Jimmy mumbled.

He ran his fingers down the bare flesh of my arm. I pull away.

"Ha, ha, tetchy, are we?"

Tetchy? yes, I suppose I was.

"What is wrong with you?" The patience had left my friend's voice "How can you be cross in a beautiful place such as this?"

"It is a prison."

My friend popped the last squidgy square of chocolate into his mouth, let his eyes fall onto the rippling water of the lake, before lifting his head to the serene mountains in the distance. Chinese psychology dubbed this scene the 'perfect landscape'. He swung to face me.

"This whole scene troubles you. Only you know why, but let me tell you, everyone is someone's slave."

I coughed on the chocolate slithering down my throat.

"How many women were denied complete freedom? Objects to their male counterparts."

It sounded good, took me away from my *real* problem of this place, or even this holiday.

Jimmy shifted slightly to my left, edging himself more into the shade

"You think so. Have you ever thought, for one slight moment, how many of those women's male servants who lived within the walls of the city, in these beautiful gardens, were wishing they could regain what was rightfully theirs?"

I scowled (as he does when he is perplexed). A question answered by a question, what fair play is that?

Reader, sniggering is not allowed. Neither is the large 'O' a mouth makes when dumbed into surprise by Jimmy's next remark.

I was mortified, embarrassed into good behaviour to the point where my mother would have given the guy a badge, just for putting me in my place.

I flounder to know what he was referring to. Jimmy intimates his head. Still no wiser. All of a sudden his hand fell to the zip of his trousers, and the meaning became clear. Eunuchs. Men whose sexuality would account to nothing more than a dream. I eyed the tourists around us, still doing their own thing, not looking our way. Oh shame.

"You mean ..." I stumbled. "Don't you?"

"I do," pleased he had made his point crystal clear. "Castration was the thief that stole not one, but thousands of men's freedom. They, as their mistress, had to manipulate a form of freedom."

I wanted the earth to open, the wind to howl, anything that would extract me from this conversation. Nothing happened. Jimmy was waiting for an answer.

"I did not think." First thing that entered my head.

"You never do."

My friend stood up, made his way to the steep ascent toward the 'Hall of Benevolent Longevity'. One or two steps from where I was sitting, he called across his shoulder.

"A Chinese proverb. Be not afraid of growing slowly. Be afraid only of standing still."

He continued upwards, ploughing stealthily up the 68.9 feet from the bottom of Longevity Hill. I stared at his back. I could hear my father's voice. "A riddle is only a riddle if the listener wants it to be."

Half way up the steps Jimmy turned and smiled. Outlined by the glimmer of sun beating down on this building I could not help the fluttering sensation rising within me. Time to upbraid myself, transferred emotions and all that rot. I ventured upwards, holding my hands out in submission. The way he saw this lifestyle of absolutes *was* as a personification of a regime who believed in oppression, yet at the same time gave freedom to those who sought it. Time to up the pretence.

12

Next morning the tension that had dogged us the previous day had disappeared. We were back to our normal selves (whatever that was). This may have been due partly to there being no tête-a-tête the previous night. I had decided not to give my friend a chance to crow, expand on my run-away tongue, although I doubt I said anything incriminating. He would have told me – yes? Instead I ate in my room, feigning a headache and exhaustion. I had expected Jimmy to do the same. Should have known better. He, from what I gathered, dined, dressed and spent the night with other tourists out on the town.

Do not say a word. I will call him a traitor.

The good news: on meeting for breakfast I could see no sign of over indulgence. Good one to talk I know, but at least we can do something interesting instead of mopping up a splitting head.

Please do not look at me as though I am a selfish, indulgent, bitch. I have no patience this morning for sullen men.

No need to worry, my friend was bubbling to tell me of the excursion he had undertaken. I listened intently, actually felt excited at his suggestion of shopping in the old quarter of the town.

Emerging from our hotel, ready to shop until I dropped, we entered the hustle and bustle of Beijing life; cars, bicycles, rickshaws and market traders vying for their section of the busy streets, students performing martial arts, chanting the philosophy of life as they thrust an arm or leg high into the air. Financiers skittering to work with briefcases swinging by their side, humming or whistling a tune that was non-descriptive and jolly. Children of middle class parents being shunted into cars as mothers rushed them to school, checking watches in their hurry to beat another fixed deadline. Endless tourists clicking cameras, blocking pavements for the sake of celluloid keepsakes, calling to each other in their own tongue to pose, smile or jump about. The city was a mass of active life played out to the low strains of the country's national anthem.

We made our way through the cacophony of noise until Jimmy found the alleyway he remembered from the night before, pulling me after him. I closed my eyes, sick of memories that will not leave me alone. Only as the noise grew louder, and the smells stronger, I opened them onto a courtyard crammed with merchants of old China; tables of herbs, medicines, creams, potions, jewellery and stationery, clothes stalls full of traditional Chinese dress. Ceremonial outfits, peasant garments, court outfits, old army regalia. Women in gowns of fine detailed embroidery, with stone encrusted combs in their hair enticed tourists to, "Come take look," at the old ribbons, rings, necklaces given to the family of a girl chosen for court life.

Adjacent to the rows of sacks and tables doors were flung open where the smell of cooking emanated from within, all decorated with colourful Chinese lanterns, their tiny paned glass windows holding notices inviting people to enter and enjoy the art of home-made sushi or green tea. Large scrawling signs hung above the doors with traditional Chinese names of favourite flowers: 'Lily Palace', 'Orchid House', 'Jasmine Rest', decorated in the old style with small tables and a carpet to sit upon.

The allure of the past was strong.

In the background, hidden under large awnings were more shops. These doors were draped with beaded curtains, and dim lighting. The proprietors, clothed in lower class traditional dress, invited tourists to, 'Try his massage parlour'. Jimmy watched the expression of surprise run across my face and whispered, "A pleasurable experience."

Save me the explanation, friend. "For who?" I retaliated.

My eyes would not leave his, my time to question.

"No," Jimmy answered. "No, I did not, but would you care?"

Before I could return his jibe a woman of eighty plus years (if not older) emerged from what I can only say was an off-white tent. She was covered from head to foot in what I now know to be a Sheni: the famous tunic and skirt sewed together that the majority of Chinese elders wore. I could see the black material was cotton and well worn.

Her bright diamond eyes shone in the deep-set hollows of her face, her long black hair (yes, I too thought a woman of her age would be white or grey) was tied tightly in a low chignon, pulling every feature of her face into a startled expression of alarm.

She stepped up to me, repeating over and over again in her own language. I took a step backward. From inside the tent a scrawny child appeared and proceeded to translate for her: "Man, meet, you like."

The child pulled my thigh length blouse, causing me to stumble. Trying to defend my racing mind, and pull Jimmy from her I cried, "Not today," in the loudest screech I could muster. Picking up on my distress, my friend decided to intercede. "Thank-you, save your runes for other tourists."

The woman thanked him, indicated to the child to whisper in his ear, and shuffled away.

Pulling him toward her the child babbled in his ear (yuk), then just as quickly disappeared. "What did she say?" I was annoyed. "Cheek of it."

Jimmy steered me through the various stalls. "Nothing of importance."

It was one of those dismissals that makes a person ask if the truth had been withheld.

We came to another alleyway.

If I did not know better, I would define my friend as having a warped humour.

Determined to keep my eyes open I prayed the stupid woman, and her sidekick child had not mentioned anything to do with Kurt.

You pull up your nose.

Excuse me, I have been told these soothsayers – or whatever you would like to call them, are brilliant at tuning into a person's psyche.

As we left the old market behind and sauntered down another street we were confronted by the hugest tree anyone could imagine. Startled at its enormity I was even more taken aback when I spotted red ribbons, all lengths and shades of crimson, tied to its overhanging boughs. Jumping around, in what I must describe as jovial glee was the funniest man I had ever seen. Think of the pantomime 'Aladdin' and the humble Chinese servant – I tell you, this man was living proof! His slanting eyes peered over the top of a pair of round spectacles in wide expectation. On his head was a round skull cap poised over a long grey plait, sweeping his shoulders like a horse's mane. Tiny beads of sweat trickled from his forehead, sinking, the faster they ran, into the creases of his puffed out cheeks, and wrinkled neck. The long buttoned silver cotton coat covering his short black trousers was threadbare, matching (in a way) the tatty silver leather sandals wrapped around his feet. These were held in place by a piece of old string. Poking out from the cut off toes were longer than average toe nails, painted bright red, resembling the long talons so loved by fictitious witches.

He whistled – well, as best as he could through a mouth of broken teeth. Dancing around the tree he sang, shouted, "Foto, you want foto?" whilst waving a black boxed camera in our direction.

"Jimmy," I stammered, looking at my friend in comical dismay.

"Trust me."

He secured my hand in his grasp (not going to let me run away then). "It is an old tradition to tie a ribbon to a walnut tree for luck."

I squeezed my friend's hand. "You know how I am with photos. Hate the things."

"This, girl, is different. You want a memory, you shall have a memory."

Now, until this very moment my friend had appeared fully in possession of his faculties. Maybe I was wrong.

I watched the little man as he delved into a bag by the side of the tree. Pulled out a length of red ribbon, and dangled it before my face.

"Long pieceee," he croaked, holding up the scarlet silk.

Jimmy smiled.

"Does it matter?" my voice shook.

"Oh yes," Jimmy said, nodding to the man, pushing us both nearer to the tree trunk.

In my opinion Jimmy has had some zany ideas throughout our friendship, positively mad ones, yet this one – this one has got to be over the top, my friend is well aware I hate cameras.

"Gooshed, gooshed," the man was hopping from leg to leg holding out his hand. "Yuan, Yuan."

Jimmy produced four paper notes (expensive or what), rolled them up and stuffed them into the old man's top pocket.

"Just smile." My friend proceeded to put his arms about me, and embrace me tight. The old man continued to dance round the tree, clicking the camera first one way, then another. After five minutes of this absurd behaviour he stood in front of us, leaning his head to the left, then right. Cross my heart I wanted to laugh, he was *that* funny. He held one of Jimmy's arms. "You kish," he commanded, spitting white foam through his broken teeth. He put a bony finger to his mouth, pursing them for all he was worth.

"What?" I exploded turning my face to my friend, whose lips suddenly covered mine in the ferocity of a lightning strike.

I could not explain that moment to myself, let alone describe it for you. Repulsion – this was my best friend. Sweetness, a lingering sensual simplicity. A moment of complete madness?

Jimmy removed his mouth from mine. He neither apologised, explained, or burst into laughter. He just clasped his hands together and bowed to the old man, in the traditional mode of old China (similar to how they show you on the films), wrote his name, hotel, and room number on the pad provided, tied the brilliant ribbon to a bough, then began to walk away.

We were half-way down the alleyway before I heard the strained sound squeeze pass my teeth. "Was that my souvenir?"

No turning to look at me. "Why, do you want it to be?"

I was fighting for restraint.

"No," I squealed. "Not on your life."

"Fine," came the answer. "Let's search."

It was not so much the attitude that put me off balance. More that *he* had kissed me – full on the mouth at that.

'*Nothing out of the ordinary,*' you sigh. '*He is your friend.*'

So tell me: why then does your comment irritate me?

I think of Kurt, his shadow enticing me to hold our passion sacred.

It was one kiss. Not the shared excitement of Berlin.

A gesture, maybe, given in the form of friendship. The memory will fade.

How does the saying go? Making a mountain out of a molehill.

My friend is already striding in front, forgotten, not looking my way.

The damn kiss was a joke.

We re-enter the main city. "Keep up," my friend hurls.

I knew it; as always, worrying for nothing.

I rub my lips, willing the soft sensation to go away.

—

The day before our homeward journey my parents arrive back at the hotel in a state of confused irritability. Evidently, walking the Great Wall of China had left them (as far as my mother was concerned) with sore feet, aching bodies and blinding headaches, a far cry from the athletic woman she presumed herself to be.

From the moment she spotted Jimmy and me waiting patiently in the reception area she started to moan. "The sun was too hot, the nights too cold, the paths too dusty."

Moan, moan, moan. The smallest detail, to the most mundane activity, expressing herself in a tirade of frenzy, berating every small obstacle that had crossed her path.

Longing for her to take breath, clasp me in her arms, ask what I had been up to, was in all honesty far more than I could expect. This was *my mother* after all. She looked in the reception mirror.

"Oh dear," fingering her sun-bleached skin, "There was no time for my daily make-up routine. Look at my skin shining from lack of cleansing and toning."

On and on her lips moved, believe me when I say the five thirty express to Scotland could have gone no faster.

Okay, I will agree, she was speaking the truth. I could see the 'disaster' as she called it. How the powerful Eastern sun had caught her nose and cheek bones. I could even show a speck of alarm at the bright pink spot making itself at home on what I always thought was a bulbous chin, and yes, I was unable to count the freckles congregating on her nose – shall I continue, better not.

Father, in his usual laid back manner claimed it was her own fault. Mother had ignored the advice given by the guide, foolishly removing her wide brim hat at the hottest part of the day, casting him an obnoxious glare, and stating in her usual 'know it all' voice that her moisturiser was 'top of the range', and would prevent sunburn no matter where she sunbathed in the world.

My eyes became saucers.

"Not the best," my father was whispering. "Oh no. Add this haughty attitude to her argument of no double bed, no en-suite bathroom, no scented sheets, and we were the laughing stocks of the party."

Although he had whispered this information into my ear, Mother still ranting on about the crudeness of it all, I gathered he fully enjoyed sleeping in the ancient road side watchtower.

My mind was striving to conjure up the scene: Mother with her mattress on the floor, Mother and the pee pot in the corner (behind a curtain), Mother and the lack of light, just an odd candle, Mother and pouches full of clean water stored in the care of the trekking helpers for careful use, out of her reach!

From what I gather she drove my father to the edge of despair.

All I can say is ITALY.

She herself admitted arguing for a whole week; a 'yes please', and 'no thank-you' over the group meal being the end to their daily tiff.

For the socialite who was my mother, it must have been hell on earth: for my poor father, poor guide, poor tourists; rather you than me.

Once the flame of blame and disgust had burnt itself out Mother headed for her room, no doubt to lower herself into the watery world of perfume and eau-de-Cologne she knew so well, leaving behind my father shaking his head in confused annoyance, and a daughter and friend doing their best to hide their amusement.

—

It is said that truth hides its face when cornered.

Following my father and Jimmy to the lounge area, we ordered coffee and talked nonstop about the Forbidden City and Summer Palace. The highs and lows, gaffs and arguments all laid bare for my father to mull over. Jimmy's conversation was light, skittering over the little old man and his walnut tree; a subject I did not wish to expand upon. The conversation moved on to the camera and the picture, definitely an area I wished to forget. So much so, that when the pictures had arrived at the hotel late the same day I stashed mine at the bottom of my suitcase.

'Out of sight, out of mind,' my grandmother would comment.

Jimmy neither mentioned or joked about them. Guess he was as embarrassed as me.

Now, he was telling my father it was a joke: embarrassment confirmed.

We sat there a good hour, father not offering to go to his room, Mother not imposing further moaning upon us. When she did finally join us, her mood had changed, along with her clothes, make-up and hair. Her re-entry into the civilised world had been secured by a scented bath, heated rollers, and a cucumber face mask. Behind her those trekking days, never to be repeated. Before her, her self-righteous status seeking friends, all but an aeroplane flight away.

Stories of her expedition would fill each week, each sherry party or bridge night; stories that lengthened with each telling where stark nights would turn into romantic evenings, hot blistering days into incredible fantasies. The tales would stretch by the telling, igniting the gruesome with rainbow colours, until in the end they would become fact. Talks for the Women's Voluntary Service where the organisers would beg her to excite their monthly gatherings, selecting the 'right' audience, brandishing their listeners with tea and scones. How my mother would revel in it, dressed in her best Hartnell or Jaeger outfit.

The ear to suffer: my father, weary at what the Joneses or the Smiths thought of her travels. No mention of her poor daughter's worries, spinning somewhere between a German alleyway, and a man with broken teeth and red painted toenails.

13

It took six months of fretting and arguing with myself over whether I should visit Alexander's studio again. What instigated it in the end – boredom.

No need to remind me, I know I said 'Never again', but like my drinking – well, I am sure you have been there.
Life had carried on in the usual way.

The errand running and tea making at the beck and call of my bank colleagues paid my salary, the once a week barrage of insults from my mother over the 'low class' work position of her daughter, the lack of attention on her part to grasp my father's truthful, yet hurtful point of view, that *her* only daughter actually needed a 'kick up the bottom' to get herself motivated.

"Unlike Jimmy," she would preen, "Up, up, and up the ladder of success."

Good for him, and yes, I agree – sour grapes.

I believe my friend to be good at his job, top of the class among the old artefacts and paintings.

"Got an eye for masterpieces," my father commented the day Jimmy was promoted from ordinary curator to specialised expert.

My friend trawled all over the country to find objects of interest, bring them home, collate them with tender loving care, and exhibit them.

Instead of excitement I found it boring; old dusty relics – **boring**.

Time was taken away from me. Monday, Thursday and Saturday evenings being his 'loose end' periods.

Could he not understand it was just work, work, work, and more bloody work?

We began to argue over silly things, the weather, the time of day, each other's likes and dislikes. Today, I needed to find freedom before I blew a brain valve at him.

You gulp – exactly my reaction.

What game was he playing, and to be truthful I missed how we crossed swords in humour, not this bickering and throwing insults.

You raise your eyes.

No need, as already stated – he is my best friend!

Convinced Alexander's needle would drive my boredom away I deliberately cajoled my mother into believing I was shopping for her Christmas present and set forth on my quest.

—

Stepping inside the heavily scented studio, I quickly registered how every picture and piece of furniture were in the same position. Almost as if I had been nowhere, or the clock had stood still. I wondered if Alexander and the 'Bumble-bee' (as she still sprang to mind) would be the same. Would they remember me? Would they even be as accommodating as after Berlin?

Mozart filled my ears, calming the tempest within, drifting me to a place I frequently found myself of late. There had been no discovery on my part into where Kurt had gone. Jimmy never mentioned him, therefore, I was certain he knew nothing.

The television news reported on Stasi members imprisoned. Kurt's name was never among them.

I can see you shaking your head, dear reader.

Please do not. Since that day under the walnut tree I had vowed to track my lover down. Where? who knows, How? Yet to find out, but life throws these cards our way, I knew the time would come.

'*Jimmy?*' your eyes are bright as you gently ask the question.

Jimmy, do not worry about him. I have everything under control. Kurt had to be innocent. His father was the problem, as my friend will understand in the end. Jimmy was wrong, Kurt would not hurt a fly.

I leant back on the velveteen cushions. Funny really, the last time I came the weather was 'yuk'. Today, rain is falling again.

'Tears and pain, guilt and deceit.'
I cast you from my mind.

"Hello." The cheery greeting swept over me.

I quickly sat upright, scouring the hazel eyes smiling into my own.

"Alexander."

"Rhia, I believe, how are you?"

From the soothing voice to the hippy clothes, nothing had changed. Behind him the loyal 'Bumble-bee'.

"Hi," she said her sugary smile and batting eyes as big as ever.

"Hi," I replied.

Alexander lowered himself onto the sofa. "What this time?"

Red lips moving in my periphery view mouthed, "Another landscape?"

"Rosie, get a drink." Alexander's voice ripped through the air.

The poor girl moved away, a smirk of, 'I told you she would be back,' spreading across her lips. It was almost as if she had guessed the conflict taking place inside me. Could her own longing make her susceptible to my need? I settled my eyes on those fleshy lips and found they disturbed me. Brought to mind a small Chinese man, a moment in time.

"I'm not sure," was all that sprang from my throat. "I have a postcard."

Alexander held out his hand, took the card. He pondered for a moment, held it at arm's length, then lay it on his lap.

"To reproduce all four images would be quite expansive. Is that what you want?"

"Not really. A memory."

The 'Bumble-bee' handed me the steaming drink. I nodded, not so much in approval, as in fear of what her canny mind had gathered.

"No worry," Alexander stood. "Come, tell me all."

He began to walk toward the studio, his young assistant promptly stepping in between us.

—

Alexander drew four tiny rough sketches as I talked. Each in a small box to fit neatly down my arms. His plan was to etch his idea within square diameters, superimposing them from shoulder to just below the elbow.

"This," he was saying, "would allow me to be neater, and –" I shook my head. He stopped mid-sentence. "You do not want my work on show?"

Being truthful to oneself is hard, uttering the absolute truth to someone else is very often nigh impossible.

"It is not your work, it is me."

The girl shot a quick glance at her boss, moved one step nearer to his elbow, sough, as a mother would her baby, to protect him from harm. Keeping her voice light, she asked, "Do you wish us to suggest another place?"

Alexander groaned. "Thank you, Rosie, I am sure you have work to do."

"No, please do not scold her, that is a good idea."

She patted his arm, which he abruptly pulled away before scanning a wary eye over my robust figure.

"Right," he smiled. "If I were to sketch all four images the way I landscaped the Berlin Wall it would cover a large amount of your body."

Now, there is no argument it would not look superb, what else would you expect from my artist? However, where and how large were another story.

Collecting his tools and gloves he requested me to lay on my stomach. The 'Bumble-bee' covered my lower body with the designated 'modesty sheet' before showing me once more why I had thought of her nick-name. Removing, fetching, cleaning, answering the phone, serving clientele, she succeeded in flying in and out the room at such break-neck speed. All this exerted energy passed Alexander by. He made no comment, neither praised her or nodded a 'thank you'. Typical 'take for granted' attitude. I could not stop myself from feeling sad. The

'Bumble-bee' tried so hard. To be so smitten at her age must be painful.

You laugh; every right, knowing this profound statement came from one who is hardly five years older, and incarcerated in **1989.**

Still, the girl's jealousy was obvious. Yet, I could not help but sense the 'deja vu' that bound us together. We both longed for a relationship beyond our control, fantasy or fire, who knew?

Drying his ink-smudged gloves Alexander demanded the girl fetch a mirror. He took it sharply and held it above his finished work. I twisted my head, gasped as my eyes fixed onto the apex of my copious ass (whoops sorry, not very ladylike). Perched alone, and more lifelike than I wish to admit was the red-bedecked walnut tree. Either side in medium sized boxes stood the Forgotten City and Summer Palace.

Real – too damn real.

I choked on my intake of breath, coughed as if my lungs would burst.

"Do you like?" Alexander's glare implored me to nod.

"A postcard to remember," I joked, nodding like mad.

"You are pleased?" he asked again.

The 'Bumble-bee' interrupted. "As you can see, Alexander is brilliant, and so undeserving of the criticism he gets."

I lay back down on the couch. The emotion Alexander displayed in his work shook me. "Brilliant, have you never re-submitted your art?"

The girl ceased wrapping my upper backside, let her gloved hands drop to her thighs. She caught the sigh of her boss, caught it and held it in her own repetition.

Alexander cut through the ensuing silence. "I cannot be bothered."

"Be bothered," the dismayed sound reverberated around the room.

He smiled, excusing himself. The 'Bumble-bee' continued to bind me tight. As her boss left the studio she bent nearer my ear "He has lost his nerve to display. Shame really."

"More than a shame."

"Mind," she continued, nervously looking toward the door "When his 'art' is hidden away ..."

Ouch. Then, the idea. Oh boy, my mind was tripping over itself.

Curious to know? In that case, I will spill the beans.

'So?' I hear the squeal.

Shall I tease?

'No.'

I laugh. This guy is from a painting calibre only the Jimmy's of this world would appreciate.

'What?'

I laugh again. Wait and see.

14

The opening for my plan came a year to the day after my visit to Alexander's studio. Our sweet talking Irish postman dropped dozens of letters, bills and junk-mail into the elaborate postal box fixed to the main door wall.

I cease writing for a moment to giggle, for I can see my mother in my mind's eye, boomeranging here and there to collect the post.

I breathe, collect my thoughts and gather myself to put pen to paper once more.

"Look," she screamed. "Joe has left us a mountain of post."

Noting that we were on first name terms I walked into the vast lounge. I never felt truly comfortable in this room, far too sparse. Mother would often comment with pride on its spacious layout. To me, it was cold, clinical, drab in its beige and cream colouring.

"Rhia, Rhia." Her voice followed me. "You have what I presume is an invitation."

Taking the huge white envelope from her excited hold I tore it open. Written in gold bold lettering and signed A.C. was the most ornate printed card.

"Well?" Mother stood on tiptoe to peer over my hand.

"Nothing," I lied. "An invitation to meet a friend this Saturday, that's all. You don't mind if we postpone our shopping in the city, do you?"

Mother's face fell, then lifted. "Jimmy?" she asked.

I paused, saw my escape. "You've guessed. His art gallery, umm – a surprise for you."

"Oh, then you must go," walking into the kitchen to open her post (heaven forbid, paper may drop on the floor).

I took in the time, the command for my presence, and wondered if this was the 'Bumble-bee's' trickery.

—

Reader, I put this to you. Be truthful, have you ever taken a journey in the knowledge that somehow the course you are on is about to turn your life upside down? I believe you would say, "Yes."

Saturday arrived, and no rain.

My plan not quite formulated, only the thought of Jimmy's sojourns to Paris to observe artefacts of interest. I could hitch a lift.

Can you see where I am taking this plan?

Pretend to see the sights, all in the course of freedom (of course), find an art collector, one who may be interested in Alexander's work. My pattern was weaving, I would shift my sackcloth and ashes, make one dream come true. I never doubted Alexander's brilliance, he was waiting to be discovered. All I needed was a simple sketch, then Jimmy to believe my lie.

Hard job? No, just need to 'up' the deceit.

OK, not in all things. 'Materialise from nothing,' as they say.

At the exact time the bell eased its clanging the door to Alexander's inner sanctum opened and out popped the 'Bumble-bee'.

"Hello."

"Thank you for the invitation. Has he changed his mind, showing his art work?"

Rosie ran her thumb along the edge of the desk. "Not exactly."

"Oh."

She did not look at me. "It was what you said the last time you were here."

I frowned.

"You remember, about showing his work."

Now, it was my turn to act apprehensive.

"Well, Alexander had to go away for a few days, family matters, so, I thought it a rare opportunity to show off his work to you, and follow it through. Yes, he will sack me if he finds out, but he is really that good."

I was stunned, the girl trusted me.

"How many more people are coming?"

She shifted awkwardly. "None," the voice hardly above a whisper. "I know it was elaborate, but I did not think you would come if you had thought –" she trailed off.

Dead right.

"Bum. Rosie, I do have a plan. Not sure it will work, but can think of nothing else at the moment."

The girl was mesmerised.

"Quick, lock the door." I sounded bossy even to myself.

On hearing the 'click' of the bolt I began to share my idea. The girl's face passed from wonder to awe, until finally the red mouth broke into a large 'O' shape. Not one word left its gaping orifice.

Leaving out Jimmy, Paris, and certainly the cajoling I would need to put into practice to get there (cannot have her thinking I am a low cog in this plan), I revealed, shall we say, half of my idea.

"Sounds great," she muttered.

"Only if we keep it under control, then nothing can go wrong."

'*Famous last words,*' you offer.

I tremble as I write.

'Thrilled' is such a poor explanation of the 'Bumble-bee's' antics. She jumped up and down on the spot, running round the reception area picking up certain sketches in a duplication of my mother's postal dance.

I waited for her to stop.

"Forget the black and white sketches, has he anything else?"

She hesitated, her eyes as furtive as a rabbit's, then opened a locked door within the sterilizing room. From the bottom of a large pile of canvases she took three.

"He must never know, unless you get lucky."

I stared in disbelief at the paintings, a collection of oils. Landscapes of immeasurable beauty, a portrait of the 'Bumble – bee' herself. Unable to speak I walked up and down the reception area, choosing one for my favourite, then another; stunned by the perfection of art before me. From where she stood at the desk following my every move, smiling at the different expressions dancing across my face.

"Impressed?" the voice cut through my thoughts.

"An understatement," I replied. "Why does he not sell? His customers would love them."

"Pain of rejection," was her simple reply.

"Rejection be blowed, the man is in a class of his own."

I decided not to ask for one of these paintings, he may count them, instead removing a small painting from the wall.

"Can I please take this one?"

Her face froze. The moment had come.

I was so sure of my plan that to let it slip without even trying would, in my eyes, have been ridiculous. "Trust me, I promise you, it will bring about his dream."

I had never been confronted with 'scared.' I will actually go further, the girl was petrified, her red lips trembling as she asked, "What shall I tell him?"

"Nothing." I let the exhilaration of the plan wash over me, it felt good.

"Nothing?" Her head fell to the left, her brow a mass of lines. She was so young. I looked into her eyes, gave in, and told her everything.

Rosie muttered something I could not catch, rolled up the canvas. "Can it be done?"

"Promise," I said cocking my head in the way Mother did when determined, fingers crossed behind my back.

"Here, take it, I will replace it with a spare painting from the drawer."

"Will he know?" I queried.

"Not if I use the duplicate."

"This man duplicates. Whatever next?"

We both laughed, exhaled the tense emotions building inside us. Who would have thought, the 'Bumble-bee' and I had become partners in deception.

—

For me coercion and deviousness were becoming parallel to a second skin. While this may be the case it had still taken me a good six months (that figure was beginning to haunt me) of nagging, plying my charm, and using endless lies to persuade Jimmy to let me accompany him on a week-end to Paris.

Why had it taken so long?

I had not realised how difficult my prey would be.

Do not believe it when you are told a pretty smile can get you anything. I will correct it right now. Some guys (Jimmy) have a barrier, I swear, for an appealing smile.

To start with, would my friend see my point of view?

No, he thought I was up to something, which I was, but that is beside the point.

OK, my cajoling may not have been the smartest; actually, he repeatedly questioned why I had suddenly taken up an interest in art. I told him I had always been interested, just not to the level he was. That surprised him, I think. Then, I told him I was in great need for space from Mother's nattering. His argument? I was used to it, before laughing his socks off when I explained my desire to research French paintings.

I was seriously running out of ideas and excuses.

Last, wrenching his sides in jovial pain when I told him I could audition at the famous Moulin Rouge. I suppose that was a step too far, and yes, I could see his point, their dancers were slimmer (skinny in my eyes), and taller – who cares? But, when all was said and done, I was desperate.

I was seriously beginning to think French girl, stashed away, does not want me to know. Then I switched back to the district of Pigalle (topless dancers and all that), before I settled on Jimmy being awkward. *He* took to the habit of looking at me down his straight aquiline nose. Pumping querulous words at me in quick succession, until I told him to shut up. Anyway, in desperation I threw a huge tantrum, asked my friend if he was ashamed of me, poked about over the girlfriend thing, and yep, that did it, hurray. I got my own way!

Now the truth is – I may, just *may* have told him my little plan when we arrived in the country if he had been a trifle more accommodating. After everything I had to go through to get there –what do you think?

I can hear you reason, '*Why did the silly cow not get on a flight and just go? With her father.'s wealth, it was not a money issue.*'

Maybe you are right, but that would have blown my plan apart. Understand, Jimmy was my introduction to the art world.

While all this coercion was going on I found myself at Alexander's studio every Saturday afternoon for coffee. As the weeks passed Mother became less convinced with my excuses. A visit to a cat sanctuary, a hair model for a student. You name one, I told it. I kept up these visits for two reasons – one: to chat, two: to make sure the 'Bumble-bee' had not confessed to giving me the print, three: to hide from coercion. At least on the second score I am glad to report both boss and assistant were shuffling along as usual. No spilling the beans; two people lodged in the halcyon days of peace and flowers; neither aware of my hard struggle. However, tattoos were catching on fast much to Alexander's pleasure, giving him any excuse to be more flamboyant.

"A protest for creative freedom," he spouted.

I would hold up my hands in the protest gesture, knowing each 'coffee spot' that loomed ignited an insatiable curiosity inside me to see what outlandish art had been hung on his walls in the past week. In truth, my Monet was rapidly turning into a Picasso; the fight within his head was appearing on canvas. This four thirty slot was becoming what I nicknamed 'my dumbing down hour'. No nagging, no lying, no anything out of the way I was. Mother shopped on her own (spent more money sad to say). Jimmy, if he was not at work or flitting abroad, joined my father at the local football match.

In due time my two days in Paris had been sorted; the most outrageous concocted story yet. I led Jimmy to believe I was considering a painting for my parents' anniversary (most years I forgot to send a card, never mind a gift), fingers crossed he did not remember this, and I needed to speak to a Director of Art over its worth. Jimmy 'tut, tutted' for aiming for the heights, and he himself could guide me to a good buy.

"Not a brilliant idea," I groaned. "It had to be my choice." Fighting for ground here.

'*Tell him the truth,*' you scoff. '*The tattoos, the painting, Kurt.*'

"One day," I breathe deeply, "one day things may be different."

'Too late.' Your scorn is obvious.

What do you know? I shift uneasily. Back to the present.

I had booked into a French spa on the Saturday night. Refused flatly to accompany Jimmy to a business dinner. He complained, I brought up his arty mates, an offensive amount of wine – not quite my scene.

'Say that again.' Go away.

The scene 'eyes popping out of head' clouded my vision, and I have to admit that the wine sounded alluring, his mates – another thing.

Another fact: it was to be held in the district of Pigalle. Now I know that Jean Baptiste Pigalle (1714-1785) was a famous sculptor, but the district named after him was a well noted 'working' district. Relaxing on my own is not quite my thing either, but at least I will be pampered, and not worrying over the scanty dressed females promising a world that does not exist. I was absolute in my resolution to hand over Alexander's painting.

Paris April 1993

The Rue De La Boule Rouge, just down the road from the Folies Bergeres Theatre, filled me with a pleasure I had not expected. It was not the French perfume that lingered in the air of my room, or even the sparkle of the midday sun as it lay across the white linen on the bed, or the regal design of the armoire and dressing table (both in the period style of Louis XIV): it was an unexplainable trembling that had taken control of my body.

Leaning against the long casement window I let my gaze wander up and down the busy street. The whole debacle that was my plan had started to worry me. I had worked every move out in my head, ridiculously overlooking Jimmy's continual questioning, and what I generally tabbed nosiness. My friend had not given up. Whenever he had seen me it was, "Why the sudden interest in painting?" "Why the nagging to visit Paris?" "Surely if you were *that* interested you would join me on the arty dinners?" Repeat, repeat, repeat.

I hate to say this, but Jimmy, my best, best friend, got on my nerves.

On arrival in the capital Jimmy had been summoned to a meeting at the Louvre. He was not happy. His plan to have coffee with me before depositing me at my selected spa had backfired. I, on the other hand, was pleased. Told him not to fret, that by the time he had finished his meeting I would have found the place myself, and, if by any chance I got lost, there was such a thing as a taxi. My friend wished me well, checked in his diary for the spa's name and number, and made me promise to be back at the hotel by Sunday lunchtime. That suited me: the less I saw of Jimmy this weekend, the less I must lie.

Turning from the window I decided to have a bath. Indulge myself before the heavy hands of a French masseur pummelled my skin. Goodness knows what comment would be made over my tattoos. Letting the hot steamy water run into the oversized bath I tipped in a whole bottle of French bubble bath (it was free), scattered my clothes on the floor (think French film), and lowered myself into the frothy depths. Resting my head on the soft silky bath cushion my eyes closed. What occurred now was of my own making.

Heaven. Parfait.

—

Emerging from the bath I dressed quickly in a white, slinky strapped dress with swirls of lavender on a full swing skirt. To look good would make me feel good, and besides, I felt like Audrey Hepburn in the film 'Roman Holiday'. Okay, enough giggling; a larger Audrey Hepburn, with red hair, but the same intention – to do her own 'thing'. Selecting a chunky white cardigan (April is still nippy) I twirled in front of the mirror. My red hair swung around my shoulders, and I was positive it had grown at least six inches since the new year. It actually needed trimming, but to be honest I could not be bothered. All that fuss over something you could wrap in a band and twist into a bun was by far too time consuming to me.

My eyes were bright, glinting like emeralds. Pushing my feet into white cotton pumps I felt sixteen again. With my small, neat overnight bag I skipped toward the door. Strutting into the street I was pleased that I had made a space in my busy schedule to have that promised coffee, albeit on my own. The French knew their priorities. I would sit in a pavement café watching the world go by. Sheer relaxation, what more could a girl with a plan ask for? Head held high, I swaggered like a model, skirt swaying, chest heaving. The whistles thrown my way both surprised and thrilled me.

'I must look good,' ran through my head, pulling the low-cut dress over my ample bosom.

It was not long before I found a street café with wooden tables, draped in pure white tablecloths, spilling from the door beneath the seclusion of huge beech trees. Accordion music drifted from an old gramophone placed on a long counter, just visible from the table I chose under one of those trees. I looked around me. To the left, and fanning out onto the cobbled pavement couples sat heads together, chatting intimately. To the right, an elderly couple sat in silence, evidently enjoying the sun of this spring day and allowing memories to overtake their thoughts. Behind me, tucked around the trunk of another beech tree sat a noisy group of young men, tittering and chatting amongst themselves.

At first my thought was to move, but that would only draw attention to myself, and I wished for solitude, so let them enjoy themselves. I was here to savour the coffee, and bask in the French way of life. Even more so when the good-looking waiter delivered my coffee atop a highly-balanced tray. His smouldering eyes and fluent French tongue sent my trembling heart amok. Think, 'yummy' and you would be right.

Fantasising? You bet!

Stirring sugar into the hot black liquid I listened to the clink of stainless steel against a white china cup, the reflection of the late afternoon sun mingling with the steam rising before me.

Male laughter reaches my ears, creating a strange tingling inside me. Without knowing why, an invisible hand squeezed my heart. I eased myself around to scan the table of young men.

'*Why?*' you ask.

My answer? "I don't know. a premonition?"

It was then I saw him, light bouncing on the fair head, mouth open to the heavens in a roaring gesture, eyes alight with pleasure. Breath left my body, the spoon clanked to a standstill, the invisible hand squeezed tighter as I took in untidy hair, rough stubble, drab clothes, worn shoes, large hands waving above his head. I blinked, was this an apparition of my imagination, that solitary wish I had buried deep inside me, a hope that had never died? The laughter grew louder. Tankards clanging together. It was impossible to avert my eyes. Could this be the youth of my memory, this unwashed, untidy figure?

I stir the cooling liquid in agitation. Go – stay – I play with these words – what *if* (not just for an empress or concubine) it is not him? and yet ...

Jimmy would be livid at my behaviour. Question my reasoning, remind me of honour and pride (fuddy-duddy), little did *he* know. My reply: "What good is pride when your body is on fire with infatuation and passion?"

I watched as the young man stood on his chair, tankard above his head, mouth open ready to yelp in a victory whoop.

Then he was staring at me, the expression on his face one of startled disbelief. He grimaced.

Here, I have to write that the young man's face contorted, his lips took a downward turn, his eyes registered the fight or flee movement of momentary panic before –

He begins to wave, slowly to begin with, then in a frenzy of recognition. I gulp, submit to the obvious, and Jimmy flees from my mind.

Clambering down from the chair he moves it aside, the scrapping twanging every nerve in my body, in between tables, over spare chairs, closer, closer, blocking the sun as he stands in front of me.

"Rhia?" Spoken as if not a hundred percent sure, the German accent gone, replaced by the heavy vowel sound of French.

He sat as if I had opened my mouth and invited him.

"Kurt," was all I managed to mumble.

"Yes," he laughed. "You look good, my very good friend."

The eyes bored into my body. Friend. The word grated.

So many things I wanted to ask him, so many things I could not.

He turned, shouted back to his fellow companions. "Rhia, my friend. We had fun, I remember it well."

They raised their tankards my way.

Fun? What an understated expression. He could view, what was for me a life changing experience, as *fun*.

Jimmy bolted back into my mind. "Traitor," he was shouting. "Black hearted dog."

I pause. My next move on balance would be to stand, say "Goodbye," then phone Jimmy pronto.

Shame life does not quite work out that way.

'*The picture,*' you remind me.

"A propaganda stunt for his father's political whim," I reply.

'*As you wish,*' you snap.

Throwing his head in the direction of the other young men he whispered, "They know nothing of Berlin, or its crazy politics back then. They paint for a living, as do I. They would not understand."

A meaning had entered his tone; a forceful suggestion telling me what I had believed all along: my lover was a cog in a wheel, involved through parental obedience. Jimmy was wrong.

'*Delusion,*' you whimper, embarrassed.
Go away. Leave me alone.
You shake your head.

I was fast slipping into that black hole that suffers a stable conscience to forget its rightful place.

"How is Jimmy?" his fingers entwined in mine.

I fought with my reply, fought and won. "Fine," the answer was evasive.

"Is he here?"

"No." There, it was done, the lies upon lies that add to that web of deceit.

"Good, no need to worry." He looked around.

"Kurt," I began.

"Shh. That is no longer my name." He took a breath. "It is great you are here – on holiday?"

"I – you guessed." I bit my tongue.

"Then you have time to spare? Your parents?"

Believe me when I tell you I really was fighting within myself, yet to this day I can hear the answer I gave. "I am alone, all yours. I go home Monday."

The spa – Jimmy – the truth.

Kurt, as I will call him for the moment, popped over to his companions, spoke in a low voice, joined in their laughter, then summoned the waiter on his way back to my table. He ordered wine, two bottles at least, winked in my direction, then said in a soft lilt, "My name. It is Jules."

"Jules," I repeated.

"Yes, Jules Dragner."

"Why?"

"As I told you, I am a painter."

Before you get ready to hang me, think of my reason for coming to Paris. The gods had dropped a gem in my lap.

'*The price?*' you ask.

Kurt – sorry, Jules, tightened his hold on my fingers.
"You are so beautiful, Rhia, and I was sad to lose you. My father made me run. I was innocent."
PROOF. I knew it. Wait until I see Jimmy.

We talked, anything and everything while the sun sank to its vermilion closet. His friends left, raising their hands in our direction. The spa floated into my head, floated out again.

I am going to prostrate myself on the mercy of the reader. Plead with those who have experienced that craving; a fantasy or a need they believed to be their destiny.

As you are already aware I never made it to the spa, or back down the street to where Jimmy would be waiting.

Instead I followed 'Jules' to his shabby flat.

15

How many times do I have to say it? I could not help myself!

How many times do I have to say it was me, but not me? I was living out a fantasy.

Still the frown.

The flat was a hovel, dirty and untidy, paint brushes all over the place, turpentine everywhere. That alone made for a beating head and high spirits. The bed, a mattress thrown onto the floor, covered with an old white cloth.

Hardly a desirable boudoir.

My stomach churned as the rising of the new day highlighted its true condition. There had been no tenderness, for we had set about each other the moment the door had found its hold.

I think of a lion, preying the scent of an in-season female, performing his duty, then drawing away to prepare himself for his next conquest.

I move slightly under the cloth, trying hard not to disturb the male by my side.

Too late, he turned my way, the stubble even more prominent on a face reddened by the exertion of lovemaking.

"Awake."

I wished to tell him I had no way been to sleep. How could I, the guilt was mounting by the second. I thought of Jimmy and the spa – still said nothing.

Kurt – damn it – I mean Jules – **Jules** – stroked my exposed flesh (which was abundant), down my back, circling the small walnut tree.

"You remind me of a landscape painting," his lips dipping between my breasts, moving sensuously round to my back and downward toward the tree. I wriggled, suppressing the growing desire that engulfed me with each kiss. With angst, I pulled myself free, sat up, and as best as I could covered myself with the flimsy cover.

Minutes passed before he yanked himself up onto an elbow.

"Fed up with me already?" The chuckle seemed almost a sneer.

"Don't be silly – I'm –"

"Guilty. Exactly like Berlin, worried what little Jimmy might say."

That stung.

"No, just upset that I have to spend today at a spa, Mother's present, and tonight with a friend of hers in Paris."

Lies and more lies?

"Pity, we could have continued where we must leave off."

His voice was both sarcastic and non-committal, yet washed over me like rain on a hot summer afternoon, and I had moaned at the 'Bumble-bee's' adoration.

My lover laughed, grabbed my arms and pulled me to him, his hand travelling down my back again. "This artist, whoever he or she is, is good. Very good."

Get ready to be amazed. I thought of Jimmy, in this room, in this bed, why?

I moved away from the tempting fingers, saw the anger in my lover's eyes, said the first thing that came to me. "Alexander Cromwell, that's who. A brilliant artist."

Jules (gets harder every time I write it, I want to shout Kurt, Kurt,) kissed my shoulder. "Yeah, well the guy needs to be in a gallery, not a tattoo shop."

A thrill I could not explain ran through me. It seemed Alexander's destiny had found me, no need to pester Jimmy. Luck was on my side, for once.

"You're right," I said in the sweetest voice I could find.

Like an eel, he slipped back under the cover dragging me down with him.

The guilt side of my brain wished to curl up and die, right there, right then, yet I longed for the touch of those fingers setting me on fire.

I searched the eyes no longer angry, felt the roughness of his touch, knew he was peeling away my fragile resistance.

—

I waited for my lover to haul himself from the bed, throw on the same clothes he had worn the previous day, and bid me 'Goodbye' as he left for a meeting, vowing we would continue our wanton reunion another time. Little did he know this was impossible – in the near future at any rate.

The moment he had gone I rushed from the dishevelled mattress, and found my abandoned clothes. Hurriedly pulling them on I noticed the dress was crumpled, and the pumps gritty and dusty. The youthful implication both had given yesterday had lost its hold. All I could see in the broken mirror balanced against the wall was a woman surrounded by lies. I snatched the cardigan from the floor, threw my arms into the dusty sleeves and searched for my hairbrush. Tying the red tangled mass into a ponytail I made for the door. I thought of Jimmy. He would be wondering where I was, phoning the spa if I did not hurry. Casting an eye back on the shabby room an all-consuming shame penetrated the fragile excitement I hid beneath. Suddenly remembering Alexander's sketch I penned his contact details on the flip side, propped it by the mattress, and ran into the street.

—

Pandemonium greeted me as I walked into the hotel foyer. Reporters everywhere. Flashing lights, walkie talkies, bobbing heads, screeching voices, all synchronising together.

"What do you think of the painting?"

"Mr Grant, what do you think of the Balthus painting? Funny name don't you think, 'Princess of the Cats'? Tell us."

The question being hurled in the direction of a figure behind a silk draped table stopped me in my track. It was Jimmy, and if truth is the key factor to this journal, he looked important, self-assured, and extremely good looking in a way unknown to me. I was astounded. The ease with which my friend spoke to this gathering, the relative calm of his answers left me with a strange admiration. I am sure he would not wish to see me in this state of dishevelment. Maybe, if my luck prevails, I could slink past unnoticed. Edging to the rear of the crowd I began to creep toward the lift.

Wrong. "Rhia," rang through the mass of bodies. "At last."

All eyes turned my way.

"Thank you for honouring me with your presence."

Could I note sarcasm?

At once the sea of microphones turned my way, all together, all at once, I don't care how you view it, the noise began.

"Have you seen the exhibition?"

"What do you think of the painting?"

"Are you a close friend of Mr Grant?"

"Isn't he great?"

"What is your name?"

"Are you French?"

"Can we interview you?"

Question after question tumbled into the air.

Jimmy walked through the crowd.

"Come, come, ladies and gentlemen, leave the young lady be. Our museum is funding the exhibition at the Hotel de la Monnaie, she has nothing to do with it."

I swear, the noise those simple words created was like the burring sound of a plane engine.

Again.

"Are you on holiday?"

"Have you known Mr Grant long?"

"Are you an item?"

An item, after last night? I was furious.

Sidling further into my friend's space I hissed, "If you had told me you were involved in a project this important I would have stayed at the spa another night."

A look, a concern, something I could not quite put my finger on, filtered through the stare my friend threw my way. "Bet you would," he whispered.

A tremble I could not explain attacked my legs. What did he mean, had he guessed? Said it before, Jimmy has a knack of 'nailing the flag to the post'.

"What do you mean?" I whimpered.

He slid an arm through mine, drew me to the lift. "Nothing." He stopped, I am sure he went to add to his previous snipe, but thought better of it. "You just look tired. I thought these places were supposed to refresh you."

I let out a sigh of relief.

"Uncomfortable bed, you know how it is. Toss and turn. I need a shower."

Jimmy smiled, sort off, more a snigger thinking back. He turned to the microphones whilst whispering out the corner of his mouth. "If you wish, when I have finished here, say about an hour, I will take you to see the painting. We can joke over its true meaning."

I nodded, anything to get away. "Paintings? If we must."

My friend's curious gaze did not register straight away due to the young girl loitering behind us pushing her microphone into my face. "Miss, have you heard of the painter Jules Dragner?"

I wobbled, pushed the lift button in such a hurry that Jimmy answered for me.

"Jules Dragner. Mmm, is he new on the scene?"

The girl, delighted to have Mr Grant's attention, tweaked her dark rimmed glasses until they sat close to her heavily mascaraed eyes. "Yes, sir, I have heard he is brilliant."

"Really." Jimmy pulled her toward the awaiting crowd, winked at me. "Tell me more."

Leaning back against the mirrors in the lift I kicked myself for the faux pas I had just blindly fallen into. Paris had started out as my coercion trip. It should have been my suggestion to visit the exhibition, (painting for my parent's anniversary). More deceit to lie my way out of. Please!

I say, "Remember the guillotine. Robespierre. The sword corollary." That had got to be my fate! My heart beat with anxious fear, my legs went from trembling to jelly, I grabbed the bar around the lift, I had entered a new dimension, that state where one lie falls on top of another, and the deceiver is transformed from a casual dreamer into a true object of deceit.

'*Poor you.*' There is no sympathy in your tone.

I feel the sting of tears, the ecstasy of my fantasy, the hand of friendship, the thrill of my memories; all leading to a day somewhere in the future where fantasy and logic will meet, and the choice is mine, all mine.

For the moment, I descend the hypothetical wooden steps, back from the bloodied oozing steel teeth.

16

'Life is what you make it,' we are told. If this is true – why do we make such a mess of it! Why do we jump into the vast river of life without that precious paddle that would steer us to the bank? We flounder, eventually sinking to the bottom, held down by an assortment of deceit and lies.

Listen to me. Philosophical or what.

The shower taken to clear my head was working, making me piece together my present situation. Kurt (blast – Jules) had changed. By that I mean my lover was a slave to the Bohemian lifestyle, so much that I knew he and Alexander would instantly hit it off. Besides, he was protective of me, his friends I mean, no gawping from them. Loving I call it.

You snigger; ask, '*Loving, have I never heard of an easy lay?*'

Reader, I am fuming. Are you suggesting he thought I was easy, a libertine, as my mother would tag a woman of loose morals?

I step from the shower, glance at the body that bears the hallmarks of deceit – Berlin, China – quickly dress. I will not give Jules up. Keep faith, we will be together, how else could it end? My lover is no traitor, his father was to blame. Jimmy is wrong.

I know you agree, reader.

No answer.

—

Jimmy spoke of work, work, and more work.

"The meeting went well. The dinner was fascinating, topless dancers, scrumptious food, and the painting – wow, drawing in the crowds."

I would have loved to stop him mid-sentence, describe in gory detail my night of passion, wallow in the sight of his stunned reaction (spite has many outlets), yet nothing under heaven would make me lose Jimmy's friendship, he *is* my comfort zone; that is unnegotiable.

"The Princess of Cats," Jimmy announced proudly, twisting my head in every angle.

"A painting," I joke.

Exasperation eclipsed my friend's smile. "An arrogant face don't you think?"

I twisted. "If by that you mean beautiful, yet haughty, then yes. If you mean ugly and mean, then no."

Jimmy fidgeted with his programme. "I meant neither. You are right in claiming it beautiful. To the eyes of certain be-holders it is more than that. I meant arrogant in what lies beneath. A secret perhaps?"

My friend moved closer to the painting, while I tried to stop the blood rushing to my cheeks.

"You arty people see what you wish." I moved further back. "The face probably hides nothing, unless the painter is putting a label on all women as spiteful."

"Um, could that be the answer?" Jimmy faltered here. "Do all painters mark women in this way? Mr Jules Dragner for a start."

I shivered. "What has Mr er – Dragner to do with it? Who is he anyway?"

What other way could I respond. Ignorance, my ace card.

"You do not know about him? Mmm. The reporter says he is the talk of the town, his name is everywhere, cinemas, bars, spas."

That stupid fluttering eyed, soppy faced **** (too rude for the pen) Keep composure.

"Nope, never heard of him. Is he famous?"

"No idea."

Jimmy sauntered to a bench, sat down and continued to search the painting.

The five minute interlude stretched my nerves to the limit, if I could get my hands on that girl.

Jimmy coughed. "I had an idea these spas were a hive of gossip."

I *am* going to hit him!

"The spa was busy, and I went to bed early, I needed to relax, then got up early for this morning's session. I never saw any posters."

My friend bristled "I just thought you may have noticed."

"No, sorry."

"Never mind." His eyes narrowed, moved to a more sedate landscape. Settled into what those readers of a more astute psyche would label 'thoughtful'.

A quiet five minutes gave me a temporary respite until: "The picture you wanted for your parents?"

Talk catapulted back into reality.

"That," I laughed. "Think I may change my mind."

I pretended to search the 'cat' painting closer. Jimmy brushed his long fingers through his dark hair. "Wasn't that the reason for you coming to Paris?"

Reader, it appears I am in a war zone – a place where I must stay one step ahead of my best friend.

I pretended to be coy. "Not the only reason."

"Then what?" the tone was brusque.

"Oh, this and that, knowledge, time with you."

"Really?" He stamped his foot. "Come on, the more knowledge, the better we can judge freedom."

"Freedom?"

"Yes, everywhere we go, dear friend, our pact goes too."

"Really?"

If he says that word pact once more ...

Jimmy stretched, his full six foot frame across the bench.

"Are your feet up to walking?"

He had to be joking, I have had no sleep for twenty-four hours.

"Now?"

Jimmy took my hand. "Come, my best, best friend, I am overcome with madness!"

—

The rest of the afternoon and evening we walked, examined masterpieces of stone, paint-works of nobility, any monument the French could be complimented upon.

First, the Gothic Cathedral of Notre Dame, 'Our Lady' in French. Restored by the architect Eugène Viollet-le-Duc. Jimmy pointed out the naturalistic windows and stone buttress moulded with such excellence.

Second, the famous 13th century fortress full of western art known as The Louvre.

Brainchild of Phillip Augustus II. Purposely built to defend the river Seine from any Norman or English invasion. Its glass dome, designed by the Chinese/American architect Leoh Ming Pei affected me; no doubt, as it had those first visitors on its grand opening as a museum back in 1989.

I gasped in wonder, sighed at its beauty, questioned its magical hold over me. Asked my friend if it was the sheer volume of priceless art that caught me unaware, including that bewitching smile of the Mona Lisa, or the fact that its elongated galleries stretched (in my mind) to the edge of the earth. Whichever was the correct answer, we sauntered along corridor after corridor, admiring one painting after another.

As darkness fell we filtered out onto the Paris thoroughfare, there to be greeted by a fairy-tale sky, filled with a mass of stars winking down from a navy blue abyss. Along the Champs Elysées toward our third landmark, the Arc de Triomphe, a monument to the fallen in war. Reading, as best as I could, the names of those who gave their lives for their country (wear and tear of many hands and industrial dust) I took particular note of the vast number that had fallen in the Napoleonic conquest. Young, old – age had no preference, hewn into the solid arches. I felt no victory surge; only a sad realisation that the fight for freedom (whatever or wherever it is) touches all our lives, even to this day.

Jimmy, standing with his hands on his hips was umming and ahhing in melodramatic style. "Can you believe it?" his voice rose and fell with each pronunciation. "The tombstone of the unknown warrior (the remains lay buried beneath the heavy pillars) was inspired by the Roman arch of Titus."

I tried to imagine the Arc guarded by a Roman centurion, shield on chest, sword held high by a muscular brown arm, silver helmet with its red plume fluttering in the light breeze. Of course, if I wished to be pedantic I could turn the plume into an imaginary flag – 'Viva le France'.

"We all know the Romans were oppressors not liberators. Yet," Jimmy removed his hands from his hips, "even that could be argued. They designed the bathing chambers, the buildings, and roads wherever they went." He turned toward me. "A thin line I would say between oppression and liberated. What do you say?"

My friend touched the stone perimeter, shaking his head from side to side, and I had to agree. My hand that seconds earlier had lain comfortably in his own had been dropped, allowing his fingers to travel up and down the stonework.

"Fabulous piece of architecture. A contradiction and a triumph."

He stopped for breath. "Evidently the Arc in Rome is engraved with Titus, Emperor of Rome from 79-81. It depicts his triumphal procession displaying his spoils of war taken from Jewish temples."

Jimmy continued his digital march around the pillar. "Actually, how is that freedom?"

I was tired, no way will I be getting into a debate tonight.

"As you told me in China, freedom means different things to different people."

Jimmy frowned. "What is wrong with you? That is the answer of one who sits on the fence, not the friend who took the pact."

Now, forgive me having a strop, but everything I say here is wrong. If I agree my friend will dig up another argument, if I disagree the same will apply. Funny really, if I could put my finger on an exact second in history that Jimmy's and my relationship hit a turning point I would have to submit now.

He withdrew his comments, slouched to the other side of the Arc, and deliberately ignored me. A feeling of discomfort settled over me; there was no conclusive proof, no spoken reason for my belief, but I *knew* Jimmy, I was convinced a fragile thread had been severed.

I have no doubt your advice would be to, '*Talk, explain, beg for understanding.*'

157

Do you think if life was that simple I would not be side-stepping over the minefield that plagued me?

We walked back to the hotel in silence, both preoccupied with our thoughts.

From nowhere voices began to squeal, "Mr Grant, stop. Please stop, Mr Grant, spare us a moment."

Flaming reporters... and would you believe the be-spectacled young woman, waving her microphone for all she was worth.

"Mr Grant – Jimmy," she was panting. "Jules Dragner – September 24th – here at the hotel 10am."

Other reporters were closing in behind her, pushing their dreadful lollipop sticks in our direction.

Jimmy did not look at me, did not ask the mob to excuse him, did not signal to the receptionist to come and retrieve us, oh no, he listened with avid interest.

The girl was waving her microphone (wish I could grab it, know what I would do with it).

"The painter," she was shrieking. "I told you about – *the* gorgeous Mr Dragner."

Jimmy became instantly professional, his face giving nothing away. He asked no questions, quietly confirming he would be there.

The girl gave him a radiant smile as he edged a pathway to the lift. With a quick nod of the head he placed me inside.

"I must go, speak to my boss."

"Your boss? It is nine o' clock. Is he still at the museum?"

I received no reply. Our last night in Paris, and Jimmy is chasing shadows – my shadow.

He strode through the reception area, by-passing the ever attentive news crews. I longed for something, anything, to repair our easy, casual existence.

—

My heart hung heavy as I turned the key in my bedroom door. Barely twenty-four hours ago I had dressed, packed my bag for the spa, and set out to drink coffee. On the choice of one small street café everything had changed. I was committed to a relationship that would horrify my parents, and lose me my best friend. Flinging the keys onto the bed I let my weary body follow.

It was then – perfume filled my nostrils – incense sweet. I sniffed again; stronger and headier than usual. Sitting upright, my nose working overtime, I trawled my eyes around the room, locked them onto the largest vase of roses and lilies I had ever seen; pink and white flowers, bound together in a bed of dark green foliage. Thank God for friends, he had pre-thought my mood. I told you we were close; his sensory perception had told him I needed cheering up. I remember his excuse earlier in the evening to visit the toilet. The toilet indeed – he was ordering flowers.

Hidden between the leaves a cream card beckoned me. I made my way to the dresser, breathing in the intoxicating scent. Slipping the card from its resting place I tore it open. The emotions came as an onslaught – joy, disappointment, passion, tears – guilt.

I read, 'Thank-you Rhia, I enjoyed last night' A multitude of kisses – '*Jules.*'

I can find no adequate words.

The knock on the door startled me. Jimmy, back so soon? Hurrying to the bed I hid the card under the pillow. "Come."

A dark curly head shot round the door. The maid.

The oval face looked drawn, the black and white outfit a little crumpled. Bobbing a curtsy, she asked, "Can I get you anything, mademoiselle?"

"No, merci."

She bobbed again.

"Wait, when did these flowers arrive?" I asked.

"Late this afternoon, mademoiselle. The bell boy told me the scruffiest man handed them to him after enquiring after you at the desk."

He found me.

"In the guise of a painter?" I queried.

"Not sure, mademoiselle. The bell boy does not pay attention. I will report him."

"No, no, please do not bother. No harm, curious, that's all."

She curtsied, eager to be gone, long shift I am guessing.

"Wait –"

There was a resignation on her face, clearly she was used to awkward guests.

"Have you a mother?"

I know – insensitive or what.

"I have, mademoiselle." A puzzled expression stealing into light blue eyes.

"Please take these flowers. Wish her well."

"I cannot – the Directeur will not agree."

"Please – you will, how shall I say it, save my face."

The girl moved to remove the flowers, curtsied. "Thank you, mademoiselle," and slid out the door before I could utter a word.

My fingers sought the tell-tale cardboard under my pillow. How did Jules (must get used to the new name) know which hotel I was staying at. Had I mentioned a name in those hours of passion?

Am I that vulnerable?

What if Jimmy has suspicions about Jules Dragner. Informs the authority of a new painter's whereabouts? What shall I do?

I throw myself on your mercy for my next action, this is fantasy at its height, one soul in purgatory. I took the card from under the pillow, wrote the address on an envelope, placed a warning inside, sealed it, re-called the maid, asked for my message to be delivered immediately.

Forgive me my weakness. I cannot wait to get home.

Part Two

1

There are years which demand to be described as 'brilliant', and other years that beg to be chronicled as 'disastrous'. In my mind 1993 belonged to one of those unfortunate years that began with a 'd' and ended with an 's'. Everything was floundering, including my self-esteem, my fighting spirit, and my belief in mankind. Newspapers carried stories of devastation and damage in America's mid-west; quoting how the rain falling from May to September was the heaviest rain on record. Back home (yes, you have guessed) we also had mixed weather, sunshine, thunderstorms, sunshine, thunderstorms, on and on. It was becoming clear that the years' natural elements were at odds with the world's inhabitants – that's me! Things got worse. Early October saw snow in Scotland, with temperatures dropping to an all-time low. Even around London the thermometer crashed to a sickening chill. Ample curves or not, nothing kept me warm, and to add to that list, my mood – zero!

For a start I had surrendered, if you could call it that, to Alexander's ridiculous cajoling. You might have known it was impossible for me to resist a visit to his studio, fair enough, it was my task to find out if anything had arisen from that print I had left behind in Paris, but another tattoo, this time just a small one, the Arc de Triomphe engraved on my upper arm. Anyway, trying to be nosy I drank enough coffee to cast me afloat, so I suppose I needed another diversion – my excuse. Long sleeved tops were now a 'must' cover up asset. Mind, I have got to admit my mother was pulling me down, repeating four or five times a week, "You have beautiful arms child, show them off to the world."

Her reasoning? Office parties, the attention of young men – **help!!**

Not long after my latest tattoo I reinstated the Saturday coffee trips. Not wishing to outstay my welcome, and to be blunt, just a few hours in the company of the ill-starred couple was a maze game no sane minded person would wish to play, I told myself it was important work and I must suffer it. Mind, I did find it rather funny in a peculiar fashion to watch the 'Bumble-bee' rush round her beloved boss, dreamily gazing into his eyes, laughing and cooing, feigning feminine weakness.

You remark, '*You haven.'t lost your mean streak then.*'
I must rebuke you here, state – where is your sense of fun!

The really odd thing, and I stress this emphatically, was the way she acted toward me. She hovered, hummed, literally buzzed around me.

Flee from her path? No chance.

Where I sat, she sat. When I spoke to Alexander, she was by my side. When Alexander asked (ordered is the accurate term) her to fetch something, she never failed to make sure I had coffee in my hand. Going out the room was a task in itself: she would double her speed. To my mind's eye it became a party game, more to be tolerated than endured. Deciding I was way overdue putting a halt to her silly prancing I contrived one Saturday to arrive early, shock the daft girl out of her stupidity.

This particular Saturday I was greeted at the door with a huge grin. "Come in."

She guided me to the sofa, slapped a coffee cup in my hand and sat down beside me. I was immediately thrown into confusion, more so when she added, "Clap your hands when Alexander emerges from the back room. He has heard from Paris."

My face lit up. Jules (still not used to the name) had come up trumps.

The 'Bumble-bee' took my hand "Say nothing, *please,* I have informed him it was me."

Repeat – whirlwind in my ear – whatever makes you think, 'gob-smacked'?

Yes, I've used it before, and yes, I realise it is a slang word, but how else can I explain stunned – especially in the condition I find myself – paralysed.

The girl had got to be kidding.

Her hold got tighter. "*Please,* do not spoil it."

Spoil it? How dare she. What was her game?

"I –" the sound died in my throat.

Alexander stormed from the back room. "Rhia, welcome, has Rosie told you the news? who is a clever girl then?"

What do I answer. 'Bumble-bee' had betrayed me. Made me a prisoner of my own actions, out-manoeuvred me on the chess board of life!

'Fixed smile,' you suggest, trying hard to suppress a grin.

Say nothing. I will get my own back.

The emeralds sitting in my eye sockets pierced the young girl's own.

Alexander began to ramble (surprised he actually had it in him). "I had a phone call two months ago (that long) from someone whose name escapes me. A male," Alexander paused. "The laugh was he was supposed to be French, but if he was French then I am royalty. Anyway, he is considering setting up a commune of talented artists in America. would I be interested?" Again a pause. "I asked him how he knew of me. He said a woman. Putting two and two side by side I stumbled on Rosie. Who else, no other person was allowed to show my art? She was naughty, but clever at the same time for finding this guy, bless her."

Bless her, my head was spinning.

He stroked the 'Bumble bee's' cheek.

I wanted to spit. *She* was walking in my shoes, taking credit where it was not due. *S*he would be going where my lover was fleeing, leaving me behind, for I had not heard.

The 'Bumble-bee refilled my coffee cup, her eyes silently pleading for me not to drop her in trouble. Her fate in my hands; a satisfying thought.

My heartache – Jules was widening the gap between us. Was this Jimmy's work? Perhaps he had guessed, reported him, set about tracking him down, yet my friend had not made the September meeting. He had been sent to another exhibition much to my delight. I cannot remember where he was; not really bothered, he was not in Paris – to me that was heaven sent.

The 'Bumble-bee' was talking.

"Alexander has left me to deal with the finer things. He has also asked me to accompany him."

Well, hooray for her. The girl was a common thief, and a – a – bloody deceiver.

"It will not be a quick transition, Rhia, so feel at ease to have further artwork," Alexander was almost hugging me. "This painter has to find a venue, set the scheme up."

"Great," I managed to mumble.

What was wrong with me? I felt abused, my wings clipped, my heart broken.

I can sense the 'tut, tut' of your voice, the shake of the head, probably deduce it is my own fault.

Well reader, let me say, you can be the first to pass sentence *if,* and I mean *if,* you have never made a bad choice, or chosen the wrong path.

'If?' you ask.

Yes, that word, so appropriate for this discussion.

I believe by notifying Alexander my lover is calling me.

'Calling you?' incredulity spreads across your face.

Correct. let us be sensible. His offer to me will follow.

'Right, for what reason?' You seem mystified.

I block you from my mind.

"In the meantime," Alexander was commanding my attention, "he has offered to sell my work."

"Your paintings?"

"Yes," the 'Bumble-bee' broke in. "We are to send them to the address he gave us."

"An address?"

I was so beginning to sound like an echo.

I glared at the girl.

"It's hu – hush, hu – hush," she stuttered.

"Right," my reply came swift as I rose from the sofa. "I am very pleased, believe me."

Alexander appeared a little shocked as I hurried to the door, but I – Rhia Bryant had her own agenda.

—

Can a year get out of hand? Yes, it can.

By October 93 my father was complaining each moment he saw me that the mood hanging over the house was my fault. *I* was the bad tempered one. *I*, the miserable and lethargic one. Lethargic indeed. My job had me running up and down stairs like an Olympic athlete, charging round the vaults of a musty old bank. Sitting boringly at a cashier's slot until the very rustle or tinkle of money drove me crazy. Begrudgingly making tea when Lily, the office junior, was pulling a sickie. With everything else on my back (the preening 'Bumble- bee,' not a word from Jules, and Jimmy's extra working hours) what *if* it was me who was miserable and supposedly lethargic?

To insult my intelligence even more my paternal grandmother is visiting at Christmas. I have been told she will share my room. My mother will not take the, "No," I keep screaming at her. This is not fair, and it is happening to **me.**

I imagine you casting an eye to heaven, in the guise of one who is tired of moans. So you should. Not for what I have said, but for the sake of my sanity. Let me inform you this is the woman who since childhood has insisted I call her Mattie. Grandmother or Mathilda is old fashioned and 'soo uncool' (her expression), plus she compares herself to the fashion icon Vivienne Westward.

Come on – she is seventy-two years old!

That sorted (in Mother's eyes) I grew grumpier. That was until last week when a small pink envelope arrived. The insignia was type written and franked by an American stamp. Impatience made me steal to my bedroom to tear it open. As I had prayed.

Dear Rhia,

I received your note. Sorry I have taken this long writing. As you can see by the address above I have moved. I had to leave France in a rush. If you are ever in the free world look me up. Please write. Let me know you think of me, as I think of you. I am quite busy, in all things.

By the way, the roses at the top of this paper are in bud, ready to burst open in expectation. They remind me of you.

From me to you. Jules. Xx

How many times I read it was impossible to count. I cried, brought on by a sense of deprivation. I moaned, at the thought of lost pleasure. I screamed, at the degradation I felt. It was a foregone conclusion when I look back, that so much meaning would be read into that letter.

Taking a mental note of the address, I slipped it into my handbag; found paper and pen and wrote the longest letter possible. At least five pages of what I had been up too, what Jimmy was doing, asking for us to find a way to be together.

I waited and waited for an answer...

Busy I decided: not a lot of time to write. In the meantime I prepared for my grandmother.

2

Mattie arrived two days before Christmas. There she stood in her usual flamboyant style; a huge fox fur draped across her shoulders teamed up with three quarter silk gloves. Peeling them off slowly (how many years had she spent perfecting the femme fatale display?) she revealed long red fingernails that sparkled under the hallway light. Smiling, the red lips moving in an abandoned way to retain the long cigarette holder securely, she had Mother flapping around her in animated irritation. It was so funny, this eccentric woman fluttering her black caked eyelashes sheltering the palest blue eyes, taking in the world around her, while those of us on the – say, more conventional path of life, were horrified at her antics.

Those of you that cannot remember the silliness of childhood would call her a batty old fool. I assure you she is nothing like that. Mattie, who is enough to drive the Almighty mad, is one shrewd female. Those eyes, believe me, see everything. Those lips speak nothing but the absolute truth, hurt or otherwise, and that mind is faster than a top speed computer. This grandmother of mine can read me backwards which makes me loathe her presence, yet love her to bits; she would find that admission an honour.

Standing by her suitcase in the hallway, Mattie reminded me of an unexploded bomb, ready to rain her terror down on everyone. Today there was something about her. She was bubbling like a fizzy glass of champagne, falling over herself to exchange some secret held within. My father caught my gaze and rolled his eyes in the way an only son would. My mother slammed shut the heavy door against the sleet and snow of the cold December afternoon. I slumped into the 'thinking chair' and waited for the explosion.

"Guess what?" Mattie's tubular voice rang out. "I have sold my house."

Here we go. Mattie's house was no three up, three down and a cloakroom job you would buy in haste. Oh no. It was a six acre dwelling in the country. Seven bedrooms, three sitting rooms, the largest kitchen and dining room, and a bathroom to die for; an estate I suppose. Inherited from her father she had always joked that one day she would sell it to a foreign diplomat.

They say you can cut atmosphere with a knife. If I had dared I would have had a go. My parents looked at each other, then to me, and full circle back to Mattie. Nothing was passing my lips.

"Mother." My father leant on the name. "Have you completely lost your senses?"

Mattie resumed the same face movement she had adopted before her announcement, this time showing her perfect set of white teeth (all her own I believe).

"No, Henry, I have not. You have money – sometimes far too much, and I – I want adventure."

I wish you were able to be a fly on the wall, take advantage of my parents' disconcert. This was pure drama.

My father fidgeted with his tie. "Adventure, what do you mean, woman?"

Oh dear, this was his mother – respect and all that. I had never seen my father act in this way. Funny what money can do.

"Henry, I realise this has come as a shock, but I have decided life is far too short to waste myself away enclosed by bricks and mortar."

Mattie's grey head bobbed up and down flicking the long plaited tassels of her fur pull on hat from side to side.

"Well, dear." My mother stepped forward, a hasty warning glance shot in my father's direction. "You may have gained far more interest if you had waited awhile longer."

Mattie wagged her finger. "Death duties? I don't think so. not for what I intend to do."

"Which is?" my father snapped

"Trek the Himalayas, stay in a village there for at least three months, and – and purchase a flat for my grand-daughter."

The last sentence clanged to the floor like a steel girder.

Mouths like craters appeared to fill the hall. A noise not unlike a wounded lion bounced off the walls. This time you *could* have cut the atmosphere with a knife!

Things were about to escalate, or down-slide, whichever way your sense of humour rolls. Mother laughed out loud, oh yes, and spoke the only words she knew in time of trouble. "Tea Mattie?"

Father's eyes became a pair of burning coals, glaring at his wife, holding her fast to the punishment stakes. After all, it was his inheritance!

My grandmother ignored him.

"I thought you would never ask, Philomena" (yes, yes... very strange my mother coming from a working class family. At least you now understand why I have not mentioned her name before).

"Mena will do," she said with a swagger toward the kitchen, a slight upper-class pronunciation on the ending.

Mattie followed, father in hot pursuit.

I made my way to the kitchen table, kicked out a chair (father glared), threw myself onto it in jovial display. I was determined not to miss the second act of this play, no-more than finish this journal now, before you know the outcome.

Mattie removed the fox stole, laying the poor animal across the arm of my seat. There was something mischievous in the way she placed it, urging me to deliberately spy its exposing tag. Out of curiosity (follows me around) I scanned the embroidered material. The stole was a fake, created from synthetic fibres; a fantastic copy of the real thing. Mattie winked at me. "A game," she whispered as she read my thoughts. "Keeps them on their toes."

Easing off her brown leather ankle boots Mattie snuggled her toes up to the Aga.

"How I miss the open coal fire. One could toast one's toes until they thawed."

Mother hurried to pick up the boots and dispose of them in the hall cupboard. Father sat at the table muzzling his head in his arms.

"Henry, I have my Christmas presents in my bag. Be a good boy and fetch it from the hall for me." Mattie's eyes shone, relishing each moment of her 'game'.

I was enthralled as I watched my father obey. The woman had landed at our door an hour ago, and the place was in an uproar.

Dropping the large carpet bag at my grandmother's feet Mattie delved inside. There were scarves, gloves, sweets and papers flying in whatever direction they were flung. Mother's face – a picture. If I waited long enough I would not have been surprised if a sink and drainer had followed.

The kettle whistled.

Clutching three envelopes, Mattie made a resounding "Merry Christmas," as she slapped them down on the table.

"What are they?" my father's voice was cold.

"Look dear boy, look," my grandmother answered.

He scooped up the envelope with his name on, tore it open and gasped. "£500,000 –"

My mother was next. "£300,000."

My turn. I slowly peeled the glue that hid my own cheque, gasped, "Mattie?"

She nodded, ignoring the glare of her son, and the astonishment of her daughter-in-law. "Yes, dear, enough money for your own pad," (another of her co-ool words, I found out) "and an invitation to trek in the Himalayas. Invite that boy of yours – what's-his-name – Johnny?"

"Jimmy."

"That's him. Nice boy, just your type!"

She raised the tea cup Mother had set before her. My parents did not utter a word, how could they?

However you perceived Mattie's game, and let's be honest she had played it to perfection, she had won. What a woman. It is no wonder my father is astute, he had an excellent teacher.

'*True,*' you agree, inspired by her sense of practicality mixed with fun. '*What will you do?*'

I will go to the Himalayas, feed off her intuition, sort Jules out, deal with Jimmy.

I raise my tea cup (poor substitute) in recognition of her wheeling and dealing, smile to myself and conclude. 'Come to think of it... not a bad year after all.'

—

It unfolded on Christmas day 1993 that my grandmother *had* sold her 'house' to a foreign person. Not a diplomat as it happened. One better than that – a Hollywood starlet. A woman, whose name escapes me, but desired, even more than her fame, an English heritage. She paid over and above the selling price, just to secure it from the grasp of that elusive foreign diplomat. My father (due to Mother's nagging) came round to Mattie's way of thinking. In truth, he weighed up the cost of upholding such an estate, even though Mother was secretly annoyed at not being able to move into the place, and deduced it would have been an anchor around his neck. Once or twice my mother – Philomena – cannot resist saying it now – naughty – could not resist asking my grandmother what the actual selling price had been. She received no answer. Mattie was keeping her own counsel, not divulging a single numerical figure.

Good for her, I say.

What is inheritance anyway? Paper money, weighed down with the usual bad feeling.

Jimmy landed on our doorstep mid-afternoon in a right happy mood, bearing his own festive offerings. Having spent Christmas dinner with his parents, his brother and sister, their families (a curse of older siblings), numerous uncles and aunts, he was a trifle tiddly. Mattie spoiled him, monopolising his company every second she found him alone, while Jimmy responded with polite entertaining chatter, telling her stories he had never told me. I stood by the lounge door, laden with a tray of mixed drinks (cocktails that came straight from my mother's imagination), and felt a surge of overwhelming emotion. My best friend was being really attentive. He cared not if she slipped in the odd squeeze of the arm, or the tweak of the hair. He was bowled over with her attention, and from where I was standing, the whole scene looked genuine.

Something inside me twisted – think elastic band.

'*Your heart,*' you snipe.
I pretend not to hear.

It was during one of these chit-chats that Mattie jumped to her feet.

"I have it," she shouted, forcing the speediest flick of heads I can recall. "The three of us will trek the highest mountain possible. Freedom or bust!"

Her drink splashed over the grey tight curls as she threw her arms in the air. Jimmy and I spluttered on our Martini cocktails. Mother glared in disbelief.

"Mother," my father commanded. "Sit yourself down. Trekking indeed. Can you not realise this holiday is not viable, or sensible?"

"Sensible – why?" her voice thundered from deep within her.

"You are seventy-two, and too genteel."

You decide, reader. Was it the drink or that Christmas stress factor that brought on the 'put down' tone?

Mattie's eyes flickered. "My dear boy, I am neither too old, too genteel, or as you put it in not so many words – a simpering fool. I am –" the longest pause possible – "impatient to depart."

The atmosphere was ripening.

Mother, wafting her arms in nineteen twenty custom, spangled and sparkled over the drinks tray. "Drink," she warbled.

I promise you once more, this was theatre at its best.

Raising her glass above my mother's sequinned top Mattie's claret drink tipped upside down. I sucked in as much air as possible.

Danger alert – that top was expensive!

It would be hard to imagine what happened next. I will dub it, 'World War Three.'

My ears smarted from the mudslinging. Mother began to cry, clinging to the designer top with its huge alcohol stain down the front. My father began to berate his Mother, in between humouring his wife, while chiding his side-splitting daughter. Jimmy cleared the coffee table as quick as he could, crystal glass saved by his fast thinking. Carols blasted from the radio: 'Peace on earth'; 'Goodwill to all men'. I am sure they meant women as well – at least I hope – until 'Silent Night' chorused in the sweetest tones, and I thought 'if only'. Then doors started banging as bodies rushed in and out of the kitchen, bedrooms and bathroom; food, neatly laid out on the worktops became scattered across the floor. Wave after wave of insults filtered through the level of noise already permeating from each room. Faces that would look better stuck on a broom end for Halloween night, glared and contorted.

What a sight, a slapdash pantomime skit.

If I had been fortunate enough to be a writer, the first episode of a farce was being played out in front of me. The argument, if that is your term for it, took three hours to settle. Three hours, numerous drinks, and the repeat of the Queen's speech.

The clock actually struck eight sharp when we sank onto the sofas. Worn out from shouting, screeching and laughing, the usually neat house resembled a back street of the city of Beirut. Jimmy, from his corner by the television (he had hidden there throughout the turmoil) weighed up his options, discovered he could emerge in safety to join us in comparative comfort. A fragile truce had sprung up between my parents and grandmother, each party agreeing to disagree (one blessing at least). I, through this scene of undisputed bellowing knew somehow, as you will discover, that Mattie held the key to my own frantic search for inner freedom. Whatever my parents thought about this trek, it was an unavoidable part of my grandmother's and my destiny. There was no outward sign I should feel this way, but it was one of those moments in life when the hand of providence beckoned me on.

Before Christmas day had come to its conclusion Mattie set a date for the trek: May 1995. I nagged Jimmy to accompany us. It was not as though he had to delete his current entries in his diary, there was a good seventeen months to prepare. We all settled for the last hours of a hectic day.

You may say, 'peace at last'. I would say a fragile truce!

Father propped his head on Mother's shoulder, inched tight between the two women who controlled his life. Mother, resplendent in a new cashmere jumper, showed no sign of her earlier trauma. Jimmy, who had selected to kip on the chaise longue by the window, made himself comfortable, tucking into the 'refreshed' ham sandwiches and cake. Mattie, was just Mattie; the largest grin in the world, her eyes the shadow of that independent soul.

To drop a spanner in the works (father's own take on a person who deliberately causes trouble), would be a sin, and I have too many of those already.

3

The following year was to set my heart and mind in a terrible spin, have me anxiously waiting for my three month stint in the Himalayas.

Jimmy had taken to swimming regularly on a Sunday morning at the nearby pool. Mother was aghast, especially when he invited me to join him. It was public, did not belong to a spa, had no terraced cafeteria, and no annual fee to join. Queue, pay your money, share a room with other members of the public; a cubicle if you were lucky – afterwards washing in a public shower. The whole process was alien to her, it lacked finesse and class. With Mother's warning of germs, verrucas, athlete's foot ringing in my ears I accepted the challenge Jimmy threw my way to join him.

A frosty February morning, faced with a two hour swim. Jimmy had already booked us in, collecting the red pin label we must wear in the water, plus a key to a locker.

As I joked: set, sealed, and ready to go.

Finding a cubicle, I poured the items from my bag onto a wooden seat – towel, shower gel, shampoo, brush, ponytail bands, clean underwear, and my nineteen thirty vintage swimsuit.

If you giggle I shall put my pen down, leaving you only to guess the outcome of my story, so there!

There is sense behind my crazy purchase, I promise; I needed to hide my tattoos. This creation of navy blue cotton was, in my mind, a practical step. With its boat shaped neckline and three quarter length sleeves my friend would be too taken aback by my swimwear to worry about anything else. Clever – you bet.

Not once did it cross my mind that female figures had changed. The three quarter sleeved full bodice and tiny skirt were designed for a figure – um – not so generous. Obviously, the girls in the thirties ate like flies.

I pulled and pulled, clasping it tight in those places that teased it to fit snug. It had got to stretch. Tugging it until I was fearful it would 'ping' I slid it into place. Here I must own up to feeling sorry for the Christmas turkey again, trussed and tied.

Walking out of the cubicle I pushed my bag into the locker, turning the key and clasping it to my sleeve; through the cold (and may I say it was very cold) shower area, and onto the pool side. Jimmy was nowhere to be seen. Sitting on the edge of the pool I dangled my feet in the bright blue/green water. Resisting the urge to jump into its depths I looked again for my friend. Where could he be? Five minutes, ten minutes: far too long. I crammed the mass of red hair into my floral swimming cap, and was about to jump into the water when the question hit me hard.

"What the hell are you wearing?"

Jimmy was at my feet, a grin the size of the river Thames across his face.

"A swimming costume, idiot."

"Right. I thought it fancy dress."

The laughter echoed across the chilly water, inspiring those swimmers ducking and diving to stare. Heat crept up my neck, infusing my face, causing the head beneath the rubber cap to sweat.

I jumped in, swung toward my friend and lost my footing. Down I sank, flailing at the numerous feet flapping, walking, moving in a fish-like beat on the stone clad bottom. Water was rushing up my nose, stinging my eyes, clogging my ears. I grabbed for Jimmy's leg, sliding downwards to the ankle. It was then I touched something, an etching on the skin, standing proud above the bone. I moved my fingers over it, gulped, forced my eyes to open. A tattoo.

The swift ascent to the surface winded me. Gasping for breath I held tight to the arm of my friend.

"You," I panted. "You have a tattoo on your ankle – four markings."

"Yes, it is Chinese for a name."

"A name?" My heart lurched, winding me further.

"Just a name," he repeated.

"Who?" I inquired, trying to keep up with him as he waded deeper into the pool.

"No-one. Just a name."

Irritating. The guy had not told me he was thinking of a tattoo, and after all I was his best friend.

I watched as his head floated on the iridescent surface, arms stroking the water. Those black marks had a familiarity to them, a careful precision I had seen before – oh no. The world around me began to fuzz as the noise of other swimmers faded into the distance. My back stung, not because it should, guilt was kicking in – a croak left my stinging throat. "Alexander."

I prayed no-one had witnessed my outburst: not Jimmy, he was far ahead splashing and diving in the deep end; not those around me, who by now must surely have deduced I was from another era, living a life I could not return to.

My whole body shook. Jimmy had found my Saturday hideaway, no doubt spoken about me, and guess what – that girl... the 'Bumble-bee', *she* had pounced upon the link between him and myself. The little cow, wait until I get my hands on her.

You wheeze in the guise of a teacher explaining to a five-year-old.

'Customer confidentiality, she would lose her boss his reputation. Think.'

My breathing slows. I blink, rub water from my stinging eyes. This time you have to be correct – no need to panic. I swim a little further – stop – float on the spot – the name – who? who?

'Someone he admires?' you ask.

I thrash around. Admires – without telling me.

'Indeed,' is your answer.

I start to move slowly up the pool. People are staring at me, casting their eyes over my shaking head, my costume, my floundering arms. I am in agony. Jimmy, a secret love. Never!

'Why not?' you interpose.

We swore to be truthful.

'And?' you throw back at me.

I continue to swim, head for my friend, wrap my hand within the warmth of his own.

—

Every day since that swimming debacle Jimmy's tattoo has haunted me, to the point of trying to sneak from the house on a Saturday to 'shop' by myself. As you will no doubt figure out shopping was the last thing on my mind, more running to Alexander's studio, discovering the truth behind the four lettered name. My grandmother had other ideas. Flat hunting, trek booking, and lastly a rented apartment for herself.

Why does nothing go right?

We plodded around estate agents, lunched at backstreet cafés, choose various house furnishings. The list – never ending.

Mother complained she was being left out. Mattie's dismissal was short and sharp; precious time between grandmother and granddaughter. After six weeks of groaning, moaning, and asking, 'What we had seen, where we had been,' she said what she really meant.

"Rhia would be better staying at home. I can keep an eye on her eating habits."

The fact was, once I was no longer under her roof she would be unable to appraise my letters, my going out, and my coming in. Any other time I would have considered these ramblings ridiculous; a good laugh. At the moment, not funny. I need to be in one place, and one place only – the tattoo studio.

Jimmy's tattoo was tormenting my mind, for I cannot think of one good reason why he would etch a name on his ankle.

'To hide it from you.' The snide is clear.
Ridiculous suggestion, honesty is best.
'Remember that.'
Your meaning? Mine is different.
'Different?'
Yes, it is a secret, a – a –
'Fantasy?'

I contort my face, remind you Jimmy and I are best friends, and all that means.

You appear impatient.

'Yes,' you shout.

I hate this journal. A tear escapes; I drag my mind from our imaginary conversation.

—

After a month of running here and there on a Saturday, my grandmother was struck down by a cold. One of those winter bugs that are best contained in bed (my suggestion), and fed with honey and blackcurrant, along with a huge box of paper tissues. Extricating myself from 'sick' duties, I assured Mother I needed to see this certain flat- today. She grumbled, said, "Shall I arrange a nurse and join you?" sulked for the whole of the country when I insisted to go on my own. After much conniving, I persuaded her to play nurse for a day, and made my way to Alexander's studio. Planning my course of action, I promised myself this was the day that cunning 'Bumble-bee' would face her nemesis – ME. Not considering anything could stop my intentions I came to a screeching halt outside the door. The studio was closed, no lights, no music, no anything. I rattled the door, knocked as hard as I could, trying not to draw attention. Searching the door and window I spotted a sign.

NOTICE FOR REGULAR AND NEW CUSTOMERS
WE ARE CLOSED FOR ONE MONTH DUE TO ART EXHIBITION IN PARIS THANK_YOU FOR YOUR LOYALTY.
FURTHER DETAILS LATER.

Underneath there was a signature (of a sort), followed by the extravagant lettering A.C.

Shock was my first emotion, quickly replaced by what I can only describe as undignified abuse upon my senses.

This exhibition – was Jules involved?

Why had I not been informed?

How could I discover Jimmy's Chinese lettering?

What was I to do?

I do believe curiosity is like an old-fashioned poker, the more a fire is prodded the greater the flame. The next step on – Malice – the vengeful assumptions from the mind of one who feels discarded. Alexander and the Bumble-bee have flown the nest, for an exhibition, the sign suggests – rubbish – Jules is in America – unless – unless he has returned to Paris. Under the name he fled with? Never, and Jimmy has not mentioned any new artists. No, there is more.

I ponder walking to the library, researching through the books on Chinese lettering, consider how long it will take me to discover the name – rule it out as the pain of Alexander's whereabouts hits me. Irritation floods my soul. It is imperative I find the meaning of those letters, for if Jimmy has a secret I need to know but also, at the same time I fretted over the love bird and her master – it is not fair.

Here I must halt your outburst of indignation. It is simple really. Jimmy is important to me, you understand, and my secret weighs heavy enough for both. My artist has flown without informing me.

'Jimmy.'s ankle must irk a true friend, and the empty nest of Alexander and the 'Bumble-bee.' Fascinating!'

Fascinating? How could you? It is downright infuriating. Bloody girl.

Your sarcasm grows. *'The provocateur blames his tools.'*

Fuming, I turn from the window, walk back the way I came.

4

It took Mattie and me exactly six months to find a flat Mother thought inhabitable for her only daughter. We settled on the upper part of town, near the railway station, and only a stone's throw from the shops. We spent an exciting three weeks moving furniture, accessories, and essentials into its hallowed rooms. My huge iron bed from home took over the smaller space it now found itself in. Mother suggested a new bed, I refused. Nothing on this earth could have tempted me to leave it behind. Monstrosity it may be, but this object had eased my sulking after my tattoos, my protests at Jimmy's long work hours, and several hours of cursing the postman's flippant attitude on informing me of 'no post'. On the good side, it had enraptured my dreaming, helping me indulge in its silk eiderdown my deepest fantasies. Coupled with the large purple chenille sofa (Mattie's choice), piled high with a collection of sumptuous cushions, these two items stamped my mark on this new adventure.

Mother relented after much crying, berating the place as, 'Too small, and the colour scheme outlandish.' Father tried hard to wish me well, even though on the morning I moved out from under his feet he left for work exceedingly early. Probably annoyed, to my way of thinking, at the thought of having Mother's cantankerous temper all to himself.

I laugh. Shame.

Then there was Bhutan.

Mattie chose the order and the community we would lodge with for, believe it or not, three whole months. We would work, trek, literally encompass the way of life we confronted.

My parents flipped. Mother nattered; I think that is the right word for someone who goes on and on. Father, he protested, in the only way he knew – he refused to give me spending money. Mattie rebuked him, explained money would be the last thing we would require – think graft, mucking in, becoming part of a community that till the land, and brew their own wine.

A calamity, occurred you could say.

Mother went on and on about the trek she and Father endured along the great wall of China, forgetting the main mishaps were her own fault. My father was in turmoil, blaming his Mother for filling my head with silly notions. Mother calmed his fury in her usual manner, before turning her own displeasure upon me. She nagged, about the bank, the journey, the conditions of our board, my grandmother, and anything else she laid her tongue too. Went as far as accusing me of being downright lazy.

"Slumming (it sounded funny in her pronounced tone) is not the 'thing' to do. You have not been brought up a loafer."

To stop myself falling into fits of laughter I excused myself and headed home; it sounds really odd. Opening the door I searched the post cage. No post. again.

Upset – that is mild, I was livid. Jules appeared to have dropped from the planet; no letter to invite me to his commune, no word to express his love for me – nothing. Not even a note from the 'Bumble-bee' to enlighten me over Alexander's flight, and to cap it all Jimmy was acting really strange. He had asked no questions about the trek. I was beginning to wonder if my friend was interested. Could the name on his ankle be adding to his disinterest? We shall see.

—

By November 1994 Mattie and I were well along the road of preparation, passports up to date, flights booked, with one on hold, taxi to and from the airport sorted. Full steam ahead, I thought, that was until this particular Saturday evening.

I had invited Mattie and Jimmy for an evening meal; my trekking buddies. Gone out of my way to produce a meal that would delight the palate, no processed meat, frozen vegetables or cubed gravy. I will call it my 'piece de resistance'; fresh, and by my standard this chef's best spaghetti bolognese. Actually, if I sum it up in truth the hob was smelling, bubbling away, in the way of a witch's cauldron. My eyes took in how the spiky hands of the clock wobbled across the eight and the six – Jimmy was late.

Mattie had arrived an hour ago, sat down on the purple sofa, accepted the large glass of wine I had given her, and settled down to await my culinary masterpiece. Time was moving on, running in fact, making me stir hard and release the bulk of meat from fastening itself to the bottom of the pan; the spaghetti bubbling in its salted water also was a slight cause for concern. The doorbell rang. Jimmy flashed through my mind, bottle in hand, huge bunch of flowers. I rushed into the lounge, tripping over my own feet to get to the door before Mattie. There stood Jimmy, no bottle of wine, no bunch of flowers, instead an expression of downright misery. He came through the door, chucked his jacket onto the arm of the sofa, and threw himself into its depths alongside Mattie.

"Work problems," I groaned before hurrying to the kitchen to check out the 'offish' odour.

I could hear Mattie's loud, "No," her follow through of, "Poor you," and finally, "Do not worry."

I suppose you would expect me to show sadness at the catch in her voice – not at all – I was elated – my friend would be free to spend three months without begging those fusty people for time off.

I poured *my* bottle of wine into large tumblers (considered the wine glasses a little small for this grand occasion) and carried them through. The sight that greeted me would have turned the wine sour.

"Okay you two, why the glum faces?"

Jimmy averted his eyes, looked toward my grandmother, fumbled with a cushion.

"That bad," I hissed, passing the tumbler into his outstretched hands.

Jimmy took a long gulp of wine, then blurted, "I will not be going to Bhutan."

My glare was one of disbelief.

Not going? I did not understand. If it was money – ridiculous. Mattie had set aside enough money to cover the journey for three. If it was the living – poor excuse. We had bartered in a style I thought was top of the class to set up fantastic working/living accommodation. All *he* had to bring was spare cash, himself and luggage.

If he had no job, all the better – what was the guy's problem?

Jimmy closed his eyes, let out an exasperated, 'she is not listening' whistle, then gabbled, "I have got to work."

"Work," I exploded – this was a joke.

"Seems so," he muttered.

"I thought you were taking a break."

"I was, but someone has gone missing which leaves me to do the Paris trip again."

"Paris – go back and tell your boss this is not fair. You are going on a trek!"

Jimmy laughed. "If only it was that easy."

I could feel the anger rising from the pit of my stomach. I had deluded myself into thinking Jimmy had lost his job. My voice rang round the flat. "It is easy, Jimmy. It is."

Mattie moved slightly in Jimmy's direction, opened her mouth to speak – closed it as I let out a scream. "You have no backbone."

Jimmy raised his head. "Backbone? You are a good one to talk."

Struck with the scorpion's tail I shouted, "Me, I have backbone, trust me."

Jimmy's face became a set mask. "Is that the way you see it?"

"See what, you fool?"

"This and that." His tone lowered. "I am tracking down a painter."

"A painter?" Mattie intervened.

"Yes, someone who is not quite the deal."

My heart raced.

"Unavoidable then." To me my grandmother was plastering over the cracks splintering our friendship.

Jimmy poured all his attention onto Mattie, ignoring me completely.

"I am afraid this is one job I cannot avoid. You see, they need my expertise."

The sound that left my throat would have suited a witch more than a concerned friend. "No one else will do then?"

"No," he clipped.

"Well, you are a coward, a beastly coward, not the friend you pretend to be."

Jimmy's eyes narrowed. "Think before you speak," he threw at me. "I am the true friend."

"Right," I threw back.

A strange hissing was ejecting from the kitchen.

"Blast." I ran into the adjoining room.

"Now look." I banged the saucepan as loudly as I could. "My beautiful kitchen represents the soil from the red desert."

Not a sound from the other room.

Grabbing a cloth, I began to mop, scraping the reddish-orange mess from the floor. The more I rubbed, the more it stained the cream tiled floor.

"Damn you," I was at fever pitch.

Not a sound.

Throwing cold water onto the already bubbling tiles I screamed, really screamed, "How long will you be gone?"

A rustle. "Not sure," came the reply. "Only Mona can tell me that."

"Mona?" Scooping minced beef from the floor, I let it slide back. "Mona?"

"That's right." His tone had a ring to it – what kind of ring I could not fathom out.

"Who the hell is Mona?"

I should have moved my body, poked my head (at least) round the kitchen door.

"Mona," came the reply, "is – wow, how shall I put it? One hell of a girl."

Chinese lettering was running high speed across my vision.

I kicked the oven door, threw the cloth I was holding into the sink, and raced back into the lounge, my rage was cut short. No friend, indentation on the sofa from his weight, but no Jimmy.

"Where?" I exploded.

"Gone," Mattie said matter of factly.

"I can see that."

"You," came the accusation.

"Me?"

"Too hasty, too hectic, too everything."

Mattie stood, pulled her coat on. "I will fetch fish and chips, do pour more wine."

Incensed, I stomped back into the kitchen.

The flat door slams. I shake myself from my melancholy state, allow a pang of hunger to overtake me.

—

The months preceding our trek to Bhutan both my grandmother and myself forged a special relationship of honesty (to a degree), and an intimate understanding. Our 'tremendous trek' as we both called it, loomed on the horizon in a haze of excitement and trepidation. In the bedroom of our flats suitcases lay open, as each day we stuffed (this is so true) jumpers or trousers into their already overflowing base. We laughed, we joked, generally made fun of every item of clothing we considered appropriate. My grandmother was turning out to be the friend I needed. On the other hand, mine and Jimmy's relationship was nothing short of rocky. Oh, he visited, we spoke, laughed now and then, discussed our daily events, but nothing of value passed our lips. Sentences were fragmented, at times funny, but also strained. We skimmed over Paris, discussed the ongoing search for 'the painter;' this subject needs to be in inverted commas because Jimmy was cagey and I too smooth. All my friend indicated was he was not working alone.

Tell me, does that mean MONA?

I tried to ask about his missing colleague – guess what? Nothing forthcoming. I gave up, concentrated on myself.

You shake your head. I raise my nose in the air – question in no quiet manner, ask: "Why not?"

Listen reader, I have come to one important conclusion. I am entering the phase in a female's life when one can definitely be labelled a 'woman'. Apart from turning twenty-eight I have grown in wisdom.

Silence!

Okay, think what you will, but if Jimmy is maturing (Mother's take on my friend) so am I, and let us be absolutely up front with one another, if my so called 'best friend' could not be bothered to choose us over work, by that I mean the wretched Mona, he did not deserve one iota of my concern.

The wonderful news is the letter I received on the eve of mine and Mattie's departure. It was from Jules – at last –

In full (if that is what one can label a five line letter):

Rhia,

At last a free moment to drop you a line. I have settled in America. Created an art commune, people of the same mind as myself. Loved your artist. The more I see of your painter's art, the more I think of your body.

If you are ever on this side of the Atlantic. look me up. Address below.

Jules♥

and, before you utter one word like, 'tell Jimmy', let me say I am well aware my lover is the painter my friend is searching, but – and I feel adamant about this, I know Jules is innocent. Wrong time, wrong place.

There is a bitter cynicism in the exasperation I hear.

Tell you what, I don't care, for the next time I will read this letter I will be sitting in the tiny airport at Nepal, waiting for our trekking guide.

Bhutan, May 1995

Mattie was dozing on the bench beside me, catching up on the forty-eight hours spent travelling, and the hard to forget dinner party Mother had made us sit through the day before our departure.

"Three months," she had consistently repeated. "Three months in hard conditions."

I got to a point where I thought this woman believes we are going for a stretch in the old American State Penitentiary. She had sobbed uncontrollably, much to father's annoyance, and Mattie's delight. Three hours we had to suffer her whining and nattering. Three hours of punishment, enough to make us run for the plane.

I pulled the folded paper from my jacket pocket, read the scrawled writing over and over again. I glowed in its warmth, convincing myself he was hinting I move to be with him, become part of the commune with Alexander and 'Bumble-bee'. That will stop her in her tracks!

'*Jimmy,*' you remark.

Who?

You scowl.

Only joking. I do miss him. I have no explanation why the guy is acting so ridiculous.

Mattie stirs, opening one eye as a cat from a quick nap. She smiles; an expression of knowledge behind the beam.

"What are you doing, child? Is that a letter from that lad of yours?"

By this she meant Jimmy.

"No, Mattie, I have heard nothing since he last left for Paris."

"Oh dear, you should not have kept on at him. He is on important business."

She closed her eyes again, fanning herself with a magazine taken from the next seat. Jimmy on important business – what does my grandmother know, he collects old relics.

Re-folding the letter, I tuck the pages into my back pocket. I must be more careful. Mattie, bless her, is one clever cookie; cunning and astute. Not in a bad way, just out of her inbred curiosity. A surge of affection floods through me as I watch her out the corner of my eye. I had found in these past months she was far more than a grandmother, more a confidante – in some things. If I just had the nerve to be honest, let her into my deceit; allow her to rejoice with me. If only I could make her understand that Jimmy is wrong in his accusation.

'If only' are two life changing words.

—

Dusk was settling as a tiny Nepalese man scurried across the tiled floor to where we sat. He kept bowing and bowing, throwing his arms in the air, and in the best English he could muster stuttered, "Sorry, late," "Sorry, late." In his grasp a card with our names on it. Mattie nigh on hugged him, especially when the young boy by his side produced two flasks. I can honestly say the fruit juice within those containers, at that moment, was the freshest and best drink in the world. Within seconds the man, evidently our guide to the village, commanded his army of young boys to remove our suitcases. With his next breath, he indicated we follow him.

Outside we were greeted by a line-up of noisy pack-horses, neighing, jumping, and generally disobeying everything the tiny man shouted at them.

First thought – Thank God they are looped together by a strong rope, for otherwise I am certain they would have bolted for the dark, forbidding mountains in the distance.

Second thought – No way are we going to trek these mountains as dusk descends.

Third thought – I wished Mother was here. Nothing on this planet could have replaced the look that would have settled on her face.

Fourth thought – Trekking in the dust? Yes, we are!

Bhutan, we were to discover, had no railway, very few roads, and the route to our village was only accessible on the back of these pack horses. Four legs, a tail and a mane, plus a fiery temper – great!

Taking hold of Mattie's arm, I whispered, "How long do you think the journey will be?" She in turn asked our guide. He, running up and down the line as if practising for some sort of race shrugged his shoulders, and with difficulty pronounced, "A day – and a half – two days."

My heart sank, my bottom twitched.

Mind, from the moment I was strapped into the saddle-seat atop one of these moving fire-balls, adrenalin started to pump through my veins; all tiredness gone,

The guide informed us the village was awaiting our arrival, and they were honoured we had chosen them. He was difficult to understand, but through repetition, hand signs, and lots of bowing he got his message across.

We began upward – steeper and steeper.

My question – why my grandmother had selected a village so far off the beaten track, what was her reasoning?

Tramping our way up steep mountain paths, chiselled from the landscape, these dusty, rocky and daringly narrow roadways gave no protection against the chilly night air. For once in my life I was pleased, as was Mattie, that I had taken notice of the travel company and brought various weight jumpers. The 'boys,' in what seemed to us to be thin trousers and tops, found our red cheeks and padded bodies a constant source of amusement. Running back and forth along the line of pack-horses their rounded cheeks and long sticks (supposedly used to show the animals who was in control) wobbled with glee. Even more so as we began to rock from side to side as the pathways grew narrower, and I screamed the horses' hooves would any moment slip over the edge of a steep ravine.

Ten miles into our journey (that's how long it seemed to me), we came to a stop, indicated to dismount, the guide relaying, in his own peculiar fashion, that it was time to sleep. I looked at Mattie in dismay. Here, in the open, on these dangerous pathways? Mattie smiled, dismounted, and offered me her hand. Sliding from the now still horse (must be tired) I limped to a small indentation the boys were preparing at the side of the road.

Here, description is paramount so you too can sympathise with me – a blanket, a sleeping bag, hard ground, and if you were lucky a sky full of stars.

The good choice, I suppose, was staying in the Central Highlands; the part of Bhutan where the majority of the population lived. Mattie had shied away from the south's sub-tropical humid conditions, the north's year-round snow, and the west's heavy monsoon rain. Our weather, according to the man from the travel agency, would be more temperate. Less rain mixed with warm and cool air. I say, 'Thank Heaven' at this moment.

Mattie, stretching and bending (someone needs to tell her this is not the place for yoga), flapped her arms around her bulging padded body. There was no tiredness in her eyes; just a light burning in their depths, matching the newly lit fire the boys had built. A little further on, tucked at the side of a bush a screen had been erected. Mattie caught my quizzical glance. "The tent? For us to wash."

"What about the toilet?"

Mattie nodded toward the young boy digging a hole, among the trees.

"That's it. He will fill it in before we set off in the morning."

"Great."

Mattie saw my alarm and took my arm, led me to the tent, turned her back, and let me get on with swilling my face, and other things.

This was all carried out under the detached presence of our guide; near to us in case of danger, remote enough for privacy.

—

As the morning sun peeped above the mountains our guide gently shook us by the shoulder. Clothes from the day before, slept in, crumpled, and beginning to hold an odour of their own, if it had not been for the breakfast of small pancakes fried over an open fire, bound together by corn and cold meat, followed by the same fruit juice we had drunk at the airport the previous day, I would have cried. Eating as ravenous children, we cleared our plates, bowed our heads to our guide, and drank until our stomachs ached.

Glancing at my oiled lips my grandmother laughed.

"Eat while you can. I am sure we will be ravenous again before this day is out."

I guessed she would be right, but I smell and I am weary, and yes, I will hold up my hands, sounding every inch my mother.

After the breakfast, the journey continued, more arduous, steeper pathways, breathing intense as the sun rose higher; the dust and buzzing flies adding to my discomfort. One bonus came our way, the guide relayed to Mattie we had made good time, cutting our travelling to the end of the day. He had sent a boy on ahead in preparation.

Morning became afternoon, the sun at its pinnacle, beating down on us poor travellers with no mercy. I prayed for nightfall, a warm shower, a soft bed.

I know, my mind was working overtime again. One can dream. If you could connect with me even you would shed a tear or two for my sore bottom. Mattie consistently chatted to the young boys, made them giggle with her improvised hand actions. They spoke in a language beyond her understanding, but she answered with an 'mph', or 'ahh'; almost as if she understood every word they were saying.

I sank into my own corner of seclusion, touched the precious note burning a hole in my pocket, swore a year down the line I would find a way to my lover's side, somehow. I made a vow – to break free from the silly pact – Jimmy was not interested in our search for freedom – Mona had seen to that!

By late afternoon sun shadows tipped the top of the mountains, dipping its rays out of sight, drenching the snow peaked tops with a mystical golden halo, catching my breath at the beauty before me. The travel brochure had branded this part of the country 'Lo Mon' – the Southern Land of Darkness, land where the Mongol and Tibetan overlords down the centuries ruled with a rod of steel. To me, on the night of our arrival it was breath-taking, a landscape painting waiting to be captured.

Snow-capped mountain peaks, fast flowing rivers, deep gorges winding their way through emerald green land; lush pastures, grazing land for the many cows and sheep, waterfalls falling into streams of translucent rainbow ribbons.

Mattie and I had been shown a short documentary of the Himalayan Mountain Range, 7,000 feet above sea level, with mountains such as the Kula Kangri rising to 24,780 feet, and the Gangkhar Puensum at 24, 835 feet; ownership argued over by Tibet and India. I thought of the Eric Clapton song, "The Stairway to Heaven" – it fit it perfectly.

The air, at higher altitudes, was so fine that I craved more; remember to breathe slow and shallow until accustomed, fingers crossed that altitude sickness will pass me by. The sheer absence of factories belching out smoke, blaring car horns, or screaming mouths was a haven of tranquillity. Peace lay over everything. Bhutan – Druk Yul; otherwise known as the 'Land of the Thunder Dragon' must surely be the most perfect place on earth. It was easy to see why the travel company had named it 'the last Shangri-La' – paradise on earth.

Sitting atop my packhorse, the boys scuttering as field mice, the guide with his broad genuine smile, Mattie awash with delight and wonder, I could not help but plead to whatever spiritual overseer that defended this realm that at last I would find the meaning of that seven lettered word (freedom) – find it and own it.

5

We reached the village east of Dhur as the sun cast its last 'goodbye' for the day. Dark clouds, heralding the long night ahead skimmed across the sky. From the moment we entered the small hamlet rapturous clapping and screaming accompanied the few yards to the centre of the village. Looking around the crowded excited faces it was obvious the conversation my grandmother and I had at our last 'nature' stop was not going to happen. All we wished was to wash and sleep, pour warm water, if they could supply such a luxury, over my now red raw bottom. I felt stiff. My back, legs, arms, and body, were set in a position I did not believe I would ever recover from.

Our guide was busy running in front of our horses, shouting out commands as he passed. All the boys were gabbling at once, jumping up and down, whilst hugging anyone who thanked them for delivering us safely. Mattie, at her age, appeared far more agile than me, sliding down from her horse with the grace of a woman half her age; briskly enveloping all the women who stretched out their arms. I put it down to those years of horse riding in her youth Father had tormented her about at Christmas.

My descent was far more dubious, letting the thick hair of the horse's mane hold my weight. The poor horse neighed, stamping the ground and swinging its head side to side. I fell – tripped over my stiff feet and landed with a thud on the floor.

'History repeating itself.'
I can imagine the scoff is hard to hide.

Mattie extended her hand, laughed out loud. "Rhia, time to get fit for the hard work we agreed to take part in."

Bhutan, sandwiched between India and the People's Republic of China earned their living in accordance with the land, agriculture and farming. We had landed on their doorstep in the busy season, to help as Mattie said, and to encourage them to mix with the outside world. Mother would call us work chattels.

Suddenly there was a commotion – voices raised as a young woman was dragged to stand in front of us. She was small, dark in colouring, and dressed in what we later discovered was the traditional ankle length dress known as a Kira; tied at the waist, and clipped at the shoulder over a long sleeved blouse. The texture, colour and decoration was determined by social class within the community.

Even here I cannot get away from the rise and fall of class status.

The woman, introduced as our hostess was the young wife of a leading tribesman; a high ranking village official. Due to her place in village society she wore a scarf and shawl, plus one earring, which we were told she had received on her wedding day, and represented her rank. The older women of the village were bending her in half, shouting "Bow, bow," in a strange tongue they insisted was English.

Holding tight to Mattie's hands she lowered her head. "I am Choo, my name by Mongolian tradition, but please, call me Lotus – my mother's favourite flower. I am your hostess whilst you stay." Pausing for a second she did exactly the same to me, her English practised and understandable. "Follow please."

Lotus pointed to a tent, closed on all four sides, a short distance from the crushing crowd.

Inside a trestle table (of a sort) was simply set out with two huge bowls of water and cloths; soap, I presume made by the women of the village due to its shape and colour, glistened in tiny pots at the side.

Lotus bowed, this time more a little curtsy, retreating beyond a screen.

Mattie plunged her hands into one of the bowls. "Warm – ohhh – not quite the depths of beyond."

I could not help my lips puckering as I squeezed the cloth in its warm depth and patted it over my face.

Our luggage, unloaded from the pack-horses, was stacked neatly to the side, ready for us to slip out of these smelly clothes and into clean ones. Girls, summoned during our preparation by Lotus, held large cloth robes to wrap us in when we had peeled (sorry, my humour) our travel clothes; their form of modesty whilst we sponged ourselves?

As soon as we had re-dressed, may I say in thick jumpers and trousers (between my sore bottom and the cold night air I wished for comfort) Lotus clapped her hands for the water and luggage to be removed. I was astonished to see girls, as young as ten, puffing and panting under the weight of our suitcases, dragging them to wherever we would eventually lay our head.

Lotus bowed – head tribesman's wife or not, she was our servant; held her hand in the direction of the entrance. "You would like to eat?"

"Yes, please," I sounded eager to fill the yawning hole in my stomach.

Holding the tent flap our hostess was greeted by a roar as she presented us to the excited crowd – heart sinking moment, no peace or privacy.

The village officials had seated themselves around a long table, beckoning us to sit and eat. Fish, meat, soup, corn rolls and tiny moulded sweet bits (sugar sweeties) shone in the light of the candles and lamps like jewels. Lotus escorted us to our seats, then placed herself at the right hand top corner. In the all-important chair at the head of the table (or the boss's chair, as my father would say) was a young dark haired man of average height, clothed in what appeared to be an official robe, the insignia of high rank, and Lotus's husband – "Welcome to our humble village."

Casting my eye over Lotus's face I thought of the 'Bumble-bee'; another searched for Mattie. She had been seated in-between two elder women, at least ninety years old or thereabout. Catching my gaze, she indicated to put food in the mouth with my fingers.

This I did with more stamina than I thought possible.

—

Sleep on that first night in the village was deep and satisfying. Mattie and I had followed Lotus to her house and into a bedroom off the large stone kitchen where two beds and our luggage awaited us. In the dim oil light we threw off our clothes and clambered into bed, ignoring everything but the need to lay our weary bodies down. One good part of our 'goodnight' conversation with Lotus was her assurance that large gatherings, as we had just experienced, were for special occasions. The norm was to sit around a fire outside our allotted house and talk with whoever passed our way, sometimes for an hour or two, other times into the early dawn. This, we would do with continual drinks and tit-bits from our hostess. It was beginning to grate on me, even in the short time Mattie and I had been in the village, how much work Lotus was required to do. Apart from bending to our whims, the poor girl had her husband's position to think about, with cleaning, cooking and village duties on the top.

Mother would have labelled our hostess a true slave.

Mind, if I had known as much about Lotus on that first night as I did on our last night I would have made it my aim not to be so bossy, arrogant, or snooty.

Anyway, that is jumping ahead, and as we learn life will never let us jump, only stagger at its own pace.

As dawn broke over the mountain peaks on our first day we woke to the sound of bamboo pipes, played by the older men of the village, shaking us from the deep sleep we had fallen into. My body ached, legs trembling when I stood on them, stiff from the hours of gripping the horse as we swayed and wobbled along the narrow paths. Throwing on the clothes from the night before, we sat down for breakfast, while Lotus explained our duties in the village – and I thought this would be a holiday!

Time would be spent with the women of the village baking, cleaning, child minding (would you believe), and generally mucking in. Dress would be a traditional long skirt, a long sleeved top, a shawl and fabric slippers, laid out daily for us by Lotus, only deviating if it was a day trekking the surrounding mountains, then jeans, T shirt, jacket, boots and a hat. Can you believe it – I – bought oodles of new clothes – not fair!

You smile.

I am going to shout. "Stop it, this is *my* 'freedom' quest."

I hear you draw breath, reprimand me. Try, I am sure, to explain real freedom is found within.

I stamp my foot. Hit back with, "Have you ever heard such nonsense?"

I whine about the beds, the dust underneath my feet, the sun glaring through the window – everyone and everything shares my displeasure.

I can see you grit your teeth, look at me with distaste and say one word. '*Mother.*'

I cannot believe you pair me with my mother. – How could you.

We move from the breakfast table, go back to the bedroom and change. I begin our three months in a savage mood, unlike Mattie, who is relishing every moment.

—

It was the first week of the second month of our visit and a letter from Mother had been delivered by the guide who scores these mountains as if he was playing snakes and ladders. Four long pages of her usual rubbish – reels and reels of it. Her friends at the social club were helping her cope with her daughter's absence (honestly), telling her how brave she was to allow me to travel to such a far-flung place. How so and so would not be able to manage such a parting, and (of course this had to come), so and so's daughter was marrying or having a baby. It could have been the new TV saga, instead, and I stress this word with unbelievable annoyance, no interesting gossip – i.e. news of Jimmy, as nothing from my friend has been heard in this quarter. Odd really, she was completely tight lipped; maybe my friend had fallen from the planet.

In such circumstances, I came to rely daily on reading the folded, finger marked piece of paper in my jacket pocket. Each night on entering my room I lifted it (not in Mattie's sight) from its hiding place, read and kissed it.

Frowning – so what?

Penning Jules a letter of my whereabouts I wished he was here as the landscape alone would inspire him, asked him to write, and put in black and white that we would be together. Pleased with myself I gave the guide my letter for posting, promised myself I would write to Mother (sometime), and perhaps find time to scribble to Jimmy.

Best friend – wait until I see him.

One evening as we dressed for dinner (hey, we were allowed to choose our own traditional dress colour.) Mattie suggested that Jimmy was holding fire to see who would be the first to write, him, or me.

"Is it important?" I asked.

"Oh, yes," she replied, confusing me further. "I am sure he awaits your apology."

Did I hear right? Apology? My grandmother had got to be kidding!

He was the one who chose work over us, chose to ignore my pleading; the one who never did state clearly why Paris was so damn important.

Well, let me state loud and clear – first to write – **"It will not be me."**

—

Thursday of the same week Mattie and I had been assigned to assist the women of the village sew, paint, and decorate the houses in readiness for a masked dance. A week-long festival, granted by the elders to celebrate our visit to the Taktsang Monastery the next day. This holy site, perched on a cliff 900m above the Paro valley was a must, and although the trek would be tiring, it was a journey we were expected to make. According to village tradition the monks who lived there would help us to gain a deeper insight into the age old rituals of Buddhism, Shangri- La on earth.

"Lots of spiritual favour," Lotus kept telling us, "and, when you return the Chaam dance will be given in your honour; your sore-torn bodies showered with herbal scented water."

Around dusk, finding myself clapping Mattie, in her usual style and flair, gyrating round and round in the young women's fertility dance (do not ask me to comment) I noticed Lotus was missing. Beginning to feel dizzy with the task of catching my grandmother's head, and depressed at the thought of the long journey on the following day, my parched throat was desperate for a drink. I knew Lotus would not deliberately ignore her duties, after all the girl was our servant. Mattie hated the whole servitude business. I, sad to say, enjoyed it immensely. Inching my way through the clapping women I briskly (more a huff in the step than a gait) walked toward the house.

Outside the door I came to a halt, ready to confront the girl, ask a reason for leaving us; then as my hand held the latch I heard sobbing, heart wrenching wailing. Pushing open the wooden door I stepped across the stone threshold. Pooled in the rays of a dying sun, Lotus was lying on the floor, arms outstretched in supplication, beating the boards beneath her. My immediate reaction was to quietly leave, suffer the dryness of my throat, and re-join the dancers. Grizzling women – no time for them.

'Arrogance,' you mumble.

I press the latch, ready to creep away.

"Go away," the voice screamed. "I hate you."

I was stunned. This woman, who was my hostess, my general slave, was barking at me in a manner that a guest (me) found offensive.

"Lotus?" The biting retort was sucked into the tiny room.

She shot up, her dysfunctional sentence breaking up as in fear she tried to say everything at once.

"Oh no, no, no – Miss Bryant – sorry – please not tell husband."

Grovelling – that was better.

"What is wrong?" I snapped.

"I thought you my – my – how do you say it – crassy husband," the furtive eyes flashed past me to the half opened door.

Lotus jumped to her feet, ran in circles around the sparsely furnished kitchen, and started to prepare food, presumably for us, before grovelling again with the offer to sit on the extended stool.

For some unknown reason Lotus's actions brought the Bumble-bee to mind once more – Alexander's vassal as I will call her.

Mother's training came to the forefront – clear, unsentimental, banal.

"Lotus, I demand you tell me what is wrong."

The young woman swung to look at me, her eyes slits of accusation, her sun-darkened skin smeared with the wetness of her tears.

"My – husband – is to re-marry."

Forgive me – I laughed – divorce has found its way here!

The first thing that enters the head is not always the most positive or kindest.

"Soon mended," I barked.

"What you mean?" she struggled with the coldness of my reply.

"Better on your own." I let it fall as snow on a winter's day, chilling the heart with the promise of freezing misery "Not good," I continued. "A man who cannot see past his own needs."

Lotus whimpered.

"Think," I said. "You can find another husband."

'Please,' you grunt.

What is the matter with you? I was helping.

'Please,' you say once more.

Fool – is my backshot.

Lotus was literally screaming, banging pans, hugging herself for comfort. I remembered my kitchen and the spaghetti debacle. I must do something.

"Run," my mother would advise. I could not, this last tantrum being partly my fault.

I closed the door, and moved to her side. "Please stop. I was trying to help."

"No help," she wailed. "You no understand."

Lotus put space between us, and I had to admit what she had said was true – Jimmy, of all people would fully agree with her.

How do I know this? My friend had often told me I was emotionally stunted (cheek), and that compassion was beyond me. As we know I could argue the case, but at what cost.

Why was I thinking of Jimmy?

"Forgive me. I was tactless and rude."

Me, apologise? What else could I do? What I did next will make you clap – or squirm, I put my arm round her waist. Lotus shivered. "You guest. I will be in trouble if husband catches us."

"Do not fret, I will deal with him." How? No idea.

"He chose other wife. She will live with me," her voice quivered.

"Live with you?" the sound echoed around the stony kitchen.

Lotus nodded. "Yes." She grasped the hand that had slid round her.

I felt sick. "He has put you aside, and still wants to live here?"

Her head shot up, her shoulders straightened themselves. "I am wife number one."

I tell you, Jimmy would have jumped up and down in sheer joy by the incredulous 'thwack' that had hit me. I could not, for the life of me, marry (spontaneous phrase) what she was saying, when that word, 'polygamy,' floated through my mind – the sheer meaning of it grabbed me as unfair. Here was I, trying to find a civilized route to the guy I was meant to be with – and here was a young woman about to share her husband's bed, and claim the honour her status kept.

I say the world stinks!!

I am not surprised if you look me up and down as you would an inflamed child; my answer – so what!

Lotus moved back to the sink. "Must get meal, husband will be home."

I moved with her, thirst forgotten.

"You accept this arrangement?" My voice is small, very small.

A querulous look enters her eyes. "We have been wed three years, husband can wait no longer."

I stood, looking out at the extensive mountain range. "For what?" the question is harsh.

"A child," the soft voice drops into the air.

"That is bad?"

"Yes, he important man. Must have child."

"You are important too?"

"Yes, I first wife."

"He loves you?"

"Yes, but need child. Second wife may give child."

I study the pain on her face, quiz her unmercifully. "You can have child." "You are not barren." "Can he not wait?" "Selfish man."

Lotus hesitates, turns my way, tears start to fall again. "I pray Buddha can help."

Buddha? My mind reels, I would have said a good bottle of wine, and a candlelit room.

'For heaven.'s sake,' I hear you moan.

I reflect on my opinion of this perfect part of the world. Beauty, mysticism, a simple way of life, freedom overshadowed it seems by that age-old obligation for an heir.

I subconsciously hear Jimmy's warning – different perspectives.

Different perspectives indeed. More male virility.

Returning to the woman before me: "I will light a candle to Buddha for you tomorrow."

"You will?"

"I will."

Lotus bowed, continued to mix the corn meal, brushing aside the falling tears.

Had I finally lost the little social grace Mother had instilled into me, she would say, 'yes.' This girl was our servant, how they conduct their life was their business, not ours; there again, my mother was a snob.

I took a pinafore from the peg on the wall, and amid her protestations began to help with the evening meal.

6

It really was a long trek to the monastery at Taktsang, hot, dusty, and incredibly back aching. How Mattie coped I will never know. I heard not one complaint drop from those rouged lips; she laughed with the young boys running at her side, explained to me during our very short breaks what the guide had told her concerning this holiest of holy places, pronounced she was in seventh heaven.

Her life, according to my grandmother, had never been so free from worry.

To say Mattie was revelling in this existence would be an understatement, she was slowly becoming a part of it.

For me, the sad picture of Lotus crying kept me quiet for the majority of the journey. It had taken me a full hour to calm her down, another half an hour to ease the sobbing, and a good deaf ear to ignore her cry for me to go. As you can guess I am very good at doing exactly as I wish. In the end I moved from one job to another teasing the problem from the young girl's quivering lips. This was it:

Lotus's husband, had been advised to consider his standing in the village, and although the government of Bhutan did not condone polygamy, in extreme circumstances it was accepted. His virility (men and their prowess) had to be shown through the birth of a child, he being among the official leaders. Poor Lotus had prayed, petitioned Buddha for a child, often until her knees were sore, but nothing had happened.

On special days she gave offerings, and only as a last resort did her husband consider taking a second wife. This, he had informed Lotus, was his duty in producing an heir. She had agreed (I cannot believe it), and set the wedding date, where they would lay on their wedding night, and, when his latest wife would move into his marital home.

"Another sister," Lotus had cried into my blouse.

"Another sister," I muttered, secretly wishing I could burn her in oil.

This morning as we mounted our horses to begin our trek Lotus handed me her floral offering for Buddha, which I tucked into my saddle-bag. On the way up the craggy track of the Paro valley I struggled to piece together my own mess.

1)   Mother, in her snobbiest voice possible would have demanded to know where 'my sensible head' had gone. What was I doing carrying flowers up a mountain side for a girl who was clearly not only my hostess, but also (in this environment) my servant. To that I say, Mother has a lot to learn.

2)   Jimmy, and his letter writing: a childish act over a problem that was created by his desire to work.

3)   Jules: the very name sets me on fire.

           Alexander and the 'Bumble-bee': *She* cheated, took my plan and made it her own, that alone causes me to think of revenge.

           Maybe Buddha could help me.

           I watch Mattie, hope one day I could be as free. Of course, when my dreams have been fulfilled, and Jules, Jimmy and me are the friends we should be.

'*Dreaming?*' you may ask.

Carry on, I return, you are no fantasist. Shame!

—

What can I say about Taktsang?

From the moment of our arrival to the hour of our departure spirituality wrapped itself around us. No matter that the crumbling building needed repair, or that life here was suspended between the past and the future; the fragile string of life melted into the vaporising mist floating across the mountain tops. Known as the 'Tiger's Nest' to the local people, the legend of a Buddhist saint Padma Sambhave, alias Guru Rinpoche, cannot be overlooked, as according to legend in the eighth century this holy man flew to the cliff where the monastery is now built on the back of a tigress. His aim, to meditate, pray in its caves for the woes of the world. Ever since the monastery has become emblematic to a sacred sanctuary.

Positioned 10,000ft above sea level, with a 1,200 drop down the cliff-side to the valley below, the views are breathtaking. Many tourists, in the words of our guide, do claim that this monastery is the original Shangri-La; that I can believe as the sound of monks chanting, the wind whistling, and the faint trickle of running water, give this shrine an enigma of its own, and I would have been shocked to be told the legend was not true, for Taktsang was a place of peace. I will call it a harbour for the troubled soul.

On arrival we were welcomed by a party of twenty monks, adorned in maroon robes, bowing their shaven heads low, and greeting us, 'welcome' in their nationalistic tongue. They held a mixture of instruments – metal horns, three metres long, large standing drums, cymbals, temple bells, hand bells, gongs and wooden sticks. Behind these twenty, on a raised wooden plinth, stood two broader and taller monks. In their hands they held cream coloured trumpets, of which our guide leant forward to inform us on their origin.

"Conch shells, human bones."

Noting the slight shudder pass through me Mattie took hold of my hand, and in a whisper stated, "Thigh bones."

"Thigh bones?"

"Thigh bones," she repeated.

Our guide made a gentle 'shh' just as the resonating sound of the trumpets drifted over our heads. The sound was wonderful, like the wind it was competing with, it held our attention.

From the moment of the first chord I knew my understanding of freedom would turn another corner.

—

It is said that time 'flies on golden wings'.

In this place of spiritual enlightenment it had to be true. There were no clocks, every meal and prayer call came via the ringing of a bell, or the blowing of a horn. We were informed of the importance of Buddhism in Bhutan.

From the region of Bumthang district of Jakar, where the present government headquarters reside, the monastery has continually played a main role in the politics of the country. The monks, practising their policy of internal peace, believe in the ten stages of enlightenment, previous existences and reincarnation which lead to the 'subtle mind'. Their goal is to end suffering, find nirvana, and not repeat the cycle of re-birth they truly believe human beings go through. To achieve this awakened mind is the pathway to true peace; paradise on earth. Whether it be over many lifetimes, the core result is the same, letting go of life's cravings and dependencies (does not fit very well with Jules and me). It is a complete opposition to materialism, with no belief in an immortal self, and the gaining of a disciplined mind.

'*No craving,*' the subconscious voice insists.
I fold it away as I would fold the note in my pocket.

Our guide, an experienced monk by all account, instructs us to follow him into a building that reminds me of a cave, known as Taktsang Pelphi.

"Very sacred," he explains "Guru Rinpoche meditated here, saved Bhutan."

I looked at the temple, built in 1694 to the honour of the holy man, back at the 'ihakhangs' guarding the entrance. Removing our shoes and socks Mattie and I were asked to seat ourselves on the floor alongside a row of young monks in deep contemplation. These boys were novices, fresh to the monastic faith, their voices ringing out in a deep pulsating, melodious flow, which upon the end of each chord the boy at the end of the row struck a small gong, informing the rest that they should lie prostrate in supplication.

I must say at this point I was transfixed, noticing the tourists around me were almost in a trance. Clutching Lotus's posy (wilting in the heat of the temple) I found myself mumbling, entreating Buddha's aid in the young woman's cause, every now and again giving up my own troubles, sinking further toward the floor on each entreaty. Pulling myself upward from what I can honestly describe as the most uncomfortable position I had ever allowed myself to be in, I cast a quick glance at my grandmother. Her eyes were tightly closed as she sat with no imploring on her face, only that of pleasure in her surroundings, chanting in rhythm to our young companions, under the piercing gaze of the beautifully painted Buddha.

On our exit from the chapel (cave) we were invited to wander, inspect our surroundings, digest the breath-taking views, with the added warning not to stray to near the cliff edge. My hands empty after leaving Lotus's flowers at the door to the holy shrine, I swung them above my head. Mattie had not spoken since we left the temple, preoccupied it seemed with her own concerns. I would leave it at that, for my grandmother was her own judge and jury, but after a small picnic, distributed by each tourists' guide, she sought out the head monk and was deep in conversation. I know great strength was given to the spirituality of our surroundings, with each guide setting themselves apart from their group to talk if a person wished, so Mattie deep in consultation was no great shock, my grandmother always took her opportunity; in my mother's words, 'One nosy lady'.

By mid-afternoon we began to ready ourselves for the descent down the mountain. The monks 'blew' us on our way with their conch shells, and our mule-pack guide detailed the time spent in the saddle, to the time we would arrive back in the village.

Now, here, I must tell the truth: if the upward journey was sore to a certain part of the anatomy, then believe me, the downward spiral was positively horrendous. Parts of the pathway sloped, so the pack-horses slid us forward, throwing us back again with what I am sure was animal delight when they straightened up their necks and bodies. I wanted to squeal, pull on the reins with all my might, and show who was boss. Not possible – oh no, these prancing animals, and the giggling cloth-footed boys were completely in control.

In conjunction with the sun burning the already dry earth to a cinder, our horses sense of humour went wild. They kicked dust in every direction, covering us with a fine spray of reddish sprinkles. Our saving grace was the large brimmed hats we had been advised to wear, and the huge cotton handkerchiefs used to cover our mouths and noses. Talk looking ridiculous –anyone trekking this mountain could be forgiven if they associated us with common bandits, ready to attack them at any time.

After an hour of sitting atop this bucking horse my three quarter sleeved blouse was stuck to my back; my only consolation its colour – black. Before you remind me that black and the sun are not supposed to mix I must remind you of my art work.

Your answer: *'Sit back, no grumbling, and swallow my pride.'*

At last, the lengthening shadows of night crept around us, cooling the air to a breathable temperature. Nearing the village we could see lanterns sparkling from doorways and doorsteps, smaller versions hanging from selected tree boughs. Bonfires sprang into our vision as the horses clopped their way over the bracken paths. The atmosphere was sizzling. Party celebrations were ready, waiting for our return. For the first time since leaving the monastery Mattie spoke. "Wonderful," she sighed, "Wonderful."

"You bet," I flung back. "I could do with a drink."

My grandmother seized my arm. "Rhia, darling, it is time for you to decide."

"Decide?" I laughed. "This girl needs a drink."

'Strange,' shot through my mind as I disconnected my arm from her hold.

Trekking was supposed to be fun, right, if you sit on a multitude of soft cushions.

—

The night sky finally hid those impenetrable mountains, shrouding them once more from the human eye; a curtain drawn, separating our world from the monks that lived in that paradise.

In the village the lamps and bonfires threw shadows onto the women dancing, men smoking and drink flowing. I was exhausted, and as the bath of warm water Lotus had organised soaked into my aching muscles, the day's activities astonished me. Mother would never believe her daughter could endure those precipitous pathways, never (and I can see that look now) believe I prayed to Buddha for a servant girl. Now, there is something to brag about at her social evenings!

For privacy, Lotus had shrouded each wooden tub with a screen of bamboo, along with a young girl (ten at least) to pour water as quickly or slow as our held up hand demanded. I silently thanked her for closeting my tattoos from all eyes, apart from the child, who I have to admit, did not know where to avert her eyes. I could hear Mattie splashing, dropping the odd snippet into the air, as the child inside her giggled.

Outside the Chaam dance was in full swing, and I had noticed on my way to the bathing tent the women were wearing their best Kira. The men, dressed in their finery, wore a garment known as the Kera; an ankle length dress-robe tied at the waist by a cloth belt, lending them the Mongolian stance of old. All wore masks and danced around a tapestry (sacred to the village) uncovered on certain nights for prayers and dancing. Drums beat out a sensuous, throbbing sound; powerful spine tingling rhythm that played upon the mind. Stepping out from the tub I wrapped a large robe offered me by the young girl around my body, her head turned to the side to avoid my nakedness.

I did not hear Mattie slide around the screen.

"I have a letter for you."

I jumped, pulled the robe tighter before turning to face my grandmother.

"I was miles away, one, as they say, with the music."

"Yes, it's alluring. Lotus gave it to me" she pushed the long white envelope my way.

At first I thought, *he* has put pen to paper, he is here, in the village, now.

This is where you try and talk sense to me?

"Your mother?" Mattie spoke matter of factly. "I would know her hand anywhere."

"Oh."

I slumped onto a bench, and tore the envelope apart.

Darling Rhia,

Your absence is worth noting. It is strange how quiet both your father and I have become since you left. We miss you terribly. Your father constantly watches the television for news, more grateful than ever that you both had the common sense to change your mind about camping in Nepal (who wouldn't, confronted by Mother's tantrums). It appears from his tone that there is violence there, and the natives are revolting (give me strength – only my snobbish Mother could have written that!) over Maoist insurgency. Therefore, I pray you are both safe.

This letter is penned in the hope you are eating properly, and Mattie (stress on my grandmother's name) is behaving herself. Thank heaven her son is not tarred with the same brush! (always thought that a ridiculous saying)

Well Rhia, I had a phone call today, July 6th, from Jimmy in Paris (good for you, Mother).

We had an issue we wanted to discuss (secrets?). He said he was fine, which I would imagine he was, for between you and me I could hear a woman's shrill in the background (Mona???). He asked me to wish you a good holiday (his hand must have fallen off), and he is looking forward to your return (yeah, yeah); also to let you know he had found the painter (what?). Sorry he could not write, he is extremely busy (if he says so), but sends his love, or I think that was what he said, the line was crackling, and Mrs Willard across the road knocked the door for bridge, so had to hurry him.

Do not let Mattie bring the name of Bryant into disrepute. Hope you have running water, mirrors, and toilet facilities. Can the locals utter a word of English?

All my love
Your mother

For goodness sake.

I stuffed the Basildon Bond watermarked paper back into the now wet envelope, and stood as if to dress.

"Parent trouble?" Mattie asked, lifting up an outfit of pink and green.

I peered into the 'see all, say nothing' eyes. How much should I confide, that Jimmy had not bothered writing to me, enjoying the company of Mona instead? That Mother was a complete pain in the rear" (polite) "that I wanted this letter to be from Jules, whom she knew nothing about? That I wanted to get drunk?

"Don't worry, my Rhia, it will all turn out right."

"Will it?" I answered in a dejected voice.

Mattie twirled, her outfit fusing into a vibrant spectacle of colour.

"Tell your young" (twinkle in her eye) "grandmother," she fiddled with the mask resting on her forehead, ready to slip it over those knowing eyes.

"Mother."

"Say no more, but remember, tonight is ours – ours and the mountains'."

She slipped the mask into place. "Ready to dream?"

She gave me a look, the one I, as a child, shied away from.

7

Sipping butter tea, I gasp as the sweet honey liquid drizzles down my throat. Made from the many bee hives dotted around the village, this pure nectar was an essential part of Bhutan farming. Although I thought it delicious, in my downcast spirit I would have given anything for a 'proper' drink, but that was many miles and many weeks away. Running my tongue around the top of my cup I could see Mattie smiling at me. One of those 'ummm' smiles that bond close relatives together, loving and warm. In my mind there was no question to be answered, my grandmother was a woman of substance. Living her life, especially after the early death of my grandfather, by the rule of 'tomorrow never comes'. This woman never judged, never saw fit for others to judge her. She was the ideal prototype for old age. Looking at her now I followed her gaze toward my outfit and giggled. I had refused outright to wear the pink and green Kira she had chosen for me, selecting instead a colourful two piece with woven hooks like her own. I thought this suited me better, moulded my shape into a small semblance of the femininity I craved. Curves, in the right or wrong places speak for themselves; you either feel good, or you don't. I was in-between!

We had been seated at the head table (a privilege, our guide soon informed us), served with food of such flair to what Lotus cooked for us (small pastries resembling fountains or flowers, meat covered in a certain spice, corn baked in their outer leaves – shall I continue?). Mattie, I noticed, was eating heartily, clapping her hands in odd little spasms at the whirring dancers. I chose to eat little, much too absorbed in my own troubles to even think of food or dancers.

You have guessed. I had sunk into that pit of self-despair.

The moon had crept high in the sky, showering the tiny village in a pool of cream light, good job really otherwise we would have struggled to see what we were eating, even with the firelight and lanterns. From her position to my left, Mattie leant my way.

"Life," her breath tickled my ear, "is to be lived. Here, drink this. Think no more of what could be, or should be."

Taking the tumbler from her jewelled hand I gulped it down. It was vulgar, yet fantastic at the same time, igniting something deep within.

"What is that?" I shot the question like a fireball straight at my grandmother.

"Rice wine, my dear," Mattie giggled before she headed toward the ring of dancers.

"Wine?" I gasped for air. "These people make wine?"

"Where do you think you are, space?" her tone was mocking. I thought of my mother – chased the thought away. "It kicks like a mule."

The men at the table laughed, the women sniggered.

"What the heck," my voice rang out. I drank more, the taste biting my tongue in a series of sharp waves, yes, yes, yes, magnificent, addictive, compelling.

Before you glare at me, and shake your head... before you raise your eyebrows, and whisper to whoever is by your side, hear me out.

I should have upped sticks, gone to bed, shown I had matured, if only. Have your actions always been above the line of judgement? If only ...

—

The dance exploded in my mind, each movement an illicit suggestion. Throwing my tightly encased arms above my head all I could hear myself screeching was, "Go, Mattie, go."

My grandmother sped in and out of the crowd; spinning like a child's whizzing toy, her shadow chasing the one before her, blending colour and movement into one rhythmic pulsation. I waved her on, pulling my arms upwards, my feet pounding hard on the ground. Sparks from the raging bonfires sprang into the sky, frizzling away as they united with the cold night air. I was alive – dreaming, buzzing with the sensation of rice wine – down my throat, piercing my gut on its journey to my stomach; my aching arms collapsing at my side.

Hearing the sniggers of laughter, I twisted my head toward a group of young boys hovering under the trees. They were pointing at me, mumbling among themselves, using their hands to gesture, movements of undisciplined coarseness. I leant toward Lotus. Time to complain, cheeky kids. My mouth full of wine I felt that subconscious need to look downwards, gravity pulling my head to seek – what? Nestled in the sapphire blue toego (silk jacket), a bulge of white. Casting my eye further I saw three flowery buttons, starting to open in expectation of freedom.

I choke. "What? What the ..."

The rice wine found a route down the side of my chin; a gushing river from a mouth unable to stem its flight. The toego must have sagged due to my upward sweep of the arms, fallen lose at the heaviest part of my body. In the light of the moon, a raging fire, and coloured lanterns, there for all to see were my breasts, unrestrained, alabaster white, chilled by the night air.

Loud shouting blared in my ears, as out of nowhere a figure jumped to its feet. From where I sat in the huddled position of a cowered dog a silhouette was moving, gyrating in a sensual mass of movement. It had to be female, for I could make out curvaceous proportions casting their shadow across the table. This moving, swaying figure hypnotised my brain, with long ebony hair provocatively stroked by slender fingers, suggestively unwinding each strand. Arms began to reach out to the male sitting at the head of the table. All I could think was – cobra – alluring, beguiling and preparing itself to strike.

Moving in time to the drum beat the figure moved nearer the man; wilder, beckoning, enticing. As quick as the woman's movements all heads turned that way, away from me. I waited – bated breath – as ribbons slid from the hair, teasing themselves around the man's neck. Mercy – this was sexual (blow any fancy words) – erotic – of the like I had never seen before. Those not dancing were captivated, my capacious chest very much in the background. Without speaking the man placed his hands on the hypnotic hips. Began to gyrate in unison with the rhythmic throw of the dance. As he rose from his seat and passed the other men a cry went up – a battle cry?

Content to cease their talking the remaining men sought women, the dance their new desire. The circle was rotating; a creation of dark figures chanting to the increased banging of the drum. Whoever that figure was (and later I would be told it was Lotus, of all people), had defused my situation.

Clutching my jacket to me I stood (as best as I could) and quietly (or so I thought) left the table. My aim, to find my bed, lay down, let my rotating head find a mooring. The dance quivered, the beat of the drum pounded, I was gyrating in an alleyway, thrusting in a shabby room; the pleasure of abandonment and the warmth of togetherness holding me upwards. I stumbled, hit the ground with a resounding "blast" – into arms, strong and supportive.

I knew it was impossible to think, rice wine searing my throat and gullet, but I knew *he* would not let me down. The tightness of the arms – hands stroking my head – easing their way up my back – slipping to the intimate part of my stomach. No-one else had ever filled my fantasies with such pleasure. I applauded his timing. Jules, I wanted to fall into him, sink under the momentary pleasure he was offering.

Plunging toward the stiffened body I whimpered at the rush of heat scorching my lower limbs. I was not afraid, I had been here before. This burning need was lifeblood itself, tearing me away from an existence of deceit into the promise I had pleaded for. Buddha was answering my request. I drew my lover to me, waited for the taste of his kiss, the sigh of united release. I was lost in the sweetness of my lover's arms.

My lips grew impatient, my nose twitching at the distinct heady perfume, a flower, grown in the fields surrounding the village. I fumbled for his arms – thin and wrinkled. I moved to touch his face – lined and edgy – aged. Terror set in; this – person – was not Jules. I tried to scream – nothing – the paralysis of fear burying my protests.

Lashing the ground I tried to fight, hit out with clenched fists, bite with my teeth; we struggled, neither relenting, neither submitting. Hands became tighter, holding me down, the awkwardness of protruding bones strapping themselves across my legs, fingers began to peel away my modesty. The top that had been my undoing gaped even wider, my breasts escaping as I strained against the forceful hold. Foam formed in my mouth; a mixture of the rice wine and food, dribbling a drop at a time down the side of my lips. Nausea was overtaking me – I was drowning, delusion and passivity submerging as one.

What must I do? Give in, help the abuser to perform? In the distance I could hear the drums stirring up echoes in the night, bidding the dancers to thud the ground in a show of solidarity. I was without fluidity of mind, my limbs, once used in the guise of weapons, ignored my bidding. How could I fight?

I eased the contortions. my will already suspended, my attacker had the advantage. Cool hands were caressing me. From the dark cloister where I had shrunk I registered a continual rubbing of my back – up, down, round and round. An image loomed – one I did not know. The arm tightened around me in the form of a rubber band, encroaching my waist, ensnaring me, seducing me. The voice was willing me – let go – let go.

Jimmy galloped through my mind.

I murmured his name, rolled over and was violently sick.

—

Life itself has no greater friend or enemy than the mind in full blown creativity.

Someone was talking – an instruction – the voice to soothe all fears. Mattie.

"What were you thinking, child, slumped in the undergrowth like a wounded animal?"

Mattie had walked into my bedroom, shaking her head at someone hovering near the door.

"Oh," was all I could bring myself to say, still burrowing under the comfy pillow.

"Lotus." She inclined her head backwards towards a figure hovering at the door.

"The girl is worried you are troubled and embarrassed."

She was right there.

I raised my hand in what I considered to be an acknowledgement of thanks. It seemed Lotus thought it was go away.

"Better then?" my grandmother asked as the young woman tiptoed her way back to the kitchen.

I turned onto my back, still gripping the cotton blanket for all I was worth.

"A little," I croaked, my throat sore from the return of the fiery liquid.

"What do you remember?" Mattie patted my hand.

"Most of it, I think." The bed creaked as I threw myself onto my side again. "I will never be able to face these people. I must go home."

Mattie squawked out loud, in the vogue of an impatient magpie. Inconsiderate of her in the state I was in.

"You are quite the little actress, my darling. These people saw nothing."

"My breasts," I said. "The – the aftermath of the rape."

I really thought my grandmother was about to have an epileptic fit. Her body bounced up and down in convulsive tremors.

"Rape? Will you never leave your fantasy world? The person who found you was no abuser. She was the 'anchor mother', a friend and wise woman."

"Anchor mother," I muttered.

Mattie thumped herself down on the end of my bed (as I say, no consideration for my predicament).

"That's right, a woman of pure genius."

"Did she?" I was about to query.

"Yes, yes, rub your back and stomach, keep you still, loosen your clothes."

Somewhere in a dark recess of my mind I brought forward an old woman, had to be eighty years at least, her face a patchwork of deep-seated craters, emphasised by hair the colour of the moon on a cloudy night. She had no teeth, for her smile, if I recall correctly, revealed the hardened lines of well used gums. What held my imagination the most were her eyes, two black pebbles, bright and intuitive, staring into mine like the posters advertising alien films. I recall a house in the confusion of my struggling, the place my mind told me I would be held prisoner – a sex slave. It was there on a tiny stool someone proceeded to feed me – all I could remember was the spoon – the feeding.

'*You had just thrown up?*'

Your face, dear reader, has got to be a picture – one of disbelief, yet do not wince, for what I thought was food ran down my throat, I am sure, in the gush of a waterfall.

I can remember gagging, coughing, crying, spitting out the awful tasting poison. What I cannot run away from is how this galling substance slowed my heart racing, and stopped the nausea. I do not remember much after that.

"What did she do to me?" the loud cry bounced around the room.

Mattie gave me one of her 'know-it' smiles. "A potion to relieve your symptoms."

"Disgusting."

"No Rhia, a potion. I helped her."

"You were there?"

"I was. I help the anchor mother in my spare time."

"I was unaware."

"You are unaware of a lot, child. I have been taught to mix potions, cook herbs, help the young girls of the village, who are raised for marriage."

"You never told me."

"You never asked."

Mattie pulled herself up from the bed, slowly headed for the door.

"Lotus?" I threw at her.

"Ah, Lotus," she smiled. "The fire and the flame."

"I don't understand."

"No, too busy lashing out. Ooh, Rhia, what were you doing, lost in yourself you missed Lotus's seduction."

"Seduction?" This I must sit up for.

"Oh yes, our hostess seduced her husband. The wine and Buddha worked."

Light flooded my brain. "She took the heat away from me?"

"She did. A wonderful hostess."

"How – how did I get into my bed?"

"With great difficulty," she laughed. "We struggled."

By-passing the drama in my eyes, Mattie leaned toward the chair by my bed. She gently lifted the dark blue toego and skirt, folded them neatly and slid them across her arm. "I promised to return our outfits and collect new for tonight."

"I am not going," I snapped.

A mask fell over Mattie's face. "You most certainly are. How could you think otherwise, your hostess would be insulted."

"But, *Mattie*," long pronunciation on her name. "I will be the joke of the party."

Mattie stood, in what, to this day, I would call a 'livid temper'. I had never seen her like this, not with me.

"Why, child, is everything about you?" (Heard that in another place, another era).

Stunned at this outburst, I apologised (yeah, yeah, yeah. *I* apologised).

"Think, Rhia, about what you were told last night. Those that demand are deceivers; those who wait are lovers. Your problem, my child is in your mind. Your heart has not stumbled across the truth."

This worried me, reader, had I ranted in my hallucination? No time to discover.

Mattie slammed the door, shaking the frail wooden frame.

8

The storm came around midnight, rumbling and clattering over the mountain tops. Rain hurtled from the high peaks, streamed down the rocks, gushing dirt over everything; lashing the small ravines, fields, gardens, herb patches, and flower beds on its way to its final destination. From my hide-out under my bed I could hear the men of the village running here and there, tethering the horses and locking sheep sheds tighter. The women battened the windows and doors with whatever they could find in their endeavour to avoid flooding. Barrels were rolled, kicked, pushed into place under eaves to collect extra water splashing from the dipping roofs. Sand bags were everywhere, piled high in the previous days, and in anticipation of an early monsoon.

I was scared. I had heard thunder before, it was part of English summer weather, yet, I have to admit, nothing like this. It was treble the noise back home, each bang rumbling over and over, lightning making this midnight hour as day. Mattie, who could not stay mad at me for long, lay at my side soothing her granddaughter's tormented soul, and boy, did I need soothing. I thought of the rice wine, its effect would be gratefully received at the moment. I mentioned this to Mattie, who obstinately refused to leave her hidey hole. Spoilsport. When I think how I had gone, at her request, to the week-long parties in our honour, agreeing grape juice to be the only sweet liquid to pass my lips.

The thunder clapped, resounding on the mountains that surrounded us; lightning still whipped the sky in blatant abuse – you could feel the tension. I jumped at every bang, Mattie squeezed me tighter, Lotus, moving in the kitchen as if nothing untoward was happening, sang at the top of her voice. I imagined Jules, held tight to his image; emotions had been stirred. Truth is, no letter had found me, from him, or Jimmy. I was beginning to wonder if one had found the other. Yes, I know what Mother had put in her letter, and yes, I know she enjoys rubbing my nose in the gossip, but no, 'Hello' or, 'Guess who I have discovered', from my friend at least meant he was still digging. With each clap that shook my body I promised myself upon arriving home I would visit Alexander (his return from Paris, umm, would be secure) and make discreet inquiries. A small tattoo would suffice.

Back to the thunderstorm. It went on crashing over us. It would not be hard for an outsider, such as myself, to deduce Buddha was angry with me, and he could see no other way than to wash the village away. Had the God of those serene monks unearthed my deceit, considered my family and friend were on the end of a raw deal, dislike the way I was pressing him to help me? Knew I should have pleaded for Lotus alone? Hour after hour the fear built up until I thought I would burst. Then, just as I was about to scream, "Get it over," Buddha decided to move the monster to the west. Letting go of my arm Mattie left the bedroom, wafting out the candle in her wake. Wriggling out from underneath the bed I grabbed the first thing to hand (which happened to be my trekking weatherproof), threw it over my flannel pyjamas (I know – Mother's idea. Cold nights, funny bugs, you name it), and fumbled my way across the cold flags.

—

Mattie and Lotus were crouched in front of the fire, whispering and – cheek – drinking rice wine. Shuffling to sit on the spare stool Lotus placed for me, I stretched my cold toes.

My grandmother took up a bottle that had been balancing in between her feet. "Drink?"

I shook my head. "Why should I, you refused to get any earlier."

Mattie made a noise akin to a snort. "Oh, Rhia, you are such a child, you would have been sick."

I sniffed. Lotus had been so kind to me, and I had no reason to be churlish. I had eventually found the courage to thank Lotus for her quick forethought on that dreadful night. She took my hand and pressed it to her forehead; a debt returned.

Mattie's eyes were glinting. Lotus was grinning. I had no idea why, for three weeks had passed since that night, and seduction or not, Lotus's husband was still going ahead with the wedding. The young girl, whom I had met, was no more than a schoolgirl passing into womanhood, *and* would be living in this house.

"Let's have a small celebration," Mattie raised her glass.

"Why?" I was mad.

Mattie paused. "Lotus is having a baby."

"A baby?" My face contorted. "Are you sure?"

"Ninety-nine per cent," Mattie giggled.

"How, where, when?"

"The night you were drunk," Mattie almost shouted.

Selected images of those bushes, swaying hips, enticing arms.

Lotus interrupted our giggling. "Husband not know."

"Why?" I exploded. "No need for that damn wedding now."

Mattie downed her drink. Grasping my shoulders, she twisted my body until I could see nothing but her beaming face. "It must be a secret. Lotus cannot tell him until she is three months gone. She has been there before, and lost. This time she must be sure."

"But –" I began.

Mattie shook me hard. "This time no 'buts', Rhia, no 'whys', and definitely no self-indulgence."

I was hurt, who was better at keeping secrets? I sank within myself.

Mattie chuckled. "I say, thank God for the rain. Early it may be, yet the cooler weather will aid Lotus and her cause."

"Right," was all I could find to add, raised the tumbler and drank.

—

The day before our departure *that* wedding took place.

'Hustle and bustle' will cover my general oversight.

Starting with the village men carrying a large carpet into the square to cover an area of ground where the bride and groom were to stand, the erection of a canopy covered in flowers of every scent and colour, to placing chairs in a curve for the elders to sit upon. Tables positioned around the village centre, covered in old tapestry cloths (used only for weddings, births, and official funerals), displaying food and drink of every flavour. Each door displayed a white garland, while the wedding night tent, hidden beyond the trees, was decked with bells and more garlands. The area smelt and looked wonderful.

"Fit for a King and Queen," Mattie kept saying, and if the rain eased for an hour or two, this wedding would be positively regal.

None of this hectic activity made me feel any sweeter toward the child bride.

I could not see Lotus's viewpoint in allowing this nonsense to take place. In all respect to her, she was pregnant, the man's number one wife. They, according to our hostess were very much in love, so can anyone tell me why, why, why?

'Tradition,' I hear. Well, let me say one thing.

"Sod it. Who cares about laws and traditions? I don't."

The rain had decided to slow as dawn appeared, and now, as the hour approached, nothing but a trickle. Mattie and I selected our outfits, mainly to please Lotus, *and* to prove to the grinning elders that as foreigners we accepted their customs (think again). We had spent the morning, along with Lotus, gathering flowers and herbs to display in our hair, and hold as a bouquet. At times, as we gathered, I could not help noticing how close my grandmother and Lotus had become. Anyone would think she (Lotus) was her granddaughter, not me. Was I jealous? Well, if one must split hairs – yes. Lotus's Mother had died when she was twelve years old, and the young girl had been reared by the anchor mother to be an elder's bride. I knew she had no other relatives, and I suppose Mattie filled that gap, but in the days prior to the wedding Mattie had become more Lotus's grandmother, less mine. *'Be kind,'* you might say. *'The woman has problems.'*

So what? Haven't we all?

You may think I am selfish – go ahead – I need a shoulder to lean on – JULES. Finally the hour came to dress. Slipping off my dressing gown I examined the kingfisher blue skirt with its darker blue silk top.

Problem. The top had straps, no sleeves, no back even. It was tied round the neck in halter style. Can you imagine my horror? My tattoos on show.

I stomped my foot on the ground with a mighty thud.

Mattie, who had already washed, dressed and adorned herself with the traditional white garland, came rushing into the bedroom. There I sat, top clutched in my hand.

"Whatever is the matter?" Anxiety was prevalent.

"This," I cried, holding the top up in temper.

"It is a top, Rhia," she advised, in her wisdom.

"Yes, but –"

"Here we go again," Mattie sighed. "Ducking and diving."

It was one of those moments when your inner self hears the fast intake of breath before it actually releases itself. Looking down – my 'art' – blatant to my grandmother's eyes.

"Phew," was my grandmother's immediate reaction. "what is this?" I shrank back into myself, in the manner of a wounded dog. "I say your artist is so-o clever, a master of his craft. The story he spins is old though, a lover, a friend; emotion between you all, and so on. One genius of the shadow."

My hands grew clammy as she brushed her gold rings over the expanse of my back. "The anchor mother was right, your heart has taken a different path." She circled the walnut tree. "This tree – ingenious," ceasing her brushing and poking. "Who knows?"

I snatched the dressing gown from the floor. "Only you, and of course, that anchor mother."

The voice was accusing. "You did not say."

"Why should I?"

"Honesty." Her tone was harsh.

Guilt gripped my heart. "Sorry."

Mattie lifted the top from my grasp, walked into the next room, spoke to Lotus, returned with a long sleeved silk shirt, which I hastily put on.

"Tell me, child, have I read your 'art' correctly?"

I gave a small inclination of my head. "Apart from the tree bit. That was silly as far as I am concerned, a moment's ridiculousness from a friend who cannot be bothered to write to me."

"Ahhh." Mattie let her hands drop to her side. "I will say nothing. Who am I to incur further upset on your socialite Mother? Just one question. Whose heart are you breaking?"

I had heard it all now. "No-one."

"No?"

She kissed my forehead, and made her departure. I continued dressing.

—

The bride and groom stood on the square carpet. To their right was the anchor mother; to their left, and a step behind her husband, Lotus in full traditional dress. The child bride, as I shall call her, was standing slightly in front of her, fidgeting, whereas Lotus was calm, composed to the point of being numb. I wished, at that moment, I could stop proceedings and ask, 'What is it with the upbringing of these females; isn't this the point where that freedom my grandmother and Jimmy bangs on about steps in? Can we discuss it?' Jimmy, get out of my head! Then, I think of earlier in the day, one of my trips back to the house from carrying food. Lotus was laughing, hugging Mattie in what can only be called a suffocating bear hug.

"Great news," Mattie exploded. "Lallah" (the child bride) "she has to live with her new husband for six months before the union is registered."

"So – how come?"

Mattie twirled me round. "Lotus went to the anchor mother, she in turn went to the religious tribal leader. He saw fit to halt the unification."

"Why are they going ahead with the wedding, then?"

Okay, so call me awkward.

Mattie gasped impatiently. "Face, Rhia – face."

"Sod face, stop it now."

Mattie frowned. "This will all turn out for the best." Now, many readers might presume me to have no idea of tradition, and probably they are right, but can someone, anyone, explain the 'night tent,' if time was on Lotus's side? Picking up on my train of thought, Mattie quietly took me aside. "Nothing can happen tonight, as unification has been halted."

"Then why the show?" I sounded exasperated.

"Face – all face."

I was sick of hearing that word; besides, my grandmother was becoming every inch the Bhutan elder. Where was the 'co-ool' extrovert I had started this journey with? I suddenly had a vision of my grandmother living here. One thought to completely toss away.

"Law, tradition." She took hold of Lotus's hand. "We must conform."

I was amazed. My grandmother had never – and I repeat, *never* conformed. Anyway, there I stood, dressed in what I can best describe as the heaviest outfit ever, waiting for a wedding I thought unfair and ridiculous. Hot, perspiring like a fountain, my flesh covered to the neck. Judge me the most suffocated, miserable, moody guest in the history of weddings. Afterwards, I will head for the shelter of the old cypress tree, pray I keep cool, and watch my newly found friend and hostess deceive everyone over the child she is carrying, where is freedom in that? The pen hesitates. I need to re-group my thoughts. The wedding began – lots of talking, lots of solemnity, the exchanging of white scarves, and the joint sipping from the customary cup. At the end, clapping greeted the final words from the elder. Out the corner of my eye I could see Lotus allow a tiny upturn movement to pass over her lips. Wrong or right this was her blessing toward years of tradition. Laying a hand on her stomach the young woman eased forward, led the child bride to the table to collect her celebratory drink. There was no acrimony on her face, as the women of the west would have worn in similar circumstances, just a warm knowing – a contentment.

The party, as all things in this remote part of the world, lasted long into the night. Horns and hand bells rang out their congratulatory message. We danced, sang (Mattie and I hummed), showering the couple with flower petals. Rice wine constantly swished in the tumbler in my hand, I constantly tipped it into one bush or the other, Mother's odd saying of 'Once bitten, twice shy,' ringing in my ears. Lotus sat with Mattie and me until a signal from the anchor mother brought her to her feet. The whole village began to clap, louder than during the wedding. Our hostess moved forward, again nodded her head in consent for those who had been dancing to pave the way for the couple to retire to the flower strewn night tent.

As they disappeared through the flap Lotus was nowhere to be seen. It did not take Mattie and me long to find her in the anchor mother's house, at the same hearth I had sat on the night of my disorder. Mattie hurried to Lotus's side as the young woman's sobs racked the tiny kitchen. The anchor mother gave her honey tea, and pronounced all would be fine. FINE.

I could show them fine, that husband and me, in a boxing ring (where do my ideas come from) belting out insults for all I was worth.

I closed in on the crying figure. "If it is any help, Lotus, I have a friend, a best friend." Where is my mouth going, what has Jimmy got to do with this? "His philosophy on life is cynical to the point of painful, yet he argues love seen as a possession is soul destroying. You are not a possession in your husband's life, remember that." Why are you glaring at me? I am helping, is it my fault Jimmy is full of this kind of mumbo jumbo? The two older women flapped their hands my way, whispering to the sobbing girl in a low, melodious monotone. Me? Dismissed as the unruly child in the classroom. I moved to the window. On the outskirts of the village our guide and those chirpy boys were readying the pack-horses for our leaving, using whatever means they could to keep the spirited animals still. My eyes fell on the misty mountains. I would take the heart of this village home with me; the awareness my trek to Taktsang... had given me the spiritual freedom of the monks, the small offering of Lotus's flowers to Buddha.

As you know, I had come to Bhutan dogged by my mother's snobbery, full of spiteful thoughts toward my friend; a yearning for my lover. Nothing had changed, yet the outpouring of a young woman's thoughts had touched a place inside me, pleaded with me to re-evaluate the pact between Jimmy and myself.

My friend and I had vowed to find freedom, to discover its different meanings, and in what context it applied to us. I know now. Oh yes, I must follow the path that leads me to my desire. Time for fantasy to enter the realm of reality.

—

I did not hear Mattie creep to my side. "We all run from our demons. A long day, and an even longer night, don't you think?"

There was no smile, unusual for my grandmother. "I have been thinking, Rhia. I am not coming home."

I reeled as a child smacked, spouted the first thought. "Mattie, have you lost your senses?"

Mattie flinched – too late – re-reel.

"What about me?" I cried. "I will have to face the wrath of my parents on my own."

229

She flipped the grey strands of hair that persisted in escaping the scraped back bun. "What about you, Rhia? Has this holiday taught you nothing?"

"Of course, I know *my* mind."

"Do you?"

"Yes, you wait and see."

Mattie exhaled, casting an eye toward the girl by the fire. "You may choose the wrong path."

"Ah, no, my mind is made up, I have worked that seven letter word out, wait and see."

Her mouth showed a slow, deliberate smile. "You are very keen on the, 'wait and see', not so forthright on, 'I may be wrong'."

How ridiculous. "Father is correct. You are selfish."

I couldn't believe it.

Mattie shifted her stance. "Is that what you think?"

"Yes, no, yes. I don't know," I wailed.

Mattie headed back to the fireplace, took up the vacant stool next to Lotus. Help me.

Is it possible you shook your head? I hated myself. Hated my egotistical tongue.

I crept to her side, knelt. "Mattie please ignore me. I didn't mean it."

Her breath came quickly. "Yes, you did, but my mind is made up. Lotus needs me, and besides, I have watched you these past months. Something has got to change. Go home, sort out your life. Take care of that friend of yours (forget him at this moment), keep clear of the wrong path (riddles again). I *will* come to the airport with you, phone your father, sort the authorities. I have money, that can speak volumes."

"I am your granddaughter," I urged her, no love lost for the woman at her side. Trust me, if she had not been in the condition she was ...

"True, and you have family. Lotus needs me."

Lotus, Lotus, I am sick of hearing the name. "Please, Mattie, please." I was the next best thing to a raging bull.

"Go home. You are your own worst enemy."

The anchor mother made her way to where I was kneeling, her outstretched arms finding me, a soft humming I found irritating and intrusive clashing in my head.

Here, I have to confess I was rude, pushing her away from me, the woman collapsing in a heap on the floor.

"Rhia!" My grandmother let out a squeal. "Go. Now."

I rose, vindictive cannot quite relay how I felt. "Stay, let Lotus take my place. Enjoy your freedom, what do I care? It is a word, do you hear? A stupid, selfish word."

Tears streaming down my face, I ran into the night air.

9

Have you ever noticed that going home is by far quicker than the journey out? As a child, my mother always commented on this fact, much to the annoyance of my inexperienced brain. Funny really, to this day I cannot fathom out why children will not admit to a higher knowledge, their Mother already having travelled down the road of disbelief. Nepal airport was crowded (still the holiday season), bodies pushing to and fro, pressing close to us in their impatience to slip through the cordon of officials, reach what they thought would be the cooler air outside (fools). Leaving our guide to tether and water the horses, Mattie and I stepped into the chaos. Throughout the journey from the village we had not spoken a word, not one comment over the clattering cymbals and wooden sticks struck with unnerving ferocity on my departure. I had waited patiently for Mattie to joke over the bamboo pipe that carried liquor for my father, or the beautiful hand woven basket for Mother; even over the miniature key-ring of Buddha, whose eyes I had said would keep Jimmy under surveillance at all times, no comment passed her ruby lips.

Throwing ourselves down onto a seat I thought back to my leaving. To Lotus and my parting handshake. *'Handshake?'* you query. No way was I going to hug her. She had stolen my grandmother. I was curt and short, fitting I told myself for a thief. She had waved 'goodbye' in a pleasant enough way, assuring me Mattie would be taken care of. Traitor!

"Do not fret," Mattie patted my hand.

"Please come home with me," I begged.

My grandmother wiped away the tears that begun to fill my eyes.

"No crying, Rhia. Lotus needs me."

"I need you."

Her hand dropped as she looked around, at last settling on the phone booth. I write in the singular because that was it: one phone in this crowded airport that connected us to the outside world.

"What you need, Rhia, is the vision to see what you will lose if you are not careful. You are always the victim of fate, never the one who controls it. Can you not see what is staring at you?"

"Please Mattie, spare me." *'Rude,'* you may say.

Suppose it is. And? "That means you are still that child, the one who always wanted her own way, the one who expected to get it." Unable to take my eyes from her rigid back, I watched as she headed for the phone, and dialled, tapping her foot as she waited for the 'pick-up' answer. Roller-coaster emotions that filed my 'so-oo coo-ol' grandmother under the heading of 'nutty'. Mattie's grey curls shook violently as she nodded in mockery at the voice on the other end of the phone. Loud speaker: **"Boarding for London, fifteen minutes."** Mattie slammed the phone onto its old fashioned hook, presumably cutting my ranting father's fast flow, made her way to my side. Loud speaker: **"Passengers for London, board now."** Picking up my hand luggage, we fought our way to the door. Clasping me to her, she stammered, "Write to me, tell me about the wonderful awakening you will have."

Striding toward the tarmac in a haze of salt laden mist I mumbled, "The only awakening for me, Mattie, will be two raving parents in twelve hours from now."

—

Whenever my spirits are low the blasted weather goes one better. Lashing rain pounded crashing waves into the chalky white cliffs of Dover, creating a spray to soar upwards before falling at rapid speed. This naturalistic movement, I can honestly write, was in tune with my own spirit – one moment soaring high to be home, the next 'down in my boots' at the thought of my parents.

The intercom was spluttering, crackling as the plane began to drop. **"Fasten your safety belt prior to landing, and collect all hand luggage as you depart."** Hand luggage. It was not hand luggage I should be taking from this can of sardines, it should be my grandmother. All around me families were chatting and joking, exchanging holiday snaps and reports. The remains of the free meal provided were quickly being cleared away by the stewardess, while a steward began the final preparations to help us leave the plane in orderly fashion. By now, Mattie would have phoned everyone, the British Embassy, the travel agent – who knows, even the Office of Fair Trading. These people would be only too happy to be of assistance, she was spending more money. *'Cynical,'* you observe. The last sighting of Mattie flashes before me; a slight wet eye, kisses blown in that over the top dramatic expression of hers, doing anything she thought would calm me down, anything but get her elegant painted toe nails up the mobile steps.

The plane dips, glides along the runway, judders to a halt. Out of a steamed up window row upon row of faces swim before me. She would be back in her beloved village by now, taking tea with Lotus, visiting that famous anchor mother.

My head was bursting, I would give anything to scream out loud.

The child across the gangway wafts his arms for my attention, shouts in the high-pitched screech of a three year old.

I wish I could join in.

—

"It's true then. No Mattie?"

The voice shook me from my composure.

"What do you think? She rang. What is their excuse for not coming?"

The lean body bristled. "Busy. It is a Friday after all."

He picked up on my look, added, "The bank, bridge, that kind of thing."

"Of course, how silly of me, after all I am just the daughter."

My friend frowned. "No need for that."

"Oh dear, it was wrong of me to want what most children get, emerge from a plane to be greeted by a parent."

"A mood, I detect." The curled lips smirked. Sorry about this, reader, but I would be covering up if I did not tell you exactly what I thought, in chronological order. 'Bog off – damn you – sad sod.'

My mother would faint at what she calls 'lower class language'.

234

Jimmy tracked down a porter, whistled him to be correct, asked in his new commanding tone to load my suitcases onto a trolley, and steer us through the crowds to the car park. The young boy, in his smart dark grey uniform, gave a small salute (manners or messing?), led us to the entrance, and proceeded to flip open a huge umbrella. Covering our heads, as best as he could, the poor boy pulled the trolley across the inlet road to the car park. Jimmy, trying his best to keep dry, and help with the trolley, came to a halt against a shining new car (a Mini) with the registration 'JIM ME1'.

Impressed? Personalised number as well. I simply said, "Job going well?"

"Not bad," he answered as he unlocked the door for me, stacked the cases in the boot, and shook any surplus rain from his suit.

Tipping the young boy, a substantial amount I would say by the grin on the receiver's face, he sat in the seat beside me. Turning the engine key, he let it run for warmth, revved it, then released his foot gently from the accelerator, and reversed into the lane that proclaimed, 'Way Out'. I fiddled with my fingers, my damp hair, the latest up to date radio, anything to hand. We have not seen each other for three months, parted in what is known as acrimonious circumstances; friends, but not friends. Something must be said to get us back on track. *'The painter,'* you remind me. Stupid or what? "You did not write," I moan.

"No, I did not." He fiddled with the clutch. "Nothing to say. I have been very busy."

"Like my parents."

His head shot round, the dark eyes solemn.

"Try and be more sensitive, Rhia. Not like your usual 'I don't care' attitude when you get home. Your father is appalled over Mattie, worried sick I would say. Your mother, quite frankly, in a panic. They can do without your flippant questions and injurious opinions." Now, let's get this straight. My parents' anger over Mattie's impetuous behaviour I could understand. Laid squarely on my shoulders? No, no, no. My grandmother, as you can gather, has a mind of her own. I am not, if my parents and friend do not realise it, her keeper. Father must know his Mother is no roll-over when it comes to walking the 'good parent' tightrope.

Jimmy accelerated harder, revving the small car to full capacity, slipping into the stream of traffic on the motorway. He began to hum the French anthem.

What was he doing, panic breeds nonsense. "Paris," I said. "Was it good?"

Jimmy overtook a lorry (it is raining my friend, bucketing down), clamped the third gear into place, and shot past two more cars in the style of a rocket speeding into space. Clasping the steering wheel he nodded, "Great, apart from that damn elusive painter."

At last, an answer. Mother, not for the first time, had been wrong; always the same, too busy with her social life to listen properly. I fingered the note, rammed at the last moment into my coat pocket, thanking providence all could be pronounced normal.

"Oh, I am sorry." (Let's play the game.)

"What is queer," Jimmy overrode my cynicism, broke off to rudely signal to the driver of a car that had cut in front of him, "this so-called master painter has dissolved into thin air, where he has gone – your guess would be as good as mine."

If only my friend knew.

Jimmy braked, swinging to miss the bumper of a Mercedes Benz.

"His problem," he continued, "I believe, is he does not want the world to recognise him."

I quickly turned my face to look out of the window, follow the shafts of rain sleeking their way across the glass, and down to the ground.

He slowed slightly, enabling me to ease my white knuckles from around the door handle, before swerving left and right at 60mph.

I could not help but wonder if work or Mona was Jimmy's main concern, for unlike now, my friend had always shown such tactical observation of the road.

With every swipe of a window blade the name Mona drummed in my brain. '*Mona, Mona, Mona.*' I took a deep breath. "How is Mona?"

A look of surprise filtered across his face, creasing the corners of his mouth, and his eye sockets. "Yeah, fantastic."

He said no more, and I asked no more. For the first time since I had known Jimmy I considered him to have betrayed me, kept me in the dark, said NOTHING! You splutter in amazement.

I gently remind you my circumstances are different.

That sickening question, '*Why?*' falls from your mouth.

I default in answering, just think of '*that*' picture.

'*Conscience, conscience,*' you accuse. Is it impossible to make you understand that my circumstances are different? I ease my head onto the black padded headrest, close my eyes against the berating rain. Jimmy slowed down, turned the radio on, and was listening intently to an American interviewer on the subject of art (what else!). Not for one moment did the words or voice penetrate my weary mind, until Jimmy, shrieking at the top of his voice, hurtled me back into life with a bang. My friend was laughing, laughing as I had never seen him laugh for a long time. "My dear girl." His gaze was intense. "Life is a peach!"

—

Was it so impossible for Jimmy to deposit me at my flat? Truth? No. Fact? Yes.

His argument – I must see my parents. My counter re-action – it was not him who was in for a showdown. No avail, here we were, the speedy Mini, my friend and me, outside my parents' house.

I stepped from the car, repeating over and over again, "Not to worry." Silly really, for I must know the imminent bomb would drop the moment I stepped through the door. Although the rain had eased a little, Jimmy ran from boot to threshold in the guise of one ducking a soaking; still wearing the gaping grin of the cat who fell from the tree and landed in the bowl of milk. Blowing the raindrops from my eyes I rang the bell, waited a good five minutes, (surely my mother, who was always peering behind the smart new blinds, had seen our arrival), until the door swung open and I faced my parents' glare. Mother, resplendent in her smart navy two piece, glowered. My father, who I must admit reminded me of the boys I had just left behind – no shoes, trakkie bottoms, roughed up hair – also glared. I managed to stop myself from spluttering out, which way would they like me to stand for the mugshot? Ummm, a bit rude I suppose.

Keeping my voice as light as possible, I sauntered past them both with, "Hello, you two."

Jimmy snorted.

"Let us go in," Mother snapped. "As you can see, your father has been gardening."

Never one to own up that her spouse just wanted to slob around, she raised her hand in greeting to the family across the road, calling, "My daughter ... home from the Himalayas ... tiring journey," and quickly closed the door.

Taking hold of my arm she hurried me into the kitchen, sat me firmly on a chair, no chance for me to glance over my shoulder for my friend, no chance to give her a hug (a dream, I know), or dive into a monologue of my activities these past three months. My parents were in no mood to be haggled with.

"What was your grandmother thinking?" my father ploughed in. "How totally irresponsible can a human being be? She is out there, age seventy plus, and we, her family, are here. Stupid, stupid woman."

Believe me, I felt his pain.

"Do not worry." I gestured in the best light-hearted manner I could muster. "She is well cared for and happy, with many friends."

Looks ... kill. Get the picture?

"Cared for?" he exploded. "Friends? She needs to be here, **here,** do you hear me? Where someone can keep an eye on her."

My father began to march the kitchen, throw his arms in the air, thump a folded fist down onto the table; Mother shadowed his actions, albeit a tad slower and out of time. Together they resembled that pantomime comedy duo I associated them with.

Jimmy filled the kettle with water. Tea, the British cure for all ailments.

The next words to fall from my mouth rumbled round the kitchen in a copycat version of the thunder that had bounced around the Himalayan mountain range.

"Mattie may stop longer than three months. She has taken Lotus and her unborn child under her wing."

I had reneged on my promise not to say anything, to save my own skin. Do not wish to hear your disgust. Three bodies sank onto three chairs, three heads turned my way, three sets of eyes bored into me. (Boring, repetitive.) I counted the clock hands as they ticked into memory, waited for the explosion. I silently implored Jimmy for help. Reader, I am ashamed to admit there was more chance of me boarding a plane whence I had come than my friend being my champion. He said nothing. Sat there, hands folded on his chest, frowning (it seemed) from a very great height, 'I told you so,' stamped upon his features.

It could not be any plainer if he had been a parcel passed over the post office counter. Oh, for an object in my grip. My father raised himself up to the pinnacle of five foot nine, set himself in my direction and barked, "Unborn child and its Mother – y*ou* are as stupid as your grandmother." (That hurt). "The woman needs control. She is a menace. Every penny she owns will be squandered." Ah, the truth seed. That green, brown and pink paper. In other words, the universal corruption – money! My demeanour changed: fidgety, upset, livid – choose. I eyed my adversaries, my parents deep in conversation, Jimmy resuming his tea duty. Mother was the first to speak.

"I suppose it is not fair to blame Rhia, it is not her fault" (come again?) "for we are well aware your grandmother has a mind of her own. It has always been her problem. The woman has never toed the conventional line."

Cups clanged onto a tray, a biscuit canister scraped along the tiled worktop.

Jimmy is warning me.

Confirmation: my parents are tyrants, old fashioned, whimpering monocrats.

Mattie should be condemned to sit and knit, play the nineteenth century elder, swaddled to the ears in black satin and a lacy bonnet.

Were they really that blind not to see that if my grandmother's spirit was kept under a barrage of conventional red tape she would wither?

Jimmy, forget the warning.

"Stop there, both of you. Can you not see your view on Mattie is wrong, way off the mark? She is not your ordinary sit at home female, she is a wise woman, a joy to be around. In my estimation it is Lotus who will gain, and us? We must hope one day she will return."

Three heads turn my way, turn back to look at each other. Mattie, in her absence had been pronounced guilty, of what? Falling from the social ladder?

The *four* of us drink tea.

10

What is going on in my brain?

You would probably file it under 'world summit.'

I had resisted the temptation to visit Alexander, for now, made excuses to myself i.e.: 'Had he moved?' 'Do I really need another 'art' masterpiece played out across my body?'

But just when you think you are going nowhere, those sliding doors that manipulate life select a path, order you to sit up and take notice.

In the last six months not one word relating to my grandmother or Bhutan had passed my parents' lips. I would say this was mainly down to me not giving an inch on the mudslinging scenario. At one point I had thought my father would take time from work, and journey to the country himself; demand my grandmother accompany him home.

Anyway, that was not going to happen, he had no spare time. The bank was expanding to such an extent, that extra staff were needed, and even if I had resisted – well, we will not go there. Simple answer: I needed money. Mattie's kind nest egg was being saved for a rainy day, and my parents refused to keep giving me handouts – miserable.

To extract myself from their bad books, I walked on hot coals; my definition of monotonous hours.

Mother thought it her duty to slip into Mattie's shoes, whizzing through the flat with a duster every other day, straightening my clothes, continually moaning that my long sleeved, high necked tops gave her nightmares of bin dusters. She rubbed and cleaned the bathroom until it gleamed. I suggested a cleaner, but she derided me further, accusing her inconsiderate daughter of showing her up.

Jimmy ... oh boy, what can I say about him? We had lapsed into an apology for our former friendship. No arguments, no opinions, no bursting into that harmonious laughter we were so good at – something was missing. Saturday nights, when he was home from Paris, were a whirl of theatres, meals (no trust in my cooking since the 'Bolognese' incident), cinema, and clubs; the close harmony between best friends had vanished. In fact, I could categorically state that absolutely all things my friend and I once got up to had disappeared. Jimmy was a different human being, and *I* missed the fun.

Am I the only person, friend, comrade of old, to blame MONA?

One Saturday morning, six months after my return from Bhutan, Mother arrived at the flat in a flurry of bemusement, waving a white envelope in my face. "Mattie has written to you via our address," she gasped in irritation. "Silly woman. Here."

I tore the sticky gum, and withdrew the sheets of paper.

My Dear Rhia,

I am praying all is well with you, and that your parents have come to their senses. I have not forsaken them, how can you leave children?

I am in good health, so happy. Lotus expands daily. Her husband cried when she told him. The child bride has gone home to her Mother. She is a notable girl in the eyes of the elders, so when the marriage is annulled she can be brought to another union.

Writing via your mother and father's house shows them I have not fallen off the planet, and may inspire them to write. I wish they could accept my mad-hatter ways.

How is Jimmy? The dark horse (I tittered at that: Mother grimaced). Hope he is not pining too much. (What does she mean? Mona?)

The weather here is ...

There unfolded each individual day's weather since I had left, the daily chores of the women, her growing friendship with the mysterious anchor mother, and the possibility of prolonging her stay.

"Is that it?" my mother snapped.

"It is," was my curt reply.

"Glad I kept it from your father."

"Why?"

"The hurt. A mother possessed."

Cocking her beautifully made-up eyes in all directions she bumped herself down onto the sofa; not before removing my large ironing pile from the seat. She sat in her usual style, back upright, legs together, head erect. I just wanted her to flop, body sprawled and legs apart, in the manner of her daughter.

She appeared awkward, eyes attempting to entice me on another white envelope balancing precariously on the sofa arm.

"Post?" she inquired, gazing intently at the American postmark. Now, before you utter one word – Yes, it came directly before Mother's arrival, and yes, I knew its content, which for the sake of my story I will divulge here and now.

Rhia (men always forgot the 'dear')

At last I have found time to write to you, found your address out from your artist. (Alexander, no doubt). Moving around is exhausting. Would you believe neither I nor anyone in the commune could find the address you sent me? (By that he means my whereabouts in the Himalayas.)

The painting ark I have set up is going great, including an invitation to your artist (*knew it*). Funds are low, wished I had a rich daddy like you (*good sense of humour*). Hope to see you soon.

When we meet nothing will have changed, apart from my name. (Again?) I am now known as Patrice. Tell no-one. There are those who misunderstand me. (*Can he mean Jimmy?*) They cannot see my desire to serve the cause. (Art?)

Think, we could carry on where we left off. Come to me.

Patrice ♥

More questions than answers.

I snatched it from its resting place and threw it into the bedroom.

"Circular, you know. Advertisement for this and that."

I swear Mother's head swivelled 90 degrees.

I clicked the gas fire button from high to low although my body trembled: anything to throw Mother off the scent.

The Dior face changed from concerned to aggravated. "Strange writing for a circular, more personal, I would say."

She tossed her nose up into the air, then continued, "Are you planning to visit America?"

My eyes expanded. Am I so readable?

"Where do you get your notions from? Me? America? Why?"

My mother shrugged. "I don't know. Another jaunt for yourself and Jimmy?"

I tried to laugh. "Jimmy? My dear Mother, he is far too busy."

The immaculate form shifted, actually stood to leave.

"Are you not still seeking this freedom thing? Silly pair, everyone knows real freedom is inside ourselves." The mask slipped, Mother's face held pain, before lifting once more into her usual pretentious glare.

I frowned. "What a ridiculous thought," my voice rose to a pitch. Had not Mattie expressed the same idiom?

Mother moved to the door. "I am going, your mood is sour. One request. Please do not visit America."

The door opened, Mother disappeared.

I felt deflated. Visit America? You bet, Mother, try and stop me.

The dark threatening clouds of winter spread across the lounge. Soon the festive season would be here for another year, and the ground would be sodden, or else crisp and hard from the white fingers of frost. Kurt/Jules/Patrice – the assemblage of names invaded my mind; my lover was on the run, in hiding until his innocence was proven. I must be with him, help him to show Jimmy and the rest who were hunting him down like the fox in the New Year hunt, that guilt lies with those already caught.

Quickly I bent forward, flicked the switch of the fire to maximum.

—

Night was gathering, the town hall clock struck six thirty. I had sat toasting my toes by the fire for the best part of six hours, moving only for pop and cake mid-afternoon, and of course the call of nature. I was going nowhere, with no-one, and the sulkiness I had felt earlier in the day had settled upon me big-time. Hearing the phone ring, I chose to ignore it, concentrating instead on the ways I could get to America. Five minutes later the phone rang again, on and on, trilling in my ear as a robin would chirp on a winter branch.

I was losing patience, the dratted ringing would not stop. It had got to be Mother, my friend was *too* busy, my lover too far; besides, he did not know my telephone number. Ready to give her the sharp edge of my tongue, I snatched up the confounded thing, and put it to my ear.

"Hello," I shouted down the line.

"Hello, you," came the gruff response.

"Jimmy."

"Yours truly," he warbled in that voice that told its own tale of partying.

"You are drinking?" Spite was starting to creep into my voice.

"Great, a mood, your constant companion."

Did he think he was being funny? "Thought you were too busy to phone little me."

Jimmy sighed. "Okay, I will go."

"No." The scream pierced the silent flat. "Sorry."

"Better," Jimmy laughed, slurring slightly on his last 'r'.

I calculated the time in Paris being one hour in advance, concluded his 'work' was very intense (do not think), and tried (trust me I really tried) to be non-judgemental.

Did I succeed? What do you think?

"What do you want?" Gruff to the point of rudeness.

"A chat with a friend," a massive boom travelled down my ear.

"What?" I screeched.

"The band. It is p – pla – playing music."

"Jimmy, where are you? More to the point, who with?"

"The boss, his wife, a – a few colleagues," he slurred, dribbling, I am sure, down the phone.

"F- off." The half obscene phrase left my tongue before I had chance to stop it.

"What did you say?" My friend's sharp question stunned me into a lie.

"Nothing," I insisted. "Please get to the crux of the matter."

A noise I can only explain as some person (my mind flew to Mona) kissing his cheek ricocheted down the line.

I tried to laugh. No good, it came out as a squawk, a bird in a trap. Picking up on a noise on the other end of the phone, a giggle met my ears – a female giggle.

"There is a lot of noise."

Jimmy's roar was deafening. "Yes, we are all in high spirits."

"We?"

"The boys, girls, and me."

I had never, from day one, heard Jimmy like this.

"Hey, Rhia, we are celebrating my promotion."

"When?"

"Yesterday."

"No need to tell me, is there?"

"Cross? For pity's sake, what is wrong?"

"You."

Jimmy whistled. Hate it.

"Me? What have I done? Be pleased for me. It is a huge step up the ladder."

The whistle alone sent me spinning into 'temper'.

"What are you now, an older dusty curator?"

"A director of art."

"Clever you."

Jimmy rattled his teeth. "It may sound posh, but what it really means is I am head researcher."

I know I should have been 'moon-jumping', but no intelligent aphorism came to me.

"Have a drink for me."

"I will," he slurred.

"We will" a female shouted.

"Who is that?" Mind – overtime – conclusion – MONA!

Jimmy cleared his throat, and from the sound of it downed a glass of beer. A female giggled.

"Just a friend."

Yeah, a tigress in waiting. I hear music, low seductive tremors. It grates on me, pushes me into that black hole where a normal spacecraft spins out of control.

"I *need* my friend."

"Do you?"

"What are you saying, Jimmy?" He had no idea he was my crutch. 'Pardon?' I imagine you straining at the bit.

GO AWAY.

Loud music, slurring voices.

"Are you still there?" Jimmy's slur gets more prominent.

"Yes." A ridiculous pain I cannot define shoots through me.

"Come on, what is your problem?" More beer, more giggling.

"You, my friend, and – and that ugly, needy Mona."

Once said, no retraction.

Jimmy coughed. "Foolish girl, that was fo-olish."

His tone held drunken anger, shouting in my ear as an express train would crash into a barrier. It was deafening, defining, mocking, causing my hand to slip with sweat from the phone. I snatched it back up.

"Girl," (what always used to be endearing, now held a hint of irony) "You have changed, big time since that weekend in Paris. I would like to say it was jealousy, a silly craving for me" – (I know he is drunk now), – "Nonetheless we both must admit it is paranoia. A case of 'I don't want, but that means I still want'." (What is the crazy drunk on about?) "Mona, my dear friend, will still be in pristine condition when you and I are in our dotage."

Once more he laughed. The girl laughed too, calling to others to come and listen.

How dare she? That legless creature was laughing at me.

"Stop it" I yelled, willing myself to slam the phone onto its holder, not daring to let go of my friend.

A woman whispered by the ear-piece, "Let's dance."

Us girls all know that sultry innuendo, what it really asks is, 'let's get close.'

"I'm going."

Jimmy did not argue. He did not beg me to stay.

"I wilsh go, before I do leavsh you to your (hic) in – inane imagination I wish to say," (here we go.) "our Mother," (might know Mother would put him up to something) "asked me to mention our ongoing secret," (I was right, ha); "A holiday (hic) for your 30th birthday in 98," (forget it) "America."

Stunned, numb, bewildered, thrilled, those emotions that collide to scream, dream, coming true, wow.

"Speak to me, I want more." Excitement gushed down the phone. "Jimmy, Jimmy. Speak, you drunken sloth."

Nothing. The soft lyrical purring of the dialling tone.

I dropped the mouthpiece onto its hold. The sweat that had attacked my hands broke out across my body. I was fighting for air, cool air. Running into the bathroom I splashed my face, my arms, any part of my voluptuous frame I could reach.

"America – dotage – pristine – Mona – my lover – wait."
My head spun.

11

The sages of the past tell us, when a person faces a foe- they either submit or draw their sword to fight.

For me, there can be no submission or battle, to do so would lay myself open to ridicule and contempt. Since Jimmy's phone call, and my lover's short note I have been weighing up my options. The longer I weighed up, the more confused I became.

Should I apologise to my friend, whose clandestine lover I had fathomed out was not a living female (how foolish of me, and bizarre of him for allowing the contentious subject to grow), but that special lady in the world of art – Mona Lisa, hanging in the Louvre museum for all to admire on a daily viewing?

Or, should I sit down and write the most effusive lovelorn letter to America? Ask my lover to wait, for I was without question on my way.

Or, should I do nothing? Wait for my friend to limp his way back to me, and just turn up at my lover's commune?

What was best – the conundrum beset me each waking hour.

I craved to be in the arms of my lover, yet to never see Jimmy again .... *'I would have thought the choice simple.'*

Your statement is bold, and you are right, the choice should be simple, but it is not. I want my lover and my friend.

Your, *'ohh,'* blocks out my reasoning. In the end I make up my mind to write each a letter; my lover to beg him to wait, stating I would sort my life out. I used no name, for each time I went to write Patrice, the other names clouded my vision.

Jimmy was harder, five letters in all, full of nondescript rubbish, which I still cannot believe, even now I am writing it – he replied with a Christmas card; 'season's wishes, friend' – and a gift voucher.

Have you heard that absence makes the heart grow fonder? I assure you it does not.

Fed up, and ready to fall out with everyone, I hurtled into Christmas 1995 with Mother, Father and me – say no more. How we did not end up killing one another I will never know. Jimmy stayed in Paris, or I thought he did. No, he took it into his brainless head to board a plane to Bhutan. How do I know? I will tell you. I had received a card from Mattie prior to his visit, explaining Lotus had given birth to a boy. She was blooming, happy, and going to make a perfect Mother. A month of festivities had been planned, and she was loving her life in the sticks as her daughter-in-law crudely put it.

Father swore she was losing her marbles. Mother agreed, I disagreed. It was plain she had written the card in a hurry, probably realising it was Christmas and the post from that part of the world had to be early.

It was the letter that arrived in the new year of 96 that felled me.

'Jimmy,' Mattie wrote, 'had spent a wonderful three weeks with her. They had talked, and he had explained why he was unable to come on the trek, due to chasing a painter, something about an old mate belonging to the Stasi.'

My suspicions confirmed.

My grandmother continued to tell me Jimmy had picked up a clue through an American art programme: he was investigating. The rest of her letter was just this and that, which I am sad to say, I discarded as 'girlie gossip'. What worried me – not worried me, scared me to death to be honest, was Jimmy's furrowing. The more I thought about Mattie's letter, the more I was brought back to the radio in the car on the way from the airport. If only, I had listened. More determined to move to America.

—

Shopping and I do not go together; the sales in my evaluation creating havoc on the body and the brain. Unlike my mother, who is destined one-day to be nominated 'shopper of the year,' I hate other women trampling over my feet, pushing, shoving, poking anybody who gets in their way with whatever instrument is at hand. The moaning and grabbing, often the item seconds before that had been in your hands, drove me to the point of considering criminal activity. The perfume you wanted is lost in the rush; shattered to the floor by greedy hands, the jumpers and T shirts trampled underfoot; I became part of the regime who uses elbows and knees for gentle persuasion.

Mother nattered nonstop about her favourite 'exclusive' shop, pulled apart the prettiest flower stand I had ever seen, raged in loud embarrassing tones at the bakery stall, deliberately emptied her purse of pennies for the Salvation Army tin, and had an ongoing argument with the bank cashier when her machine to dispense money went far too slow.

By the third week in March, and my fifth jaunt to the shops, my blood sugar was ground level, and I craved hot chocolate.

Turning into a side street (the one where Alexander's studio was at the bottom) I marched my still grumbling Mother to a tea house. Pushing her up a corner, settling into the cushioned seats, she was astonished when I announced the cream cakes were on me. Coinciding with the waiter setting down the cream buns and hot chocolate, I stared out of the window, just in time to catch a figure emerge from Alexander's studio. It was the 'Bumble-bee', as large as life – literally, hurrying up the street, carrying what only can be described as a parcel taller than herself. *'What.'s wrong with that?'* you inquire.

Not a thing, I shoot back, if the person under scrutiny is not heavy with child – pregnant – expecting a happy event – anything you can fix in your mind to call an apple shaped female in the picture of contentment and health. I was fixated, which begs me to ask the next question. How can someone who has chosen the fattest bun, oozing with delicious jam and cream, prevent it spilling over the crisp starched tablecloth. Mother tinkled her spoon to make me look at her opening and closing her own mouth in the way of a blubbering fish. This exaggerated animation of a floundering cod was her way of asking me to eat with my mouth closed. Poor woman, there was panic in her eyes. The furtive peep behind her raised hand at other customers. It was plainly written on her face: 'Can anyone else see my daughter's mouth?'

If I was not so taken up with Alexander's wobbly assistant I would have choked.

"What is the matter?" Mother spoke from the corner of her mouth as I swallowed my bun.

"Er – nothing. Eat as many cakes as you wish."

Throwing me a glance of disgust she continued to fork her bun around the plate, tinkle her spoon, dart her eyes. Today, it did not trouble me. I had made my decision.

Tattoo studio, here I come.

—

My father in a sporadic moment of literacy had said it all.

'The ruling passion, be it what it will,
the ruling passion conquers reason still'
(Alexander Pope, 1688-1744)

If I had known the trouble caused by my inquisitive mind I may have had second thoughts. To begin with, it took two agonising months of thinking up excuses before Mother would accept I needed to shop alone, although I was not to be let off the hook that easily. She wanted to know *why, where,* and *will* this be a regular occurrence? You know a little about me by now. I lied!

The Saturday morning I eventually sloped down the street to Alexander's studio I was ready for any possibility; an expert when it comes to foraging the depths of conceivable lies. Releasing the door, and hearing the familiar ring of the bell I chided myself (maybe for a second) on allowing my incredible imagination the run against them in the past weeks.

Anyway, what greeted me caused my eyes to water.

Talk flamboyant – that is mild.

The walls, last seen as the epitome of calm, were now purple; a bright, sparkling, 'emperor's cloak' colour. In layman's terms it smacked you in the eye while exasperating the depths of decency and sickening the stomach. Alexander's creative 'art' (if creative was quite the correct definition to his new sketches – splashes and squiggles – modern adroitness) were scattered around; the powerful background eating into the ink showcases. Gone the soft pink sofa, replaced by the most gaudy patterned chaise lounge, scattered here and there with lime and purple cushions. To offset the mind altogether, a white wooden desk stood in a corner, the curved design of its legs forcing the newcomer to wonder at its antiquity. By the door to the inner sanctum stood elongated jars of lime and purple;

straight from the fictional story 'Ali Baba and the Forty Thieves'.

"At last." Alexander leaned against the doorpost that led to the ante-room, his smile one of unassuming satisfaction. In his shadow hovered the 'Bumble-bee', her embarrassed gaze looking me up and down, while her neat squared fingertips stretched across her protruding belly. Imagine eyes protruding; you have got it in one!

Her rose coloured cheeks, glossy hair, and the famous 'glow' women chat about that emanates from a female in her condition, were all there; I wanted to grab her by the smock and say, "How dare you be so happy?"

What actually formed into words was, "Get you." She simpered. (Please.)

Alexander lowered his gangly body onto the lounger, the long legs transformed from brown cord to beige/pink pinstriped flares. No baggy jumper, no long hair; the hippie of my first acquaintance had disappeared, re-birthed into a modern version of any painter putting his stamp on the contemporary system. He tapped the empty space beside him for me to sit, *she* held her hand out for my coat. I passed it to her, sauntered over to the uncomfortable looking seat.

"We have changed." My host swung his arms in admiration at his flamboyant walls.

"Change is hardly the word that covers this transformation," I sniped.

The rebuff winged its way home.

"Of course you are right, but –" here he paused, sought the eyes of the 'Bumble-bee' and held them fast. "This," he was casting his hand about him again, "this is my painting legacy. I will sell the studio to someone who appreciates my 'take' on art."

Alexander caught my staggered breathing.

"I forgot, you have not heard. I am moving to America."

The 'Bumble-bee' handed me coffee, carefully watched me as I spoke.

"You evidently have had a commission."

The girl heard my quiver, intervened before her boss had chance.

"Alexander has been offered a place in one of America's finest painting communes."

She knew. I knew. she had overstepped the mark, played me at my own game.

"You are not listening." Alexander nudged my arm.

"Sorry."

"You must have a parting gift. One last piece of art work." Alexander grinned.

I would have given my right arm to throw the girl to the wolves, explain to her boss that it was *me* who secured his swift rise to fame; his commune painter being *my* lover.

I glimpsed her sagging belly. "The baby?"

She blushed. "Paris has a lot to answer for."

"I know Paris, and painters."

The girl paled, gripped the desk she was standing by. Alexander's eyes left her face to confront mine. "Really? Who?"

Strange he is asking, my lover would have spoken about me, told him to thank me for the sketch. In trouble now, missy. The thought excited me. Alexander looked puzzled.

"No-one of importance," I muttered

Can this be believed? Had the 'Bumble-bee' intercepted her boss's phone calls, post? Had they even met Patrice (heck, what am I writing) in Paris? Someone else may act as intermediary, after all he is in hiding!

Alexander pulled my arm. "Come."

I rose from the sofa. "Maybe something small to remember Bhutan," I said softly.

He spread his hands out in a gushing display. "Your memories are usually significant. Like the walnut tree, they are your destiny."

I glared at the 'Bumble-bee' in passing, standing at the desk, head held high in defiance. "My destiny, Alexander, is a foregone conclusion."

"Not always," Alexander called from the ante-room. "Who would have thought Rosie and me?"

"Yes, who would have thought it?" I bitingly echoed.

—

I jolt as I register the 'Bumble bee's' breath tickling my face. "Your art work is complete."

The mirror she is holding in front of me catches the overhead beam of ceiling light illuminating the sweep of the Himalayas mountain range across my breasts (we will not go there... it was convenient!). Every ripple of movement from the tiny rivulets above and under each nipple, shimmering as stones in a brook, to the breastbone, with the sun to the left and the moon to the right, pronouncing light and shade according to the turn of my body. A waterfall spills between my breasts, provocatively winding its way to my stomach. Flowers, trees and bushes move with the suppleness of my skin.

I would say, emotion in all its glory, exposed. Alexander's art a monologue of my deceit. The artist was nowhere to be seen.

The girl carefully wrapped the cling film around my chest. I watch her, spot the glint of gold as her fingers move. A ring, a wedding ring. Did not see that shock coming.

"You, you are married?" The sound cuts through the silent air.

"Yes," she holds up her plain band. "A thank-you gesture."

"A thank-you gesture?"

The nod comes quick, hiding the pain within her eyes.

"I do not understand."

She clasps my hand, shaking. "Shh, gratitude for his break-through."

"You mean, the baby?"

"Too much wine, it doesn't matter."

"Doesn't matter?" I am boring myself with repetitiveness.

She speeds up, moves the mirror, collects the extra pads I am to take home.

"Doesn't matter?"

The girl is agitated. "We all have secrets, don't we? Me, you. Your friend."

I jump upwards into a sitting position, a little too quickly as my head spins.

She stumbles for words. "Ignore me, *please*."

"Friend." I feel a fear that only those who have found themselves in this position will understand. "I have no friend who visits a tattoo studio."

Glancing toward the door she whispered, "Please, lower your voice. Alexander will be so cross. Customer confidentiality and all that."

My pulse raced. At last, something to make her squirm. I seized the opportunity. "Tell me then."

Hesitation, tears, trembling. Did I care? No.

She cast about for an excuse – none. Finally, in a gush worthy of a burst pipe it came tumbling out. "Jimmy. A name in Chinese."

"Jimmy?"

"Shh."

"The name?" I sounded hoarse, even to myself.

I could see the girl was struggling, panting as she heaved her belly to come closer to the couch. "Please, be quiet. 'Rhia'. More tears were forming around her eyelashes.

"Where is your boss?"

She froze.

Ah, this will teach her, payback time for stealing my thunder.

The girl visibly shivered. "Why? He is busy I guess, always promoting himself these days."

I was enjoying this. "Did this friend mention anything?"

She almost collapsed. Revenge is sweet. "Not really, he was more interested in Alexander's work. Left a telephone number. Paris, I think."

"Has he called him?"

The tears were really falling now. "Not to my knowledge."

"Keep it that way."

The 'Bumble-bee' stuttered – words stuck in her throat? Petrified of my presence? Good!

She took a tissue from her pocket, wiped her eyes.

This moment was mine. "Alexander thinks it was you?"

I had to milk this moment for all it was worth.

"Yes."

"And you are willing to live this farce?"

"I love him," she answered, striving to stem the rising tide within her.

"Enough to move to America?"

"Yes," came the simple reply.

"Fine. This will not be our last meeting."

The girl stared at me. I hear you sigh with unease.

Do not fret, I have some decency. The girl is pregnant, and I do not wish to play midwife. I ease my body from the couch, re-dress in lightning speed, make my way to the door, twist the door handle. "Have a good life." I thrust the money owed into her hand.

"Thank you," she whimpers.

The cardigan coat hangs heavy. Sackcloth and ashes. Power tasted – ummm – horrible if you wish for the truth. I must get home, strip down to my underwear, hide away.

Out in the street I hear the rumble of thunder in the distance, leave the studio firmly behind me.

12

I have come to the conclusion that moods are a duplicate of a clock pendulum. They swing to and fro, moving you on, pulling you back. On a good day the world is your oyster, on a bad day the clouds gather; I have experienced both, and to my continual sadness, nothing changes unless you change it. By that, I mean life waits for no-one.

Make whatever it is you seek, happen.

1997 was a busy year. It began with Mattie's letter (lost in the post, found us three months later) stating that Ujesh, the boy Lotus had given birth to, was coming up to one year old. His parents, being important elders, and the boy's name meaning 'One who gives light', were taking him to Taktsang for thanksgiving. Blessed by the anchor mother, and after many sleepless nights my grandmother was considering taking a short break and coming to visit us. You can imagine my father.

"Silly woman, this is her home, not a holiday, and besides the letter is already late so as always happens with my mother, something prevented her from coming."

"Maybe we are due another letter," I intervened.

"That's right, stick up for her." The growl was accompanied by a bark.

I had only popped round to kill time on a miserable Saturday (shopping trips had petered out, thank goodness), not to be dragged into another family argument.

I know father was stressed, his bank had voted to expand for a third time, but that was no excuse to have a go at me. The work had been ongoing throughout the spring and summer months. New staff brought in, and I was selected, along with six others, to act as a training officer.

Sympathise with me. Can life get any worse?

I hated the job as you know, so what happens? They pin a badge on me and everyone is acknowledging me as Madam. The hours were longer, my work ethos grew larger, and to cap it all, the amount in my pay packet shrunk, I swear it did. 'Voluntary' became Father's favourite word.

The minutes and hours grinding my life away in bank duties meant I saw even less of Jimmy. Two hours, one day a week, when he was not in Paris. Then – and I mean this in utter disrespect – he went on and on about painters and art; what type of art, age, where they lived – you name it, he listed them. I actually asked him one Saturday evening at a quarter to nine if he was on a mission to see if I recognised anybody. My friend laughed, passed the conversation over with, "Don't be silly, you would tell me."

Well, for your information, friend – I don't think so.

Still, the months rolled on... another letter from Mattie. She was on her way, a little later than planned (a lot later), but autumn would herald her arrival. Before that, Jimmy's parents were throwing a party; their son was 30, and they had been married 30 years. Mother was taken aback, stating that children's ages and wedding anniversaries should never be weighed up together.

Silly woman. We all know why!

—

The night of Jimmy's party we all dressed up in our finery. For me that was jeans, T shirt, boots and a cap. Mother paraded in a long evening skirt and sparkly top, while Father looked (and in my opinion felt) decidedly uncomfortable in a three-piece suit. *They* were 'picture and parcel' of up-town revellers: me – more downtown disco. I have got to write how nervous I was: actually trembling. Why? After all, this was my best friend's party. and his parents' (must not forget them), yet of late I had found Jimmy a teeny bit aloof, and yes, your shake of the head could say it all. I was greeting him on the back of discovering the ankle tattoo was my name, and – this upset me in a strange way – the chump was still hunting our mate down.

Talk driving up the wrong alley. Oops, slip of the tongue!

Never mind, one thing at a time: the party first.

I knew before we arrived neither parent would fit in to the off the wall gathering; Jimmy's parents being the hard rockers of their youth. Black leather, long hair, kohled eyes, say no more. From what I had gathered this party was a celebration of their music and a bit of Jimmy's taste (which was still guitar led, but quieter). The taxi we had hired to drop us off and pick us up later screeched to a halt outside the most decorated house I had ever seen. Bright white lights hung down from the guttering, accompanied by red and blue flashing lights around the windows and door. Amplified guitars shuddered through the street, while banners and streamers spilt across the hedges and windowsills. Gaudy it may be, but ten out of ten for promoting all out fairy grotto – even if it was 'crass' in our Mother's eyes.

Mother was mortified when she realised there was no room hire, just a tiny terraced house where doors were clashing, and people dressed in rock gear from the seventies poured in and out to dance in the street. Her crumpled face was worth every uncomfortable minute of the half hour drive, especially when the driver turned off his engine to ask pick up time, and all she kept muttering was, "unwashed bodies". The man gave her his deepest scowl before adding to her discomfort.

"Hey lady, I live round 'ere." I hear your titter, and agree. 'Wet myself,' is my definition.

Father was none too pleased.

It was Jimmy's misfortune to live in what my mother considered the poorer area of town, and although she adored the son, her take on his parents was cynical, very cynical indeed. They were rockers, and *he* had allowed them to organise his party their way instead of her more upper class do. I thought this great, she was horrified.

"I will go, for it is my place, he is my daughter's friend," was her argument.

The fun, to my way of thinking, began the moment we stepped into the house. Mother was drawn into frantic dancing by a long haired bearded replica of George Harrison, while my father, cider splashing down his expensive suit had his tie yanked from him by a tipsy look-alike Purdy from the classic series of 'The Avengers'.

For me, the evening was looking up. Jimmy winked at me, I returned, "Well done, you."

Two hours of grinding and spinning saw Mother dissolve into one of her migraines, and slump onto a squashed, worn imitation leather sofa, fanning her handkerchief for all she was worth. At this point you must forgive me if I lose control of the pen, for as usual, in situations of such abhorrence, the absolute clanger of the evening comes when you think things are just settling. Curious? Have patience.

Jimmy's mates from his school days bounced him in the air; up, down, up, down, spin, spin, spin, before landing him on my mother's lap. She let out the most wailing sound (in that upper-class voice of hers), and tried with contortions known only to a trapeze artist to wriggle out of the chair.

It was never going to happen, **never.**

Mother slipped to the ground holding onto Jimmy for grim death; pulling him, bang, bump, on top of her. Skirt flew up, legs flapped, suspenders popping and pinging as they shot from their cosy home atop her black stockings. The drunken revellers clapped as if she were the cabaret.

I coughed and choked until my lungs were sore. Jimmy apologised so many times you could be forgiven for mistaking him for a stuck needle on an old fashioned gramophone player. Mother clambered up from the floor, threw back the beer she was offered, then shouted at my father to take her home. Father, who had been in another room drinking and gyrating with his new-found friend, spluttered he would phone the taxi, promptly swivelled full circle, and walked into the kitchen where he grabbed a gas lighter hanging on the wall and proceeded to ring out.

The night was getting better!

In the melee that followed, my mother and father accused one to the other of everything and nothing. They threw drink over each other, squared up with a cake, hung around each other's neck as lovers do, then in the early hours of the morning sinking onto the overcrowded sofa, snored their heads off.

By the hour the taxi arrived my head ached to splitting. Never in my life had I been witness to such frivolity. Jimmy helped lift Mother into the waiting cab, before wishing me 'goodnight' in what I now dub as a reserved manner; back then I thought nothing of it.

A party this girl will never forget! Pity, I had not cornered Jimmy over his tattoo, but all considered we had a lifetime to unearth its meaning.

—

After that humiliating night it was work like never before. Jimmy buried himself in his artefacts, Father hid at the bank. Mother, poor self-conscious creature, planned a holiday. Their excuse? Neither wished for any more arguments. It would be down to me to stay and put up with Mattie while they enjoyed foreign shores to recuperate. To my ears their reasoning was sweet music. Mattie and me, chatting until the early hours, shopping until we drop, dressing how we wish. Hours where I could learn how Mattie held her ground against my parents, for America was creeping ever nearer, and it would be time to put my own plans into action; dreams of my youth.

The downside? How to bring my best friend on board.

Mattie arrived in early October, no off-hand wisecracks relating to her new life., no criticism of my feeble effort to keep the flat tidy, no denunciation of the way I dressed. Mattie was just that, my beloved grandmother; a real example of the freedom Jimmy and I had pledged to find.

On discovering my parents' last minute holiday Mattie showed no aggrieved Mother tendencies; completely the opposite. She could monopolise more of her granddaughter. Her main concern, and I found this quite hard to fathom out, was Jimmy. She insisted I invite him over. Forgoing the gap in our relationship since that ridiculous conversation on the phone, and my antics of constant laughter at his party, my friend and I had not really spoken. Oh, reader, I know I am among many who treat their special friend as a commodity, and before you even utter the scorn you must feel, I also know upon seeing him I would be struck down with that crippling mirth left over from *that* party, and, this is where the coward comes in, that tattoo and what it means. I dare not think. In the end I gave in, left a message on his answering machine, and waited. Jimmy being Jimmy called back in his own time, arranging a day and time to please all. The thrill, yet fear of his visit stalked me up to the moment he rang the bell. Mattie and I were in deep conversation, examining Lotus and her child.

"Drat," I exploded as I unlatched the door.

"Hello, you, too."

My friend sauntered in, humour of old lighting up the dark iris of his eyes. Spotting Mattie he let out the loudest 'whoop', scooping her into his arms and swinging her round as if she were long lost family.

"It is good to see you, honestly. Thanks for your mail, interesting stuff."

This was news. I am aware Jimmy phones my mother, the on-going holiday, exchanging news with Mattie, a different scam; mind remember his visit to Bhutan.

"You love it out there," my friend was saying. "It suits you."

Beaming like a young girl, Mattie eyed him suspiciously.

"Have you told her, you naughty boy?"

Jimmy made an over-exaggerated pout of his bottom lip, dropped into the nearest chair. "No, cross my heart."

"Told me what exactly?" I interrupted.

They both locked eye contact. "Not a lot," my friend tossed his feet onto the arm. "We made conversation fly," they giggled, "from Bhutan to Paris."

"And?" My voice rose higher.

Mattie was the first to bring her giggling under control. "Don't be so serious, child." (No luck she had forgotten that pet name), Jimmy's last letter was full of the calamity at the party. It did my heart good."

Knew it. My friend is a grass!

Apart from spilling the best ever farce of the year Jimmy got there before me.

Ignoring what I will underline as schoolgirl nonsense, I grasped onto anything that would steady my nerves. *'Nerves?'* you ask. *'With Jimmy? Ummm.'*

I close you out. "You write to Mattie," voice accusing.

Jimmy's mouth fell open.

"He does," the soft lilt of my grandmother caught me unaware, "to the extent that I have placed him in the role of my advisor." (Why him, why not me?)

I gulped, she saw, I went to speak, she stopped me mid-stream.

"His level-headed prognosis of everything, and his detachment from me (detachment, like heck, the guy adores you) has brought us to this conclusion. He agrees with me. Huge breath.

"I am going to live in Bhutan."

For all I would have noticed the floor beneath my feet may have broken, crumpled away, took me with it. Marbles lost. Insanity, flashed through my mind. I struggled for something to say. "Mattie, you are seventy plus years old, is it the done thing?"

My grandmother clapped her hands, screwed her nose up. "See what I mean, Jimmy? My son's daughter."

"Not true." I cast my eyes floorward.

"Don't sulk, girl." Jimmy made a grimace with his mouth. "Your grandmother knows her own mind. She is happy, far happier than you or I at this moment in time."

"Father," vibrated the air.

"Father, Father, Father. If I hear the name once more I will scream. Do not worry. I will sort him. It is only a three year stint to begin with. It will soon pass."

Mattie made a gesture to thirst.

Striding into the kitchen I pour three glasses of the red stuff (I will not call it by its name, no room for reproval then.) I set the glasses down on the coffee table, allowing the liquid to sparkle in the light of the fire.

"Help yourselves," the tone is dull.

"Wine?" Mattie eyed me. "Thought you had given up since the rice drink."

"Rice drink?" Jimmy teased.

"Forget it." I do believe the sharpness caught him off guard.

I took a sip (OK, a gulp), fixed that glare of, 'did you' on Mattie, only to concede defeat when she held up her hands and shook her head. From the corner of my eye I spied Jimmy, lost in his glass, willing the red liquor to reveal its heady secret. Out of the blue, and really of no consequence to the debate in hand, he muttered: "This decade ends in three years, and a new one begins. Our pact is finished, what then?"

The room was warm, and the shadows leaping from the flames danced on the walls with grace and elegance. Jimmy was observing me, watching my every move. If I had not known different I would say my friend could read my past, and in all probability take a damned good guess into deciphering my future.

'Freedom,' I stammered. "What is that?"

Mattie chuckled. "I know."

She raised her glass in my direction. I took the lead.

"Let's be honest," I muttered. "When Father hears the latest news from you, Mattie, no amount of camouflage will possibly make him think you are right in the head." (Take the poker from the ashes, no more prodding today).

Jimmy scowled in my direction. Mattie smiled. "She is right, and do I care? No."

I swirled as if I was dancing; joining, if you wish, the shadows licking the wall, the contents of my glass diminishing by the second.

Now, you would have thought my past lessons are stamped upon my conscious with a meaningful promise never to travel that road at any period in my life.

Come on, this is me, and if you were to write down your own – shall we say 'hiccups' in life, I bet a tipsy turvy drinking habit like mine would be one. No? Think again. Continue.

I twirled around the room, arms outstretched, dreaming of a faraway place and a blond haired painter. The music rose and sank as the incantation of the moment filled me with longing. I felt arms, warmth, breath upon my cheek; softly I whispered, "Patrice."

"Who?" The voice was loud, dragging me from that beautiful place I had fallen into; my eyes flew open. Jimmy, eyes penetrating mine.

"PATRICE?" he asked again.

I fumbled, yanked myself from his grip. "A singer," I lied.

"A singer?"

"Yep, some silly schoolgirl crush."

My gaze darted to Mattie, believe it or not, fast asleep. Excuse.

"Keep your voice down, you will wake my grandmother."

Jimmy blew that idiotic whistling between his teeth, appeared to be fighting for words, then gabbled all at once. "I thought you had found a lover," (too near the mark), "Someone you had not mentioned, and – and as your best friend I would be the first to know, wouldn't I?"

Tricky situation! Putting my fingers to my lips I pulled him into the kitchen. Please forgive me for what I did next. I had no choice.

I took Jimmy's face with both hands and kissed him.

I can only imagine your horror, the word 'false' ringing in my ears.

Jimmy's lips were soft, yielding – do not go there.

I drew apart, dropped my hands, before forcing myself to laugh.

"Got you."

Jimmy stood in stunned silence. I began to pour more wine; a hand covered my glass. "Enough, I would say." My friend was adamant.

"Come on, a joke."

"A joke?"

"Oh, Jimmy, you can be such a bore." Mouth open, words escaped.

"A bore?"

What was this, a prelude to a quiz show?

"Look, I am sorry, never meant to kiss you." (Liar, anything to put him off Jules – blast, Patrice).

Jimmy sank onto a chair. "I gathered that. It seems your singer is much more important."

We could not head down *that* road- must lead him away- shook my head to disengage the strong influence of the wine.

"Tell me, can you credit Mattie, interacting with some pesky anchor mother, a daily workload with farming women? Suppose she is to be admired. Maybe if I had the same stamina, that get up and go determination."

My friend stared; glared is more the word I will use, his eyebrows almost meeting in the middle of his forehead.

"You would do what exactly, run for the hills?"

I floundered for an answer "I- I–"

"WHAT?" The shriek tore through my clouded brain.

"Be on the other side of the ocean, not here," an afterthought. "On holiday with you and my parents. America?"

The most sardonic grin passed over Jimmy's features. "Of course."

I moved back into the lounge, Jimmy on my heels: sat on the sofa with a 'plonk', waking Mattie as I intended.

"Enjoyed your dance?" The question bit into the overheated room.

Jimmy was quick to answer. "Yep, very informative."

Mattie took my friend's hand. "Do not lose the will to fight." Her tenderness induced a response that I would recall not

266

once in the near future, but many times when that black hole of depression yawned wide.

"Fighting is for fools, winning is the podium for weary souls, am I right?" Jimmy queried.

She patted his knee, turned her attention on me, who had shrunk among the cushions in the sure knowledge that my grandmother had planned her 'sleep;' not quite the outcome she required. 'Ha.'

"I must go." Jimmy ran his fingers through his hair. "Too much wine, sorry. Prepare for my return to Paris. I will see you."

My friend was up and out the flat door in the seconds it took me to ease myself from my corner.

"You quarrelled?" More questions.

"Mattie, he has become what I feared, a museum fuddy-duddy."

My grandmother laughed, draining her glass in the age-old habit of one who thinks they know what is to come. "My dear, move your chess piece carefully."

I hate it when she flips her droplets of wisdom into my befuddled brain.

Brushing off Mattie's suggestion to ring Jimmy, explain everything, we sit and talk. She makes preparations for her return to Bhutan. I tell her not to worry over me: circle on my heart the date of my new life- November 12th 1998.

13

New York, November 1998

We flew into John F Kennedy airport in Queens County, New York, at exactly 4am our time (around 10pm their time). Everything, from the moment I stepped onto the plane had been amazing: the care, the presentation, the comfort; even, may I say, the buoyant spirits of Jimmy and my parents. This was a surprise after the fiasco that followed their return from their holiday. Discovering Mattie's plans left my father in no doubt about his Mother's sanity, and try as I might to enlighten them of her new-found freedom, they brushed it aside and claimed once she came home he would seek a way to take control. This I wrote and told her, so heaven alone knows when we will see her, if ever.

His reaction to my wish to leave the bank sent Father into overdrive, as he would not budge on the issue that it was my fault that Mattie was so silly; I should have taken a sterner stand in Bhutan.

My own reaction: "Everyone is entitled to freedom."

"Freedom indeed." He had slammed his hand down firm on his desk. "Freedom is for children."

All staff were made to work harder, play less, and know their place (including me).

Jimmy and I spent no time together, he running round Paris, and me too tired to think. Even so, Mother connived and contrived to stop the rot she said was growing between Jimmy and myself.

"Firm friends do not act so silly," was her insight into the problem, and in her view this holiday in America would cheer us up, for full celebrations were in place for the forthcoming festive season.

Funny how this woman with all her ups and downs grabs life by the horns. She won father over, and added two extra weeks to our holiday, or shall I stress, *my* farewell tour! With these problems sorted we passed from 97 through the months of 98 in comparable harmony, until now.

—

One small problem on the plane was Jimmy's constant nagging over a student rally against a Russian sub-critical nuclear test taking place in the United States in two days' time.

"Students across America are marching." He was excited. "Let's join in, show our support as of old."

March? I had no time to march. I had arranged to meet my lover, run away to the commune, telephone my parents from there. I hear, accept, comply. *'Jimmy?'* you ask.

Deal with him later. My answer to the protest march. "Go fly your kite!"

Jimmy was taken aback, yet he must understand marching had to stop sometime. I was thirty, he was thirty-two; cannot protest forever- can we?

Mother had agreed, the, 'Please don't sink so low,' expression etched on her face.

Subject forgotten.

So, here we are, outside the airport, hailing a cab, around twelve miles to our hotel in Lower Manhattan. It is true, American cab drivers chat incessantly about everything and anything; the streets (or walkways), roads, bars busy with late-night party-goers, stragglers from work or people who just found the evening an excuse to walk or cruise in a car. I was entranced by each flickering neon light and crazy road runner. A corner of my heart wanted to yell 'Yippee' out loud as dates and venues of meeting with my lover had arrived at the flat prior to leaving.

16th November, name of a restaurant in down town Manhattan where I will be met to discuss the next date on 17th November.

My thoughts? No need to discuss. I am here.

The worry, Jimmy and my parents, especially after Mattie.

Still, they could visit us often.

"Penny for them," Jimmy whispered.

I froze as his fingers touched my arm.

"Nothing."

My friend looked troubled, shifts his feet to avoid stepping on my toes, and settles down to gaze out of the window once more.

Father points to a building. "By the time we leave this city, our feet, and pockets will be sore."

Mother laughed, wrapped her fur coat (wish I could note it was artificial; I cannot) closer to her body.

Jimmy mentioned the art work rendered on various buildings, and the painters behind the brush. I gave up listening, buried in my world of fantasy and dread.

I sigh, splodge the paper bearing too hard with the pen ξ *'You are uncertain.'* Your cry catches me off guard.

I am never uncertain, you are judging too early.

'Am I?'

Wait for the end.

'You asked me to stand as judge and jury.' The cab pulls up outside the classiest of hotels. Mother smiles, Father nods, Jimmy holds his tongue. A doorman holds the door, asks us to enter, where we are met by the hotel manager. You wonder how I can tell all the uniformed bodies apart? Simple. He wore a black three-piece suit, sporting a single white rose in his lapel. Important? I would say so. Sinking into the reception area carpet we are welcomed with enthusiastic exuberance, registered, and as it is late, shown to our rooms. Large, expensive fitted rooms, boasting a double bed, streamlined wardrobes, classic drawers, and a large sofa. The bathroom; exclusive in black and white.

The maid, a girl in her late teens, informed me breakfast was served between nine and eleven, and if I needed assistance I was to ring. Thanking her I called 'goodnight' to my parents and Jimmy, locked the door, and scrambled onto the bed, pouring myself a glass of champagne. Testing the fruit residing in a diamond cut glass bowl, I lay back to think.

My lover had demanded secrecy, a large sum withdrawal from my bank, and a need to know I had upheld his wishes. This I had managed without alerting anyone; the hardest part would be the lies for the meeting, then the parting itself, for if Jimmy found out I was to stay here, live with the man whom he believed spied for the Stasi ... I dare not go there.

I hugged the pillow, torn between friendship and desire.

—

The restaurant in down town Manhattan sparkled with festive glow, the windows adorned with twinkling coloured lights, the walls with holly wreaths and scarlet ribbons. Candle logs burnt in a huge open grate, throwing their heat around the shivering diners. Balanced on the small oval tables, covered in damask red tablecloths, were tiny lanterns, creating a shimmer of shadows on the cream papered walls. Two chairs, one either side, evoked a feeling that this restaurant was mainly a couple place, a lovers' lair. Art designed name cards wished customers a Happy Christmas, and ceramic pots, placed in certain positions emitted the nose-tingling scent of frankincense. This was Christmas as it should be: scented, designed, and very much romantic.

I chose a table out of view of the window, removed my beret and gloves, placed my coat over the back of the chair, sat down and waited. Around me couples were talking: two women engrossed in their shopping list, a young man and girl gazing intently into one another's eyes, two men sharing a flagon of mulled wine, a husband and wife (newly married I guessed, for her ring was sparkly and bright) talking intimately. The monotony of working in a bank and calculating figures induced me to count the tables; twenty. Forty people would fill this quaint suburban eating house to capacity, any more and it would burst at the seams. I ordered a hot chocolate, accepted the kind query, "Is Madam waiting for someone?" mumbled, "Yes," and proceeded to sip the sugary drink; a huge pendulum clock ticked the minutes away.

I had lied to get here, fabricated a story Mother had not been too happy to hear.

"Shopping on your own?" she had questioned. "We have only just arrived in the city."

"A colleague at work," my voice broke, "asked me to pick up a catalogue as soon as I arrived. I promised I would post it to her straight away. I thought it would be better to do it on my own."

Mother was furious. "Hear that, Henry? That is cheek. Sort whoever out when you return to work."

My father asked the name. I made one up, praying he would not check until he arrived home, then, it would not matter.

Turning her back to drink the small cognac father had ordered, her voice was haughty. "If you must, but make sure you are here for supper."

Jimmy had not uttered a word.

I took another sip of hot chocolate, breathed deeply, and grew impatient.

—

The door flew open, and a girl hurtled inside. Rushing to my table she flopped down in what I shall express as the end of a race against the clock, stating as matter of fact, "At last. I thought I would never make it."

The large brown saucer eyes looked into mine as she threw her hand across the space between us. "Sharaz, you must be Rhia."

"I am." The sound was small and pitiful.

"This is an arty meeting place," she panted, looking to either side of where she sat, ignoring my inability to speak. "The place we all hang out."

My expression changed. "Right, you must be a member."

"A member?" The face lit up as the proverbial penny dropped. "Oh, you mean, am I with Patrice?"

She picked up on my disquiet, a laugh leaving the smooth swan-like throat, her eyes dancing in the dusky light.

Withdrawing a cigarette from a silk pouch she had been struggling to release from her handbag, she balanced it between her ruby lips, lit it, and inhaled.

"You are the image of what Patrice said."

Clicking her fingers she indicated for the waiter to come our way.

As waiters do, he obeyed, took her order; another hot chocolate for me, a fruit tea for her, before swaggering through rustic double doors. My face contorted at the ease of her authority. "He said you were a flame headed actress, beautiful and transparent. He was so right."

Cheeky cow, sitting at my table. I *know* my lover would never talk like that!

My tone was low, severe in its brutality. "Are you a painter?"

She exhaled – slow – inhaled deep – exhaled – taking her at least five minutes to answer.

"I am a painter. I am also Patrice's lover." I cannot use the 'Gob smacked' word again, yet I need something in line with my exasperation and disbelief.

She was joking. Like me I can almost feel your incredulity at this girl. What was she on? The cigarette had got to be a spliff, the mind blowing sort that made her talk utter and complete rubbish! For the first time since she entered the restaurant I studied the whole of her. Oh, she was pretty, too damn pretty, with the dark brown clipped bob and large hazel eyes. Her ruby mouth was rosebud shaped, that seemed to part and pout to order. Sliding my gaze downward I could see she was slimmer than me, skinny in fact; one of those girls that would need a padded bra to even suggest she was female (catty). Guessing, I would say the long legs beneath the short pleated skirt resembled vaulting poles, curved in the right direction, flexible, yet strong to withhold her weight and movement; covered by thick black hosiery (tights or stockings, you choose).

There she sat with her hands spread-eagled across the table, making me nervous. One of those people who did not give a hoot what anybody else thought; self-assured and self-engrossed.

Patting my hand, she giggled. "Do not look so shocked. We are a commune. He is the head of that community. Lord and master if you like. You thought *you* would be his only one? Oh dear, the answer is 'no', a definitive, underlined 'no'." Sheer amazement fell from her mouth.

Somehow a raw sound left my mouth. "It is a joke?" Reader, this had got to be a joke, a sick perverse giggle to welcome me into the pack. She tilted the perfected bob. "No." A slight strain entered her voice. "It is the truth."

Sharaz – I will call her by name, if only to remind myself how much I disliked her, stubbed out the cigarette, blew the remaining smoke into the air. "Look, I should not have said anything, but I thought it only fair. Patrice belongs to the firm." She caught on to my blank face. "Back home, in Germany, he gets money for them; travels back and forth to recruit new members, spies for them. He is dedicated to restore the old order. He lives for them. *We* are his – how shall I put it? His entertainment, if you like, a pastime."

She took another cigarette from the pouch.

I was fuming. "What about Alexander?"

Her brow puckered, relaxed, creased once more. "The new couple?" she bit her lip, shrugged her shoulders. "The guy is OK, the girl – another story."

I felt hot, this girl was getting to me.

"Yes, Patrice again mentioned you knew them. Anyway, the girl is a silly ass, packed her bags, upped sticks, and went home, baby and all. She complained Patrice fancied her. So what? They were living rent free."

"The 'Bum ...' Rosie? Gone home?"

"That's what I said, stupid mare. Still, one out the way."

The question burned on my lips. "And me, what is my part?" Go ahead, Miss Brain Box – get out of this one. You must know he has proposed to me (in a roundabout way). She flicked the bob from her eyes as her arm swung upward for the waiter. I waited for my answer until more drinks had been brought, and the second cigarette was lying with its counterpart in the shell shaped ashtray.

"Patrice also said you had wool between your ears. You will share, of course. Live with us in the commune."

"You are lying," I mutter.

"Lying? Why would I want to do that, I love him." Now, I am no judge of character, but I would say the whole of this conversation has the hint of sour grapes. As a matter of fact, does Patrice (oh, call him what you will) know she is here? "Have you known him long?"

Sharaz sat back in the chair, near enough whistled the waiter to bring *another* drink, and rolled her eyes heavenward. "As long as we can count."

She waved to one or two people, before eyeing me up and down.

"I am his second cousin. We grew up together." The statement was one of resignation.

Floor – open – swallow. I had detected no accent, presumed she was American.

"Your meeting with Patrice," she interrupted my thoughts. "I will give you the place, time and day."

This is better.

"Okay, I thought it would be him today."

She lit another cigarette. "No, no, not how we work, he must be careful."

"Tomorrow then, where, time, etc?"

Sharaz (wonder if that is her real name) leant across the table to get nearer to me before mouthing, "Empire State Building, 2pm."

I am sorry if I cannot take this girl seriously, but her every movement smacked 'spy game', yet, instead of being intimidated I wanted to snigger.

She wafted the smoke from the space between us. "If you go after what I have told you, please do not tell him, he would become upset."

I knew it, she was clearing the field. "Did *he* send you?"

"Yes." There was no overtone of concern as she dispensed her third cigarette. "He sent me to ask if a certain 'friend' was suspicious. He said you would know what he meant."

My mind reeled. Jimmy? What had he got to do with anything? If she thought I would disclose any facts to her, think again, Missy. You may say, no wonder the 'Bumble-bee' legged it; a spider like this. Stop, pen. I retract the 'spider' moniker. She is a PIRAHNA. Realising I was a closed book on the subject of Jimmy, she stood to button up her long fitted coat, pull the small knitted hat over her perfected hair, sling the shoulder bag across her chest, and ease on her gloves.

"This holiday is for your thirtieth birthday?" The sweetness was sickening.

She had caught me of guard. "True."

"The pact then, is nigh on finished?"

Pact? Who the hell told *her* about the bloody pact?

"How do you know? Who – who? Kurt/Jules/Patrice?"

She laughed, that full throated pleasure when someone has won something.

"Heaven help me, no Are you kidding? We, by that I mean the women of the commune hang onto his every word." She paused to lay money on the table. "Chocolate," she indicated with a thrust of her head. "Alexander spoke about you, pointing out an old picture from Berlin, you were there."

I could not help myself. "Were you?"

The perfected bob glistened in the fairy lights as the head rose in triumph. "I was, it was me that helped Patrice escape, anyway Alexander told me your problem is two men, a split heart."

There were noises in my ear, the carol singing outside the window was not one of them, or the clanging of Santa's bell.

"He is deluded." My voice was shaky. "Fool of a man."

Cannot believe the hippie sold me down the river; to the point of being a confused, lovesick fool – never!

She brushed aside my astonished stammer, wagged her finger side to side as if to a naughty dog. "Sure?"

"Jimmy is my *best* friend."

Sharaz smiled "So, you don't want my cousin out of spite, or to hide from your true feelings?"

Bitch comes to mind.

I licked my dry lips. "No." The word falls between gritted teeth.

The river behind my eyes pleads to be let loose. I thrust my head forward, compel myself to seek eye contact. The creature does not move. "Why do *you* stay with him?"

"Me?" Her eyes hold mine steadfastly "I *do* love him. Always have, always will. Simple."

A cold numbness crept over me. I felt cold. The door clanged, the robust figure of Father Christmas rang his bell, adding, "Ho, ho, ho," to the chatting and carols. I drew my attention back to the girl opposite me.

The bobbed head was already in the street.

14

By morning I was exhausted. Raw emotion had kept me awake during the night. I had cried, railed at the image of a girl with such confidence and pizazz, that I had punched my pillow until my knuckles were sore. Finally, wrapping myself in a huge fluffy dressing gown I had sank into bed. The phone had rung once, twice, three – four times, the door rattled from my mother's knocking, annoyance creeping into the concern. I covered my ears.

My saving factor, my friend. He would have the sense to inquire at the desk, gather the information given to them. I was not to be disturbed. I had returned with a throbbing headache. Jimmy would suggest I sleep it off, wait for breakfast when more information could be gleaned.

I had spent my time alone scratching at the dregs of my memory and emotions.

If the German authorities were searching for straggling Stasi, silly of the cousin to mention Jimmy. Let's be honest, my friend is a museum curator, not the F.B.I nor Interpol for goodness' sake. Even so, *what if Jimmy had visited Alexander.'s studio again, what if the two had talked, what if the 'Bumble-bee.' had phoned him? What if? – round and round, on the merry-go-round of what ifs.*

The girl had to be lying; my lover could not belong to the shadow of the past; a firm that killed and maimed. He could not do that, any more than take other lovers in the way a person would spoon sugar into a coffee cup. He wished to marry me.

I tossed and turned.

I convinced myself the image she portrayed did not fit with the lover I knew. *If* he did need money, it was for his commune, *his art,* not some underhand dealing. Cousin, or not, this girl was a threat to my happiness, and the Jimmy thing. I rest the pen. Doodle – aaaa,ddd,ffff,ssss.

'Significant,' you remark. *'Are you swearing, knowing a modicum of truth is hidden in her words?'*

Fool, I shout, snatch the pen, and hurry on. My body aches, weariness my closest companion. I must get up. Today is that day when I choose to hide in the shadows, at the beginning. A new life; freedom found. I will tread in Mattie's shoes, live my dream, what more could I ask?

I think of my mother, the devastation she may feel. Think, and then conclude – she will get over it!

My father, how angry he will be? That's life!

Jimmy, what can I say? He is my best friend ever, yet of late we have crossed a line. The pact? Who knows?

Inside my heart was clawing, dragging me down into a pit. I had weaved a web, deceit was second nature, art its communication, and today was its fulfilment.

—

"Morning, dear, do you feel better?" Mother was as buoyant as ever, a tactical approach. My mother smiled, not the sugary kind, but for her as near to genuine as she could get, someone had warned her. I slowly moved my head toward Jimmy. He was talking to my father. They had pamphlets, planning their day.

"Where are we going this morning?" I queried, the could-not-care-less attitude plain.

"Does it matter?" Jimmy's voice was strained.

"You and Father are choosing."

"Not for you," my friend was agitated. "We thought after your headache, you ladies could browse."

"What a good idea," Mother intervened. "Let's shop, Rhia. A small birthday gift."

"If you like," I answered.

Breakfast was served, Mother eating her toast and marmalade in quintessential fashion, small finger stuck out as a yacht flag would salute the sky. Father, head buried in the national newspaper. Jimmy, scouring through the numerous art gallery brochures stacked at his side. No-one spoke. This was agony for me, with the knowledge of this afternoon. Jimmy glared at my sullen cheeks and dark rimmed eyes.

"Are you still feeling under the weather, or is something worrying you?"

"Whatever makes you think so, I am fine." Two seconds later, "Thank you."

Silence.

Eventually breakfast was finished, the crumbs of the piece of toast I had forced down me scattered around my plate.

Mother was the first to stand. "Settled then, meet me in the reception, Rhia, in fifteen minutes."

I stood and saluted, to nobody's amusement; humour off the menu today I see.

Walking toward the lift, Jimmy laid his hand on my arm, halted my movement.

"Let's take the stairs, it will suit us better, and besides you have eaten nothing."

"I am not hungry." Spoken with childish sullenness.

"OK, your choice." (No argument, wow!)

He led the way to the stairs. "You had no dinner last night either."

"Too tired," there was a snap in the answer.

He slowed down for me to catch up. "I took it you were meeting someone."

I tried to laugh. "How silly can you be? Who do I know in this city? The catalogue, remember."

"Ah, yes."

I sensed my friend was unconvinced, so I changed the subject. "What are you and Father doing today?"

"Oh." Jimmy paused. "Here and there. Museums, paintings. A game of basketball."

"Paintings on holiday?" The incredulous tone grated on him.

"OK, OK," he smirked, "but, you know how it is when we need to view something."

"Such as what? oh, Jimmy you can be such a bore."

The arrow flew home, hit its mark. "Yep, but an honest bore."

I refused to confront him on that issue. Reaching the first landing he stopped, took my hands, cold in his grasp. "Please tell me if something is wrong. We are best friends."

Tears stung my eyes as I nodded and thought, 'I will miss you, Jimmy,' unlocked my arm, and disappeared through the beckoning doors.

It took five minutes to pack the small canvas bag I had brought with me for this occasion, rolled up trousers, rolled up jumpers, and essentials; each item ticked from a mental list within my mind. Hat, scarf, coat. Check in the mirror.

Looking back at me – a mess of womanhood. Eyes, tired and sore. Face, pale and drawn. Hair, a tangled bush. Not quite the alluring coquette I had in mind. Placing the canvas bag over my shoulder I made my way down to the reception area.

Mother was waiting, in a coat of grey wool, pink hat and gloves; an ever present reminder that her daughter had no fashion sense at all.

"What time is it?" I ask in the most nonchalant way I can summon up.

"10 o'clock." Mother stretches forth her Gucci watch, sparkling in the morning sun.

"Four hours," I mutter to myself. "Four hours."

—

One o'clock and the shops were heaving. We had trudged through each department store before trailing back to the first for Mother to buy a scarf. Coffee at eleven thirty was taken in a small uptown diner (my choice) blaring out jukebox favourites. Mother was appalled, though the funny side was she made no comment or wise-crack (my opinion of her sarcasm) in my hearing. It was during coffee that I dropped the bombshell of visiting the Empire State Building on my own. You would have thought a hurricane was about to strike. She moaned, argued, and, for the sake of a better word, bloody demanded she accompany me.

What was I to do?

If I refused she would be on the phone to Father, wailing and complaining.

If I accept her company she could discover my plan, and Hell hath no fury ...

Fate was not playing a fair game.

The clock struck one thirty. I submitted to fate.

—

It rose before us, the pantheon of structural elegance, the Empire State Building.

More than one quarter of a mile into the Manhattan skyline this national landmark sported 6,500 windows, and 73 elevators. Designed top-down by William F. Lamb from drawings taken from the Reynolds Building in Winston, Salem, North Carolina, and Carew Tower Cincinnati, Ohio. Construction began on St Patrick's Day 1930, coinciding with the Great Depression. According to history a stream flowed on the site beforehand, and the land was occupied by the Waldorf-Astoria, catering for the city's elite (just up Mother's street). In 1931 the then president, Herbert Hoover. switched on the lights of this impressive building; plus the action was repeated the following year when Franklin. D. Roosevelt toppled him from power. The 86th floor observatory tower stands at 1,050 feet, with an open-air promenade, partly enclosed by a glass pavilion. The 102nd observatory floor is a spectacle that enabled the American Society of Civil Engineers to dub it one of the seven wonders of the modern world. The Art Deco spire, (originally designed to be a mooring mast for airships) salutes the city and its inhabitants in an unobtrusive fashion. The whole building is a beacon to man's superiority over bricks and mortar.

I had made Mother promise to wait in the lobby, convincing her it was a secret wish to view Manhattan on my own, and after all, this trip was for my birthday. Guilt for the days she had coerced me into shopping, or fed up with arguing, she was lulled into agreeing. I promised her, if she would wait in the lobby, while I viewed the city from the observer's tower, afternoon tea awaited us at the most expensive hotel she could find. Boy, did she bite the bait, my mother loves 'regal'. She chose the newly furbished Peninsular Hotel. Swanky, smart, and very expensive!

By the time we had reached 350, 5th Avenue, I was glad I had worn flat boots; the wind was howling, making the thick trousers and jumper a heaven sent choice. Leaving Mother in the Art Deco lobby, furnished with paintings of the seven wonders of the world, and two large American flags hanging beside a metal relief structure of the building, I headed toward the lift. I had worked this moment down to the last detail.

As follows: after my meeting with my lover I would have tea with Mother, where I would try and explain my intention to stay in the States, arrange a time and place herself and my father could meet him, and beg her not to worry.

Jimmy – a sigh – not sure. I did not want to lose him, but if he was going to be awkward ... I guess the suspense of our parting would soon make him sit up and see how wrong his judgement had been. I inhale, exhale, tell my heart to slow down. I push my way into the crowded lift. Once again in this story I imagine the men, women and children resembling the proverbial sardines squashed into *that* proverbial can.

The doors clang shut; the lift starts its journey upward, scent and sweat of bodies in close proximity drew me back to a narrow alleyway in the back-street of Berlin, to a drab bedsit in Paris. Ecstasy shot through my veins. the dreams of youth played out among this echelon of history. In front of me a man holding tight to his grandchild's hand lurched towards me as the lift jolted to a stop on the 86th floor. Apologising, he ruffled the child's hair as the large doors clattered open.

I emerged onto one of the most breath-taking spectacles I had ever seen. Excited children ran here and there heading to the vacant viewing binoculars dotted around the platform, adults fumbled for loose change; upon finding the correct amount inserting it into the waiting slots, drawing in their breath as the state of New York swam before them. Deep in thought, I found a deserted corner; with the wind rattling in my ears and the birds soaring above my head, the city below faded from my mind. My body tingled as it felt a slight shift; almost as if the elements were teasing those of us who dare stand at such a height, infinity made by human hands. Lost in thought I did not hear the tread behind me; gasped as a slight pressure bore down on my shoulder. Swinging round, I am startled by the man standing before me; not my lover of Berlin, not the painter of Paris, but a dark haired figure whose bronze skin gave him the appearance of an exotic nationality. The fine cut suit and trilby hat completed his transformation.

"Kurt?" the name rolled from my tongue.

The pale blue eyes took in those around us, the hardness buried within eventually finding my own; the voice stern. "Patrice" as he pushed me back onto the strong railings and kissed me, a roughness, undiscovered in our earlier encounters igniting the embers within me. I clung to him.

"You submit?" the pronunciation of 'submit' echoed on the passing wind.

I giggled. "I never submit, I always give in."

Pulling me closer he ran his fingers slowly across my neck, downwards toward the buttons of my coat. Embarrassment made me shrink from his touch. "Kurt, please."

"Shut up," His voice was wild. "If I tell you again, my name is PATRICE."

Disturbed, I cringed at the way he looked me up and down, sneering, cruel. "Sharaz said you were every inch the child in a woman's body." Wait, was I hearing correct, that stick on legs with the bob?

"She said what?"

My lover sniggered, moved closer, barred any movement I may have foreseen.

"You heard." Still trying to loosen the buttons on my coat. "I would say you are nothing like a child – you are a worm."

Was this his idea of a joke? Please say yes.

"She – she lied to me." He will be mad at her, feel sorry for me, wrap his arms round me and laugh.

I believe the saying goes, 'Face like thunder.' (Ridiculous, I agree, no-one, not even the brainiest scientist would even be able to guess what thunder looked like, would they?) I shivered. The wind, that's all, his hands tightening on my arms

"Sharaz lied. Tut, tut, naughty girl. I know she warned you off me, the stupid minx told me. Oh dear."

He focused on a couple standing a few inches from us "Scram," he shot their way, took hold of my chin. "Never mind, she will not be doing that for a while."

The word confusion will not begin to cover my bewilderment; the tumult inside me was fanning into a fire.

"She told you?" I was stupefied.

"That's what I said didn't I? She will not leave the commune for a month or two."

He kissed my ear, laughing out loud, bitter, coarse.

"Stop." I struggled for breath, a space, to think. "I do not understand. Wh – what has happened to her?"

People were staring, he caught the darting of my eyes.

"Left, right, left," he mimicked, his tongue finding my earlobe. "Bad girl, how thick are you?" I felt the roughness of his hands as they slid beneath my coat. "She is, how do you say, indisposed, and you, a rich man's daughter, my ticket to complete anonymity." Tell me this nightmare will end soon! *Don.'t hold your breath!* He smelt of eau-de-cologne, overpowering and expensive, creeping into my sinuses, clouding my mind, attacking those emotions I could not control.

"I think I love you." Mind let loose, fantasy taking over.

He took a small step backwards. "You are stupid," he spat, my hands grasping his jacket as he shook me with the temper of a child to her disrespectful rag doll: then, I touched hardness, something that lay beneath his jacket top pocket. "What is that?" I screamed.

Heads turned, twisted in our direction.

"Mucking about," he yelled. "Being silly."

Heads turned round again, muttering to whoever they had been speaking with.

"Be quiet," his hand tightened around my waist, the threat in his whisper chilled my heart.

"Please Ku, Jul – hell, Patrice – what is it?"

"A gun." The sneer winded me. Speak to me.

Silence.

Someone, **tell me**, I will wake from this nightmare. What was wrong with me? Say anything, bloody anything.

"Sharaz. Is it true?" His face crumpled with reproachful angst. "What she told me – you and her, how long, why?"

A moment of calm. Next, I thought he would convulse.

"True? What is truth, you are the last to know. We understand each other, and the firm." His voice rose, whipping itself into a fury in harmony with the wind.

I swallowed hard. What had he said? The firm? My father called the Stasi that, the bob had mentioned it in passing. I am scared, this man – my lover – Jimmy – (why am I thinking of my friend now?)

I struggled – he struggled – people moved away.

My eyes darted to the lift.

He saw my distress, gurgled a low sickening sound, wrapped his arms tight round my waist.

Panic tore through me "What – what have you done to her?"

"A bit of roughing up... a lesson."

Fear set in, a fear I promise you I had never experienced before.

284

His hands start to roam; warm against the skin beneath my jumper. I sense the bonfire of my fantasy. I think of those letters, discard them in disgust. Over his shoulder I could see the lift doors opening and closing; people pouring out and going in. I picture Mother.

Wriggling in the warmth of his hands, I hear the bleat of my cry. "Someone is waiting for me."

He froze, clasped my hands to my side, pinning me even harder to the wire.

"Witch, and I thought you wanted me."

"I do." Once again that cry of pain.

His lips teased the side of my mouth. "You want me, and yet – who?"

"Who?"

"Who, have you brought with you?"

"My mother."

"Liar." The loud drone created a vacuum where people around us moved as far away as possible.

Patrice spat into the wind. "*He* has found me."

I stiffened.

"You have brought *him* here."

"Him?"

He squeezed the skin along my waist, I ouched, realising he meant Jimmy. Oh dear Lord, if he thinks that, Jimmy is right. You know what I mean. Answer me. My heart beat fast, fear has no concern for its victim. "No, it's my mother."

His mouth twisted. "If you say so, Rhia." (first time he had used my name). "Let me remind you. I knew back at uni how you wanted me" (make it sound grubby) "how you played out a delusion festered in the back alley of Berlin. You could not let go, could not see the act for what it was, a moment of fun." (**no...**) "Little Miss Fantasy wanted more, so much more," iron pressed close to my chest, "that longing led to Paris, and now to this, only what your head will not get, is you are my guarantee to freedom."

I feel the edge of his nail tracking my spine, creating images of what should, or could have been; my stomach lurches, nausea. I want to let go.

15

I am trapped between the real world and its surreal equivalent.

"What do you want?" I know. Could you have done better? "Cut the drama. *He,* your friend, has he found me?"

I panicked. "Jimmy? How do I know? Please, Kurt, (slipped out again) what is wrong?"

The pressure of his fingers came to rest in the sensitive part of my back.

"You. You are my problem. How many times do I have to correct you?" The menacing bellow cutting through the howling wind.

I shift from one foot to the other, try to cut through his anger. "Jimmy is not here, I came for you."

He let out a low exasperated sigh. "But, I do not want you, just the money."

I struggle with my tears. "You wrote, you sa – said."

"Fool. You are quite the little actress, always following her fantasies, never grasping what is before her eyes." Here he hesitated, moved his fingers until they rested just above my breast bone. "Not once were you able to see what was so plain to everybody else."

My lips quivered, tingling from the sensation of his roaming tongue.

"What do you mean?"

"Come on, no more games. I am sick of them. You have chased me until your feet must be sore."

"No." The tears could not be held back, they spilt down my cheeks.

"Yes," he shouted. "That is why Sharaz told you about my set up. She wanted you gone."

"And you?" my voice hardly audible.

"Me?" the weight of his body was pressing onto me. "I wanted fun, at first, but then you pursued me, so I thought, ah, this girl has a rich father; discussed it with mine."

Fantasy was becoming fact. Jimmy – hate – shame – willpower – gone.

Through the tears my words stumbled "I – it – i – is – th – the – mo – money, th – that's – a – all?"

"Wow, brain is working. Rich bitch. The odd night, but, you are nothing but a means to an end. That and two fingers to that wretched friend of yours." Don't utter a thing. I grant you have tried to tell me throughout my story that I am deluded.

Silence.

Forget the bloody non-speaking – answer. Hurry! "I don't understand." Wind whistles, people carry on walking, viewing.

He, shifts, feels inside his jacket. "What is there to understand? Through art he has uncovered many a party member, now he has found me."

"How do you know?"

"That besotted wife of your artist. She hated me."

"The 'Bum ....' Rosie!"

He side-stepped my surprise, this time literally spitting on the ground. "If I could get my hands on her ... she had the guy's personal number."

I felt the ground rising to meet me. "Rosie, Jimmy? He is *my* friend."

The wind stung my face as it stole the remark from me.

—

I thought of the 'Bumble-bee' (inside me this is what she will always be – a false, hypocritical, double-dealing bee, with a deadly sting). She had not told me Jimmy was on pally-pally terms with her. I remember her mentioning my friend's tattoo, fretting in-case I said something to her boss (disclosed confidentiality, wish I had), certainly not told me she had his private number. I would have remembered.

I thought of myself, trapped between a thousand feet drop and the Devil's advocate. My fantasy died, there on the 86th floor of the Empire State Building (thank my lucky stars it was not 102nd floor). I could see now, everything about this man was false, the world he moved in, his friends, the way he swapped names, his love for me. *'At last,'* you breathe. I think of Jimmy, hiding behind the tag of museum curator while tracking his prey like a hunter in the wild. The 'Bumble-bee' personally dialling *my* best friend. Sharaz, stupid to the point of certifiable, and – Kurt/Jules/Patrice, damn his chrysalis/butterfly status, swapping persona and country just to aid his bloody cause.

Somewhere in the city a clock struck the hour.

The fingers penetrating my skin pinched, made me squeak.

"Are you listening to me?" The rough tone made me snap back to the present.

"I – I was thinking."

"Well, think on this, I need money, lots of it."

My heart flipped, pained at what I had lost, longed for a pathway of escape.

"Money?"

His contorting face reminded me of a Halloween mask, his voice of a wounded animal.

"I will kill you. Do not think you would be my first." His hand began to move inside the jacket. "You are my escape route. Do not –" his eyes saw mine dart to the lift – "for one moment think of shouting, making a fuss or that woman thing of fainting. I have it all covered. I –" he paused to look around – "have aided interrogations for the cause with my father. I really would not consider anything foolish." His hand held me, pushing my body in a vice-like grip, further back toward the barrier.

Funny really, to others we gave the impression of bonding, fused in the heat of the moment. People were nudging each other as they past us in a pre-conceived notion of agreement or disgust; avoiding two people they suspected were locked in consented desire.

"Please, I must go." Desperation filtered through my heavy breathing.

"Go where?" his fingers dug deeper.

"My mother." Pause. "She is waiting for me, believe me when I say she will raise the alarm."

"Raise the alarm, for a woman of your age, come again. Do you think I am a dreamer like you, one that will be taken in – and spat out?" His voice rose. I was sinking fast. "Do not make fun."

"Make fun? What else can I do, Rhia. You are pathetic, take the blinkers from your eyes."

Crippling shame made me cringe. The twisted mouth let out an expletive. Children hid behind their parents.

"You were always my plaything, Rhia. A stab in the back for upright Jimmy. I hate him. I gave him the chance of freedom. All he had to do was leave you."

"You offered him a role in the –"

He roared, "Firm, say it. I did. Especially as he had already put two and two together on the afternoon of the Berlin wall. Waiting for me in the hall on my return to the house. I told him shopping me would break your heart. Silly ass couldn't bear that. Told me to go to hell."

My awesome surprise made him laugh out loud again. "Oh yes my lover, you were my tool."

The sweating hand pinched and squeezed, fumbling for the desired effect.

"You are such a spoilt brat, protected by the friend who is afraid to tell you he adores you, kept afloat by your rich parents, what do *you* really understand about freedom, or for that matter, love?"

I went to speak; blown away by the accelerating wind, forced the words out.

"You said you loved me."

Dark head shook in the wind. "Did I? You dream. I took you because I could, not because I wanted you. I have had enough of this, you are not worth the bother." He dropped his hands from my waist, removed them from under my coat. "I want money." The weapon sparkled in his hand.

"Please let me go." My knees were starting to sag.

"Pay me, yes you will. Shall I let you go? Ummm, let's see. It will depend on the amount."

I fought to be free, search in my handbag, found my phone, he slapped it back, I found my chequebook, my shaking hand writing the chit. I had to act quick. "Here, take this." *'The amount?'* you ask.

I pretend not to hear. Let's just say Mattie's money is no more. "Generous," the dark head nodded, in that desperate way of an irritated horse.

"I have made it out to you, today's date, please. Let me go."

'You begged him'

Yes, I was beside myself with fear... and my heart was breaking.

'Here we go, drama queen.'
CRUEL

I cannot say for sure, so therefore cannot write it down, why or at what precise moment he decided to let me go. Maybe it was memories (I like to think so), or the guard began to stroll; large, shall we say heavily built man, around the platform. He had a truncheon at his side, and a bulging holster on his hip.

Kurt (sorry, I refuse to call him by any of his ridiculous names any more) leant back against the railing; room for me to pass? I eased around him, making ready to run. As a shaft of lightning he grabbed my arm. 'Done for' as they say in a gangster film – then, pulled me closer. In a low menacing voice he hissed, "Do not say or do anything you may regret." He caught my puzzlement. "Jimmy. I have your address, and something for him. Now, get out of my sight, you creature of easy virtue. Oh, by the way, the party will be grateful."

The snarl evaporated the last shred of emotion I owned; without another word, tears of relief and humiliation cascading down my cheeks, I ran to the lift, flung myself inside, and pressed the ground floor button.

—

I am scared, this fight between desire and rejection holds me in its grip. The lift doors clanged open, tourists pushed past me, no thought for those of us who wished to step out as they chatted, bumped and squeezed into every available space.

Out, onto the marble tiles, lost and alone; buried in my own thoughts.

"Rhia," The high-pitched squawk elbowed its way through the gathering crowds to my side. Congregating visitors swarmed across the lobby, waiting for lifts, visiting the shop, raising their voices in melodious rapture at the sights and sounds.

"Rhia, I was just telling that polite guard over there that my daughter had probably fallen off the balcony." Whatever your thoughts, reader, please, keep them to yourself. I flinched. "How silly, Mother, the platform has a glass panel and nets."

Mother bristled, cast her eyes to make sure no-one had heard me, then led me to a bench, where she proceeded to ease me down, then sit herself.

"You, young lady, appear to be distraught. Are you still in possession of your purse, or your expensive jewellery?"

Expensive jewellery? A few tatty bangles. I could think of something that would aid her flapping – my honour in shreds!

The guard (presumably the one Mother deemed polite) had decided to saunter our way, presumably to ask Mother if I was her child.

"Madam, is this your daughter?"

"Yes. Thank-you. I over-reacted I suppose. I am sorry for the things I said." *'What?'* Curiosity getting the better of you.

This time I warn you don't go there, Mother is Mother. Say no more! "Not a bit." The guard tipped his cap "The pleasure was mine" (men – creeps); anyone who has had the enjoyment of my mother's 'panic' would not call it a pleasure.

Mother fumbled with her coat, her boots, hat, scarf, the least little thing to waver asking me outright.

"As I asked" she tossed her head in the air. "Have you lost anything?"

How do I tell her I have lost my heart? *'Repeat, drama queen.'* "I am still intact." Start counting, "Purse, bangles, head, fingers."

"Stop it, Rhia, I was worried."

Guilt seized me. "So-rry."

She slipped her arm into mine. OK, I will give her this one. She looked worried.

"Fine, although you seem to have been crying."

My mother should have been a spaniel, the springer breed that sniffs out trouble. I clothe myself in pretence. "The wind stings your eyes up there."

It is fine for you to sit there and look at me in that way. I can tell you quite frankly that if I say anything else we would be facing a battle more fierce than anything we could imagine. Her screeching, my blubbering, would bring the secret service out in force, running round in circles, sunglasses and guns pointed up everyone's nose.

Moving slowly out of this magnificent building the fleeting shadow of a man scurrying past caught my peripheral vision; the swagger I knew only too well, fear leapt from my stomach into my throat. I fastened my hold on Mother's arm, slowed her to almost a standstill as he vanished out of sight.

"Coffee?" The intensity of my mother's voice made me jump.

"A drink?" The question was flat.

"A promise is a promise," she fired back.

My world had fell apart, and my mother wanted coffee.

She smiled sweetly. "Come on, this is as much for you as me; take the sting from your eyes."

I shudder in the afternoon temperature, visualise that cheque. *'Cancel it,'* you demand.

Not possible, the cheque book left by my grandmother, all signed with her signature, needs her authority – not going there. Mother hailed a cab, literally threw me in, and applying her swankiest style, demanded to be taken to the Hotel Peninsular.

This girl would have been a fool, miserable or not, if I had not grasped why Mother chose this hotel. Exclusive? You may prefer 'out of this world.'

The foyer could easily hold sixty people at leisure, with two double ante-rooms to either side sprinkled with chairs and sofas of brocade damask and velveteen, scattered with cushions of matching colours. Either side of the sweeping staircase a tall round pedestal, topped with vases full of seasonal blooms stood on parade, inviting their clientele to step onto the gold carpet, while placing our hand onto the gold and black bannister rail – sophistication grand style! This led to the upper landing where more gold, in the guise of foot-wells fanned off to the right and left. On a par (only more elegant, if that is possible) with the building we had just left, the design was 1930's art nouveau.

Mother came into her own, raising her hand to the boy, in his extravagant uniform, reclining by the desk.

"May I help you, Madam?"

"You may." She flashed a daunting smile his way. "My daughter" (hanging my head to hide my red rimmed eyes) "and I require coffee."

"Of course." (More than his job was worth to glare in my direction) "Follow me."

He led us to a lift (is everything in this city obtained by standing in a moving iron cage), pressed a button and waited for the doors to open.

"You require the top floor, Madam. Fives Restaurant. Beautiful views over Manhattan."

"Thank you." Mother brushed him away, her overbearing snobbery played to its full potential. "Come along, Rhia, let us partake of the view."

She really was in her element.

There would be no time to sit in contemplation, not one second would be spent in silence. She would parade, exhibit like a débutante at her first dance.

Damn the lady in waiting; the mess in the background whose mind was a mixture of scathing lies and dying fantasies.

16

The passing of each day brought its own disquiet. Don't get me wrong, I joined in the planned pursuits. Walked, ate, drank (more than I should), clapped at the colossal amount of shows Mother booked us into, and on the whole acted as normally as I could. Mother did not breathe one word about that afternoon on the 86th floor observatory platform (a side of my mother I did not know). However, the coffee hour (that's what she says – I say it was more like two hours) at the Hotel Peninsular was dragged out at every chance.

On the Wednesday of the second week I propelled my feet to the nearest bank under the pretence of checking my funds. I requested a run-down of my expenditure into the account Mattie had set up for me. The money had gone three days after that dreadful afternoon.

After 'Black Wednesday' as I will call it, my moods were up and down. Mother, father, and Jimmy had not the slightest idea how to please me. Jimmy, especially, received the raw edge of my temper, such as when he asked me to visit a new art gallery on the other side of town.

"An exhibition of new painters," he chirped, dropping a few names into the conversation.

That's right, Alexander and Jules Dragner were among them. I feigned boredom, stamped like a child, and reminded him it was *my* holiday, and how could he be so selfish to think of work? Jimmy gave in, amazed more than he dared to say over how vehement I was.

It was Father's suggestion we visit the Statue of Liberty and Central Park on our last day. When we all agreed, the poor man fell back in a state of shock. I could not care less where we ended up, as long as there was no painting in sight.

'Painter' to me was a dirty word.

Mother nearly threw herself into the wardrobe to find the fur stole purchased the day before at one of New York's exclusive stores. Enveloping herself in the brown mottled skin

(I have commented on this before, fake does not belong in Mother's dictionary), she announced, "We should take a carriage ride through the park."

Father conceded to this last expensive treat – for if Mother suggests, you can stake your life on it oodles of money is required – but only on the condition that we visit the Statue of Liberty first. Mother hesitated, lifted her new shoes out of their resting place, and slipped her tiny feet into the brown patent heels (think blisters, think pain). Jimmy, in a sheepskin hat and coat, offered me his hand to start the journey. I swallowed hard, glad I had put on some dark glasses against the winter sun, and, for once, accepted gracefully.

I suppose at least I have my friend, even if Kurt grassed up his feelings – if that was the truth – *if, if, if.*

—

New York harbour was a mass of bodies. Before us, positioned on a twelve acre island, stood that symbolic statue of freedom, titled by many as the 'Beautiful Lady'. Aloft a rectangular stonework pedestal (her foundation is shaped in irregular form as an eleven pointed star, moulded from a sheath of copper patina) the lady held a stone tablet against her left side, engraved with the month, date and year the United States gained Independence: 'July IV MDCCLXXVI'; July 4th 1776. Her extended right hand gripped the famous flaming torch, originally copper, later altered to hold glass panes in gold leaf. Presented by the French in 1886 as a gesture of friendship, this impressive lady welcomed tourists, immigrants, and returning Americans with the same confident smile.

Jimmy, who stood behind me followed my gaze to the seven spiked rays around her head.

"They symbolise a halo," he was informing me. "A gesture of liberty to enlighten the world. Created by Frederic Auguste Bartholdi and Alexandre Gustave Eiffel. It stands about 305 feet from plinth bottom to the tallest ray. Some say modelled on the statue of Helios 292-280 BC, otherwise known as the Colossus of Rhodes that was destroyed in an earthquake in 226 BC, or the statue of Saint Charles Borromeo, Archbishop of Milan 1584."

As in France, Jimmy is a fountain of detail.

All around I could hear the snipes or recommendations for such a huge figure.

"Look at that," one woman griped. "Have you ever?" another's brash voice entered the furore. "Typical," another hollered. "The yanks always go that one step extra."

At the same moment a group of American students chanted in full volume, "Land of Liberty, Home of the Free."

My stomach squirmed. Freedom should have been mine – with him – here. I paused to think of the seven lettered word.

How many times do I say it to myself? It is just a word, flat, meaningless, unobtainable.

Others think differently.

"What do you think?" Jimmy was close to my ear.

My brow furrowed.

"The statue. Is she not beautiful? What she stands for, do you believe it?"

His gaze searched my eyes staring out across the Hudson River.

"Freedom, you mean?"

"Yes."

"We took a pact on it." What kind of answer was that?

His brow furrowed.

"I know. Fat lot of good that was."

Jimmy made a three point turn, there and then, within the jostling crowd.

"Where did that come from? All according how you size it up."

"Is that your opinion?" I cry into the deep crowd he had delved into. My friend did not answer, did not even turn around to see if I was following.

The word 'adore' crashed into my head as a wave crashes onto a beach. Kurt had lied AGAIN.

Jimmy cared for nothing, unless it was a thousand years old, and cracking down the middle!

Mother came tottering over to where Jimmy had finally settled himself on a seat at the side of the harbour, her new shoes pinching her toes, causing her legs to redden. Actually she looked cold, silly woman, however smart the stole it cannot compensate for a coat. She pointed to where my father had joined a group of foreign students, clicking his camera, and trying to spout history.

"Those kids" – as she politely put it – "are egging him on," catching her breath. "Jimmy, make him stop."

Placing her hand on her head in dramatic fashion she sat down to wait, the word, "Vulgar" falling from her red painted mouth. Vulgar Mother, what is more plebeian than a woman of your age strutting her stuff on a rostrum of ice, wobbling all over the place, wet brown fur sticking to her expensive make-up?

'Nasty.' you remark.

Listen. Do I care? Jimmy pounded over to my father's 'playground'. Good thing he did, for Henry, as Mother was chirping into the wind, slipped on the ice. My friend (if I could find it in my heart to call him that at this very moment) saved him from hurting himself (worse than his vanity that is), retrieved the camera, slapped him on the back as men do, and directed him to where we were waiting. Gathering his breath, my father ordered us to follow him to where a yellow cab sat revving his engine. Mother tripped herself up trying to keep up, the wobbling heels straining at their connection point in a way that made me suck air. I brought up the rear. (Good word for someone who had stuffed every cream cake in sight since that blighted day, and was expecting to have gained at least half a stone).

Our destination – Central Park – a flat piece of land to add to my misery.

—

My verdict on New York.

It is a city of cabs. Thumbs up everywhere, mouths whistling or hailing. The truth – if you have not joined this throng before the end of your American holiday, you certainly have not lived. These enclosed pods of given and received information (most American cab drivers talk nonstop) are a law unto themselves. They blare horns, spin round corners, and brake at an instant's notice. It is a miracle the passenger does not arrive at their destination in a state of convoluted disembodiment. The up-side, as seen through the eyes of one who has used them to excess, is the ease at which the driver moves through crowded streets. Give them a name, and no matter how you pronounce it, they will get you there.

Conversation is the key, that and the ear they offer. It might as well be a long-lost friend you are talking to, not the ear of a complete stranger. One might go as far as to say the life of the cabbie holds much to be admired, yet, as with the hairdresser at home, the burden of gossip could also foul up his life; if only in an extended situation. Mother loved the cab, and I am sure in the duration of our ride to Central Park our driver (young man, twenty something, Irish descent) had gleaned the full story of our visit to his beloved country. On Mother alone he would have been half way to writing her biography.

—

Central Park spread before us like an oasis in the dessert. A surprising green belt of peace and calm in the metropolitan madness of Manhattan. As we drew closer Mother clapped her hands and eagerly pointed to the entrance. In full glory, swishing their tails, and tossing their heads were a pair of white horses and a black carriage. Now reader, if it is true what many in the equine world say about horses and head tossing, this pair have already decided that there will be no unity between themselves and us – oh dear, fun all round! By their heads, a man in a dark blue uniform was enticing them to munch on the odd sugar cube. The swirl of gold on his epaulettes gave the impression of an important person within his chosen work.

A guess – the owner of these two fine beasts?

Father paid the cab driver, and we all clambered out, swapping our warm enclosed gossip hub for a runny nose and shivering body. Once settled in the carriage, the man proceeded to wrap us in thick woollen blankets. Mother gave the appearance of a small springtime animal, caught in the winter chill, clothed in a thin layer of fur. I wish you could have seen her: the pinched nose, red at the end, the trembling chin; a rabbit trapped for the pleasure of mankind. The man mounted his seat, wound the reins around his hands, clicked his teeth in response to the horses' head rearing, and set off at a leisurely pace. I was certainly unprepared for the sights that met us. Lakes, ponds, walking tracks, wildlife sanctuary, ice skating rinks, conservatory gardens, areas of natural wood, and running tracks, an outdoor amphitheatre, a zoo, special oasis for migrating birds, major and minor grass land for team sports, enclosed playing parks, a 106 billion gallon reservoir, a castle used as a nature centre, the Swedish marionette theatre, and a beautiful carousel.

Boy, my mind was whirling. Never, in my wildest imaginings could I have expected this piece of flat ground (as I had put it) to be everything the city was not; calm, peaceful – an expanse of nature within a rambling riot of commerce and trade.

It was hard to take everything in. Even more so when the carriage suddenly came to a halt under the branches of an evergreen tree. The man jumped down and ran to the back of the carriage. 'Great,' was my first thought. 'Spoil it by breaking down.'

Not so. The man unroped a large wicker basket strapped to the footboard, which he placed between our feet. Opening the lid he took out four champagne glasses, handed them to us, and filled them to capacity. He then saluted my father, made sure the horses were tethered properly, and disappeared into the trees.

I was amazed. Clutching fast the glass in my cold hand, a chorus met my ears.

"Happy birthday, Rhia."

I looked at the three people in the carriage raising their glasses, wishing me well.

"Enjoy your surprise?" my father winked.

"To remember this holiday," my mother joined in (she had got to be joking).

"To rid yourself of the past, only the future counts," Jimmy added.

"We love you." Father patted my knee.

A small tear pushed its way through my eyelashes. I quickly wiped it away.

"We did not –" my father began.

"Hush, Henry." My mother chinked his glass with her own.

Jimmy put his arm around me (I let him). In an odd way, it felt good. *'A safe haven from the tribulations of the week gone by?'* Your question catches me off guard.

I refuse to reply. Moving to the edge of the seat so the arm fell behind me, I drank the sparkling wine.

Jimmy's brown eyes rolled, he whispered, "You are very sullen these last days."

"Fed up with the sound of your voice on freedom, freedom, freedom."

"Right." He scooped the last drop of champagne onto his tongue.

Uncalled for I know, but the warmth of his arm, the nearness of his body was disturbing my composure. I had still not forgiven him for the drama at the ESB. *'Jimmy?'* you quiz. *'How was it his fault?'*

He persuaded me to go to Germany.

I can almost feel your disbelief. *'Your choice, your pact.'*

No, I inwardly scream, his.

For the first time since beginning this account of my tribulations I sense you would like to give up on me. Please don't. Our picnic was accompanied by low strains of music; a background for the many skaters floating across the ice rink. Children as young as four or five move warily under the prodigious eye of a parent, while couples interlink arms as they dance with the grace acquired from many years of practice. A light wind rose, tickling our faces, and causing us to shiver. Mother snuggled up to Father, and out of need, I inched myself closer to Jimmy.

The man in the blue uniform re-emerged from the trees, packed the picnic basket, and removed it to the back of the carriage. He jumped up into the driving seat, and we set off once more. Mother snoozed, snug in the blanket tucked around her, protected from the wind by father's arm. Jimmy was studying what I would define as the hairs on my neck. My next sentence is going to sound so silly, but I dare not look my friend's way; a dread was beginning to fill me, a dread I could not justify – my friend had somehow withdrawn into himself.

"Something wrong?" I spoke as quietly as I could.

"You could say that."

I screwed up my nose.

"We come on holiday, you hardly speak. You go wandering at the beginning. What do you expect me to think?"

"Enjoying it," I mumble. How feeble is that?

Jimmy made no remark. Father leaned in our direction, trying hard not to disturb the woman on his arm. "Tell her about that obnoxious painter."

"Painter?" My stomach sank.

Jimmy stared over the park. "I doubt Rhia will know him."

"Who?" The rabbit, headlights – get the picture?

"A guy called Alexander Cromwell." The flippancy in Jimmy's tone did nothing to relieve my dread, as a matter of fact it embedded it further.

My father was laughing. "A real oddball."

"More than that," Jimmy said through clenched teeth. "He was a downright liar."

I pretended not to understand. "You have lost me."

"The day you and your mother went to the Empire State Building –" Father began, only for Jimmy to intervene. "I had asked your father to accompany me, on a quest for the museum" (act normal, say nothing) "to track down, or pick up clues, concerning that mate of ours, Kurt. Lives here, in the States." (Heart thumping... pulse racing) "Anyway, the only person we saw was this guy, to my utter amazement the tattooist who had etched my ankle. He told us he knew no-one by the name of Kurt, or Jules" (please... I must get home) "said he was in charge of the gallery. Did I believe him? Not on your life!"

Father nodded in agreement.

"What really capped my distrust," Jimmy was now full in my face, "was this guy – Alexander – pretended he had never met me, acted strange, his manner darkened when I asked if a girl named Rosie was with him. Vehemently shaking his head, said he knew no-one of that name. I had the wrong commune, and slammed the door in our face."

"More to him than meets the eye," Father declared.

Trying to make light I giggled (in a way). "Detective now."

Jimmy was in no mood to play. "No, the director of the museum in Paris asked me to do a bit of digging. The art world is a good cover for traitors." I thought of my breasts, my back, my waist, arms – every intricate drawing. Think. Fly to the web. Over the next hour the clatter of the horses' hooves echoed in my mind, the clickety click noise escaping from my mouth as it did when I was a child.

Jimmy spoke first, "Sobering thought, Rhia, you making childish noises. Better than enquiring over that silly tattoo of mine, the one you made such a fuss about before Bhutan."

Another move on the chess board!

"The name, you mean, gave up on that score. It is up to you what is etched on your body."

Jimmy looked surprised. "Right. How did you know it was a name?"

I stumbled. "Saw it when we went swimming."

"Ah, you can read Chinese."

Panic, sweat, headlights getting nearer.

"I guessed."

Jimmy came nearer to my ear. "Well thought out."

Double alarm bells – I feign tipsiness.

Noticing my drama Jimmy pulls a face. "Shame, are we a trifle queasy?"

It was getting chillier; the television at the hotel had warned snow was on its way. I had no reason to believe otherwise. Actually the wind was not alone in its chill factor. My friend's tone was blowing cold – easily –2 Fahrenheit, the inflection forming its own iceberg between us. The chance to bite back at Jimmy passed, Father engaged him in a discussion on rare birds – two feet, but with wings (I am sorry, anything to restore a fraction of humour). Mother awoke, embarrassed at her short nap, complaining she was cold. Her moaning and huge pretence of shivering was a forewarning the trip would soon be over. This time I will silently thank her. We trotted to the entrance of the park.

Coming to a standstill, the driver jumped to the ground and opened the carriage door for us to alight. Father eased himself down, thanked the man for his display of attentiveness, then offered Mother his hand. She, and it will come as no surprise to you, took it readily, before lifting her head in the air to act every inch the grand lady.

I promise I did not laugh, let out such a huge bellow that the champagne I had gulped would cause me to burp. Jimmy stepped down from the carriage, and immediately threw his arms wide to catch me if I fell.

What was he suggesting? I really was tipsy? Try again, pal!

Spotting my annoyance, he grabbed me and pulled me to him, pretending to steady my descent, at the same moment planting a kiss on my cheek. His action had been deliberate, much to Mother's amusement.

Apart from my friend being the most ridiculous human being on the planet, the thought of Jimmy's kiss, as in China, left me – cold? muddled? excited? Drat, I cannot think.

Father hailed a cab, we piled in. I counted eight feet over and over again, memorised the twists and turns in two sets of shoelaces, took in the inadequate amount of leather in the whole of Mother's shoes, spotted the marks making funny shaped circles on the toes of my own hiking boots, memorised the tapping of those feet as we all sat and listened to the driver. "Snow tonight, snow tonight."

We arrived back at the hotel, consumed by the driver's incessant chatting, informing us how he had made the switch from stuntman to cab driver: with his driving, he most certainly was telling the truth. Mother inched her way out of the cab, still shivering, still holding her fur stole up to her chin (1930s style). Jimmy crept after her, waylaying the hotel door before she had the chance to uncover her muffed hands. Father was paying the driver, giving me room to alight with ease.

Father came up behind me. "Hope you have enjoyed your day, Rhia." He stopped, then started. "Jimmy's idea for the champers. Happy birthday, the best is yet to come, and when we fly home tomorrow our lives will never be quite the same."

I wished to reply, 'That is true, it will never be the same,' but the words would not come. Instead I smiled sweetly, ran for the lift, my hand touching the cheek that stung from Jimmy's kiss.

17

The smell of vetiver oil was strong; acknowledged in aromatherapy circles as Vetiveria Zizanoides, the oil of tranquillity. Thank goodness it was, for I certainly needed something to ease my mind through this unfamiliar territory chosen for my tattoo. *'What?'* I hear you exclaim in surprise.

Time for me to explain. Music was playing, soft and low, the singer accentuating each vowel of the tear jerking modern ballad. I felt the crisp cloth beneath me, smelt its aroma, focused on the sweep of a name *'**Pen to Skin**.'* sewn onto the linen edge pillow under my head.

Realisation was slow, creeping into my fuddled head like a gathering storm. Impulse had brought me to this destination (that all too frequent sentiment that ruled my life), as impulse had opened my mouth to ask for... wait and see...

Had I lost my senses?

This was not Alexander's comfortable studio, but a tattoo shop tucked into a street I had never walked down before.

Why?

Because I needed a statement, an act of defiance, a proclamation saying, 'Rhia Bryant's life is in a mess. There is no need for pity, please. That would be the end of my determination to finish this story – all in good time.

What I can tell you is the apothegm of 'Kiss my Ass' stands out on my buttock exactly as I have written it.

You shake your head in disbelief.

Don't. Either way it does not matter to me, for the tattoo will incorporate all my emotions. The up-side of this errant visit was no-one knew me.

The owner, old enough to be my father, completed the cheeky eulogy in relative quiet.

"May hurt a bit, dearie" he warned. "But, never mind you have more than your share of flesh."

Thoughtless man.

On finishing his female partner soothed, covered and collected the money, an older 'Bumble-bee'?

Six months it had taken me to gather the courage and fortitude to find another tattooist, and apart from its backstreet location the place was clean and quiet.

I have got to admit I had roamed passed Alexander's studio. The place was gutted; builders everywhere, a board the size of a mountain proclaiming the forthcoming dress emporium! I recalled the American holiday, a fiasco if ever there was one; wait: I will be brave and re-label it a humiliating shambles. The meeting with Kurt had frightened me, crushed me to face the truth to such an extent that I wanted to curl up and feed myself a continuous stream of hot chocolate. *'Revenge,'* is bounded about.

Have no fear, all you iron-minded women, I tried to plan revenge. Nothing.

'How come?' you sigh.

I did not know where my lover was, or more important, what name he had taken. In all probability *my* money had paid for him to cut and run once more. Let me lay the facts bare – the longer I pondered over that day at the ESB I should thank my lucky stars I was here. Whether he would have used the weapon is open to everyone's guess; we must remember he had been raised within the field of torture and death.

I was just another number; another 'Bumble-bee', a besotted fool.

My other problem, pressing down on me like a ton of bricks, is Jimmy.

What Kurt said.

My friend's loyalty.

Those kisses.

I re-live China and America over and over again, and yes, you have every right to howl.

'I told you so.'

All I can ask for is patience. I am trying not to let tiresome reminders get in the way of my story.

Silence from my sternest critic?

"Wow."

Jimmy had not wasted a single moment of our homecoming. From the plane landing at London's major airport he had literally run home, re-packed, then flown to the French capital the next morning. Gone, in a puff of smoke.

Please do not deride him, he still phones me every Saturday night, half past six on the dot, surrounded by his work friends. His conversation is light, we joke, we chat, we share work stories, we are (what terminology shall I use) acquaintances.

The sad part of all this: I miss him. *'100% turnabout.'*

I hear, accept, comply. At work I became known as the 'saddo.'

If you thought 'downright rude' join me, if you do not – well ...

Churlish protests met my father's ears of me being grumpy, miserable, gruff with customers, rude to staff.

You think of it, made up or otherwise, and I am accused of it.

In the end, Father had to transfer me to a smaller bank on the other side of town.

Here, the days get slower, the work is far more mundane (if that is possible), *and* my colleagues are all the kind that moan for no reason, and groan out of necessity. I am incarcerated in a tomb.

I write to Mattie, ask for her pity, wait for her sympathy: none.

May 1999 a telegram arrives.

Rhia – I have been busy –Your supposed feelings for this man never existed – a cover up for the person you really want – stop – Listen to your subconscious – think of Jimmy – stop – Thousand year party on its way – that pact – don't leave it too late – stop – Mattie – x- x-- stop.

If this is my grandmother's wisdom (evidently the above was important to *her* to pay through the nose for it to be sped down a wire) I will sleep the rest of 1999.

—

Walking in a strange pattern I concentrate on the stinging of my nether region. This tattoo hurt, throbbed as if my skin would burst. It was smaller and by far the simplest, yet the ache resonated with my heart. I began to limp, dragging the right leg at a slower pace. People were staring at me, making a wide berth as if I had a placard hung around my neck. I held my head down, thought how Mother would fuss. Instruct me in that ostentatious voice of hers to 'hold my head high' as only guilty people gape at the footpath. How do you explain to someone that a person can leave fantasy behind, and still wallow in deception; somehow still collude with trickery and hypocrisy?

I continued to lie to Mother, today, and as many Saturdays as I could manage.

Sugared over the cracks in my father's temper by spying on his staff.

Fed Jimmy any nonsense I could think when he phoned.

Above everything. I lied to myself, over Berlin, Paris and America; basically over my life in general. Absorbed by ice-cream splodges, pop splashes, trodden-in cigarette ends, I did not see the woman in front of me, pushing a pram, humming a tune. When I realised two feet were stepping into my space it was too late – slam – trip – I fell 'whack' onto my backside.

The scream of pain would have stopped the London traffic. Thank goodness I live in a suburb.

"Rhia?" the name crashed through the barrier of pain.

Rolling onto my knees, rubbing my backside with no thought to the tattoo, or common decency, I came face to face with the 'Bumble-bee', Rosie Cromwell.

She had lowered herself to my height, the mirth of old spreading across weary eyes. Without even thinking of the derisive sting in my yell I shouted, **"You."**

She tried hard not to burst into full blown chortling. "It's me, sorry, you look so funny, grovelling at my feet."

"Glad you find me funny."

Her face was all contrition. "Here, take this, wipe your jeans. All I have I'm afraid." A baby wipe fluttered in her hand.

I snatched it with the disdain I felt. "I was thinking about you." Panting heavily, I struggled to my feet.

"Me?" She sounded surprised. "How strange. I also was thinking of you."

Gripping my hands around the pram handle I stood, pointed to the baby. "Yours?"

The 'Bum – Rosie – pointed to the pram. "Meet Oliver."
Oliver? Different circumstances, different memories, I would
have laughed out loud. Silence descended.

Oliver was the image of his Mother, large eyes, round face,
dark hair. The one disparity was he was a bundle of cooing and
merriment, whereas she had always been solemn. "Could not
resist," she was saying.

"He will be tormented," I muttered, cautiously moving to a
bench tucked onto the end of a shopping arcade. We both
collapsed; me with a gasp of pain, her with a drawn out sigh.

Rosie (my first grown up step, use the girl's name) rolled
her eyes upward. "Probably, but you must admit you would
have done the same."

I smiled back in confirmation, relaxing in her company.
Stretching forward she began to rock the pram. From the skinny
infatuated teenager I first encountered, she had blossomed into a
young woman. Flesh had settled on her scrawny frame, lending
a softer, gentler persona to the once flashy girl. Her hair was cut
short, feathered onto her face, highlighting her eyes. If anything,
it was the change in those eyes that startled me. A hard, 'don't
mess me around' glare looked out onto the world.

Was this the girl I had poked fun at in my mind, the
simpering, smitten teenage romantic? I wanted to ask so many
questions, yet at the same time run away from the answers. I
wanted to find out her connection with Jimmy.

She caught my hesitation. "Surprised at the change?"

"Yes, and no." Lying again.

"Of course you are. All down to Alexander, I'm afraid.
Well, America and that man."

She means Kurt. Change the subject.

"You came home?"

Rosie leant into the pram, stroked the now sleeping baby's
head, her voice cracking under emotion. "*He* – tried to
blackmail me – your artist friend."

Please, don't. "Weather, not sure what it is going to do."

Her eyes opened wide, she continued rocking the pram.
"Weather? No, not sure." Her voice was uncertain, unsteady
"*He* said if –" she paused, "if I would be his lover Alexander
would make the grade as an artist. Oliver was *two* months old."
She glared at me, challenged me to answer.

I felt the grip surround my heart, the squeeze of exhalation as my breath left my body.

What could I say? Words stuck in my throat.

She moved to raise the hood of the pram, protect its precious cargo from the noise around us.

"He lied to me also." More a protest than a statement.

Wiping a straggling tear from her eye she muttered, "Bewitched women. We deserve what we create."

The spasm in her throat touched a chord I wished to keep hidden. I sat there, twisting the handle of my bag, feeling sorry for myself.

"I came home," she whispered. "Alexander had a choice. Life as a painter, or Oliver and me."

I grasped her shaking fingers, could not help myself. "And?" It shot from my throat as a bullet would leave its gun barrel.

She shrugged. "Who knows? He hasn't returned yet. I don't think he will."

My heart burst for her pain, for it was me – *me* who had led them to that man; a selfish act that created a lottery of broken lives.

Satisfied Oliver was in a deep sleep, Rosie leant against the bench support.

"I thought of you often in America. Blamed you for our situation" (what have I just said) "told myself not to be so stupid. If you knew what was going on, you were that cold calculated bitch I had took you for, you would be making quicker tracks than you were. It was then that I phoned your other friend." Is it possible to see stars in daylight? She means Jimmy.

'Pretend. Lie, if you must.'

Do not judge me, dear reader so severely. I am who I am.

'The lull before the storm.'

That idiom again – I refuse to believe it. "Other friend?"

"Yes, Jimmy. He gave me his phone number the day your name was tattooed on his ankle. Told me he was searching for a painter, if I heard anything, or needed help – phone, so I did."

My stars turn to storm clouds.

"When did you call him?"

"Before he went to America. Your birthday present, wasn't it?"

Her words were confirming my fears. "Did he help you?"

"Of course he did. Funny how I believed he would, a kind nature I suppose. Anyway, we met again when he was in the States. I had moved out of the commune by then. They thought I had gone home. The man with him was bewitched by my son. Your friend and the other man paid for my return tickets. How kind is that?"

Neither my father or Jimmy told me they had met up with her, or paid for her ticket home. They knew everything.

Rosie was still talking. I honed back in on her explanation of her escape. "The older man amused Oliver while your friend and I talked. He asked me various questions: 'How did we find this painter, did we receive help, did I know a woman of your name?'"

"Of course, you said you did." It had become an effort to speak.

"If you mean did I mention you, the answer is no. We discussed *him*" (she too found the name difficult to utter) "where he was, what name he was using. I thank God to this day that he asked us if we knew a painter by the name of Jules – that he said 'people who deceive get caught in the end'."

"You told him you did not know me?"

Rosie leant into the pram again. Satisfied all was well she returned to the subject in hand. "As I said, I could not see the point in involving you, after everything you were going to go through. That girl, Sharaz told me you were a ticket to money" (the cow) "I did not answer Jimmy's question about you. Anyway, your friends" (she has no need to know one was my father) "suggested I return instantly to England. Escape while I could. Jimmy," the name was used carefully, tentatively, "assured me he would inform the authorities."

"Did he?"

"I would say yes. Mind, who knows if *he* ran, especially if *he* got money."

Life ties us in knots, deceit more so.

Rosie had finished her tale. The baby stirred: his Mother, lifting the small body from its nest, cradled him to her breast. "I live with my Mum. She loves Oliver."

"Alexander? If he comes home."

"We will see what happens."

"I'm sorry."

Oliver gurgled, she exchanged him to her other side. "Don't be, you are lucky."

"Lucky?" I eased my poor bottom further onto the wooden slats. "I would say we are both lucky. Free from the Devil's hold."

She kissed the crown of her son's head. "I did what I did for a man who told me he loved you. Repeated not once, but twice. He said the real you was kind and considerate, and he was sorry I did not know you."

Again she kissed her child, her lips snuggling into his pale blue suit.

Standing as best as I could (stooping would be more accurate) I thanked her, and wished her well, instructing myself that curiosity could ask nothing else. Yet, there is always one last query.

"Do you like my friend, Rosie?"

She eyed me, in that way she had in the past, uncertain, problematic, caged.

"No, just grateful for his help, but you," the young mother held my gaze, "you are a fool if you let him go."

She popped the boy back in the pram, waved her hand and Oliver's, saying, "Goodbye" in the way young Mothers do.

I thanked her, and walked away.

—

"Loves me?"

These two words assemble in my head, line up as soldiers on parade. I staggered home, full of remorse, and a feeling I could not quite describe. Rosie Cromwell's innocent declaration had caught me off guard. The card she had dealt me tore at my soul. Was it possible my friend loved me?

Me, who lived in a shadow world, me – who regarded duplicity as second nature, scored top marks on the fantasy front.

Me, who had pushed my best friend aside, spurned any small gesture of affection.

The pain from my tattoo, like the pain around my heart was unbearable. I clasped my hands together in front of me, hobbled from room to room. With each rumble of 'he loves you' I was transported to a time and place where Jimmy's odd behaviour

311

became clear; kindness on the morning after my sojourn into the alley of Berlin, more than friendly attentiveness as we toured the Imperial Palace, a kiss under the walnut tree, fathomless questions in Paris and, the irony of America.

My heart struggled for anything I could use as a tool of argument. I closed my eyes. I mentally scream.

It is Saturday night, and six o'clock is creeping up on me. Jimmy will be ringing, guess something is wrong, how can I tell him?

I will play the cool friend, talk of work. I will not give him an inch to ask me how I am, for dear reader, I do not know.

I walk (OK, hobble) into the bathroom. I need cold water on my face; get ready. That task takes me an enormous ten minutes, another ten minutes to sit, prepare and relax.

The phone rings, rings, rings.

I am rooted to my seat, hear the honking horns in the street, the flat window shows up the flashing lights. I still do not move.

RING, RING, RING.

I will convince him I was ill, in a deep sleep. The eyebrows are raised.

Oh, reader, what can I do? This weak, deceptive woman; all I know is *my friend* is in love with me.

How will I get through the next nine months to Millennium Eve!

18

New Year's Eve, December 1999

Have you ever anticipated an event with such strong feelings that the tiniest action or word could make you cry; a turmoil so deep inside your stomach that when it arrives you want to turn and run? That was me on the morning of Millennium Eve. Although my meeting with Rosie Cromwell in May was what the wise dub a wakeup call, I still torture myself over this evening's get-together. *'Why?'* you ask, and I retaliate with, "That is a very good question, because a lot had happened. *I* was a different person."

'Changed.'

Correct, in many ways. First, Kurt – the fantasy had ended; abruptly.

Second, Rosie Cromwell – the picture she painted of Jimmy; add this to Kurt's stinging words.

Three, Jimmy – separation had forced me to untie the ribbon of deception that held my life together.

It started the morning after bumping into the young Mother; an urge to unravel the past ten years of my life as though they were an old newsreel. The fantasy world of my lover (of which my body bore the markings) crumbled into the rubble it had always been. Truth became my assailant; a total execution of my pride, nowhere for my self-indulgent ego to hide. It was easy to see how I had put my lover on a pedestal, disregarded the obvious clues – uniforms, pictures, name changes – need I go on? Ignoring the symptoms of my delusion I had provided the stepping stones for a brilliant artist to be torn from his comfort zone into the hands of a traitor. In this downfall a besotted girl lost everything.

Many a night I would pretend I was speaking to my grandmother, ask her to forgive me over the money I gave away in fear, help me to choose between the friend I had known, and the man I was informed loved me. Mattie would know, for she scolded me often for tossing him aside, her affection for him enduring, her common sense to see him as a stalwart human being.

Around September I begged Mattie to come home.

Can you believe it? She argued her heart was secured in Bhutan at the moment; Lotus (Lotus this, Lotus that) and the anchor mother (here we go again) depended upon her. She wrote as an afterthought (my take on the slow arriving letter) to assure me I could cope with the thousand year turnover in my usual secular way, and one day we would be re-united; then added a 'P.S': 'When Henry and Philomena acquire prudence'.

I so wanted to write and tell her I had changed, for the better?

Would she believe me? I doubt it.

Truth – the real reason I am so jittery tonight – a feeling I cannot describe!

I have been writing to Jimmy, this friend who has phoned, of late not every Saturday, but once a month (cheek, don't you think?)

Please do not look at me in amazement. I convinced myself to write; pen a series of light, non-committal letters, nothing in particular, mainly about work, and asking after his days.

I know, he probably wondered if I had lost the last vestige of sense. *'Answers?'* you sound impatient.

Not one, I inform you. Not one.

Your response will be, *'Can you blame him?'*

Actually, yes I do. I had penned nothing derogatory, as a matter of fact each line had been full of compliments on his work, interspersed with jibes concerning *my* work and workmates.

Best to play light. The over-ruling factor of tonight is *my* love for my best friend.

Silence.

I will say it again. *I Love Jimmy.*

Do not ask me when the penny dropped, it does not matter, the most important thing is Jimmy will meet me tonight, and the fuse, torch, firework, will explode.

Explode into millions of shooting stars.

I tremble and laugh, whisper, "Trust me, I know him."

Your forehead crumples.

—

Standing before my mirror at exactly five o clock I shudder at the thought of dressing. My wardrobe is bursting with tops, jeans, skirts, blouses, and jumpers. Rummaging through old suitcases, I had hurled the clothes labelled. 'Never Wear Again' into a pile by the door for the charity shop. I so wanted to look good, not scare my friend into catching the tube to the airport (joke). Nothing satisfied me.

Women in general will feel for me. How could I meet my friend on this last day in December in something that would show my over indulgence of food at the Christmas period? Show my artwork (which he has not seen), and show how I wished to entice him into my web (another joke – maybe not).

Flinging the last few articles of clothing onto the floor I spot a very ordinary long sleeved cream jumper and a pair of boot leg jeans.

You sigh (as Mother would).

Come on, both are new, and are perfect for my mood, new clothes – a new beginning.

It is now seven o clock, and my stomach is in the curl of my throat.

Scary is an easy word to utter. not so simple to rid the body of its grip.

The twirl in front of my bedroom mirror suggests plain, dowdy, frightened; all my mother's nightmares rolled into one. Unlike the dress she would be wearing for my father's 'end of the year' bank spectacular.

Full marks, it fell from the rail of a Parisian designer; a sleek offering studded with rows of beading, Mother's way of out-shining the other women.

She had practised of late to have patience, consideration, understanding for the daughter who was her constant headache. When I asked her opinion she would tweet like a hungry bird: "You are my child," "I admit your faults, but ..." "No-one can always be *that* choosy." before running her fingers round my flat and adding 'dusters' to her shopping list.

315

At eight o clock I close the flat door, edge my way down the stairs into the street. The small town is throbbing with people, dressed up to the nines and sparkling as if they were the fairy atop the Christmas tree. Many were rushing to catch buses or trains into the capital, determined not to miss the fun that awaited them there. Others, gathered in family groups to admire the activities taking place, jugglers, fire eaters, acrobats, singers, dancers; any amount of amateur and professional artists, all working together to make the suburbs a part of this wonderful night.

Jumping onto any bus that sauntered in my direction I was not surprised when I had to stand, jostle, push through party hats and streamers for the ten minute ride. Another night sprang into my head. A night I would do anything to forget. We shunted along, the driver blowing his horn at the slightest show of camaraderie from passing cars. The man standing by my side uncovered a football rattle, swung it, deafened my left ear. Those surrounding him cheered. I was glad to escape onto the embankment of London, with its muddy water below. A desire was rising inside me; a desire so strong, yet fragile in its conception. I re-lived those two kisses, remembered the sensation beneath the walnut tree; the sweetness of central park. Re-lived, and dreamt of nothing else; and before you mention it, there was no cause to assume I was jumping from bad to good in retrospect – Jimmy had been there all along. Reader, I can honestly hold up my hand and say, "It was me." This glorious sensation of loving my friend, completely right! A real new beginning.

—

We had arranged to meet at Parliament Square at twenty past eight. I say 'arranged', what I actually mean is Mother had given me the message. *'Strange.'*

Thought you may say that. I thought so at first. My friend was busy.

'Not too busy to speak to your mother.'

Ummm, I will forgo the peeved act. Amid the bright yellow police jackets the crowds swarmed, as bees gather around pollen. Whistles dangled from their mouths, strips of coloured paper adorning their party clothes, the implication of expectancy in every sentence they shouted. Towering above them in the way of a lighthouse beacon was the glowing face of Big Ben, resolutely ticking away the passing of a thousand years. I arrived at the spot Jimmy and I had agreed to meet, screwed up my eyes against the flash of cameras or bouncing coloured lights.

No Jimmy.

My legs started to wobble. I must do something, anything so patience can take its course. I look back to the clock. Four dials, twenty-three feet square, clock hands, fourteen feet long, each figure a height of two feet.

There – wouldn't Sir Benjamin Hall (the man who the thirteen ton bell was named after) be proud of me? Then, I imagined his face, the contours of his mouth turning into a downward, 'What have you forgotten?' Of course, oops, the stack of coins placed on the huge pendulum in an effort to keep the right time.

I would chuckle under his auspicious gaze. Apologise for my lack of memory.

He would forgive me.

How do I know all this? A pamphlet thrown into my hand!

No Jimmy.

I stood there, staring into the dark sky, not hearing or sensing the figure that crept to my side.

"You should be proud of me, I have survived the incendiary bombing of the Houses of Parliament in 1941. I am the sound of hope. Tick, tock."

My heart fluttered as the deep lilting tone washed over me. There was only one person who spoke in that way. I swung round – lost in the dark eyes – my stomach lurched – "Jimmy."

"Hello, girl." Old greeting.

Sounds good, yes?

"Jimmy." I let his name roll from my tongue. "Where were you hiding?" I felt shy.

He shifted a little. "I was watching you."

"Watching me?" I pushed a creeping uneasiness back down inside me.

"Yep, making sure you would wait for me." To say I was perplexed ... I recalled the letters, my friend had only to read between the lines.

'Do you think he got round to reading them?' you ask.

In desperation I seek assurance. "Did you read my letters?"

He stroked his chin. "Yep." (Irritating.)

"You didn't answer?"

"Nope."

Jimmy was pointing skyward, flexing his fingers to mimic the 'tick tock' action of the huge iron hands. What was wrong with him?

I tried to relax a little, let my heart soar on such a night. It was not happening.

Lowering my head I caught his gaze, no laughter; replaced by a weary, worn out face.

How ridiculous of me. Jet lag. Phew!

Jimmy suggested we walk, soak up the atmosphere. "Talk." He appeared to be gabbling.

Jimmy curved himself in and out of the jostling masses, making me run behind as a puppy being led. Throwing his voice back across his shoulder the comment hit me like the roar of Eastern wind. "Bit like Berlin, don't you think?"

Not sure of the comparison. "Yes," I whimpered.

His meaning? the crowds, the expectant upturned faces, the singing, the noise in general, me? him? Not sure, dare not ask.

The pact, our friendship, surged into my head.

For a reason beyond my control I screamed, "Jimmy, wait."

He stood still, looked at me for what I swore was forever. Continued walking, shouting something. I lost its meaning in the volume of noise.

Silly damn shoes.

My friend found a table outside a bar draped in red, white and blue to resemble the Union Jack; very English for such a momentous night. Kicking the chair aside he slumped into its depths. I followed. Heaven alone knew what was running through that crazy mind of his.

OK, we had only seen each other at intervals these past months; no time to question him over the letters. Besides I was scared. Had he displayed moods on these *rare* visits home? I cannot remember. Tonight, he is a stranger.

I chose wine. A large glass.

"Still drinking, I see."

"Not so much." Defensive.

"Liquid courage."

His declaration could not have been nearer the truth. I shrunk further into the heavy black cardigan coat I had thrown over my casual outfit.

He fixed his gaze squarely on my face. "Rosie Cromwell."

The organ in my chest doctors insist is a heart began to beat at a rate that could outdo any seafaring wind. "Pardon?"

This was not how I had planned tonight. Where was the fairy-tale ending, the falling into my arms bit, the sneaking away to make everything right? "Rosie Cromwell," he repeated. "Do you know her?"

"Rosie Crom...?" second cardiac thumping. I swallowed hard; hate the stickiness of underarm sweat when the flight/fight mechanism kicks in.

Jimmy was getting impatient. "Please spare me the act. Of course you do – the tattoos?"

She *had* told him, lied to me, said she had not.

"A good customer, were you?"

Two faced hussy. I need time. *'To think of a lie?'* Jimmy swivelled in his chair, stirring the coffee he had ordered.

I coughed into a serviette placed on the table. "I knew her slightly."

His face clouded over, his hand pounded the table. "Liar. You were one of their best customers. Helped Alexander break into the art world."

Bitch!

I swigged the wine in a gulp; felt the smooth texture of grapes slide down my throat, pray it would ease the elastic band squeezing my lungs. Jimmy flung his cup into the middle of the table, threw back the chair and started to walk again. I ran after him.

How could she? Lie I mean. Be as nice as pie to me, while informing my friend.

How much did Jimmy know? What did he think?

How will he understand? Back and forth, back and forth.

Catching up with him, my friend turned into an alley.

Heart thumping, mind registering – 1989 – 1989.

Without thinking I avoided bottles and streamers, stepped deeper into the stench.

—

My stiletto heels sunk into the unpaved earth; swallowed into the mire that equalled my deceit. Jimmy did not look back once, just pushed the rubbish out of his way as he forged ahead. If only I could get my hands on the 'Bumble-bee's' throat. *'Rosie?'* you question.

Forget the niceties, how could she do this to me? *Me,* who had fixed her 'love' affair in the first place. *Me* who had overlooked her stealing my glory. I wanted to cry out. Big Ben rang out ten o'clock. Reaching Jimmy's side, I noticed he was leaning against the wall, a childish poem chiselled into the brickwork. I could not stop myself from reading:

'If you can git a gel
Bring er don the ally
Kis er on the lip
She'll sone hav a big beli'

Any other time I would have laughed until I cried, poured contempt on the spelling; tonight, all I could see was the displeasure in my friend's eyes.

"Why are you such a cow, Rhia?"

The inflection made me snatch my breath. Had I heard right?

"Jimmy," I began to pant. The wine, the air, the contradiction of this special night.

"I have no idea what that girl has told you. Believe me, I came to meet you this evening in faith and honesty."

He twitched. "Honesty? Leave that for true friends, you have no moral justification to use it. All these years I thought you were my friend." He paused. "More than that. I found myself loving you. Instead I find you have deceived me." Now, as you are aware, I detest the effect wine has upon me – gushy, loud-mouthed, argumentative. Pushing his edict to one side I saw an opening.

"I have done nothing of the sort. I came to tell you I loved you."

I have said it. Three cheers for me!

For the rest of my life I will remember that howl. "You stupid, silly, brainless, immature, inconsiderate, opinionated cow. How can you love me? You lied to me."

I felt the strands of my ponytail (yep, 30 and a ponytail... so?) fall free of the tight band, my mouth working nineteen to the dozen. "Rosie Cromwell says the first thing that enters her ridiculous head."

He glared at me. "You think so. By that I take it you are owning up to deceiving me."

I let out a growl. Believe me, it sounded like one.

"Let's get this straight. I do not know what the stupid girl has told you, but whatever it is, *please* do not believe it. She has not long had a baby, and fled from her husband. What has that got to do with us?"

His look was withering, showering me with a contempt I had never witnessed before.

"Ah, you do know her then?" Venus fly trap. Caught.

'What goes around, comes around,' you whisper.

I tell you in no charming manner what to do. Jimmy leant his head against the wall, actually swung it forward, then drove it backward with a bang (ouch). His eyes were closed, a faint line of wet slipping under the edge of his lashes. The devious part of my brain told me to stumble. He could do no other than grab me, unclasp his hands and hold me to him. The sensible part suggested I leave, go home, start afresh from there.

This girl has a habit of not listening.

One of the houses adjoined to the alley threw open a window. Music blared: trumpets, violins, drums; a soprano voice warbling the notes of a broken love affair. The dark eyes open, search my own, before closing once more. Big Ben struck eleven o'clock.

19

There is a saying. 'Laugh and the world laughs with you, cry and you cry alone.' With the striking of the clock the booming music stopped. It was as though the world had receded, and two solitary figures stood in a back alley, the choice of exit lay in the outcome of their argument. Jimmy's eyes suddenly flew open.

"Are you OK?" My concern was futile given the fact that his head must be paining.

"What is a headache compared to a decade of lies?"

The shrewd eyes caught the darting of my own. "Touched a nerve, have I? About bloody time."

"Jimmy." (Too sweet, even for me) "All of this is silly – that girl, the alleyway, us, wasting time." I stepped nearer to Jimmy's side. He recoiled. I tried again. "We are friends, yes?" He recoiled again. I continued. "The pact?"

"What about it?"

"Freedom cannot be found, you and I know that, it is within us, and –"

My friend did not wait for me to finish. He grasped my shoulders, shaking me backward and forward in a frenzy. My eyes rolled past the tiny trickle of blood on the wall where his head had lain. In a daze I caught the flash of his distorted face as my head, as a child's rag doll, waited for the torment of his temper to recede. The stench of the alleyway, the sight of blood, the fire that was fully alight inside me. I managed to struggle free, spotted a pile of rubbish up against the wall and quickly disposed of the ruby liquid turning sour in my gut.

Jimmy pushed past me, muttering something, louder and louder with each intake of breath.

"You and that scum."

Wiping my mouth on my sleeve (no hankie to be found) I raised my spinning head. Pretence was my only shield now. Struggling to keep a little composure, I sniffed.

"What do you mean?"

Jimmy tugged at my cardigan. "Listen to yourself. Lies, lies, and more lies."

"What do you want me to say?"

"The truth," the boom resounded around the alleyway. "The full blown fucking truth." Jimmy slammed his arms to his sides, his exasperation mounting. "The tattoos, the pact, the cosy meetings. What happened in Berlin, Paris, America – everything." Is it not said that if you give a man a spade (the term is metaphorical) he will dig his own grave?

My spade would be to tell my friend the absolute truth.

My grave? To lose Jimmy. "The odd tattoo hurts no-one. You yourself have an ankle name. That is where I met Rosie Cromwell. Suggested to Alexander that you could help him."

"Liar." This time I really thought my best friend was having a brain storm.

"Sod the calm, you will not listen, I am trying to help," my voice rang out in frustration.

"HELP ME – I want the truth," Jimmy fired back. "The truth, truth, truth."

I had never seen Jimmy like this. It was as though his fury had no limit.

My friend sucked in his breath. "Lies roll from your tongue as water from a pitcher."

Scream, spit, screech. "They do not. You would rather believe that- that hussy."

His eyes narrowed. "Yes, and the word hussy, hah- that is rich, falling from your mouth."

Control was fleeing... "How dare you say such a thing?"

"Is that a glimmer of fire, is it? I will tell you why I can say it. Because it is true."

I stepped toward him (always heading into the battle, never backing away) scared where this conversation was going.

Realisation: it needed to stop, now.

Mattie would say, 'There would come a time for souls to relinquish their sorrow.'

What can I do?

Urging myself to grasp any chance to bring this conversation to an end I forced my nail to trace his lip, drawing my body nearer to his own. *'Wrong move.'*

SHUT UP. I felt the quiver, sensed the anger. Jimmy swept my finger away, pushed his hand into his coat pocket and produced an A4 sheet of paper. "Read this," he exploded.

Fear gripped me, the cold hand of justice squeezing my heart. Through the mist of tears the long, scrawly handwriting floated before me.

"Open it," he shouted.

Slowly I unfolded its torn corners until I read:

Jimmy Mate, how are you? (swine)

Thought you may be interested in what I have to say. I am sitting in a German police cell, but come on, you already know that. You finally found me through that stupid girl Rhia introduced into my life. Oh, yes, Rhia. (NO – noooo)

If I tell you all maybe you won't be *so* pumped up with pride, *so* full of yourself, and the freedom thing- it never lives up to expectations – Right, here we go.

I took in line after line of intimate details, starting with the alley in Berlin, going onto the bedsit in Paris, and that doomed day at the top of the Empire State Building. On and on, revelations of acts, letters, thoughts- the past ten years of my sordid fantasy.

Tears dropped onto the page.

Rubbing my eyes, I felt Jimmy snatch the paper from my hand, tear it into tiny pieces. "Don't think of denying it. I have it in black ink. The colour of his soul." I had never seen a man cry. Often, Father had been near; Mother drove him that far. Not like these sobs, wrenching my heart, ringing around the alleyway. Jimmy took my hand, squeezed each finger until the pain made me gasp.

"I shopped your lover," (please do not call him that) his voice broke, "for what he was- a Stasi traitor. He spied on innocent people, gave their names to his high-ranking father, who passed them on to his superiors in Berlin."

"I did not know," came my faltering reply.

"Did not know – LIAR. Know this, he witnessed people being flogged." Caught the shock on my face. "Whipped – I said whipped as a peasant of old, and eventually killed." He dropped my hand, tilted my chin upwards. "I say, thank God for the Rosie Cromwells of this world. Not so wrapped up in herself she would let a low-down skunk like him ruin lives. From the moment she phoned me and described the slime trying to ruin her life I knew it was *him*. What she didn't say was how you were mixed up in it all. I found that out through *his* letter, and the German investigators tracking him down."

Trying to remove my chin from his hold I choked, "They knew me?"

His patience (if you could call it that) was running out. "Knew you, me, me, me, not you in person, but some poor fool who had succumbed to his threats, given him money."

"My money." How insignificant terror is when rebuked from the mouth of someone you love.

I would do anything to run from his contempt. "Provided for him and his cousin" (she stayed with him?) "to hide in Norway."

"I was scared, he- he was threatening me."

Jimmy laughed aloud. "Your precious lover?"

I cringed as his knuckles hit the wall. My hand found his. He slapped it away, laughing and sobbing at the same time "Admit it, you were his lover. Your deceit drove Rosie Cromwell into his arms, who is the hussy now?"

"NO." Pain hurled through me. "It was a fantasy."

"Boy," he exploded, "the excuse of all time," ricocheting down my ear drum. "Is that the best you can come up with? Oh, excuse me Jimmy, you are my best friend, *but* I am living a fantasy." His voice got deeper, more deliberately taunting. "It doesn't matter if I keep secrets from you; pretence and ignorance you see, are part of our agreement."

"NO." Panic was rising within me. "I DID NOT THINK, and- and I did not know you loved me."

Jimmy moved, floundering over his own feet to miss the rubbish on the floor. He steadied himself, rubbing the cut on the back of his head. "DID NOT KNOW. DID NOT THINK, here we go again." His voice was louder than ever. "GIVE ME STRENGTH." quiet once more. "I could not have made it any plainer. Still, don't worry, Jimmy. I will betray your trust, throw your love back in your face."

He threw his hands up in the air, aimed toward the wall.

I cried out, "Please no, please." What shall I do? My mind is blank. I re-read the childish poem, in an effort to stay calm. There was no humour. Emotion had left me.

Big Ben chimed a quarter to twelve.

I was losing the compulsion to stay sane; frustration and desperation walking hand in hand. *'Time to do the right thing,'* you advise.

I nod in agreement. "OK, you win. I lied to you."

Jimmy turned, his eyes glaring triumphant. "At last," he sighed through gritted teeth.

How do you retrieve what is slipping away from you, hold on fast to something you so desire? You talk as if you are jumping from a speeding train.

"I was besotted, thought I was in love with a no-good waster. Please forgive me for lying, deceiving you, whatever. Have you never been in the wrong?"

Jimmy's eyes were slits of glowing embers. "In the wrong, oh yes, loving you for one, trusting you for another."

His foot kicked a can from the position it was lying at, spinning it out of control, hitting the wall and rebounding it, the half drunk contents washing over my feet. Swearing, he made a deep throated gagging. I squealed. Long, high pitched, banging the earth with the soles of my shoes for all I was worth; two children in the middle of a tantrum. The more we banged the wall or jumped on the earth, the higher the sound.

A window was flung open releasing a body to hang over its edge...

"Shut-up down there," came the rasping call.

"Go to Hell," I returned.

Jimmy's bloodstained hand settled on my hair, entwined a strand between his fingers. I winced. He moved nearer, his mouth a murmur from my own.

"You have broken my heart. Just thinking about you and that traitor makes my blood run cold."

I was shocked at this new, yet mystifying friend.

"He meant nothing," I gabbled.

Jimmy snorted, more a laugh if I was honest. "Nothing... of course... is that why you were with him in Paris, in America, even worse. In Berlin?"

Words lodged in my throat, disjointed gabble pushed its way past my lips, "Believe me I hated his touch. His kisses made me heave."

Jimmy pulled harder on my hair. Brought my face an inch from his own. "Oh, how you lie. They roll from your tongue. I – I –"

Please do not go there.

Clasping my chin, he roughly pulled it upwards. "Not his version of events."

Before I could think of another response his lips covered mine, wet from his falling tears, cold from the night air. Pulling away, Jimmy cast his eyes up and down my rigid body. "I suppose that is nothing also. There we go," he threw at me. "Two kisses in an alley, compare. The pact is finished, so am I."

My friend twisted on his heels and headed for the opening. My past indiscretions, they fell over each other. My life – need I spell it out? Fragmented. The hushed cry sounded strange. "Where are you going?"

Jimmy snorted, walking at a pace my dressy shoes found hard. "As far from you as possible."

"Jimmy, I have changed."

"Changed?" He swivelled on the spot. "Of course, that's why when I asked you for the truth you were willing to continue lying."

The acrid taste of smoke settled on my tongue. People were burning wood, grilling sausages, setting off early fireworks.

If only this organ known as a mouth, at crucial moments concentrated just on taste, but that would be too easy; it has no idea when to close, when to admit it is beaten.

"I bet your jolly colleagues were a comfort to you on a lonely night."

"WHAT?" Jimmy gripped his palms into rounded balls, pummelling them as a baker would dough. "You are such a child, Rhia. If that is the best you can come up with, don't bother."

Now, how many dear reader, will hold their hand up to own up to continuing a fight when defeat is in sight? Everyone!

Defiance set in. Imminent disaster.

"Tell me I am imagining it, the voices down the phone, the giggling. Shall I go on?"

For the first time tonight Jimmy gave out a belly laugh. It was coarse, strange, and above all directed at me. "You are so used to concocting lurid lies that even innocent friendships have to be slurred. Grow up, Rhia, take a hard long look at yourself, then go to the bathroom and throw up."

How dare he, who did he think he was. Insolent, stuck up, pompous- Fury was raging through me; fury and something so fragile I could not quite put my finger on it.

"I hate you." I whispered. "I love you."

My web of deceit was collapsing, uncoiling the diaphanous threads it had spun around my heart, pushing the truth to the surface. Here I stood, his kiss still lingering on my lips, his tears mingling with my own. I watched as he walked further towards the entrance, smaller, smaller.

My mind was tormenting me, telling me to drag the hideous shoes from the filth and catch up with him, stop him, make him see remorse- ask for forgiveness. Voices began to sing. The sky erupted, charging the night's black arena with a plethora of bright colour. The sound of laughter could be heard. **Big Ben struck those magical chimes the country had been waiting for. One, Two, Three, Four, Five, Six, Seven, Eight, Nine, Ten, Eleven, TWELVE.** The thousand year passing was slipping into history, accompanied by the wailing of my heart.

"Jimmy, stop," I blurted. "I love you."

—

Standing alone in that long cold alleyway I felt as a tiny boat adrift a vast ocean. Not sure which way to steer; frightened the creatures of the depths would pull me down. I was rowing on a murky sea, no idea where Jimmy had gone, too proud to run after him. I searched in my bag for my mobile phone. Brought to mind Mother's: "Keep it near at hand, you never know when you might need it," although I do not think this was quite the situation she had in mind. Fumbling, I decided to phone Jimmy's parents. Ask them to tell him to ring me. Spin them a story of being parted in the crowds – good idea.

I tapped in their number. Ring, ring, and again, ring, ring.

"Answer," I wanted to shout. "Can you not see I am in pain?" Voice-mail. Speaking as quietly as my strung nerves would allow I ask they would kindly get Jimmy to ring me as we were parted by the riotous crowds. Press the red button and replaced my phone in my bag. Think – another resolution.

Hearing footsteps behind me my heart momentarily leapt, Jimmy had returned.

How silly of me. My friend would not abandon me. He has returned to say sorry for his temper. We will talk.

Can you not see? It is up to me to forgive him. *'It is you who need forgiving,'* I am reminded.

Listening to the sound of beating feet I realise it is not one set of feet, but many; a group – oh no, singing, shouting, blowing trumpets, and worse – they were drunk.

What do I look like? Mascara running, lipstick smeared, cheeks (I am sure) red and blotched from crying. I was every inch the backstreet girl (if you know what I mean). *'Move,'* is your warning. *'Move. Focus on the opening before you, do not look back.'* Each step was an effort, these idiotic three inch heels parallel to screws in an electric socket.

I stumbled. An arm caught mine.

They had caught up with me.

Hitting out I screamed, "Leave me alone, don't touch me," breath leaving my body in short sharp pants.

"OK, hic, lady. Happy New Year to you, hic, hic. Enjoy your job."

The rest of the group found the boys' innuendo funny, decided to join in.

"We know what you're doing, we know what you're doing."

Fear secured my answer. I let rip. "Sod off, you silly ffffff."

"Ohhh," the chorus filled the night air. "Keep hic, your hair on, hic."

A window opened and the same boom as before wailed out. "Clear off, I have a bucket of water here, kids." The voice spoke to a figure lurking in the background. "A foregone conclusion."

The 'kids' waved at the figure leaning from the open window.

"Happy New Year to you too, man – hic – it is her you need to wash, ha, hic."

"Get." The figure brandished a large plastic bucket, indicated it was about to be thrown. The group squealed and fled for the opening.

"You too." The figure pointed to me. "Hang out elsewhere."

The bucket tilted. I started to walk, hop would be nearer the truth, sinking in and out of the dirt, out of the alleyway, onto the brimming street. Keeping my head low to avoid the eyes of the curious I began to re-trace my earlier journey.

My aim – home – and Jimmy.

20

The city was heaving with excited people streaming toward the city centre. 'Oohs' and 'ahhs' mingled with new technology heralding the twenty first century. Fireworks exploded, shooting flames of coloured stars into the dark night sky. Bodies were pushing here and there, gate-crashing the street parties taking place in every side road or cul-de-sac a trestle table could be erected.

On a night such as this any time traveller from history would mistake the thousand year passing as the celebration of the jubilation marking the end of the 1939-1945 World War. Mother had warned me about the huge laser shows taking place in the city.

"Huge laser and light show at the East India Docks, then a firework display on the Thames. Crowds of people emerging from the newly erected Millennium Dome."

I could hear her breathless tone as she repeated the names and venues down the phone, begging me to 'take care' or 'to be careful of those who have not bothered to wash'.

If she could see her daughter now.

'Old Lang Syne' rang from every office building, hotel, and town hall, as parties were in full swing; their occupants dancing, 'Knees up Mother Brown', or 'The Hokey Cokey.' Not knowing the person next to you was not a problem tonight; strangers linked arms, a kiss planted on every cheek they passed, shaking hands and laughing at the top of their voice. It was the latter that got to me. How could these people be happy, where was their motive for fun? More sadness, I say. Was there no sympathy for a dysfunctional female like me? Someone must care if my heart is breaking, or my soul lost in the mire of dirt buried in an alleyway. The more I pushed these revellers aside the more they flocked around me, gripping me in frantic hugs and planting wet, mushy kisses on already bruised lips. At this rate I would be lucky to be home by daybreak.

I decided to try and ring Jimmy. He may have cooled down by now. Thought his behaviour through and decided I should not be on my own on such an important event.

I pressed the all too familiar numbers. Ring-tone, no answer.

Thought, bad signal. I will ring again.

Number. Ring-tone. No answer.

The system must be jammed.

Try again.

Over and over, the same ring tone, same ending – no answer.

I stared at this specialized instrument experts rave about –

'An advancement in technology,' they say. 'Communication at its best.'

Well can't the idiots understand? If it was I would be speaking to Jimmy right now, explaining my side of the story.

Temper set in, got the better of me. Spying the iron barrier separating the water of the Thames from the pedestrians strolling by I felt the silver case leave my agitated hand. Glide through the air, skim into action, down, down, 'plop,' sneak under the dappled brown water. Realising (far too late) that I had lost my only contact with Jimmy petulance fought sanity, mouth raging and spluttering with every name and obscenity I could lay my tongue to. *'Wait,'* you demand. *'Telephone box.'*

'Full,' I scream. 'Queues stretching the embankment. Not everyone has a mobile.' I throw the sparkly shoulder bag slung around my neck onto the ground, splitting the thin material open; lipstick, handkerchief, perfume, five pounds in change, and a bar of chocolate spew across the uneven slabs. I was steaming. People were giggling, hands were grabbing.

"Go away," I yell, my foot slipping on a patch of Coca Cola.

"Move," a teenage kid mouthed at me, trying to negotiate his skateboard.

"Move where?" I bawl. "Into the water, you fool? I have just lost everything, my friend, our pact, my heart, common sense, my temper, and **now my phone!**"

The kid scratches his head. "Crazy woman." He snatches up the few remaining coins, picks up the skateboard and climbs over me.

"Lady, you have a serious problem, here." His dirty hands poke my brow.

I stumble onto my knees. "Drop my money, you little shit. I need a bus."

"You'll be lucky. What buses?"

A gush of pain envelopes my feet. "Insolent brat, weird loser."

The kid glares at me, raises his two fingers, and skates off jangling my change.

The sorrow of my aching heart, my sore backside, my foul-mouthed rant, clog up my non-functioning brain. Tears spill onto my face, into my mouth, washing away the final dregs of the pink rose lipstick. I scream in frustration, flail my arms into the night air. Onlookers clap, cheer and jeer, imitate (in their own drunken state) the woman with the blistered toes and broken heart grabbing her scattered possessions and ripped bag. Call after her in tones unrecognisable even to themselves as she crawls to her feet, once more begins the long stumble home.

21

New Year's Day 2000

It is a strain to see the words between my river of tears. Nothing had prepared me for the truth of my own undoing.

Is it not often asked, 'Can truth be separated from fiction?'

"Can it?" is my answer. "This selfish, uncaring, puerile creature is not sure."

I wait for you to comment. 'Hard on yourself,' or something down that line.

You vocalize nothing. I cast the scribbled pages to my already chaotic bed. I have not slept for twenty-four hours; hours in which my heart had been torn from my body; my weary brain at conflict with my aching limbs.

"Jimmy," willing my friend to form before me, a protoplasm of my yearning.

Still gripping the pen, I crush it into the palm of my hand, snapping the clear outer casing, destroying the ink cartridge lodged inside. A warm black trickle slithers over my hand, stigmatizing the white sheets of my confessional papers. I scoop them onto the floor (out of my sight), ignore how they spread themselves in chaos. I care not, for after all, this is *my* version of the truth. I drag myself to the edge of the bed.

"It is finished," I call into the morning air. "The unravelling of my deception." I could almost hear my grandmother praising me. "Well done," she would say. "You have cleared your soul."

Yet, dear Mattie, if that is the case, please make me understand why I feel no better. I ponder what to do, my eyes searching the accusing paper straddled across the carpet. 'Burn it,' Mattie would declare.

I think of Mother. If she read it, my subconscious revealed, she would shake her head at every confession, prepare herself for the fastest moving, 'I told you so,' slanging match anyone could imagine. *'How do you know?'*

Reader, is your voice hard?

You inject, '*After all, she is your mother.*'

I smile (fleetingly).

If nothing else this revelation has shown my mother as a suppressed modern day puritan. There are rules to follow – *her* rules.

No-one bares their soul. In her opinion, that kind of 'letting go' is left to those poor dissolute people who frequent late night televised chat shows. Talking of my mother, she had set a time – 5pm, and date – New Year's Day, to arrive at my flat.

Mercy me, THAT was today.

You feign surprise, don't.

Come on – by now you must realise wild horses would not stop her from poking that nose. She expects to encounter Jimmy and me – you know – cuddly, romantic, everything her narrow edged brain claims to be wrong and right at the same time.

I wriggle, wishing my legs would obey.

I search for my alarm clock among the mess on the floor, find its pulse button and throw it across the room. The day is late. I know this by the dark misery clouding my bedroom. Lowering myself to the floor I crawl among the paper, one thought: clear, hide this mess before the greatest snoop on earth unravels my misdeeds. The clock hands inform me it is 4.30pm. Oh heck, Mother is on her way. I make my way to the bathroom. Confirm I look no different than I did before starting my journal; I resemble a battered burger bun (my effort at a joke – red hair (relish), shrunk PJs (the bun), and shiny, sweaty skin ('yukky' cheese), a bad description. Who cares.

More important things spring to mind. The bathroom smells; I hold my nose, the lounge is a tip, my bedroom; we won't go there, the kitchen; I want to hibernate!!

I start running around like a mouse avoiding the big fluffy cat.

'Spray anything,' whispers my battered conscious. 'Air is needed, lots of it'

I rush to the windows, throw them open, suck air, shove papers and clothes into cupboards and the wardrobe, grab a dressing gown, hide my 'art', sit – just as the doorbell rings. Deep breath, unlock the door, open it.

"Rhia, you look terrible."

Mother swaggers in, trailed by the unstable steps of my father.

"Hello, Mother. Happy New Year," I say, kicking the door closed, head throbbing at the bang.

Mother, nose twitching, lowers herself (elegantly) onto the sofa, orders Father to do the same.

"Your father drank too much last night," she declares, brushing imaginary dust from her expensive heeled boots.

"Enjoyed yourself, then," I mutter, stroking the bowed head of my father.

"Showed me up," Mother snorted. "Good job the chief executive knows his employee has a sensible wife."

"That's good then," my sympathy swamps the poor man lounging on the opposite end of the sofa.

Spotting Mother's furtive glances I decided tea is required, guide her attention elsewhere, and (sorry, but it is funny), Father's throat needs immediate attention. Shuffling into the kitchen I put the kettle on, take clean cups from the cupboard, set them on a tray, hum whilst the kettle boils, hear the clandestine chat from the other room, return to the lounge with this hotchpotch of mix and matched cups. Placing it on the small coffee table I slump down on the floor. My eyes catch Mother's indignation, oh boy, she was speaking, wafting a lacy handkerchief retrieved from her handbag in front of her face.

"Whatever is that smell? good perfume gone to waste, I would say."

I tried to smile, lost the fight. Father leaned backward, stroking his own head. "Have you heard from your grandmother?"

"Really, Henry," Mother interrupted. "That is not what we agreed to speak upon."

I passed her reproval aside. "No, she must be busy." My tone was defensive.

"Ah." My father closed his red watery eyes.

Mother let her eyes stray over my dressing gown, and past the open door of the bedroom.

I was instantly on the defensive. "Late night."

Holding the pink rose cup atop the blue leaf saucer she returned, "So I see."

We drank tea in comparable quiet, Mother prompting father not to slouch in the chair.

I was waiting, holding my breath for outpouring of curiosity. *'It is not so much how long, more how she would go around it.'*

You giggle.

I look you straight in the eye, feign surprise, acknowledge. "Straight to the point." It took all of ten seconds. "No Jimmy?"

Breathe, count – one, two, three. "Jimmy?"

Mother bristled. "Do not act silly, Rhia, you were meeting last night."

I swallowed hard. "Oh, that. Just a friendly drink."

She shifted back in her chair, crossed her legs, blew her tea.

"Your friend, as you call him, paid us a visit this morning." If a look could have flattened me to the floor, it was crossing Mother's face.

Father, poor state or not, shot her a glance, and played the finger game with his lips for discretion. Me, I must keep this light, not give an inch, for we all know what happens then – 'take a yard.'

"Whatever for?" the voice was as floaty as I could make it.

"You do not know?" she quizzed. Dear reader, I could do without all this 'do you know?' 'whatever for?' business. I hated games at the best of times. Today ...

"**Mother...**" the cry was demanding. "Just say why."

Father gave her the, 'When will you be warned' look. She completely ignored him, mouthing instead, "Tetchy, Henry, I told you something was amiss."

Any minute now I will 'Tetchy Henry' her.

Mother returned the mismatched crockery to the tray, swept a stray hair into its correct place, fixed her eyes on my own. Long red fingernails were inspected, rubbed, admired. All this paraphernalia I call it, before calmly stating, "He is leaving England for good."

My cup clinked back onto its saucer, lips mouthed, "When?" heart surely snapped. I hear you, I hear you. *'Drama Queen.'*

How can I fight when my heart wants to stop! Mother's hands trailed her moisturised brow. She was playing her part to the full.

"Oh, as soon as possible."

"Impossible," I whispered. "Impossible."

My father raised his head. "Have you two fallen out?" caught Mother's glare, then continued to drink.

She did not wait for my answer. "Honestly, Henry, what is the matter with you, is it not clear, no Jimmy. Use your brain man" (poor father) "your daughter has messed up – again."

Returning to her tea (hope it is cold) she continued, "I always said this would happen." Her little finger wagged in the air. "Took him for granted. This young woman is reaping what she has sown."

Was it because she spoke the truth, or the condescension in her voice? Either way I wanted to take her by the arm and throw her out the flat door, stamp and scream at her to stop the act, have pity for once.

"Thank you, Mother. What do you care?"

The silent whip of derision sparkled in my mother's eyes. "I love you, Rhia. *That* is why I care."

The outburst startled me, defused the fire inside me.

"We quarrelled," I mumbled.

"Ah, thought so." She motioned her head to my father, then back to me. "So alike, father, daughter." Pause – in a louder voice, "Grandmother."

She rose to her feet. "Take advice, my dear."

Here we go nag, nag, nag – WRONG.

My mother bent her head, kissed me on the cheek and whispered, "Whatever you have done, put it right. Jimmy loves you."

Had I heard right, did she not mean 'loved'.

With a quick flap of the hand, indicating my father to follow, she disappeared out the flat door.

"Do not miss a chance," she had thrown back at me as she disappeared through the lift doors, her fur stole and hat muffling her voice. My father smiled, weak, but warming.

Back in the flat I stood in mortification. Jimmy – leaving – no mobile to text. *'House phone,'* you remind me.

I will have to ask you to forgive me, for I cannot speak down that earpiece.

'Why?' The inquiry sounds sharp.

I do not know what to say. I will hear his voice. Please believe me when I say women unite in a time of trouble, and beyond a shadow of doubt I can relate to those feminine sisters who have confronted a problem and overcome it. Yet, and here is the hitch in my story. Everything that occurred was engineered by – **me.**

I sank to the floor in futile desperation.

The church clock struck seven o'clock.

—

It may be a new Millennium, but it still allows the winter darkness to steal over the land. It appears the moment the clock reaches 4.30pm the black velvet curtain drops, dispatching birds to their bed, and humans to their lairs of bricks and mortar. Lights click on, fires roar away, as the country becomes a conduit for an overwhelming electrical surge.

I find it depressive, especially today. My flat has become a vault, enclosing my heart in its centre, locking it away without air or daylight. Mother had arrived in the dark, and left in that same manner, leaving behind a soul imprisoned in the universe black hole. I crave the dawn, a new day, and if I am lucky a new way of solving my problem. Dramatic, yes, yes, you have told me – often. She made it clear Jimmy was leaving; no compunction for my grieving heart, no game plan to hand. I knew this tactic well – hit between the eyes before they gather momentum, yet, who could blame her today?

I do worry, how much my friend confided in them. *Please* not the whole sordid story.

Mother already ranked me bottom in her popularity pole. Further discoveries? Do take a guess. Running to her bedroom, refusing to come out. I am telling you she would sell up and move – do not forget the Joneses! *'Where?'* you dare to giggle.

'The Outer Hebrides' Do not forget her social standing.

The gas fire I had switched on an hour ago was at its highest point, mark six; blazing its pretend coals to bright red. The lounge walls glowed, depicting here and there shadows of a funky vase, or a strategically placed chair. I hurl myself onto the sofa, easing my head and neck into the mass of cushions. I had not eaten all day, and the empty space known as my stomach was beginning to rumble. Too much effort to walk into the kitchen, I could not even bother to move the tea tray from earlier.

The old wives' tale of 'starve the body, save the soul' comes to mind.

Twisting and turning I am anxious the buttons of my pyjama jacket stay within the loopholes of their holders. I do not wish to see my indiscretions, good or otherwise. All they interpret are the dark foreboding memories of past dreams and fantasies. I yank the jacket lapels tighter across my neck, in the hope of removing the gallery of my undoing; seek solace in the hideous notion of 'out of sight – out of mind'.

Why had they not disappeared with each sentence I wrote?

The bold, black ink would forever be a reminder of my pain and desire. I needed fresh pyjamas, a pair with tight buttons.

It was an amalgamated decision between myself and my conscious to step into a scented bath. Let the water evaporate the stench of the night before; add more perfume to the overwhelming eau de toilette already escaping from the bathroom.

Soaking my tousled hair, feeling the lap of water over my ample curves I let my mind wander, and picture Rosie Cromwell, the front runner to apportion my present state of mind. If it had not been for her Jimmy would not have found my lover, or discovered my part in the drama. I could have buried my past where it belonged, in the dungeons of yesteryear; never to see daylight again. *'Stop. Life does not work out so easy. Everyone faces their nemesis, one day.'*

Who says? I bark, a mouth full of soapsuds.

'History.'

Bah, Humbug (always wanted to say that).

'Feel better?'

No. I rub soap over my body, gather the gel into a lather and scrub. Still the markings on my skin gleam, accusing *me* of unfair play.

Why? I will give all those involved a fair trial, starting with:

Alexander. A dreamer one would say, like me I suppose, allowing nothing or no-one to stand in his way.

Rosie. In reality she was scared, who would not be knowing what Kurt, Jules, Patrice (blast the name) could do? Love for her boss drove her to the extreme.

Kurt (my, how easy to say his name now) is best left alone, his voice still sending a chill (I repeat CHILL) through me.

Jimmy. Mother said he loves me, where is he?

and last – Me. I was the one with pretentious fantasies. The dreamer who got carried away. The one who dealt that fatal card.

Me, self-centred, thoughtless **Me.**

Twisting the hot tap I let extra water run into the bath. Content with the warmth surrounding me I twisted them off, slipped down in the foam, and drifted to sleep.

—

The thud on the flat door was abrupt, and over in a second. My eyes shot open, cursing the kids messing in the hallway. Every holiday, their parents not focussing on them, they wander; play 'rat tat ginger' (Mother's title for nuisance kids!)

'Settle down, Rhia, back to the trial.'

Knuckle on wood, ignore it. Harder, more insistent, the brutal force of impatience.

Cannot be kids – continuous – Mother has come back – what for – more gossip?

What shall I do? (mind blurring). – pretend I am asleep (good idea)? Unfair (she is your mother).

Wrapping the towel around my wet body I pad over the damp tiles, onto the carpet, and inch myself into a position behind the door.

"Hello, is that you, Mother?"

Nothing.

Feet shuffling away.

I try hard to peer through the tiny peep-hole Mattie had insisted was 'a must', can see nothing.

Mistake – someone still there – they bang louder – angrier –
Silly woman, what is she doing?

My senses switch on. I am scared, decided it is not Mother – but who?

What if – scared to walk that pathway.

Thought hit me. *What if he* had escaped from jail? *Break the door down – what if?*

Grasping the hardest object I could find I commanded, "Make yourself known."

Silence.

My limbs began to shake.

A lull in the thumping, then a bitter sound from the other side of the door. "Are you going to open up?"

Jimmy.

Fingers trembled. I missed the latch twice, pulling, twisting – the door swung open, my friend hurling himself into the lounge.

Talk shambles. Jimmy was a mess.

He had not changed his clothes from the previous evening. He had not shaved. His red, tired eyes were sore and swollen. His hands were grubby and his hair uncombed. He certainly had not been home, and from the state of his once polished brogues, he had walked miles.

I could not look him in the face.

Standing by the fire rubbing his hands together he threw at me. "You got home OK."

I tried to incline my head, suddenly realising the towel wrapped tight to my, skin accentuating my markings rather than hiding them away. My eyes shot to the bathroom.

Jimmy sniggered. "Cat got your tongue, has it?"

"I should –" pointing to the room I had just left.

"Don't bother on my behalf," he snapped. "I can see nothing I have not already imagined."

"Oh." I flustered, pulling the towel edges tighter. "Drink then?"

"Water," he snapped again.

This was not easy.

In the kitchen I ran the tap, filled a cup, did not even bother with a glass, walked back into the lounge. He had not moved, still wearing his coat.

'Not staying,' was my first thought, dismissed, skipping into, 'It is cold out there' (help).

"I – I tried to ring you." The stutter was so not me.

"My mobile is turned off."

"Oh," was my answer.

"Anyway," he interjected, "we said everything last night."

Jimmy sipped the water, stared at my 'art'.

He turned his back on me to watch the flickering flames shooting in and out of the cobbled façade.

"I want to explain," I whispered.

"Explain," his cry was weary – torn. "Don't bother. I am too tired."

I tuck the crossover edge of the towel even tighter, ashamed of my appearance.

"I will go and get dressed. This towel is doing me no favours."

"Again, do not bother. I do not care what you look like." I imagine I am crossing a river of crocodiles. They lash out as I tread one way, then just as quickly swivel themselves to stop me another way. I thrash about to think of something, anything, I can say. "My mother said –"

"What?" Curt, accusing, unforgiving. "Your mother knows I am leaving."

"Yes." I swallow hard.

"Then you know why I am here."

"No."

"To say a final 'goodbye'. Your mother was persistent that I come – if she only knew."

The scathing sound made me shiver.

"I am sorry, she can be a pain."

"A pain, she at least is genuine. That woman you so disrespect is actually on your side." Misery is such an incomprehensible emotion. Shallow would cover it better. The glint from the fire, in conjunction with the glaring ceiling light, highlighted the fading mark of the tears on his cheeks; a harsh reminder of the night before.

"You have told them," I mumbled

The pain in Jimmy's eyes gave way to sheer exhaustion.

"Told them what? Their daughter is a deceiver; a liar to boot? No, my tongue is sealed."

I sigh. Why, I do not know.

I look at his hands, wish I could take hold of them, dare not. He followed my gaze, pushed them into his coat pocket.

"Thank you," was all I could utter.

We stood staring at each other. He looked me up and down, curiosity getter the better of his good intentions. Taking his left hand from its cosy hide-out Jimmy let his fingertips brush the bone above my cleavage. "The making of an artist, I guess."

I wriggled the towel a little higher, desperately trying to cover the bold print. "Guess so," shivered once more, remembered the windows were still open.

Night was closing in fast.

"You are so –" he stopped, a thin trickle of tears beginning to edge underneath his lashes.

"I must go." He headed toward the door.

My heart flipped, soared. Something had changed. There was a fire in his eyes, a promise of what might have been? Please tell me I had not imagined what I had seen there; a chance, a kindling of old. Forgetting the grip of the towel, forgetting the pain of last night I ran to his side. My friend laid his hand on the latch. I covered it with my own, held the astonishment in his gaze.

"Stay."

22

The glaring light of a single light bulb stirs me from my sleep. Slowly I drag my mind from its tranquillity, seek the clock on the bedside table. A fraction of order guides my eyes to the starry sky outside the fast closed window. Frost is my first thought, as I take in the smear of white around the edge of the pane. It was that kind of night, one where the world is circumvented by the breath of new beginnings. I acknowledge the thrill that runs through me; hugging it to myself in the disorder I dare to call my bed. The body by my side disconnects his limbs from mine, rolls over to face the other way, the satisfaction of his sigh a completion in itself. Leaving the white mist to hold the world in its glacial grip I inspect the head resting on the companion pillow. Dark hair damp from shampoo and desire frames a face I know well. My best friend and I had shared a journey – along the Berlin Wall to the grandeur of the Summer Palace, onto the magic of Paris, and the mystery of the Himalayas, ending with the memories of Central Park. We had soared the highest mountain, and delved into the deepest valley, locked in mutual curiosity of the artist's hand – the flowing landscapes. Gone were the decimated memories of pain and power, given up to that collective emotion of tenderness. My hand gently runs down the length of arm, finds the hand that explored the artist's handiwork, loses itself in the tight lock of instant recognition. We are one, this voyager and I. My soul had found its missing link.

—

I wake an hour later, the chirp of the dawn chorus echoing in my ear. The world is stirring, replenishing itself for the trauma or joy of the new day. I murmur a soft 'Thank-you' to my mother. She left her trump card until last – played the game to her rules. Makes you wonder at the woman's real character. I think of Mattie, my grandmother had no doubts on the ending of this drama. She knew human nature. She knew me!

Rosie Cromwell, who ten hours ago I would have decreed must leave this world by Tudor execution – now, it seems, according to Jimmy, is re-joining her husband in America to begin an art academy of their own; Alexander being cleared of colluding with a traitor.

As for my past lover – his future is mapped out in a German prison cell.

A movement of a hand clasp tells me Jimmy is as conscious as me. He turns my way.

Do I care it is nearly five o clock on the morning of January 2nd 2000, and the most hideous pyjamas are gracing the floor? Do I care the flat is parallel to an imaginary rubbish dump? What do you think!